The Gilded Harvest

by

Richard Myerscough

<u>**Author of**</u>

Bat Blood - The Devil's Claw
Bat Blood - Part Two - Unshackled Demons

____

Copyright © Richard Myerscough 2017
published by Richard Myerscough

first edition - November 2017

No part of this publication may be reproduced in any form, or by any
means, electronic, mechanical, including photocopying, recording or
any information browsing, storage, or retrieval systems, without
permission in writing from the publisher.

I would like to dedicate this book to the three women that supported me the most, Laurie, for enduring my day to day torment while I wrote it, Claraicy for her inspiration, and Victoria for her tremendous support.

Prelude

How It All Began

Corporations rejoiced as the last glaciers melted. Finally, nothing was preventing them from exploring, drilling and mining the rich resources that had been trapped under both poles. The surviving penguins and polar bears became zoo animals.

Unfortunately, all of the conservative forecasts were wrong. Many coastal cities went bankrupt shoring up their levees against the rising water.

Then a series of violent earthquakes ended the celebrations. No longer compressed under mountains of ice, the rising tectonic plates under the poles began to crack. The quakes killed hundreds of workers connected to the newly constructed oil rigs and mining operations. Cruise liners were overturned and sprawling communities along the shore were obliterated by gigantic rogue waves. Thousands of tourists, sailors and locals drowned.

As other plates readjusted, a global rash of violent earthquakes, tsunamis and volcanic eruptions followed. Sky scrapers in New York and Washington were demolished by massive tidal waves. Levees were washed away. Coastal cities were turned into swamps.

World-wide, over a billion destitute people had to be relocated. The scientists that were corporately paid to preach that global warming was natural and something to look forward to, were put on trial and turned into scapegoats.

As two massive plates squeezed the vast Mid-Atlantic Ridge, the displaced water elevated the sea level far beyond anything the scientists could have predicted. Tidal waves rained havoc on the remaining coastal cities. Hurricanes, tornadoes and monsoons, pushed the devastation inland. It took only a few weeks for Holland, Florida and most of Brazil to disappear.

Rivers began flowing backwards, wiping out the towns and cities along them. The massive efforts to save London and Paris were futile. The Mississippi River became a huge inland sea engulfing the rich North American bread basket. The Chinese delta and India's plains met the same fate. The majority of the earth's prime farmland was under water.

Desperate armies ferociously fought over the few remaining pockets of fertile land. The constant pounding of artillery and bombs accelerated the shifting plates. Entire chains of volcanoes exploded. The darkened sky turned blood red as the earth's surface cracked open.

The continents began to split apart. Entire naval fleets were swamped and submarines imploded amidst the violent turmoil.

While trying to adjust to the shifting plates, the planet began to wobble. One day the sun would rise over what was once true north, a couple weeks later over what was once north-east or even north-west. The disruption to plant growth was devastating. The magnetic flux created by the shifting poles scrambled the electrical pulses rendering all electronic devices useless. World-wide, nuclear power stations suffered catastrophic melt-downs spewing clouds of radioactive dust.

Cars, planes, tanks, and ships were reduced to scrap metal. As man reverted back to the barter system, money was used to light fires and gold was cast into bullets.

The planet's erratic wobbling increased until it flipped end for end. The earth slowly stopped rotating. Then it slowly began to spin in the opposite direction. During the change, month long days and nights wreaked havoc on the remaining plant life. Some mountain ranges crumbled, while others sprung up from the ocean. Hurricane force winds distributed the nuclear and volcanic ash around the globe.

Even the oceans were not spared. Heat from the volcanic activity and the depletion of oxygen caused a vast range of oceanic species to either float to the surface or sink. Their rotting corpses further contaminated the water. Thousands upon thousands of more species were obliterated.

In the frigid darkness of the global nuclear winter, thick sheets of ice began to cover the planet. On the surface, people sought shelter wherever they could. Without heat, most froze to death while embracing their loved ones.

The fortunate managed to find a place underground. They secretly turned mines, tunnels and other underground complexes into large self sustaining shelters. Limited to the capacity that their greenhouses and supplies could sustain, they had to fend off the violent mobs trying to force their way in. To help prevent being breached, they masked the openings and sealed themselves in.

The Freeze

Decades later, on the surface ...

Small bands of scavengers hauled their air-tight shells over the ice searching for food. The thick walls of the lightweight shells were made from multiple layers of hide, fabric and salvaged building insulation. A section of the thick floor was folded inward and tied to the sides to allow them to push the portable shelters from place to place without leaving it. Crammed inside, the inhabitants had to plan and co-ordinate every move they made.

A single breath of raw frigid air could freeze their lungs. They were forced to breath in and out of the tubes attached to their insulated leather hoods. The baffles on the top of the domes helped to preheat the air before it entered the tubes. A metre of the exiting air tube was coiled around the incoming tube and wrapped with insulation. This helped warm the incoming air. The exiting tube then split off into a side pouch. Inside the pouch, the condensation from the escaping air was collected and used as drinking water.

They used every method they had at their disposal to retain as much body heat as possible. Through the multiple layers of clear plastic that protected their eyes, the only faces most of them saw were either frozen or about to be eaten.

Groups of shells fumbled around the icy surface bumping into each other. Limited by the rudimentary periscopes they used, the shells scoured the surface until they found something worth investigating. The shells communicated with one another by whistling through their air lines and chiselling messages and symbolic symbols in the ice.

Once a target was obtained they took turns carving tunnels through the ice and exhumed whatever treasure they found. It didn't matter if the bodies were days or several decades old. The frozen remains were chiselled apart and suspended next to the air baffles to thaw enough to butcher.

During the freeze, families and large groups tended to huddle together. Churches became sought out targets. Their large frozen congregations allowed rival groups of shells to come together. With plenty of meat to go around, a truce was normally formed. Along with it was a chance to meet, converse and size up their opponents.

The excavated caverns were turned into banquet halls for a rare communal feasts. The thick ice helped insulate them from the cold. As selected members of the different shells sat across from one another, the desire of a much warmer meal sometimes led to group murder. To protect their individual shells, normally only one armed member attended. In smaller shells, a women was usually selected. They were more likely to be impregnated by one of the healthier males, then killed. As a show of strength, in larger shells it was normally a man. During the feast they shared stories, acquired survival technics and enjoyed the warmth of each other's bodies.

Either by accident or force, shells had occasionally flipped over. In the bitter cold, if they couldn't get their floor shut fast enough, their occupants could perished within minutes. Their meat, tools, clothes, along with their shell's components would be harvested by the others.

In lean times, battles between groups of shells became common. Using protruding hooks capable of pulling apart a shell's exterior wall, opposing groups would separate and harvest their opponent's weaker shells.

The Thaw

The nuclear and volcanic dust finally began to dissipate. The sun slowly melted the ash covered ice and parts of the planet's barren surface were exposed. With the remaining corpses rotting as they thawed; Hungry marauding clans were forced to brave the radioactive ash and turn their shells into huts. As they began feeding on their own sick and dying, a new source of meat began to emerge.

The Survivors

Flooding, failing life support systems and lack of supplies forced people out of mines, tunnels, caves and deteriorating bomb shelters. To the hardened surface dwellers, they were just meat. They had no interest in the knowledge and skills the underground dwellers had used to stay alive. Like the capitalists that caused the global catastrophe, the cannibals only sought instant gratification.

The survivors tried to adapt the skills they had honed underground to life on the surface. Born underground and living on a diet of mainly root crops along with plants that required minimal light, their smooth skin developed a golden hue. The lesion plagued cannibals that hunted them looked upon their capture as a greatly prized, gilded harvest.

The Gilded Harvest

Chapter one

Gunfire echoed from the valley on the far side of a ridge. The faint blasts of the distant muskets compelled a curious twelve year old to investigate. Dressed in a tunic and pants woven from the same multi coloured thread, Steven worked his way over and around huge piles of rubble as fast as he could. At the bottom of the steep cliff he lifted his head and brushed strains of his wavy brown hair away from his eyes. Biting his lower lip, his eyes went in every direction as he tried to calculate the fastest way up.

With sweat pouring off of him, he remained on all fours until he caught his breath. Crawling to the edge of an outcrop, he peered into the valley. The skirmish was over. The mishmash of colours in Steven's outfit helped him blend in with the surrounding rocks. His wild hair shielded his eyes and golden face from the sun.

Below him, a long line of captives were being forcibly led toward a cluster of structures made from reclaimed material. The hands of a half dozen of them were lashed to the push bars of three two man carts full of butchered bodies and plunder.

From his vantage point, he could tell that the captives were foreigners. Their woven grey and brown clothes were in striking contrast to the tanned human leather the Townies wore.

A woman began to fall back towards the end of the line. Steven saw her uncover one of her breasts and reposition her crying baby. An enraged guard began to scream as he ran over to her. Steven couldn't make out what was said.

The guard grabbed the head of the hungry infant with one hand and yanked it away. While holding the distraught mother away with the other arm, he snapped the child's neck. Barely looking away from the mother, he tossed the small limp body into the rear cart.

After briefly sucking on the woman's bare breast, the guard pushed the screaming mother ahead of him. Her shrieking echoes forced Steven to look away. Beads of sweat formed on his pale forehead. "I should've never left the tunnels." After using his sleeve to wipe his forehead, he mumbled, "Maybe the elders were right."

The wind picked up and began to drift a line of dark rain clouds towards him. Looking away from the distant red flashes within the dark purple clouds, he gazed at the crumbling remnants of a once vibrant city before his descent. Earthquakes and decades of shifting ice had toppled its shiny skyscrapers. Mounds of concrete, rusted metal, and ground glass had turned the city's multi-lane roads into narrow diamond shaped pathways that funnelled rainwater towards the inland sea. The other half of the old city was under water. Along the shore, a string of large mounds defied the pounding surf and acted like a levee.

Steven was drenched by the time he got down from the cliff. All he wanted to do was to get back to the colony before he was missed.

The majority of the city's underground infrastructure had been sealed off for his clan's use. With the drains plugged, the torrential downpour turned the cris-crossing pathways into fast flowing streams. A small lake formed in front of the levee. Its only escape was through several small gaps. On the far side of the levee, fountains of water spewed into the agitated sea.

The rain eroded the gravel beneath a large slab of concrete. A thundering lightning strike masked the sound of it sliding down the side of a crumbling mound. The dam it created redirected two gentle streams down one narrow path. The sudden surge caught Steven off guard. Stepping on a smooth, thick piece of glass, he slid backward and landed against the remnants of a rusty vertical girder. Overhead, the girder slammed against a pile of concrete. The impact broke a small piece of reinforcing rod free from it. The heavy rain pushed and rolled it next to the protruding girder.

A sharp twinge ran up Steven's leg. Looking down he saw that his ankle was twisted sideways. Hanging on the girder he gingerly stood up and tested his injured ankle against the current. He clenched his teeth. As he collapsed to his knees he grabbed the girder with both hands. The jolt shook it enough to caused the small piece of rod to tumble over the edge. It fell and struck the back of Steven's head.

By the time he had regained consciousness the torrential stream was reduced to a trickle. With blood dribbling down his face, blurred vision and a pounding head, he knew that he was in serious trouble. After tearing the sleeves off his tunic, he used them to bandage the gash on his head.

Slipping in and out of consciousness, it took him nearly two days to crawl within earshot of the entrance to his underground colony. The blood covering his body acted like glue and turned the dust falling off the mounds into cracked flakes of plaster. Resting against a slab of concrete, he recalled his short life and how his rebellious six hour excursion was about to end it. Mustering up all the energy he could, he yelled out, "Please take me back."

A while later, he saw his older brother running toward him. He reached into his pocket. As David knelt beside him Steven handed him a round, flat piece of engraved metal. "Take it back. I won't need it anymore."

David looked at it and started to cry. Shaking his head all he could say was, "Why? Why did you have to go?"

Steven had no delusions about his fate as he gazed into the tear filled eyes of his parents. They tried to cover their heartbreak by dusting of his cloths and wiping the grime off his hands and face. With his arms slung over their necks, they cried as they carried their youngest child back to the entrance of their underground complex. David walked several steps behind them squeezing the medallion in his hand.

******

Behind a wall of loosely piled concrete, the sentries peered through the holes of wire mesh disguised as pieces of rubble. The tips of their muskets looked like rusty pieces of re-bar. The concrete in the large mound they were on was riddled with exposed reenforcement rods.

Stationed on top of the tallest section of the levee, the sentries watched over the flattened city. Behind them, the steep seawall protected their rear. Beneath them, their clan had transformed the remains of a gigantic, heavily fortified bank into a self sustaining underground complex.

Behind the sentries a half dozen colonists positioned curved polished metal to direct the bright mid-day sunlight at a large suspended crystal. The specially designed crystal shot a concentrated beam of light down a long shaft. Several mirrors redirected the beam into a large cavern. There, it was bounced from mirror to mirror illuminating the area for the solemn ceremony that was about to take place. The introduction of the light also gave the members of the underground colony a rare chance to gaze upon each other's faces.

Everyone in the colony wore tunics and pants made from recycled multi-coloured material that was woven in darkness. Along with their sandals, everything they wore was tied in place by strands of braided leather.

Living underground in propped up sections that were once the sub-floors of a fortified, high security banking complex, they rarely saw each other's faces. Instead, they relied on smell, the sound of a person's voice and the contours of their face and body to identify one another. The simple delight of seeing a spouse or child's soiled face turned the subdued ceremony into a joyous event.

With his head down, David quietly sat at the end of a long bench trying to ignore his clansmen's judgmental glances and sly remarks. He looked up as his mother approached. Several people began to mutter as she slightly choked on the morsel of broiled flesh she was chewing. Tears formed on the corners of her dark glassy eyes. As she bowed her head, a clump of her unkept auburn hair fell forward and covered half of her face. His father stood beside her holding a tray of sharp smelling liquid. After dipping his hands in the tray of purifying water, David used the inside of his soiled tunic to wipe them off. Seizing his parents' shoulders he pulled them closer and whispered, "I promise you, when I die, I'll make a feast that no one will question or shy from."

With a forced smile on her face, his mother whispered back, "I truly hope so." As David released his grip, she took a shivering breath. In a firm voice she spoke loud enough that everyone there could hear, "Now it's your turn. Honour your brother. Learn from his mistakes and obey the Laws of Life. They had kept this clan alive for this long and will hopefully continue to do so in the future."

David stared at the specially prepared, elaborate ceremonial plate as two women passed it to his mother. Sitting on four pillars above the pile of thinly sliced meat was a shiny convex metal plate. It not only protected the meat from falling debris, it also reflected any available light onto it. With the rest of the clan watching, David reluctantly stuck out his hand. He knew that if any family member refused to consume a kin's flesh, it would be deemed unclean. It would be rendered unfit for the rest to eat. He could not allow his brother's flesh to be degraded and treated like that of a contaminated vagabond.

As his fingers touched the meat, a cloud blocked out most of the sun and darkened the large chamber. Using the dim light to his advantage David selected the smallest piece of meat his nimble fingers could find. Holding the meat next to his chin he sat down and pretended to take a bite. He chewed as loudly as he could before swallowing his saliva.

After hearing him swallow, his mother put on a fake smile and presented the plate to the others as they formed a circle inside the reclaimed old vault. With the sounds of people devouring the plate of flesh, David was relieved that his brother would live on inside of them.

The laws they lived by were simple but David knew that Steven had broken several of them. If his clansmen knew about all of Steven's excursions, his corpse would have been tested and maybe tossed into the saltpetre pit.

As light flooded back into the chamber, a large thick chested man stood on top of a stack of concrete blocks near the back of the large vault and bellowed out the same funeral sermon his father had recited. The light reflecting off a nearby mirror made the grey strands of Joe's mostly black matted hair shimmer. Even as the chosen clan leader, his ragged soiled tunic was sewn from the same cloth as everyone else's. Instead of rewards, his title came with extra burdens. To give someone more, meant everyone else had to suffer. With limited resources, that could weaken the fragile colony and cause it to self-destruction. Being the only person without a set job, Joe helped anyone in need of guidance, advice or muscle. One day he could be helping forge a replacement part for some broken piece of equipment and the next clearing a clogged drainage pipe.

******

Like the previous clan elder, Joe was born in a large underground mining complex. He was five when he first saw the sun. After the temperatures started to plummet his parents were among the tens of thousands that sought refuge in a deep, massive gold mine. The deeper they went into the mine's labyrinth of shafts and tunnels, the warmer and more dangerous it was.

The mine was ill equipped to handle the seemingly never-ending line of refugees. The heavily rationed provisions that the ruling government could confiscate lasted only a few months. Mobs of starving refugees raided and consumed the plants sown in the underground gardens before they were ripe enough to gather new seeds.

At the same time, sections of the emergency LED lights were severed to conceal the gruesome cannibalism that took place. At first only the dead were eaten. Then came willing volunteers that could not bare the thought of consuming human flesh themselves but wanted to give others a chance to survive. After that, it became survival of the fittest, eat or be eaten.

When a large earthquake fractured the mining complex, isolated groups began taking different paths. The discoveries and mistakes the clans forefathers made formed the foundation of 'The Laws of Life'. Modified for life on the surface, the clan still revered them.

******

David looked at the small strip of meat in his hand. Closing his eyes, he reluctantly placed it in his mouth. Steven was a dreamer. His belief that there was a place where edible plants grew in the sun and strangers were not looked on as meat, was ludicrous. With the taste of Steven's flesh still on his tongue, David's mind drifted into his brother's fantasy world as Joe continued his sermon.

Raising his right arm into the air, Joe looked around the room and proclaimed, "We must all live by the Laws of Life. First, eat only meat and part of plants approved by the sacred beast. Second, reap only plants from soil harboring living fingers. Third, trust no one outside the clan. Fourth, never stray from the clan. Fifth, respect and share your wealth with your fellow clansmen. Sixth, never tread on poisoned earth. Seventh, when a clan grows larger then its resources can withstand, the strongest third must venture out to form their own colony. Our clan is living proof that it is possible."

A wide grin spread across Joe's face as he looked around the half lit crowd. "And lastly, honour those that lived a clean life and feast on their flesh so their strength and wisdom can live on within us. Beth and Daniel's youngest son Steven was deemed clean by his family. The resources he consumed over his short lifetime were not wasted. He shall live on inside us. Remember him as his body strengthens us."

David loved his brother. A lump developed in his throat as he saw Steven's remains being dumped into the giant communal cooking pot to extract all of his remaining spirit. He felt like he was being forced to consume his brother's flesh if he wanted to or not. If he refused to eat from it, his brother's cleanliness would be questioned and his family disgraced.

After Steven was carried back, he barely lived life long enough to beg for forgiveness. All that David had to remember him by was an engraved, shiny medallion. While twirling it on top of a flat slab of concrete, he remembered it falling out of a pocket of an outsider that was being tossed into the saltpetre pits. David had no way of knowing how its embedded images would affect his brother when he gave it to him.

******

Dawn broke the following morning with a worrisome low lying fog covering the ground. Sitting on top of the mound Mary took off her wide brimmed helmet and sipped on some warm herbal tea. Her wild, dust covered brown hair hardly moved as she walked from one vantage point to another. The eerie quiet made her shiver.

The calm water barely splashed against the rear of the mound. She was wary that the hunters had used boats to probe the shoreline before. The thick white haze above the water appeared undisturbed. Looking inland, all Mary could make out were the tops of the other mounds and the jagged cliffs that surrounded the levelled city.

Her eyes scanned up and down every known pathway. She froze at the sight of a twirling patch of fog. While putting down her mug she noticed the disturbed fog getting closer. She quietly slid down a narrow chute and ran to Joe's quarters. Placing her hand over his mouth, she pinched his nose until he woke. When his eyes opened she pointed in the direction of the main entrance. She then left without a word being said.

Wearing only his sleeping shorts, Joe knelt next to her behind a jagged, metre high wall. While scanning the terrain in front of the mound's obscure entrance, he barely whispered to her, "They could be following Steven's blood trail."

She turned to him and whispered back, "We should have sent out a bigger cleaning party."

Without looking away from the fog, he placed his hand on her shoulder and declared, "We may be in luck. I can only spot three of them. It is probably just a scouting party."

Beth crawled out of the tunnels and knelt beside them. "Josh and Daniel are loading their guns inside so they won't be heard."

Shaking his head, Joe whispered, "In this still air, any gunfire would give the location of the colony away." Pulling a large, angled khukuri knife from his belt, he added, "We need to go down there and quietly dispose of them."

Despite his age, Joe could handle a knife better than anyone in the clan. Seeing Beth's knife drawn, Daniel put down his musket, drew his and got down on his belly. After slithering down the partially hidden trail, they disappeared beneath the thin white haze. As a back-up, Josh and Mary guarded the outside of the entrance with their muskets cocked and flash pans primed with freshly ground gun powder.

From their perch, the armed pair kept track of everyone's movements by studying the gentle swirls they created in the thick fog. The narrow paths between the rugged mounds made the intruders' movements predictable.

Along the diagonal path that pointed straight to the entrance, a large swirl caused the fog to dance around in a figure eight. A half a minute after that another large swirl chased away the fog for a couple seconds. That was long enough for both Mary and Josh to see Joe shove his fingers up a large intruder's nostrils, yank his head back and ram his knife deep into his victim's mouth and up to his brain. As he twisted and withdrew his knife, the escaping air from the man's lungs released a gargling sound that echoed off the sides of the narrow pathway.

As the sun began evaporating the fog, Joe desperately searched for the third intruder. Suddenly he heard a strange metallic click. Beth also heard it and circled behind where she believed the sound originated. With the fog dissipating, she knew that their territorial advantage was running out.

Peeking around a sloped piece of concrete, Beth saw the kneeling intruder fiddle with a metal tube attached to the side of the barrel, of what looked like a short rifle with an oversized, awkward looking butt. The gunman's finger nervously tapped the trigger guard as Beth snuck up behind her.

In front of them, a tiny piece of rust fell off the girder that Joe's back was rubbing against. The intruder's response was instant. The first almost silent bullet whisked away the haze exposing Joe's position. The second bullet struck his shoulder and spun him to the ground.

Beth ran and thrust her knife into the gunman's back. It didn't penetrate. As they both fell forward, a half dozen more smokeless shots flew out of the strange gun's muzzel. Beth quickly grabbed the intruder's right shoulder and pinned the gunman to the ground. With the point of her knife pressed against the gunman's chin, she heard the strange rifle hit the ground and rattle off to the side. With a gleeful smile on her face, she glared into the intruder's eyes and said, "Unfortunately for you we will need someone to interrogate."

Daniel ran up and yanked off the intruder's crude helmet. It was only a young girl. "She's no Townie. Look at her eyes. She's too scared to be a hunter."

Blood was dripping from Joe's shoulder and thigh as he limped toward the girl. "Look how smooth her skin is. There is even a chance she could be clean. Have the beast check her over. We need to send out a crew to retrieve the two bodies along with all the gear they were carrying."

Beth began shoving the frightened girl ahead of her down the path. Joe bent over and picked up the strange weapon. After smelling its muzzle, he mumbled, "No gunpowder". His fingers fumbled with the different levers and inadvertently caused the tube running along the side of the barrel to fall off. As it hit the ground, six plastic coated shells sprang out followed by a spring.

Daniel picked them up. He examined a shell that had part of its plastic scraped off. "Even their bullets are different. They are light for their size, but have enough mass to cause a lot of damage." After using his knife to peel off more of the outer casing, he showed Joe the shiny etched metal it protected. "You were lucky."

Joe handed the gun to Daniel before grabbing his shoulder for support. As they worked their way up the side of the mound, he caught a glimpse of the girl. "She's certainly not from around here."

Transferring a lot of his weight onto Daniel's shoulder, Joe hobbled past Beth and the girl and sat down on some rubble in front of the main entrance. After retrieving the strange gun from Daniel, he handed it to David. "Take this to the Jacob. I need him to find out how it works." Before David could take a step, he cried out, "Wait." Pulling out the tube, spring and slugs from his pocket, he grinned and said, "He may need these."

David bumped into Jacob in the entranceway. The blacksmith took the gun and gazed upon it like a newborn baby. "I gotta get this back to my bench."

Enraged by the blood dripping down Joe's side, Beth shoved the girl against the side of the large mound and slit opened her coat. On the inside of her coat were overlapping pockets filled with thick wads of bonded papers. They had turned her coat into a flexible suit of armour. Around the girl's neck and upper shoulders was a thick collar made from hundreds of glued papers.

David joined the others that had gathered around the papers that fell out of the coat. Spotting a wad of papers with pictures on them, he stealthfully crouched down, snatched a bundle and retreated inside.

Their was something in the girl's frightened glare that made Joe feel uneasy. Turning towards Beth, he barked out, "The sooner she's processed, the sooner we'll know what to do with her."

Beth stripped the girl and tossed her clothes into a metal bucket to be burnt. Daniel tied a thick piece of leather to the naked girl's mouth and forced her onto her stomach. With her head pointed away from the entrance, he told her, "I don't think you want to see what is about to happen. For your own sake, remain still. Any sudden moves could inflame the beast and that could be fatal."

Daniel held the girl's ankles while Beth wrapped her hands around her wrists. After wrapping a muzzle over the sacred beast's snout, Mary led it to the young frightened stranger. The round coarse haired beast snorted as it smelt the bare flesh.

The drooling beast tried to chew through its muzzle. Despite the beast's shoulders only reaching midway to Mary's knees, its powerful legs made it difficult to control. Wearing leather padding on her arms and legs she found herself in a tugging match with the beast. Fortunately, the platforms smooth surface didn't allow the creature's sharp hooves to get much traction.

Again and again Mary let it approach various parts of the girls flesh with the same results. The floppy ears couldn't hide the red eyed beast's frustration as it was continuously yanked back. "I have never seen an animal so excited. She definitely clean."

Content with the beast's reaction to the girl's flesh , Joe decided, "We still can't take any chances. Give the beast it's reward and finish processing her."

Beth tugged at the girl's right ankle as Mary eased the unmuzzled beast over to her exposed calf. The beast's violent bite was almost more than both Beth and Mary could handle. After it ripped off a mouthful of the girl's flesh, two men ran over and helped Mary pull the beast away before it could take a second bite. It's high pitched squeals echoed throughout the tunnels and announced the outcome to everyone inside.

While two men secured the beast, Mary wrapped it's muzzle with a thick strip of leather. Stroking his neck to calm it down, she whispered, "Good boy, good boy. You served us well today."

Beth quickly wrapped a thick pad around the girl's injured leg and bandaged it the best she could. After wiping her brow and taking a few long breaths she grabbed the girls other leg and stretched it over two rocks. Picking up a hammer Beth drew in her lips and looked at the side of the twitching girl's face. "Calm down, it's almost over."

As the words exited her mouth, she swung the hammer and fractured the girl's tibia. The sharp crack was loud enough of everyone there to hear. Beth looked at Joe as he nodded his head, "Good job. Lets hope it wasn't in vain." Gazing back at the mound, he added, "The squeals from that beast might have drawn out some hunters. Lets wrap everything up and get back inside."

After placing the leg in a splint, in a soft calm voice, Beth told the girl, "Skin and muscles grow back. Bones mend. To you, this may appear cruel. To us, the welfare of our colony must always come first. We can't allow any kind of infection to be introduced into the colony, nor let a spy escape and tell others where to find us."

Beth washed the girl's entire body with an acidic smelling solution. As she shaved off the girl's matted hair and threw it into a small fire, she told her. "We can't be to careful. Parasites and foreign diseases can thrive in hair. Consider yourself lucky, you're the first clean stranger we processed in years."

As Beth stood up and got a blanket, the girl noticed the huge scar on her one leg and enlarged section of bone on the other. Beth watched the girl's eyes as she covered her. "Yes, I was processed just like you. Unfortunately the person that did it smashed both my tibia and fibula. After the fibula healed the tibia had to be broken in order to straighten it enough for me to walk." With a deep sigh she added, "Now, this is my home. It is all I have. There is nothing to go back to."

With tears running down her face, the girl mumbled, "But I have."

The words were barely recognizable, but Beth understood them. She shook her head. "If you did, you wouldn't be here." With a forced smile, she added, "Don't worry, I gave you a clean break. Your leg should heal straight and your muscles will grow back. Over time you will see that the pain was worth it."

Daniel and Josh placed the girl on a stretcher. As Beth removed the leather from her mouth, she asked, "What should we call you?"

With blood dripping from the corners of her mouth, she answered, "Sarah. Sarah of Coral Island."

Daniel stood up and shook his head, "Where is that?"

Sarah closed her eyes and told him, "It's a small island in the deep water beyond the sea."

Josh and Daniel carried Sarah down the tunnel as Beth stopped to examine Joe's wounds. They had only hit flesh and were clean. The bullets went in and came out without tearing too much flesh. "From what Daniel told me, you were lucky you didn't take the time to dress."

Joe felt his shoulder muscle. "I know. The shells were etched and designed to break apart upon impact in order to maximize damage. If they had hit a bone or the hem of my clothes, you would never find all the pieces."

"Lets hope that the outside of them weren't contaminated."

With Josh standing watch, Mary and two other women took no time in washing away the remnants of Steven's blood trail along with all signs of the skirmish. An hour later, the bright sun had evaporated all the wash water they had used.

Perched on top of a large rocky cliff, Daniel could see smoke hovering above a town resting on the water's edge. Every month the town's population dwindled lower and lower. Of the thousands that migrated there after the melt, only a few hundred remain. Their numbers gave them the strength. When their hunts and sea harvests failed to sustain them, their food stores were propped up by public meat lotteries. The last Daniel had heard, two sacrifices were selected from the elders plus another from the women every two weeks. Refusing to enter the lottery meant death.

Gazing through his telescope, Daniel focussed his attention on the two foreign vessels tied to the docks. Unlike the fast sloops the townies used, the large, three hulled boats were fitted with both square and triangular sails. On the street across from the docks was a solid, brick building with a gentle stream of smoke flowing out of its chimney. A gentle breeze wafted some of the smoke his way. "They wouldn't waste that much fuel unless the smoker was stuffed full of meat. Those poor fools had no idea who they were dealing with."

After returning to the tunnel, Daniel approached Joe. "No sight of anyone looking for us. However, I saw two large ships tied to the docks."

Joe stroked his beard. "Sarah said her family lived on an island. Maybe she was telling us the truth."

Daniel lowered his head. "Judging from the smoke above their butcher shop, I think they slaughtered the rest of her clan."

Chapter Two

Joe slowly limped down a long sloping concrete corridor. Most of the steel doors of the vaults that lined both sides of it had been removed. The rest were permanently wedged in place by the massive weight of the debris pressing down on them. He entered one of the small vaults. A dim light radiated out of the neighbouring room through a small chiselled out doorway. Peering inside he saw Beth checking Sarah's wounds. There was only one way out of the sealed vault, and that was through Beth's quarters.

The mattress Sarah rested on was made from broken up chunks of foam insulation encased in cloth. Despite being lumpy and uncomfortable, it was at least warm and dry. Startled by the shadowy form looming behind Beth, she used her arms to wiggle and push her back against the wall.

Beth saw her cringe and barked out, "Don't do that! Any quick movement could throw your leg out. I don't want to have to reset it. Do you want to walk again or not?"

When Joe placed his hand on Beth's shoulder, she flinched. In a deep but gentle voice he said, "I'm sorry for the intrusion but I need to ask Sarah some questions." Looking at the bewildered girl, he asked, "How did you get here?"

The white faced girl snapped back, "I already answered that question. On a boat."

Joe remained calm while asking, "When did you come ashore?"

"About a week ago."

Crouching down and looking straight into Sarah face, Joe further inquired, "What happened after you arrived?"

Tears began to flow down her face as she recalled things that she would rather forget. "When we first got here the elders thought that the townsfolk looked off-colour and sickly. They wouldn't allow any of us to leave the ships. Needing supplies and the use of a forge to repair a few broken pieces of equipment, both captains, an elder and some of the crew went ashore to barter for the supplies. When they didn't come back that night, my dad asked one of the dockworkers if he knew anything. He left and came back saying that they were still working things out.

The next morning we noticed that everyone on the other boat had disappeared. Later that day we saw some of the people in the town were wearing their clothes. After they posted armed guards, it didn't take us long to put two and two together. That's when we found out that they had chained all three of the ship's rudders to one side. We were their prisoners.

My father overheard the guards talking about some people beyond in cliffs. He figured if they could survive so could we. Using a baffling devise to silence his gun, my father and oldest brother shot and drained the street lamps along with killing the two guards. It didn't take them long before they discovered we were gone. Thirty-four people left that ship. My parents and I were the only survivors." Sarah looked up and glared into Joe's face. "Then you slit their throats and turned me into a crippled orphan."

After forcing down a lump in his throat, Joe solemnly replied, "We thought they were a scouting party. The Townies see us as meat."

"They don't even dress like us."

"Their hunters are always trying to trick us. For all we knew, they could have taken clothes off people they had killed."

Daniel entered the vault and placed two bowls on the floor next to Beth. Beth turned to Sarah. "No one can change what was done." Beth picked up the first bowl and passed it to her. "Now honour your parents and let both their spirit and strength live on inside of you. This bowl was your mother."

Sarah glanced at the thinly sliced meat. After swiping the bowl with the back of her hand, she crunched her eyes and looked away, "You're cannibals. You're no better then they are."

Beth stood up in shock. "We're not cannibals. We don't hunt people for meat. Don't you believe in letting the good live on inside you? How else can they can help guide you to a better life?" Flipping over the second bowl as she stood up, Beth turned and retreated through the hole, "She's nothing but an unappreciative heathen."

As Daniel picked the meat off the floor and put it back into the bowl he told Sarah, "She didn't mean that. Give her a bit to settle down and she'll be back."

With her left arm wrapped around her face, Sarah whimpered, "What did you do to my parents bodies?"

Staring at the dirt incrusted strips of meat, Joe stepped forward and answered, "The sacred beast has proven them clean and their bodies have been processed accordingly. Their flesh is to be consumed and their bone ground to enrich our gardens."

Hidden in darkness Sarah blurted out, "So a miniature pig told you to butcher them? I never heard of anyone worshipping a pig before."

Joe knelt on his good leg, "No, we don't worship pigs. The beasts are tools god gave us to stay clean." He saw the hatred in Sarah's eyes. "You saw the sores on the Townies' skin. Their bodies are full of toxins."

After brushing off a piece of meat and placing it in his mouth, Joe added, "Besides that, if the beast didn't like you, both you and your parents would have been tossed into the saltpetre pit to rot. The salt generated from your bodies would have been ground into gunpowder. In a land of nothing, nothing can be wasted." Watching Sarah lower her arm, he slowly shook his head and added, "Not even you."

Sarah looked at both Daniel's and Joe's faces and hands. There were no marks, lesions, rashes, hair loss or any other sign of disease. Shaking her head she told them, "We managed to stay clean without resorting to eating each other."

Joe gave out a small chuckle. "You are young. You're barely old enough to bleed. How could you know what decisions your elders made to keep your colony going?"

Daniel tapped Joe's good shoulder. "Ask her about the air powered guns. Jake is still trying to figure out how to recharge them. If the townies added them to their arsenal we might be in deep trouble."

Sarah looked at Daniel. "I don't know anything about them. I never touched one until the escape."

"How many did each ship have?"

"All I can tell you is that our ship had a dozen of them, along with a bicycle driven airpump. I imagine the other ship had the same."

Pacing behind Joe, Daniel mumbled, "If they have that many rapid fire weapons they could overwhelm our guards before we had a chance to defend ourselves."

Sarah piped up, "Most of the guns on the other boat may still be on it. We took all of ours when we escaped. Their's may still be hidden in the ship's gun compartment. They were always kept hidden at port in case of robbers."

Joe thought about the ordeal Sarah's family had gone through. "I'm sorry about your parents. Your father must've been a brave man. When we recovered his body he had four guns on him and two were covered in blood."

Sarah rubbed her hands together and muttered, "Three were from my two brothers and older sister. I watched those cannibals hack their bodies apart and toss them into a cart."

Shocked by the size of Sarah's family, Joe tried to pick his words carefully. "Four children, here you are lucky to have two." Putting his hand on top of Sarah's he told her, "In the world beyond your island people don't live by your set of moral values. Food is scarce and people do whatever is necessary to survive."

Sarah grasped Joe's hand and stared into his eyes. "My neighbours couldn't even bring themselves to pick a gun up. After being captured their infant daughter Rebecca started to cry as they were marched back to town. One of the men snapped her neck and tossed her into a cart like a turnip."

Sarah looked away. "They were out of range. All we could do is watch. We were not warriors. Even with our guns firing twenty bullets to their one, we only hit a dozen of them before being overwhelmed. My parents stuffed me into a deep crevice and shielded me with their bodies. For some reason the Townies didn't look inside it. I guess they were more interested in butchering my brothers and sister." Looking deep into Joe's eyes, she asked, "They butchered their own dead along with ours. What kind of people are they?"

Joe pulled his hand away and stood up. "A dying race of sick mutants."

Sarah lay there crying as he walked away. Daniel followed him. "Joe, if the ship's night watch were armed with a couple air powered guns, the townies may have up to eight of them already."

Placing his good arm around Daniel's shoulder Joe said, "Even more if they locate the gun compartment. We need to put a team together to make sure they don't."

Joe's leg and shoulder were still stiff and sore. He could only stand back and watch as the others got ready. Daniel looked over his shoulder at Beth as she fastened a leather and metal brace around her bad leg. "Did you get all the information we need from Sarah?"

"I think so." While securing the brace she added, "Without seeing the ship's interior, it's hard to picture the exact location of the gun compartment in my head. The ship has a lot of unusual features."

After helping Josh put on an oiled leather slicker, Mary stood in the entrance and handed him a small bag. "Be careful."

Holding onto Mary's hands, Josh looked into her eyes, "Always." He gave her a hug and a tender reassuring kiss. "Lets hope none of us need to use them." He put the bag into his coat pocket and smiled, "They won't be expecting us and everything should go as planned. We will all make it back safely. I promise."

They knew that with the town's dwindling population, strangers could easily be spotted. Fortunately for them, more dark rain clouds were rolling in. They put on the same leather coats, shirts and pants made from tanned human skin and soaked in black oil sludge that the men patrolling the town wore. Only their faces and smooth skin could give them away. After plastering their hands and faces with ash and charcoal, they checked each other over, put on their wide brimmed hats and departed.

About half way there Josh opened the small bag. Inside were three small canisters. He put one into his pocket and gave the other two to Beth and Daniel. No one said a word. The poison inside of them was strong enough to kill them along with anyone consuming their flesh.

In the rain their large floppy hats hid their faces as they entered town. The odd lightning bolt lit up the semi ghost town and gave them a brief glimpse of its ever-changing layout. Walking down the centre of the streets, they travelled several blocks before even seeing a fleeting shadow in a window. The storm made the town folk nervous. During dreary nights, poachers were known to nab people for the black market.

Most of the buildings they walked past were mere shells. As homes were abandoned, they were stripped. Anything that could help repair or patch up one of the remaining houses was taken. Daniel turned to Beth, "Their days are numbered. They can't live like this for much longer."

"We're not that much better." Facing him, she added, "Our gardens are yielding less and less. If it gets any worse, we'll have to split the clan. Finding and setting up a new garden and growing it to maturity takes months."

Josh butted in, "We will probably be leaving with you. Mary has already started training a few beasts to help us."

Daniel sharply blurted out, "Quiet."

A block in front of them, four shapes had run across the road. Daniel saw at least two more on the side they came from.

Running in single file, the trio retreated into a narrow alley between two sets of houses. Trailing behind, Beth looked back and counted eight figures running after them. To confuse them they circled back to the next block. Spotting a burnt out shell of a large two story house, they crawled through a broken window. Inside there was a multitude of hiding spots to choose from. After running around inside the house in their muddy shoes, they climbed out of various windows and hid behind the remnants of the neighbouring house's foundation. Laying stretched out along the inside of the foundation Daniel quietly spoke out, "They will be searching in there for a while. As soon as they are all occupied we can move on."

Hearing loud footsteps pounding up and down the stairs, Josh peeked through a large crack in the foundation and whispered, "I can't see anyone."

Daniel whispered back, "Lets go."

On their hands and knees, they slithered through the remains of three adjacent foundations and around to the far side of a small dark house. Between the rumbling thunder they could hear faint whispers coming from inside. Hiding under a collapsed section of wall of the semi demolished neighbouring house, they waited out their pursuers. They heard a knock on the house door and someone yelling, "We know someone is in there. If you don't open up we will break down the door."

Recognizing the voice, a thin man with greying hair lit a lamp and opened the door. "Grant, is that you? How can we help you?"

Two men rushed past the man and his frail wife while a third stood at the door. Grant's large muscular frame filled the doorway. "We were chasing three potential poachers, have you seen or heard anything in the last while?"

The frightened man shook his head, "No, just you guys."

After rummaging through the single room shack, the two men returned and announced, "The place is clear. There are just the two of them."

After examining the rifle leaning next to the door, Grant looked at the scared couple's dry clothes. Seeing that the only mud on the floor had come from his own men , he knew they were telling him the truth. "Sorry to bother you. Secure your door and windows when we leave. Illegal poachers are going to wipe us out if we don't stop them first."

As he turned to leave, the frail man asked, "Any news about some more meat. The smell of it smoking is driving us crazy. We are tired of eating sea grass, slugs and the odd jellyfish. If the mayor wants us to work, we need meat."

Without bothering to even turn around, Grant answered, "We will let you know. Maybe tomorrow."

Walking past the collapsed wall one of the men mumbled, "Why should we bother giving those two skeletons any meat. It would be like throwing it away. They should feel lucky that we are not eating them."

Grant answered, "Without it, they won't last another week. That last storm tore apart the kelp field and drove the jellyfish out to sea. Remind me to tell the mayor about them in the morning."

Another man piped up, "Remember, they are the same age as us. The only difference is, we are better fed."

Along the waterfront were a number of lit torches designed to make the town look prosperous enough to draw in curious travellers. From a distance, it appeared that all five of the town's piers were lined with boats. However, most of the boats tied to the lines of rubble were mere props. The hulls of damaged boats were resting on shelves made of debris. The hoax was only visible close up. By that time the trap would have been sprung.

The two large trimarans were secured several piers apart. Beth payed no attention to the two guards posted on each ship. "Sarah told me that they were only one pier apart. They must have moved them for some reason."

It took Josh a couple seconds to respond. "Maybe the sea harvesters needed the centre piers to haul their pontoon boats out of the water for some repairs. They are the only ones that have ramps."

The ships' elongated hexagon shaped decks were supported by three stainless steel hulls. The hulls were made from dismantled railway cars designed to carry refrigerated liquids. Two back to front cars formed the centre hulls. The single cars fastened to sides acted like outriggers in rough water. In the middle of each ship, a short covered stairway led down to their main cabins. Near the back, each had a wheelhouse and a strange metal box. The hulls were angled upwards at the front to help the ships cut through the waves. Each ship had three masts. A long bowsprits stuck out of the ships' bows to extend the reach of their jib sails. Along with the lines to support the jib sails, the front mast had three spars. The middle mast had four. Each spar was designed to handle square, patchwork sails. The rear masts were rigged to support large gaffed sails to help steer the ships.

The gaffed and larger square sails from the lower spars had been removed from the closest ship. Using her hand to shield her eyes from the rain, Beth studied the other ship. It appeared to be intact. Beth could not identify either ship. Their damp jib sails were draped over the names of both ships.

"I wish I could see the first or last letter of one of the ships. Sarah told me that 'New Hope' was the ship she was on and that the 'Fresh Start' had the guns." She twisted her head and looked at Daniel. "They had spent a lot more time on the closest ship. If that's it, they may have found the guns. Lets hope it's the farthest one."

Daniel pointed to the flickering lamppost on the far side of the furthest ship. "One of the torches is going out. When it does, the far side of the ship will be the shadows. If we can identify it, we'll know which one to scuttle."

Daniel retreated into the town and reappeared a dozen metres from the burnt out lamp. Seeing the one next to it flicker, he signalled for Beth to wait a bit longer.

After the second lamp burnt out, Beth raised her hand when she felt it was safe for Daniel to cross the yard. With a short hook shaped piece of steel rod in each hand, Daniel headed to the pier, climbed down the rumble and slipped into the oil covered water. His leather hat and slicker seemed to soak it in. The chunks of concrete, jagged steel, tires and brittle plastic garbage were covered in thick black goo. His improvised hooks made the rubble easier to hang on to. He knew that a simple cut could cost him his life and condemn his body to the pit. With the gentle waves heaving and pulling his body around, he carefully planned every move he made.

A rope attached to the jib was resting in the water. Unable to see or hear the guards aboard the ship, he worked his way towards it. With one hook caught on a piece of metal, he stretched his arms as far as he could. Swinging his other hook, he snagged the dangling rope. Using a gentle whipping motion, he tried to jiggle the sail away from the ship's name without attracting any attention. The wet sails clung to the side of the ship and wouldn't budge.

As the guards looked away, Josh and Beth snuck along the front of the buildings to get a better view of the ship's bow. Hiding under a raised porch they patiently waited. A gust of wind help lift the sail and revealed the extended bottom of the last letter of the ship's name. While shaking Josh's shoulder, she told him, "It ends with an 'E'. That's the wrong ship."

The banging of the door of a nearby structure announced the intrusion of two men carrying a ladder and a couple of containers. "These lamps have been a constant headache ever since those ships arrived."

The rear man barked back a reply. "But why are we the ones being hauled out of bed all the time. I thought everyone was suppose to take turns?"

Their loud echoing banter nearly drowned out the surf splashing against the seawall. "Right now I am just glad that I am getting my full share of meat. Even with a full smokehouse a lot of people are going without."

As he readjusted the end of the ladder on his shoulder, the rear man replied, "I guess they have to ration it. Who knows when we'll get another harvest. They are getting further and further apart."

While positioning the ladder against the post, the lead man felt a drop hit his hat. Looking up he declared, "It's still leaking. I told the mayor that both these lamps need to be replaced. They haven't held oil since they were shot up."

The other man looked around before saying, "It is not safe out here. I heard that Grant had spotted some poachers a while ago. Lets just patch it up as quick as we can, fill it and get out of here."

Seeing the ladder facing the water, Beth whispered to Josh, "They could see over the seawall and spot Daniel."

With both men gazing up at the lamp, the pair waited for the guards to look away. They pulled out their long bent knives as they leaped out. Approaching the men, they reached back and swung their knives in a wide upward arcs. Their footsteps and swishing blades caused the men to turn. Neither had time to utter a word before having their throats ripped open. Josh and Beth stuck their free hands into the gapping holes and used the men's lower jaws as handles as they dragged the dying men to the shore and rolled them over the seawall.

As the rocking ladder twisted and fell with a thud, Beth heard the footsteps of curious guards on the metal decks. Seeing the bodies lying next the water's edge, Josh and Beth jumped on top of them.

Daniel looked up as the noises drew a guard to the side of the ship. Seconds later the second guard appeared. "What happened to the men fixing the light?"

The first guard pointed to the fallen ladder. "Maybe they forgot something."

It took a couple seconds for the second guard to come up with a reply. "Could be poachers."

The guards low voices barely carried beyond the ship. Crouched on top of the dead bodies, Beth turned to Josh and whispered, "We're trapped."

On the far side of the pier was the New Hope. The staged boats along it were propped up bow to aft. "Daniel is on the other side of the pier. If we climb over these boats, we might be able to get around and join up with him."

Even though Daniel wasn't sure where Beth and Josh were, he knew they were safe. If they had been captured or killed, the guards would be more jubilant. While the guards surveyed the shoreline, Daniel used the cross braces between the main and side hull to made his way to the back of the ship. Once he got to the stern he used the docking line to climb onboard the ship. With the guards checking for any movement in the water along the seawall and pier, he stepped around the gear box that synchronised the ships three rudders and hid behind the wheelhouse.

A sharp voice rang out from the other ship. "What's going on over there?"

"Poachers nabbed the light keepers."

The other guard tapped his shoulder. "I better set up some more torches."

In defiance the first guard grabbed the second guard's arm. "I'm not leaving your side."

"Fine, we'll both set them up."

The rear facing stairwell leading down to the main cabin was positioned between the two front masts. It only stood waist high with sloping sides. Its hinged water tight door had been left open. As the guards searched the water between the dock and the ship, Daniel snuck behind the door and waited.

After a guard climbed down to collect some torches, Daniel took a deep breath. He squeezed the handle of his knife until his fingers turned white. The second guard got down on one knee and yelled down, "Don't take too long down there."

Daniel stood up, leaned over the door and wrapped the edge of his bent knife around the man's throat. With one tug, the sharp blade sliced through his neck and embedded itself next to the back of guard's jawbone. Grabbing the back of the blade with his other hand, he used his knife to help him drag the body alongside the cabin and out of sight of the guards on the other ship.

Hearing the footsteps, the guard inside the cabin called out, "Ronnie, is everything all right? Did you see something?"

Daniel used a mirror to peek inside the cabin. He saw the barrel of the guard's rifle. As the tip of the rifle's muzzle poked out of the cabin, Daniel crawled over the dead guard and rolled on to the top of the cabin. Using both hands, he thrust his knife as hard as he could into the middle of the open doorway. The blade struck the bottom of guard's right collar bone. With a strong upward tug, Daniel sliced through the man's cracked collar bone, shoulder muscles and clipped off part of his ear.

The guard's trigger finger tightened. Along with the bright flash and echoing blast, a lingering cloud of black smoke filled the doorway. As the guard fell backward, Daniel dove into the cabin after him. Unable to use his right arm, the guard reached for his knife with his left. His limp right arm got in his way. Daniel plunged his knife into the man's chest.

Daniel's eyes twinkled as pulled out his knife. With a smile on his face he watched the blood spurting out of the man's chest. As the dying guard covered the gapping hole with his good hand, Daniel told him, "To bad your body will be wasted. It could've made good powder."

The guards on the Fresh Start knelt against the railing and shouldered their muskets. "What happened?"

Trying to imitate one of the guards, Daniel answered, "We're fine. My partner thought he saw some poachers and got trigger happy. The coward ran below to hide."

"Did he hit any of them?"

"No, he just shot into the air to scare them off." While ducking into the cabin, Daniel hollered out, "I better get him back on deck before Grant finds out how useless he is."

One of the guards turned his focus towards the shore. "Why didn't he just yell out?"

Daniel poked his head out. "He was scared."

Using a mirror, Daniel saw the guards on the sister ship walk towards the bow. Casting off his hat and slicker, he layed down on his stomach and crawled to railing. As he reached up to extinguished one of the torches, he heard a 'splash' near the aft of the ship. Looking over the side, he saw Josh and Beth hanging onto the dock line. If they tried to board the ship, the light from the torches would reflect off their oily outfits. He had to hurry.

Seeing one of the torches go out, a guard on the other ship returned to the railing and yelled, "Are you sure everything is all right?"

At the same time, a window facing the shore creaked open and a woman cried out, "What's going on?"

Moments later a small cautious crowd formed along the wharf. Grant stopped short of the burnt out lantern and got down on one knee. The blood and drag marks lead to the water. "Poachers would have dragged the bodies into town, not to the sea." Eyeing the dimly lit ship he wondered if the guards could have poached them.

Several people gasped as the last torch was extinguished. A wiry man pointed to the ship and yelled, "Did you see that?"

Beth and Josh quickly climbed aboard the ship. As Beth began cutting the mooring lines, Josh told her, "But this is the wrong ship."

Beth wildly glared at him and said, "It would be suicide to try to steal the other one. We didn't come here to be butchered and this ship is our best means of escape."

Seeing a group of townies approach the ship, Josh grabbed the rifle and shot bag from the dead guard next to the cabin. Leaning over the cabin he fired at the poorly armed crowd. The bullet tore open the side of one man and hit another man's leg. While the crowd scattered, Grant's men blasted the dimly lit ship. As the surf pushed the ship's bow into the seawall, Josh looked at Beth as he reloaded his rifle. "Now what? None of us have ever sailed anything like this before."

Daniel finished loading the other guard's rifle and shot a nearby lamp. With the ship plunged into darkness. Beth looked up at the sails. "It will take them a time to regroup. Daniel, help me unfurl some of the sails. Josh can keep them at bay."

A second group of men knelt in the middle of the street and released a second volley of bullets. As the bullets rang off the hull, Josh noticed others dragging a small cannon out of a shed. After taking careful aim he squeezed off a shot and rolled towards the front of the cabin. A man with a red splotch on his chest fell against the cannon. It twisted and one of its wheels came loose. The cannon toppled over unto another man's leg. Another volley of bullets peppered the hull near where the lingering black cloud had marked Josh's last shot.

The sails were rolled up like Roman blinds with ropes woven through them and manipulated by a set of cranks attached to the bottom of the masts. After releasing the catch on the crank controlling the forward mast, Beth and Daniel tugged on the sheets of its square sails to make them taut. The sail blocked out the moonlight and the ship fell into complete darkness. Hidden in the shadows they became almost invisible, while the townies were easy targets. Another volley of bullets peppered the ship piercing through some of the freshly unfurled sails. Josh took his time picking a target. He knew the cannon could cripple the ship. As several men tried to right it, he carefully aimed and shot through the jugular of one and into the forehead of another. "I love it when they line up for me like that."

Beth grinned, "Nice shot."

Josh reloaded his rifle as Daniel aimed and fired. One of the guards on the other ship keeled over and howled in pain. As he lowered his musket he yelled out, "That makes eight, nine if you count the one with a broken leg. Is that enough meat for you or do you want us to kill a few more.”

Grant looked at the dark ship as the bodies of the two guards were rolled overboard. Behind the sails and gun smoke there was nothing but dark shadows. Without any targets to shoot at, he turned to a group of men and cried out, “Where are the rest of the cannons? Go and get them. Drag them if you have to.”

The dock grew quiet as a gentle breeze pushed the dark ship away from the pier. Grant walked towards the seawall and muttered, “We maybe out of their range, but they are not out of ours.” Gazing at the sea harvesters’ pontoon boats, he turned around and bellowed out, “Get those boats into the water and retrieve those bodies before the sea takes them.”

With the ships rudders jammed to one side, no one could steer it. Between the wind, waves, and rudders, the waves almost spun the ship around in circles as they crashed against its side. Daniel and Josh hoisted the gaff sail and tried to use it to steer the ship. They had to constantly readjust it between and after every wave.

Beth looked towards shore and saw the townies pull the dead bodies out of the water and hack them apart. The bows of three small boats were pointed out to sea. “They are not done with us.” A minute later, a cannon ball splashed into the water a few metres off the port side of the ship.

“If we don’t free the rudders we will be cannon fodder.” Josh tied a rope around his waist and looked around for any signs of jellyfish before jumping into the water. The Townies had wrapped a chain around the centre rudder and fastened it to the propeller on the starboard hull. After coming up for air, he pulled out his knife and tried to pry the chain over one of the blades of the propeller. With a link of chain caught on the top of the blade, he had to surface. Between his gasps as he bobbed on the surface he yelled out, “I almost got it.” After another breath he added, “If I could turn the propeller, I could twist it off.”

Daniel rammed the steering wheel back and forth. “It was tighter then before.” Before Josh could dive back under the water a cannon ball narrowly missed the aft of the starboard hull. The corner of the ship rose into the air along with Josh and flopped back down. Josh was tossed a bit higher and landed flat on his back. After Daniel got back to his feet he went outside and looked over the stern. Josh was floating on top of the water with a growing film of blood floating around his head.

Grabbing the steering wheel, Beth banged it from side to side. Suddenly it started to turn. “The jolt must have freed it.”

Daniel grabbed the weighed line used to determine water depth and tossed it over Josh. As it slid over his torso and pulled him closer, Josh grabbed one of the knots tied along its length. Beth lashed the wheel in place and helped Daniel pull him aboard. Lying on the deck with a stream of blood pouring out of his forehead, Josh told Daniel, "The chain is probably still wrapped around the centre rudder. If it gets snagged it could tear it away along with part of the hull."

While picking Josh up, Daniel responded, "That's the good thing about having three hulls." Placing him on the fold down seat at the rear of the wheelhouse, he added, " We just need to get into deeper water."

Under full sail the ship started to pick up speed and distance itself from the small boats. As Beth finished bandaging Josh's head she watched Daniel fight with the sticky steering wheel. "I really wish one of us knew how to sail."

Every swell tossed the ship and flailed the chain about. All Daniel could do is grin. "At least we will soon be out of their range. Beth take over the wheel. I have to try to disconnect the centre rudder in case the chain gets caught on something."

Josh flopped his head to the side and peered out the back window towards the dock. In a semi-delirious state he began to ramble, "We are not safe out here. The seabed is littered with old mangled structures that could punch holes in the ship's hull." While starring into their faces he added, "Even if we can get back, our bodies would be rendered unclean. That contaminated goo we waded through has turned us into outcasts."

Chapter Three

In the dark underground complex an oil lamp's dim light was like a beacon. Lit by its soft glow, Sarah became a sideshow attraction to the tunnel dwellers. They hovered around the hole in the wall as Mary changed her bandages and helped her dress. Every flash of her smooth skin sent them into a chattering frenzy. Their fascination with her was short lived. Days after Beth and the others left their attitude changed. She was shunned. Even Mary's visits seemed rushed.

She tried not to sob as Mary changed the bandages on her bitten leg. "I know that something is wrong. What's going to happen to me?"

"I don't know."

"Is Beth coming back?"

Mary couldn't look at her face. "They have been gone too long."

Sarah could see the tears running down her face. "As long as she is alive, there is still a chance they could return."

"You stupid child. Even if they do return, under the Laws of Life they will be deemed unclean. At their age, being reprocessed could cripple them for life and severely tax the colony's resources." As she finished tying the bandages, Mary glanced at Sarah and added, "Their bodies are not as young and resilient as yours."

Sarah's hatred for what they did to her parents had turned into confusion. She wasn't sure if Mary's tears were because of the fate of her comrades, or that their bodies would not be rendered fit to eat. Sarah had always felt safe growing up. Her extended family and close neighbours had always looked out for each other. After seeing them slaughtered like barnyard animals, she didn't know how to feel towards her bizarre hosts.

Mary picked up Sarah's barely touched bowl of food and left shaking her head. Watching her leave, Sarah wondered why she cared if her legs healed or not. Knowing that her captors ate her parents, she refused to eat anything that she could not identify as a vegetable. Weeks of not eating caused her cheek bones to stick out and her legs to not heal like they should. Looking down at the ribs sticking out of her chest, she muttered to herself, "What is the sense of eating? It would only give them more to butcher."

******

As Joe neared the water entrance of their hydro-electric power station, the smoke from Jacob's forge was mixed with the mist coming off the incoming water. Jacob's workshop took up almost half of the cavern's remaining floor space. On a table next to the wall, he had all the parts of one of the air powered rifles arranged in such a way he could easily reassemble it.

As Joe picked up and examined one of the small parts Jacob came up behind him and said, "Most of the intricate parts were cast from moulds and carefully filed down. It must have taken them years to finish the first one. Getting the precise thickness and strength in the air reservoir, along with milling air tight valves and threads would taken the most time. If their calculations were off, they would explode."

"Could you recreate one of them."

"Sure, with the right metals, fuel, time and a lot of luck."

Picking up one of the assembled guns, Joe handed it to Jacob and asked, "Can you show me how it works."

Grabbing the protruding lever above the gun's trigger, Jacob slid it back while telling Joe, "Sure, first you slide this lever back. That pops a slug out of the spring loaded magazine attached to the side of the barrel. When I release the lever, a spring pushes the slug into the firing chamber and secures it. Then you simply squeeze the trigger. The baffles attached to the end of the muzzle reduces its noise to a soft thud." Taking aim at the pool of trapped water, he pulled the trigger. "When the compressed air in the barrel passed the end of the tube below it, some of it enters a small hole and blows back against a piston that moves a series of levers and springs. They re-open the chamber and inject another slug into it."

Joe pointed at a long tube attached to the side of the barrel. "What is this for?"

Jacob put the rifle's butt on the ground and pulled the top of the tube away from the barrel. He clipped the hinged rod that came out to a shaft that slid up and down inside the stock. "It is a hand pump. It takes a couple hours and over five hundred pumps to replenish the reservoir. You have to stop every twenty pumps to let it cool down. A full tank can empty the fifteen slug magazine, however the last few will not be at maximum power."

Joe picked up another gun and looked at it. "It takes me a minute to load my musket. If I had to, I could shoot off over sixty shots in two hours."

Jacob put down his gun and reached for a small backpack. "In a battle, its better to change the tank with every fresh magazine. I can do it in less than a minute. That's thirty shots in less then three minutes. Sarah's father had two extra tanks and six full magazines in his backpack. If we had three skilled marksmen working as one unit, with these guns they could hold off a sizable attack."

Not convinced of the gun's capability, Joe asked, "Without a constant force behind each slug they can't be very accurate. Have you figured out their effective range?"

After snatching one of the plastic coated slugs from the table,

Jacob told him, "The gun's short barrel reduces its accuracy at long distances, but at short range their first ten shots are bang on." Showing Joe the much larger slug, he added, "I also found this at the bottom of his pack. See how its back end is caved inward and it's sides pre-grooved. It's designed for a single shot gun with deep rifling. A gun like that could be a match for your sniper rifle at medium range."

As Joe felt the weight of the slug, he replied, "It would require a lot of power to push it through a rifled barrel. I hope we don't face them."

"It took you years to grind and alter your sniper rifle. Using moulds those farmers could probably manufacture one in a week without having to worry about the consistency of the powder it uses. Even less if they had a stockpile of share parts."

While handing the slug back to Jacob, Joe shook his head as he told him, "I need you to concentrate on making slugs for the half dozen guns we already have. We might need them to defend the tunnels."

******

After being bedridden and shunned for almost a month Sarah's face turned white as she heard several strange voices coming from the adjacent room. Using the palms of her hands, she pushed herself up and wiggled her back against the wall.

Her fear turned to confusion as the sounds of strange instruments came together and formed a melody. The clicking and banging of strange contraptions made from twisted pieces of pipe, the twanging of plucked wires stretched inside large arc shaped objects, and the bellowing of twisted horns of various sizes vibrated through the tunnels.

With a wide smile on her face, Mary put words to the music as she entered Sarah's room carrying a platter of meat. "Praise be, this day has finally come. Praise be, the colony will be one. Praise be, your time has been served. Praise be, you get back what you deserve. Praise be, it's your time to become whole. Praise be, we welcome you to our fold."

As Mary presented the platter, Sarah looked at the meat and screamed out, "I told you before, I'm not a cannibal. I'm not going to eat anybody!"

Straightening up, Mary replied, "This isn't anybody. This is your body being returned to you. You are deemed clean. You deserve to eat a piece of the beast that ate a piece of you. That is your right." Presenting the plate to Sarah a second time, she added, "Now, we want to welcome you to your new home."

Distorting her face in disbelief, Sarah said, "So that's the pig that tore apart my leg?"

Mary nodded her head and smiled. "Yes, and now we are giving part of it back to you. When the beast got sick we were worried. A couple other beasts plus a few members of the colony began showing the same symptoms. People thought that you brought in a disease. Luckily they all recovered. Joe found out it was from bad water from one of the cisterns."

Sarah reached out and grabbed a handful of meat. "You're not trying to trick me are you?"

Shaking her head, Mary replied, "No, this is your day. You are now a member of our clan. Through this meat, your essence will be spread throughout the colony. Afterwards, no one can chastise you without condemning part of themselves."

In a state of disbelief Sarah smelt the meat. She put a piece into her mouth. She chewed it slowly and after a while finally allowed herself to swallow. "It's not like anything I have ever tasted before."

"You can have as much as you want." Mary set the platter down next to the cot. "I'll leave the platter here." Grabbing Sarah's head with both hands she kissed her forehead. "After losing four of our members, it's feels great to be adding one."

Mary retrieved a second plate of meat from the adjacent room and stood next to the hole leading into Sarah's room. One by one every member of the clan entered and was formally introduced to Sarah by their names and occupation. The first few brought with them extra lamps to help brighten the room.

Their names all blurred together but their unusual job descriptions stuck out. Professions like hydro manager, light keeper, vent controller, powder maker, excavator, electric generator and more were mixed with the ones she were familiar with, like cook, cloth weaver and blacksmith. Even with the extra lamps, their faces were like fleeting shadows. Their silhouettes and voices were the main distinguishing features. Halfway through the procession, a thin teenage boy a couple years older then Sarah appeared. Mary looked at him and smiled as she turned to Sarah. "Sarah, this is David the gardener. We are hoping that someday you can take over his chores. That will allow him to follow in his father's footsteps as a repairman."

Sarah stared at them. On the island, even the lame had to work. Why would this place be any different. Looking down at her withered legs, she asked, "How much work are you expecting from me?"

"We know that your body needs time to recover. All we ask is that you do your best." Mary saw the worried look on Sarah's face. "Since you came from a farm, we thought that you would enjoy tending the gardens."

David gazed at the floor and blurted out, "I don't dislike looking after plants. It's a great job, but I would rather be fixing things."

Sarah cocked her head to the side and grinned. "At least I'll know what I am eating."

Joe was her last visitor. "You probably think of me as the man that killed your father. That was regrettable. If things had gone differently your parents would be enjoying this feast with you." Watching Sarah's face turn red, he added, "I'm sorry they're not, but if your father felt that your home was under attack, he would have done the same."

Sarah crossed her arms. "No, he would have hid us until they were gone."

Joe shook his head. "Your siblings were killed fighting."

"We were caught in the open. They had no choice."

"Nevertheless, your father gave you a lethal weapon and you accepted it. If one of us had confronted any of you head on in the fog, they would've been shot before they uttered a word. In a world of kill or be killed, that is how people survive."

Sarah shook her head. "Our weapons were designed to protect us, not kill."

Joe looked up at the ceiling. "We don't use our guns for hunting either." As he turned to leave, he added, "Remember that you shot me twice and I never held it against you. In fact, I was the one that made sure you were spared."

After Joe abruptly left, Sarah noticed a wheelchair outside the hole in the wall. Mary saw her stare at it. "It is for you. Joe thought it was time for you to explore your new home."

The next day, as Mary tried to teach Sarah the Laws of Life, David peeked into the room. He saw her put down her food and shake her head in disagreement. "Cannibalism is cannibalism. You can't disguise it by calling it something else."

David smacked some dirt off his tunic before interrupting them. "Sorry for butting in, but I thought Sarah might want to get out of her bed for a while."

Feeling both anxious and nervous, Sarah said, "Sure."

Mary took a deep breath. "You might as well go with him."

With Mary cradling Sarah's legs, David carried her through the opening and into the wheelchair. Once she was strapped in, David pushed her up the sloping corridor towards a dim light. "I hope you like gardening. It can be one of the most rewarding jobs in the colony. You get to see things grow, plus you get to work in the light."

Gripping the seat tightly, she replied, "Than why don't you want to do it anymore?"

David froze for a couple seconds. "My parents are not coming back and the colony needs the skills my father taught me."

Near the top of the incline David zig-zagged through a number of rooms before a bright light shone through a small doorway. As he pushed Sarah through it, she closed her eyes and let the sun warm her face. "I've been bedridden so long I forgot how bright the sun was. Can we go outside?"

David straightened his body and sharply told her, "No, we can't risk being spotted. There are hunters everywhere searching for us. If they find the entrance, they will hound us until we are either harvested or forced to abandon everything that we have created here."

Hearing the fear in his voice, Sarah quietly replied, "So I will never bask in the sun again?"

"Not freely." David looked down at her and shook his head. "After your legs are healed I'll show you how to get the odd bit of sun. You need it to stay healthy."

Next David showed her the cavern where the tide was collected and slowly released. The flowing water passed under a giant wheel with a couple dozen elongated paddles attached to it. A series of gear boxes and long spinning shafts went up an incline, through a wall and into the generator room. Each drop of water that went in and out of the large cavern was funnelled between the wheel and water gates. A series of huge gates trapped the water that was left behind from high tide. That way the colony could extend the electricity output to sustain their gardens.

Jake smiled as he looked at her, "Sometimes when the tide comes in fast Jacob uses the excess electricity to fuse pieces of metal together with small lightning bolts."

Sarah noticed four small cannon's pointing towards the opening that led to the sea. Along the far side of the cavern, John was blowing through a tube into a furnace. The baffles flaming the furnace were governed by a shaft coming off one of the gearboxes. It wasn't until John pulled the pipe out, that Sarah saw that he was forming a hollow glass bulb. A bike powered vacuum pump stood beside the light maker's modest bench full of scrap wire, metal and glass.

Jacob used a pair of tongs to take a crucible of melted metal out of his forge. After he poured it into a long mould he finally acknowledged Sarah and David presence. "There's another batch of slugs for Joe to test."

Despite Jacob's smile, all Sarah saw was his marred face. Years of hammering red hot steel and working with molten metal had left behind their scars. Reminded of the men that butchered her clan, she had to turn away. Redirecting her focus, she asked David, "Why are they crammed along the sides of the reservoir?"

"It's the only place they can work without giving our location away. The mist off the water helps disperse the smoke. The crashing waves muffle Jacob's constant hammering. The duct work attached to the sides and back of the furnaces provide heat to the nursery located in the room above the cavern."

Jacob's smile disappeared as Sarah left without saying a word to him. David was about to push her wheelchair by one tunnel when she got a whiff of a putrid smell. "What is in there?"

Refusing to stop, David told her, "That tunnel leads to the pits where the unclean bodies are left to rot. The powder maker uses them to collect saltpetre. You don't want go down there. It's far more disgusting than it smells."

With one hand covering her nose, Sarah reached back and grabbed his hand with the other. "How can it be any worse?"

David stopped. "The damp air extracts the saltpetre from the bodies and deposits it on the walls. Each room in the tunnel contains mounds of rotting flesh in various stages of decomposition." He wasn't able to see the disgust on Sarah's face as he snickered, "Even the unclean are not wasted."

"So that is what would have happened to me if Joe never spoke up?"

Without hesitation, David answered back, "You would have been stripped and tossed down the disposal chute without a second thought. In a land of nothing, nothing can be wasted."

In total darkness, David rolled her down an old sewer and through a washed out tunnel that had been reinforced by crude brick arches. Sarah rubbed her hand against the brick and realised that they were the same as in the sewer. "Did your clan dig this tunnel?"

"No, we just made it safer to travel through."

The wheelchair barely had room to squeeze through a chiselled out section of a concrete wall and into another tunnel. David stopped in front of an elevator shaft that once lead to an underground parking garage. A dim light glowed from it. "We need to go down this shaft to get to the gardens."

David placed Sarah into a harness and used a block and tackle to lower her down. As she passed the tunnels containing the first two gardens she was mesmerized by the bright lights hovering over the long rows of plants. After she reached the bottom she took off her harness and was overcome by the heat generated from the lights. Seeing what she thought was a rag she took off her tunic. After ripping a discarded sac into long pieces, she tied it around her bare chest. David climbed down the shaft and removed his tunic. "You don't need legs down here. This shaft is the only place down here that a person can stand up."

The tallest of the three gardens was only a metre and a half high. Like the others, the giant slab of concrete that formed its ceiling was held up by toppled columns and piles of debris. The ice that crushed the building had also knocked its lower levels out of alignment. Unlike the upper levels on the surface, as the ice melted each of the lower levels were gently lowered onto the debris piled beneath it, forming several shorter levels.

Each row of plants was housed in long troughs made from recycled plastic. As Sarah bent forward to touch a foreign looking plant, a lightbulb burnt her bare shoulder. "Why are the bulbs hung so close to the plants?"

"Plants need heat almost as much as they need light, water and nutrients."

David grabbed one of the carts leaning against the wall of the elevator and lifted Sarah onto it. "The carts allow us to work on two rows on one pass. We have to keep an eye out for algae and fungus. Some we can eat, the rest we give to the beasts."

Sarah ran her fingers up and down several plants. "Their stems don't seem to be that sturdy."

"The colony has had a problem finding more nutrients for the plants. We can't recycle everything."

With a tray mounted above her legs, her injuries didn't impede her work. It didn't take her long to plant a section of seeds. Most of her time was spent hand pollinating plants. On the island the wind had done most of it.

Near the end of their shift she picked any ripe tomatoes, strawberries and blueberries she found in a patch near the back. After that, she harvested a section of carrots, onions and potatoes. David followed behind her and removed the stalks and roots to feed to the beasts. Sarah saw David wipe the dirt off the plants. He collected any worms he found and placed them in a pail. "What are the worms for?"

David held up the pail. "Meat."

"You eat them?"

"Worms and cockroaches are much more efficient then beasts." With a grin on his face, he chuckled, "You should see what they eat. The tunnels they root through are filled with funguses, algae, slime and other disgusting stuff."

Sarah thought of all the bowls of soup, stew and mashed up mush Mary had given her. She had no idea what was in them. "So most of the meat you eat isn't human?"

"Are you kidding? An honouring ceremony only happens when someone clean dies. We're not hunters."

As they worked David would ask her questions about the island she came from. Remaining clean while growing plants in sunlight was mind-boggling to him. He had only known of a few types of beasts and she spoke of many. The creature that fascinated him the most was a small four legged, wiry haired animal that acted like a sentry.

Feeling more at ease David got up the nerve to ask her. "Why would anyone leave such a paradise?"

Sarah froze. She didn't know how to answer him. "One day my

father came home and told us we had to go."

Mary and Joe climbed down the shaft, knelt and watched as the pair worked. Mary put her shaky hand on his shoulder and whispered, "Josh has been gone too long. If he returns, it will kill him to be stuck on a trolley."

Joe tried to consol her. "They are still patrolling the shore. That means that they never recovered the ship. As long as they remain alive they control their own future, not us."

Joe noticed David watching them. Waving back he yelled out, "How's the crop?"

"It's getting thinner with each harvest. We need more nutrients."

Joe grabbed Mary's hand. "The search party has not returned yet. The clean stuff is hard to find. It has already cost us two beasts. When they get too hungry their judgement is off."

Joe and Mary climbed up the shaft. While Mary pulled the wheelbarrows they brought with them a little closer, Joe hauled up the harvest and pig feed. After hauling Sarah up and placing her into the wheelchair, Joe wheeled the harvest away.

Instead of taking Sarah back to her room, David wanted to show her the piglets. Mary was inside of a small pen pushing their waste along a trough and into the collector on the floor below them. Sarah was surprised by the absence of any ammonia. Sarah rolled her wheelchair next to the gate. "Where's the smell?"

"What smell?"

"The smell from the pig's waste."

"Oh, that. It's in the digester being separated into plant fertilizer and methane to cook with. Like I told you, nothing is wasted."

By the time David placed Sarah back on her cot, he acquired enough nerve to ask her something that had been bothering him. "When you arrived your jacket was stuffed with thick wads of paper. Do you know anything about what was in them?"

"On the island there were ruins full of them. We read them to pass the time."

David looked at her confused, "You can read? I thought only the elders could read."

Sarah chuckled and shook her head. "We were all taught to read. How else could we understand God's word."

David stepped back. "Who's God?"

"Our creator. His work is all written down in a book called the Bible."

David wenched his face to the side. "I've heard the elders mention it. It ended with the holocaust. That is why our forefathers created the Laws of Life."

Sarah looked at the very subdued David and knew better then to pursue the matter. "Enough about religion. What did you really want to know?"

"Some of the papers showed people eating weird things and a lot of strange plants."

"I thought you were going to give me a lecture." Sarah took a deep breath of relief. "Bring me the papers and I'll read them to you."

Within a few minutes David returned with the papers he had taken. "They burnt most of them, but I managed to salvage some of them."

David placed the papers in front of Sarah. On top of the pile was a magazine with a hand clutching some long thin plants with large clusters of seeds. Pointing to the picture, David asked, "What is the man holding?"

Sarah looked at the old farmer's magazine. "It is called wheat. It's used to make flour."

David pulled Steve's coin out of his pocket and handed it to Sarah. "And this?"

Holding it close to a lamp beside her bed, she told him, "This was a third place medal for something called hockey." After pointing out the marks made when a piece was broken off, she added, "It was worn around the neck using a colourful ribbon to bring every ones attention to it. I guess the wheat somehow represents Saskatchewan, the place the game was played."

"Judging from the stalks and leaves, those plants waste very little nutrients. If we had some of their seed, could we grow them here?"

While handing the medal back, she said, "Maybe." Sarah could see the tears forming in his eyes as he clutched it in his fist. "Is there something you are not telling me?"

David lifted his head. "I gave this medal to my brother, I believe he died trying to find that plant."

Sarah grasped David's fist. "Before we were forced to leave. A couple farms grew a simular plant called rye."

A puzzled look came over David, "I have to ask you again, why did your family leave?"

Sarah let go of David's hand and turned away from him. "My father said that we had no choice. A horde of cannibals had discovered our island. When some of the elders offered them food and a better way of life, they butchered them. We are not fighters. There were only two ships at the dock. The elders selected the families that were spared. The ships were mainly used to harvest jellyfish and seaweed to help fertilize the soil." Sarah turned around and asked, "Why can't you do the same thing? It could save your gardens."

"Because we would be the ones being harvested." David put his hand on her shoulder and said, "A few jellyfish make their way into the cavern but not enough to make a difference."

Chapter Four

Outside the main entrance, Mary leaned over a boulder and studied the crumbled ruins for any sign of movement. As the rising sun tried to break through the clouds a layer of fog began to form. With both his musket and one of the air powered guns slung over his shoulder, Joe came out of the main entrance and passed her a mug of hot tea. "I used mint this time."

"Thank you." Mary looked around one last time before standing up to stretch. "It has been quiet so far. Lets hope it stays that way."

With sharp pieces of rusty metal making the ruins extremely hazardous to anyone unfamiliar with them, moonless nights were relatively safe. Unfortunately, foggy mornings allowed enough light through so that a skilled hunter could navigate the dangerous terrain without being seen.

The sentry stationed on top of the mound reached down and tugged on an obscure line. The thin rope travelled through a series of pulleys before it tugged on Mary's ankle. Joe noticed her leg twitch. They both turned and saw an unnatural swirl in the fog.

Mary yanked on the rope three times to indicate that she spotted the intruder. Joe tugged on another rope. In the tunnels a series of flags were unfurled. Feeling the rush of air and the unravelled fabric brush against them, two men and three women stopped what they were doing, grabbed their weapons and ran to the entrance. Looking at Mary, Joe whispered, "Go inside and prime the scattergun."

Resting on a stand inside the tunnel were fifteen large barrels welded together in a gentle arc. Each barrel was loaded with small pieces of scrap metal and glass. It was designed to be ignited by single spark into a common flashpan and plaster the inside of the entire entranceway with shrapnel.

Kneeling next to Joe, David saw a distant figure walking down the middle of the path towards the entrance. The figure disappeared under the fog and reappeared holding a rifle in the air with a spoiled piece of brightly coloured cloth tied to the muzzle. David whispered to Joe, "It's a trick." Seeing another swirl in the fog, he added, "They found us." David raised his rifle and pulled the trigger.

It didn't go off. Joe had jammed his hand between the flashpan and hammer of David's rifle. David looked at him in confusion. "I had a clean shot."

"No, wait. Hunters don't talk to their prey, they kill them."

"But I saw another swirl. There are more out there."

Joe pulled out a pair of binoculars and studied the figure along with the surrounding landscape. "No, she's alone. You must've spotted some falling debris. That section is known for it."

When the figure got closer David's eyes began to tear up. Beth stopped at the bottom of the grade, looked up at him and smiled. David surged forward. Before he took a step, Joe grabbed his right arm and told him, "Your mother knows the law, as do you."

Beth rested the butt of her rifle on the ground. Her gaunt face revealed the cost of the trios long ordeal. "David, your father is safe."

Hearing Beth's voice, Mary dropped her powder horn, ran out and stood behind Joe. With tears flowing down her face, she cried out, "Is Josh alright?"

"He's fine. Josh and Daniel are guarding the ship. We're all a bit dehydrated and very hungry. So far, none of us are displaying any signs of infection." She looked at Joe and shook her head, "I'm sorry. We stole the wrong ship."

"That's all right. So far we have not seen any evidence of the air guns in town." Joe released David as he continued. "In fact, there is no sign of even the guns they had taken."

As David dashed into the tunnel, Mary informed Beth, "Jake saw the ship escape but couldn't see who was aboard. I'm relieved you are all safe."

David exited the tunnel with a small sack and a leather pouch. "Mom, take this." David tossed the sack while telling her, "It was all the cook could spare."

After taking a drink from the water pouch, Beth sat down and opened the bag. Inside were several small potatoes and a half dozen beets. She pulled out a beet and started to eat it. Between mouthfuls she blurted out, "Maybe the guns are to advanced for them?"

Joe shook his head. "No, there has to be another reason." Turning to Mary and then back at Beth. "The garden isn't doing very well. We had already debated your return. Processing you would mean too many unproductive mouths to feed. Since you are all relatively healthy and have a ship, maybe it's time for another quest. The gardens are in desperate need of nutrients."

Beth looked at her leg brace. "We came to the same conclusion." Slouched over, Beth twisted her head and looked up at him. "We will need food, water, a few supplies and some time to recover from our ordeal. Our last full meal was on the day we left."

Joe smiled at her. "Of course. We will give you anything we can spare. The colony depends on your success. Even if everyone has to skip a few meals, it will be worth it."

Feeling reassured, Beth sat up and looked at Mary. "Josh told me to tell you how much he misses you."

Tears dripped off Mary's chin as she replied, "Tell him that I miss him too."

As Beth chewed on a mouthful of beet, Joe told her, "All of our previous search parties have been costly. Maybe with a ship, you might have better luck, plus a way to transport the nutrients back?"

While chewing on some beet greens, she stared at him. "The ship was not designed to be sailed by only three people. It requires a larger crew."

Glancing at the crowd standing outside the entrance, Joe said, "I don't think I'll have any problem enlisting volunteers."

Mary took at deep breath, turned and faced him. "I'll go. Someone has to look after the beasts that they will need to take with them."

Despair filled Joe's face as he rattled off, "That means food for the beasts. The remaining beasts will also suffer until another harvest is ready."

"Than we'll cull the bigger ones. Keep only enough that can survive in the algae tunnels. You may need to cull even more in order to feed the colony." Looking down at Beth she added, "If we can not find the nutrients the gardens needs, the colony may be doomed."

Joe put his hand on Mary's shoulder and looked at Beth. "It could take months, maybe even half a year. We can't provide you with enough food to last that long. After a few weeks, maybe a month, you will be forced to fend for yourselves."

After Beth devoured a small potato, she softly muttered, "I know. We will need to weave together a net and rig up some harvesting poles before we depart."

Mary grabbed and squeezed Joe's hand, "Sarah said that the ship had been used to collect Jellyfish. They dried and ground them into fertilizer for their gardens. Maybe we could do the same thing?"

"That would turn us into easy targets. The only place we saw them in any quantity was by a kelp bed in plain view of the town." Bowing her head, Beth rested her hands on her knees. "The few we saw while we were drifting about were barely enough to keep us alive. The Islanders must have discovered more swarms of them."

Joe looked down at her. "Either way, things will be tight until the next harvest and maybe even beyond that."

******

Holding a large sack of food over her head, Beth waded through the surf towards the anchored ship. "I hope you were not in a rush to be processed? As we expected, they want us to use the ship to search for nutrients. They even suggested harvesting jellyfish."

Josh yelled over the side, "Did you ask where we can find them?"

Daniel nodded his head and smiled as Beth tossed him the sac before climbing the rope ladder. The two men quietly contemplated their future as they relished every bite. After swallowing some beet, Josh asked, "Where should we start?"

Beth spoke up, "As far away from that town as possible."

Daniel sat in front of the pair. "We could just drift along the coast line."

Turning to Josh, Beth announced, "Mary has already asked to come with us. She could look after some beasts. We'll need their noses in order to find the nutrients."

Daniel smiled. "Good, they can lead us to it and make the search a lot easier."

******

Out of eleven beasts, Mary selected three to take with her and four young ones to stay. The rest she helped the cook butcher, slice into strips and hang to dry.

At the end of an old sewer far away from the rest, Jake and John wrapped wet rags around their mouths and noses. Several metres away from a small raised fire, John got on a ladder and slowly poured a bag of ground plastic into a hopper. As it flowed through a copper tube, the raised fire melted it. At the end of the sloped tube, Jake slid two sections of a four piece, double hinged mould under it. The wind passing through a porous mound above them sucked out the toxic fumes from the melted plastic and made their jobs bearable.

Jake quickly pressed the inside halves of the moulds in place. After letting the plastic cool down for only a couple seconds, he pulled the moulds apart and flipping the top and bottom halves of a large, square plastic container together. Several screw-on lids were formed by a single press. Trimming and filing off the excess plastic took longer then it did to form them. It took only two windy days to make all the watertight food containers needed for the quest.

David rationed the plant refuse given to the beasts and dried the rest for the ones that would be going with them. The tunnels were lined with strings of drying, thinly-sliced pieces of potatoes, fruits and vegetables. The entire colony knew that their future depended on the quest's success and everyone was willing to endure the personal sacrifices that had to be made.

Relying only on rainwater was dangerous. At sea, a single splash of salt water could contaminate their collection system. After studying the disassembled airgun's high pressure pump, Joe helped Jacob forge the pieces needed to build a devise that could make seawater drinkable.

Finding the right types of clay to make the various ceramic filters was left to Mary, her beasts and Joe's wife Karen. Digging into the soil was risky. It was hard to judge how far down the ground was contaminated. While excavating a horizontal tunnel in the wall off a sunken chamber, they came across several layers of clay soil. After running it through a number of metal and cloth screens, plus washing and settling tanks, it took Karen a couple weeks to extract the clay needed for the filters. By that time the men had developed moulds for the filters.

By running salt water through two ceramic pot filters first, they found it easier to pump it through the finer filters. After wiping his lips, Joe filled his flask and tasted the treated water. With a smile on his face, he announced, "Perfect, I can't taste any salt at all."

During high tide, the ship was anchored close to the generators in order to make use of the excess electricity they provided. Long insulated cables were stretched out to an arc welder onboard the ship. They needed to finish the repairs to the rudders, starboard propeller along with a few other modifications that Daniel deemed necessary. The rest of the time the trio stayed out of sight by sailing from one obscure inlet to another.

As the tide was about to come in, the New Hope approached the tunnel housing the generator. Sitting on the top spar of the main mast Beth noticed the tip of Fresh Start's mast rounding the far end of the island that shielded the opening from view. After yelling out a warning she frantically slid down the mast. As Daniel cranked the steering wheel, she ran to help Josh adjust the sails.

Stripped of its sails, a muffled mechanical rattle radiated from the Fresh Start. A black cloud obscured the ship's bow along with a loud 'KABOOM'. The cannonball splashed the New Hope's stern.

Josh yelled out, "They mounted cannons to it."

With the open sea in sight, Beth responded, "Our only hope is to stay out of range."

As the wind shifted they noticed a small plume of grey smoke rising from the aft of the Fresh Start. While tightening a rope, Josh announced, "They must've figured out how to operate the boiler. Without having to rely on sails, they can travel directly into the wind."

Beth stared at Josh. "But the wind is against us. We can't keep zig-zagging in front of them. They are going to catch us."

Josh looked up at the sails. "Maybe they will run out of fuel."

The second shot fell a long way off their port side. From inside the pilothouse, Daniel shouted out, "They don't want to sink us. They want our ship and our flesh. They are just using their cannons to corral us."

Knowing that their engine was their best bet, Beth ran into pilot house, opened the hatch in its floor and climbed down a ladder. She immediately climbed back up. "Josh must've released almost all the methane gas when he emptied the digesters to help enrich the gardens. We have hardly produced any since then."

Without looking away from the window, Daniel asked, "Do you

think we have enough for a couple quick bursts?"

Beth looked at a small gauge and muttered, "Maybe."

With cannons mounted on the bow of both side hulls, The Fresh Start got behind the New Hope and blasted two more rounds. One almost hit their bow while the other splashed a few metres behind them. Along the coast Daniel spotted a long familiar passage marred with rubble. While cranking the steering wheel, he yelled out, "Fire it up. We will need everything you can squeeze out of it."

Josh cranked the jib sails in order to catch more wind. While the crew of the Fresh Start reloaded their cannons, the wind filled the New Hope's sails. With its port hull slightly lifted out of the water Daniel spun the steering wheel. Within seconds the ship pivoted seventy degrees. As it sliced past the Fresh Start's bow the townies peppered the metal pilothouse with rifle fire.

With bullets ricocheting off the cabin's door, Daniel yelled out, "Beth, how long before we get any steam?"

Beth's answer was almost muted by the ringing bullets. "Another minute or two."

Twisting his neck around, Daniel could see smoke coming out the exhaust pipe. "They have no way of knowing how much fuel we have. If we use it wisely we can fool them."

By the time the Fresh Start had circled around, the wind had pushed the New Hope out of reach of its cannons. Standing on the ladder, Beth popped her head out of the hatch and informed Daniel, "We won't have enough methane to out run them."

Using all his strength to control the wheel, Daniel grunted back, "As long as it gets us into that passage." Glancing back at her, he added, "When I say 'cut the engine', shut it down. Josh will need your help cranking up the sails."

The passage was a narrow gap between a long, jagged island and the mainland. Both sides of it consisted of rubble from toppled sky-scrapers. The entire length of the shallow passage was littered with sunken debris and hull ripping snares. Inside the gap, the trio had previously discovered a semi-protected inlet that had allowed them to get an occasional good night's sleep.

Josh watched the black smoke bellowing out of the Fresh Start's stack as it was about to go around the tip of the island. With the passage's entranceway in sight, Daniel yelled out, "Cut the engine."

By the time Beth raced up the ladder, Josh had already started to crank up the sails. It was the fastest Daniel had ever steered the ship into the dangerous passage. Despite the gentle breeze blowing against them, the momentum the ship had built up was enough to briefly combat the flapping of the unsecured sails.

After the ship glided past a small backward angled inlet, Josh and

Beth squared off the bottom sail on the main mast and brought the ship to a stop. As the wind began pushing the New Hope backwards, they released the ropes that secured the sail. Using the current and the wind pushing against the ship's flapping sails, Daniel skilfully guided the ship around the debris protecting the inlet and gently slid it into the obscure hideaway away from the wind.

The bow of the Fresh Start had crossed the mouth of the inlet before the first shot was fired. Josh responded as its aft cruised by.

With nowhere to turn around in the canal, Daniel knew that the captain of the Flesh Star might risk backing up.

Josh ran to the bow and began securing the forward jib sail. Beth had barely got below deck before Daniel yelled down, "Engage the engine."

Bullets rang off the New Hope's side hull as it emerged from the inlet. The wind blowing down the passage caught the ship's jib sails and spun it towards the mound of concrete that guarded the entranceway. Amidst gunfire, Josh rolled from one side of the ship to the other in order to secure the bottom square sail of the main mast. As he pulled on the ropes to angle the sail, a bullet whizzed by his head and another sliced through his sleeve.

As the ship's side hull rubbed against the smooth, weathered concrete, the wind pushed its bow around and slid it into the narrow canal. With only a few metres on either side of the ship, Daniel tried his best to stave off any further damage. The pilothouse deflected most of the bullets as Josh squared off another sail. Blood dribbled down his arm as he fought the ropes attached to the sail above it. By the time it was secured, his shaky hands made him collapse against the stairwell.

The two puffed out sails gave all the power Daniel needed to steer the ship. Only the odd bullet pinged off the pilothouse's steel door as the gap between the two ships widened. With the Fresh Start stuck in the canal they had plenty of time to escape.

The tide had finished rising by the time they returned back to the generating station. Word of the ship's return quickly made its way through the tunnels. Mary and David patiently waited in the hydro cavern as Josh swam towards the entrance dragging a rope behind him. The sealed plastic containers tied to his chest kept him afloat. He grabbed a pulley tied to a buoy and attached it to the line coming from the ship.

After feeling three firm tugs on the rope, Joe and Jacob began to haul it in. At the same time, Mary swam out of the submerged opening, stood up and faced her husband. "Bad timing. The tide has already started to go out." After looking up and down the canal, she added, "Jake told everyone that you had been spotted."

As the line was hauled into the cavern, Josh told her, "Without any sails its masts blend in with the debris sticking out of the mounds. We barely saw them. Our sails made us an easy target." After catching his breath, Josh informed her, "When they get out of the canal we suckered them into, they will be searching for us."

Mary noticed the blood soaked cloth wrapped around his arm. "Are you all right?"

Josh calmly told her, "Just a scrape. It barely cut through the skin."

A gust of wind rocked the ship and revealed the slight indentation that ran along the hull. Mary caught a glimpse of it. "You got away lucky."

"Daniel knows what he's doing."

"I hope so. The entire colony is counting on his leadership to acquire the nutrients we need."

David swam out of the tunnel and popped up next to Mary. "Tell mom and dad that I'm coming with them. If you hit bad weather, you'll need some extra help with the sails."

Josh smiled at him. "Your parents may not like that. It's dangerous out there. As long as you remain here, your parents will at least know that you are safe."

David crossed his arms and shook his head. "Between the poor harvests and all the flesh hunters skulking about none of us are really safe."

Chapter Five

Using ropes and grappling hooks, the crew of the Fresh Start tried to guide the ship backwards and swing it around. As its stern was about to enter the inlet, a sudden gust of wind twisted the ship and pushed it further down the canal. The starboard rudder struck a piece of concrete and the ship started to turn. Fighting the wind and pounding waves, the ropes either slid through the men's hands or dragged them overboard as the ship twisted sideways. With nowhere else to go, the water rushed under the ship and heaved both ends of it onto opposite sides of the canal. As the water level receded, the ship formed a bridge across the canal.

Onshore the crew pulled on ropes attached to the ends of the ship in hopes of dislodging it free. Simon glanced back and told the large muscular man behind him, "We need a real captain, not some bloodthirsty blowhard who doesn't know how to steer a ship."

Patrick gave the rope another tug before answering his young slim comrade, "You maybe right, but for now just pull on the rope. I don't like being on shore unarmed while the captain waves his pistols about."

After a couple tugs on the rope Simon began to bellyache loud enough that some of the others could hear, "The only reason the captain is in charge is because his brother Charles is the mayor. He doesn't know anything about boats. If it wasn't for Patrick, the ship would never have left the pier. He's the real captain of this ship, not that fat bloodthirsty ape."

Patrick was overwhelmed and could only produce a low rumbling groan as he pulled on the rope as hard as he could. He knew that the small framed, clean faced chatterbox in front of him was probably right. Since they arrived in the town Simon's cunning wit had wiggled both of them clear from Charles's dinner plate on numerous occasions. In addition, the combination of Patrick's many skills and large stature along with Simon's savvy had insured they both received the best cuts of meat on a regular basis. He smiled as he recalled how Simon would surrender some of his meat in order to help him maintain his strength.

Simon continued to complain. "We have been at this for over hours and got nowhere. The ship has barely budged,"

The scruffy, badly-weathered man behind Patrick added to the crew's discontent. "The young sprite is right. Why don't you take over? You have more experience on the water than anyone here. It's in your blood. You came from the sea."

Another man piped up, "Just because the captain is the Mayor's brother doesn't make him the right man for the job. All it means is that he takes a larger share of the hunt and lets the rest of us starve."

Before answering, Patrick glanced back at the man behind him. Comparing his scrawny arms to his own bulging biceps, he knew the man had very little to lose. "You are talking treason. If any of what you and Simon said got back to the captain, he would butcher all of us."

"You and Simon have been secretly running the ship from the moment it sailed. Why not make it legit." The man stared at Patrick's thick shoulders as he added, "Look at me. To be butchered would only relieve me of my suffering. Starvation isn't the easiest way to die."

The captain liked to use his overwhelming size to intimidate the crew. Despite the captain's girth, Patrick was the strongest of the two. The battle scars that cris-crossed Patrick's face along with his wild tangled red hair, frightened most of the crew. However, his even temperament earned him their respect. After taking some time to think, he shook his head. "The captain will turn us into meat if he got wind of this. I didn't grow these muscles to fill the captain's plate."

Simon cocked his head back and muttered, "Not if we do it right. I'm proposing a secret vote. Everyone puts a different coloured stone into a sack. White, the captain stays, black, we elect a new captain. All we have to do is start the rumour and put out a sack."

"What if the captain finds out? He'll suspect me. He knows that I'm the only man here capable of taking over the ship." Shaking his head Patrick added, "And what about Charles?"

"Once it is done, it's done. He will have to except it. Besides, he probably knows his brother is an oaf."

"Maybe you are right. The crew knows and respects me." Patrick let go of the rope and yelled out. "This is useless. Everyone drop your lines and take a break."

From aboard the ship, the captain watched the ropes go limp. At the top of his lungs he screamed out, "What is going on? What everyone doing?"

Patrick yelled back, "The men are exhausted and the ship isn't going anywhere until the tide comes in. Dragging the ship over this debris would only tear holes into its hulls."

"You are not the captain. Get those men back on those ropes."

"Do you want a ship or a of pile of scrap metal?" Patrick glanced at the ensnared hulls. "If it sinks what happens to us? There is nothing here to either eat or drink."

Despite the captain yelling and screaming for them to get back to work, the men on Patrick's side of the canal went inland and sat under a rocky cliff. Knowing that both teams had to work together, the crew members on the far side of the canal tied off their rope and found their own haven away from the wind.

As the exhausted crew sat around grumbling, Simon spoke up,

"Where is all this getting us? The captain is forcing us to drain our bodies without giving us anything to eat. He doesn't know what he's doing. To him we are just walking piles of soup bones."

Feeling more confident about the outcome, Patrick smiled as more of the crew started to grumble. "He's not here. We can say anything we want and he can't do anything about it."

Nick, one of the older members of the crew stared at him. "They're too many snitches in the crew. They would do anything for a second helping. Everything we say or do will get back to him." Waving his finger at Patrick and Simon, he added, "If you keep this up he will turn your flesh into jerky and make boots out of your hide."

"So the only reason that we obey him is out of fear of his snitches?" Patrick looked around and saw all the nodding heads. "Well, I don't think that is the way to run a ship. We are no longer in town." Pointing to the ship, he continued, "With that ship we can forge our own future. Lets see a show of hands."

With both Patrick and Simon pacing in front of them with their arms high in the air, one by one their fellow crew members began to raise their hands. As the frightened men gazed at each other, they found the courage to join the revolt. Simon walked over and stood in front of the only two nonconformists. "Henry, Nick, what about you two?"

Henry stood up, "The captain has always been good to me. If we go against him, he will butcher the lot of us."

Patrick walked over and stood in front of Henry. "Look at your belly. I had to work hard to get the meat I needed to pad these shoulders. What have you done to earn your extra portions? How may men have you turned in?"

As the other men looked at Henry, Simon restated the question, "Tell us, how many of our friends have you helped butcher?"

Nick put his arms around his stomach as he watched the mob stand up and walk towards Henry. Fearing that they might turn on him, sweat started to run down the side of his face as he stood up.

Henry raised his head and smiled as Nick quick-stepped over to his side. "See I'm not alone."

As the mob closed in, the pair pulled out their knives. Taking a step backwards Nick flung his arm around Henry's neck and sliced his throat. The blood gushing out of Henry's throat made the crowd step back. As his friend collapsed to his knees grasping his throat, Nick's knife fell away from his trembling fingers.   Looking at him, he muttered, "I'm sorry but it had to be done." Gazing at the crowd, he told them, "There is no going back now."

Patrick kicked Henry in the head and knocked him to the ground. With his head cocked to the side, he smiled at Nick and said, "You're right, there is no going back now. We need a new captain."

Simon piped up, "You are the only one here capable of doing the job. You have more experience at sea then anyone here."

Nick stared at Simon as he raised his blood drenched hand into the air. "I nominate Patrick to be are new captain. Does anyone know of anyone more fit to be captain?"

The men looked around at one another. Barely a word was said. Simon looked down at Henry as he struggled in vain to stop the blood coming out of his throat. "Nick is right. There is no one here that is more qualified. I say lets vote right here and now and get it over with."

The scruffy weathered man spoke up, "What about the men on the far side of the canal?"

Simon looked at the ship and then at the rope tied to the far side of the passage. "They will have their turn but I firmly believe they will agree that the choice is obvious."

Nick flung up his arm. "I stand behind Patrick."

Barely clinging onto life, Henry's eyes grew wide. As he wrapped his blood drenched fingers around Nick's ankle, his body went limp. With air still gurgling out his dead friend's neck, Nick kicked his foot free and bellowed out, "Who is with me."

Without hesitation every man there threw up his arm. Patrick took a deep breath and carefully studied their faces. "It will be hours before the tide raises enough to free the ship. Lets divvy up this traitor's meat and plan our next move on full stomachs."

After washing the blood from his beard Patrick walked toward the ship. The captain saw him and shouted out, "Tell them lazy sacks of meat to get back to work before I slaughter the lot of them."

Patrick noticed the ship rock a little as the water was starting to rise. "Then who will do your bidding?"

The captain hammered the railing with the butt of his pistol. "There are plenty more where they come from."

Walking over to the bow of the ship Patrick looked up at him. "The tide is coming in. Soon the water will be high enough to pull the ship free without ripping apart its hulls."

Out of frustration, the captain fired one of his pistols into the water and splashed the side of Patrick's leg. "Get them back to work, right now."

The crew deliberately took their time manning their ropes. In that twenty minutes, the tide had risen up to their knees. With each swell Patrick could see the ship bounce a little more. Wading into the water he yelled at the men on the far side of the passage. "Watch the way the ship rocks. As it is about to go up pull on your rope and let the water help us ease her off the debris."

The captain watched Patrick from the side of the ship. "Who's giving the order here?"

Standing where both teams could see him, the men ignored the captain's rants and watched Patrick's arms. On his command the men heaved every time he dropped his arm and took a breath between each wave.

Out of frustration the captain fired his pistol in the air. Patrick glanced at him and yelled out, "Stop". As the men released the ropes the water jolted the ship back to where it was.

As the captain used the railing to regain his footing, he screamed out, "I didn't tell you to stop."

Patrick turned and yelled at the captain, "From up there, you can't see what has to be done. Do you want me to free the ship or not?"

The captain rested both of his hands on the railing and snarled back, "I'm the captain. If you don't stop undermining me, I will have you for supper."

Patrick put his hands on his hips and looked at him. "At least let me free the ship before you start divvying up my flesh."

"This isn't over. We need to have a little chat."

The man behind Simon muttered, "I thought the captain was going to shoot him."

Simon turned to the man and said, "He can't. He knows he couldn't operate the ship without him."

Every order that Patrick barked made the men grew more confident in their decision. After Patrick ordered to men to regroup and pull from a different direction, the captain rolled up his coat and tossed it onto the deck before bellowing out, "What are you doing down there?"

A mere half dozen tugs latter the ship was dislodged. With the crew holding the ship from floating away, Patrick stared at the captain and said, "I told you that I could get the ship pointed in the right direction."

With the ship's anchor holding it relatively steady, the crew climbed up the rope ladders on the sides of the ship. As Nick climbed aboard, the captain grabbed his blood stained arms. Noticing that Henry was missing and the fresh blood on some of the men's sleeves, he asked, "Tell me who is the captain of this ship and who gives the orders?"

Nick's refused to answer. Enraged, the captain wrapped his arm around Nick's neck and began to squeeze it. "You are going to answer me or I will skin you alive."

Simon was the first to yelled out, "Let him go." The captain laughed and squeezed tighter. As several members of the crew began to circle around him, he stopped laughing. Simon pulled out his knife and stepped towards him, "We have elected a new captain. We don't need you anymore."

The captain looked at Patrick. Enraged, he tossed Nick onto the deck and went for his pistols. Before he could pull them out of his belt, four knives were thrust into his torso. As he tried to speak, Patrick stepped forward and knocked him onto the deck. With his foot on his throat, he told him, "The crew doesn't have to listen to you anymore."

While watching the captain bleed out, Patrick ordered the crew, "Haul what's left of Henry's body aboard. We can feast on these two porkers for a couple weeks."

Simon smiled at Patrick, "What do we do now captain?"

With his hand on Simon's shoulder, Patrick gazed at his men and proclaimed, "What ever we want. No more lotteries for us. We could even go back to town and pick it clean if we wanted to."

Gasping for air, Nick barked out, "They're not going anywhere. They'll keep. The other ship is still nearby. We can't let a treasure like that slip away."

Patrick walked over to him and helped him to his feet. "It'll be just a matter of time before we cross paths again. Next time, it will be ours. With two ships we could scour the coast and expand our hunting grounds."

Amidst rapidly growing cheers, Patrick threw his arms in the air and smiled. His eyes rested on Simon. "You were right. I think that I was truly meant to be the ship's captain."

Nick picked the captain's coat off the deck. Pushing Simon aside, he helped Patrick take off his tattered coat and put on the captain's. Stained in human blood the leather coat had a dark red hue that almost matched Patrick's long matted hair. Nick stood back and smiled, "Now this is a coat that people will fear."

Patrick studied his reflection in pilot house's window. "It really does make me look like a captain, doesn't it?"

"Not yet." Nick went into the pilot house and came right back. From behind his back he brandished a three pointed hat with strange bright feathers sticking out of one side. "With this on your head everyone will know who's in charge."

"Where did you get that?"

Nick smiled as he placed it on Patrick's head. "I found it hidden amongst the charts in the pilothouse. It must have belonged to the ship's previous captain."

Simon saw the gleam in Patrick's eyes as he stroked the feathers. "I wonder where these came from?"

Nick stood in front of Simon and blocked his view. Patrick noticed Simon peeking over Nick's shoulder. As he began to walk towards him, Nick stepped in his path. "You are the captain now. You should take charge. You can't let a child tell you what to do. How would that look to the rest of the crew?"

Bewildered, Patrick stared at Simon and whispered, "I might as well act like a captain." Gazing over the crew he shouted out, "First, we need to check the ship over for any damages. Then we'll return to town and fill our hull with all the meat and supplies it can hold. Why should we go hungry while Charles's men grow fat? This is our time to take control."

Simon stood back and watched as the crew revelled in the thought of having full stomachs. Under his breath, he told himself, "This is not what I expected." Seeing Nick adjust Patrick's coat, a tear ran down Simon's cheek. "That conniving weasel. Open your eyes Patrick. Everyone knows he's toxic."

Chapter Six

Sarah wheeled her chair into David's room and saw him packing. "You leaving?"

"As soon as they finish loading the ship." Without looking up he added, "The gardens need nutrients and I am one more mouth to feed. My parents need me."

"Where will you go?"

David never stopped working. "I don't know."

Sarah watched David pack all his meagre possessions into a small sac. "How about the island my family came from."

David stood up and faced her. "Maybe, at least we will find nutrients there."

Sarah wheeled her chair backwards and block the doorway. "Then you would be stupid not to take me with you."

Shaking his head, he told her, "How are you going to get around on the ship? We can't take the wheelchair with us."

As her fingers squeezed the chair's wheels her knuckles turned white. With bulging eyes she told him, "I am their only hope of finding the island."

"You could draw us a map."

Sarah shook her head. "I can't. I only know the direction we were travelling when we passed various landmarks along the way."

"And why should you help us? As you said many times over, we ate your parents."

"I have to know if anyone else survived." Looking down at her lap, in almost a whimper, she told him, "I have to know if I have a home to return to."

******

The shuttle they used to load the ship was nothing more then a shallow box with a few floats attached to each side. Using rope and pulleys, it was hauled back and forth with the aid of a multi-geared hand crank. As Mary hauled away an empty cart, David wheeled his next to the opening. He looked at Jake and saw the sweat pouring out of him as he leaned against the crank. "I have some more supplies to put aboard."

Jake shook the sweat from his forehead and said, "I hope John gets back soon to relieve me, I'm getting wiped out."

David smiled at him. "I thought you just took over."

"That was a few trips ago."

"Maybe I should get my stuff in the shuttle while you still have some energy left."

With his head buried between his arms, Jake told him, "Go for it."

David glanced at Jake before he bend down and rolled a large sac out of the cart and onto his shoulder. After sliding into the water, he readjusted his load and waded towards the exit. The splashing water muted his soft instructions, "Now take a deep breath."

From inside the large sac, Sarah whispered, "On a count of three."

As soon as he heard 'three', David dove into the water. With his belly scraping the floor of the shallow exit, he used the rope to pull them through it as fast as he could. As he rolled Sarah off his back and into the shuttle, he said, "Are you all right?"

"I'm fine. Now go before they get suspicious."

Jake watched him crawl out of the water, dragged the two remaining sacs through the tunnel and into the water. After tossing them into the shuttle, he climbed in and gave the rope three quick tugs. Jake felt the tugs and began cranking the shuttle towards the ship.

The shuttle bobbed along the top of the water as the rope pulled it through the surf. The curls of the white crested waves drenched everything inside the shuttle. Hearing Sarah fighting for air, David told her, "I told you that it wasn't going to be a joyride."

With her forearms holding the fabric away from her face, Sarah replied, "Yeah, but I presumed you wanted me alive. If you wanted fresh meat, I would've volunteered."

Clinging to the sides of the craft, David muttered, "You can't show us the way to the island if you are dead."

As the shuttle bumped the side of the ship, his father reached down and grabbed David's hand. Daniel's tanned skin was so dark that David barely recognized him. As he helped him stand up, all David could say was, "Dad".

With a wide smile on his face, Daniel said, "Welcome aboard son. Now, let me help you with your things."

David grabbed the rope ladder that was draped over the hull of the ship and used it to steady himself. After tossing the two lighter sacs to his father, he reached for the sac Sarah was in. Before he could get a hold of it, a wave rocked the box and Sarah's head slid beneath the water inside the shuttle. David let go of the ladder and quickly grabbed the knotted end of the sac. As he hoisted it into the air, Daniel reached down and grabbed the rope that tied it shut. "This is a heavy one."

Between the waves and the shuttle banging against the side of the ship, neither of them heard Sarah's moans. As she clenched her teeth, she heard Daniel say, "We have to keep the box moving. Hunters are everywhere. Any delay could expose the location of the generating station."

With David's help, Daniel slid Sarah onto the deck. While Josh signalled for the shuttle to be hauled back, Beth helped her son climbed aboard. "I missed you."

While still on their knees, he gave his mother a big hug and told her, "Me too."

Cutting the hug short, David scampered over to Sarah. Once the shuttle began its trip back, Daniel turned around and asked, "So what's in the bag?"

Beth bent down and helped her son open the bag. She noticed the smile of his face as Sarah gasped for air.

Sarah looked at her and spurted out, "I'm not food." After a couple breaths, she said, "I know my legs make me a liability, but I can point you to the island that I grew up on. It has all the nutrients your colony needs. You won't be able to find it without me."

David helped her out of the bag. Daniel looked at her legs. One was still in a cast and the other wrapped in bandages. "You could have drawn us a map."

"How? All I can go by are the various sights and smells I experienced along the way. A map would be next to useless."

Daniel walked over and helped David to his feet. "You should've left her in the tunnels."

David wrapped his arm around his father and faced Sarah. "We could search for maybe years without finding the nutrients the colony needs. If we can find the island she came from, we might be able to fill the hulls and make it back before the next crop rotation. The time she can save greatly outweighs the food she will consume."

Beth stood up and smiled. Putting her head on her son's shoulder she took a deep breath. "If we find it, we can draw a map and return as many times as we need."

"It is to late to send her back." Looking down at Sarah, Daniel shook his head. "She is going to be a burden. In order to sail a ship we have to react quickly."

Sarah looked at his grimacing face, "Don't worry, I'll earn my keep. I know how to run the engine plus I can look after the digester and even the methane separator. I don't need legs to crawl around below deck."

David stepped between Sarah and his father. "She's a hard worker and she knows the ship. We need her, bad legs and all."

Daniel watched David's face as he defended Sarah. As David reached back and squeezed her hand, his father smiled. "She's here now. One more mouth for us, one less for them. I only hope she's worth more than she consumes. David, she will be your responsibility."

David helped Sarah up. With his arm wrapped around her waist and hers around his neck, Sarah forced herself to smile as she told Daniel, "I promise you won't regret it."

Beth walked over to husband and smiled as she reached for his hand. The pair watched David pick Sarah up and carry her toward the forward hatch of the port hull. Daniel called out to his son, "David, as soon as she is settled, get right back up here. We need a lookout."

Seeing her son nod his reply, Beth whispered to her husband, "David knew you wouldn't send her back. The ship is deemed unclean and he knew that you were aware of what would happen to her if you had."

Before the water flooded the cave, with John's help, Mary loaded three beasts into the shuttle. Despite all four legs being tied together, as a wave rocked the shuttle, one of them broke free and jumped overboard. She reached into the water and caught its hind leg. Using both hands she twisted it around and grabbed its ears. Its flailing hooves and sharp teeth tore off pieces of the leather protecting her forearms. Seeing Josh hanging over the side of the ship, she yelled above the screaming beasts. "I'm going to toss this one aboard. Tell everyone to get ready for it."

Despite its snapping teeth, Mary tightened her grip on the flailing beast's ears. As the shuttle approached ship, she wiggled her feet under her crouched torso and yelled out, "Here it comes."

As the shuttle was about to hit the side of the ship, Mary sprang to her feet. Picking the beast out of the water she flipped it over her head. Josh caught one of its hind legs and rolled it onto the deck. While helping Mary lift the other two onboard, Josh looked back and saw Daniel and Beth trying to catch the elusive creature. Seeing Daniel fall face first onto the deck, he chuckled as he helped Mary climb aboard. "We better get these two below deck."

As Josh picked up one of the beasts the smile on his face disappeared. Above his wife's head he noticed smoke from the Fresh Start's stack on the far side of the long island of rubble that hid the cavern from view. "They came back!"

Seeing David exit the hatch of the port hull, Josh tossed the beast into his waiting arms. "Get them below deck."

Mary put down the beast she was carrying and reached down to disconnect the pulley connecting the ship to the cavern. The disoriented beast ran between Daniel and Beth as they frantically cranked up the anchor. Josh ran and released the cranks unfurling the sails. As the shuttle was being hauled into the cavern its aft rose out of the rising water before being pulled under and into the cavern's submerged entrance. Beth looked at Daniel and said, "I hope their lookout doesn't see it."

As Josh and David adjusted the sails, Beth and Mary tried to capture the elusive squealing beast. It saw the open cabin door and darted towards it at full speed. At the sight of the stairs it turned and slid against the door. Twisting its head around it saw Beth's hands reaching towards it. After tucking its hind legs against the door, it sprang into the air and slammed into her chest. While stumbling backwards, Beth wrapped her arms around the beast. Its high piercing squeals were deafening. As she hit the guard railing the impact loosened her grip. It was just enough for the beast to climb over her shoulder and leap into the water.

After it surfaced, Mary watched it cry out in terror as it splashed around. "We have to retrieve it."

Beth shook her head. "We can't. There is no time."

******

Simon's slight but sturdy frame made him an ideal lookout. With one arm around the centre mast and his other shielding his eyes from the sun, he sat in a sling attached to the top spar of the centre mast. As the ship was about to sail pass the end of the island, he looked back and saw the top sail of the New Hope's middle mast being unfurled. "I was right. They anchored in the same place as last time."

Upon hearing it, Patrick turned to Nick. "That can't be a coincidence."

"Just think, if we didn't check the ship over where we did, we would've gone right passed this channel." Nick smiled at him and patted him on his back. "Maybe some luck is finally coming our way."

Simon saw some splashing in the water but didn't pay to much attention to it. With part of the island still between them, all he could do was give Patrick updates. Unfortunately the wind was behind their prey as they sailed around the island.

Grinning, Patrick told his crew. "You wanted a second chance at them and now you got it." Glaring up at Simon, he told him, "Don't lose them. We need to see where they go."

As the ship entered the canal Patrick used his binoculars to study the shoreline. "They seem to like this area for some reason or other."

Nick put his hand on his shoulder. "They escaped from us twice now. Maybe they picked it for security reasons."

Nick shook his head. "There has to be another reason."

After noticing some splashing in the water Simon yelled down, "Ease off the engine. Something is in the water. It's off the port side."

As they got closer, the struggling beast's squeals rose above the clanking from the engine. Nick spotted the frightened beast. Using a grappling hook, he snagged the poor creature behind the ribs. While he hauled it onboard, a dozen men formed a semi-circle behind him.

Seeing the crowd beneath him, Simon yelled down, "What is it?"

Nick got on one knee to look beast over. "Nothing I've seen before. It must have fallen off their ship while they were getting away." Looking at the men around him, he added, "I caught it so I should have the right to cut off my share first."

Simon yelled down at him, "I thought Patrick's orders were that all meat was suppose to be shared equally."

Several members of the crew pushed Nick aside and hung the small beast from a sail spar. As they cut off the beast's head, they collected the blood in a large bowl. A tall crew member handed the bowl to Nick. "You snagged it, so you should be the first to taste it."

Nick took a few large gulps and passed it back to him. The man stared at the bowl. There wasn't much left for the rest to share.

With a dribble of blood trickling down his chin, Nick looked up at Simon and grinned. "See, everyone gets their fair share."

Nick stepped aside while the crew hacked the beast apart. From the helm Patrick saw everything that transpired. When Nick brought him his portion, Patrick laid the strange meat down on a small metal counter. After hours of heading in a straight line out to sea, Patrick told Nick, "This is foolish. They are not heading anywhere. They are just putting the wind behind them to get as much distance between us as possible. There has to be a better way to capture that ship along with their flesh?" After a brief pause, he added, "In the meantime, I know an easier game to play."

******

Perched on the highest spar, David stared at the Fresh Start as it began to slip further and further behind them. "They are starting to fall back."

Daniel took out his binoculars and looked at the distant ship. "I can't see any smoke. Maybe they are running out of fuel?"

Feeling safe, David slid down the mast, opened the front hatch on the Port hull and climbed down to where he had left Sarah. As he sat next to her, he said, "We are safe. I think they are running out of fuel."

Sarah glanced at a hatch in the floor near the rear of the compartment. "Are you sure we're safe?"

"I wouldn't have left my post if I wasn't."

Sarah grabbed his leg. "You know that even without the engine they have enough manpower to catch us."

David shook his head. "I don't understand."

Sarah placed her hand on his cheek. "Help me to that hatch and I'll show you."

The hull was lined with storage compartments. With only enough room for one abreast David had to almost drag Sarah along the hallway. At Sarah's request, he opened a hatch in the floor. Chains, gears and scores of miscellaneous mechanical parts filled the bottom third of the hull. David turned to Sarah and asked, "I thought the bottom of the side hulls were full of ballast. What is this equipment for?"

"Lower me down and I'll show you." They were no stairs or even a ladder to assist anyone into the dark, shallow room. David grabbed

Sarah under her arm pits and eased her through the hatch. She gasped in pain as her knee hit a metal rod. The compartment was barely waist high. While using one arm to hold herself steady, Sarah carefully slid her legs forward as she was lowered into the chamber. With the foot of her bandaged leg resting on a pedal and the one in a cast to the side, she sat down on a padded beam. After pulling a couple levers she grabbed two handles that were attached to a piece of twisted steel. "Now watch this."

As she turned the steel handles a chain that was wrapped around two gears moved her foot in a circle. David could feel the ship rock slightly. "What's happened?"

"I engaged the gearbox to this section of the pedals. It controls the port side propeller. Even a girl with bad legs can help move this ship. There are seven stations on each side hull. These ships were designed as escape vessels. It can use sail, steam, and even human power. In fact, if the gearbox is properly set, all three could be utilized all at the same time."

After lifting Sarah out, David ran to his father, "There is a reason they need so many men aboard their ship. They don't need sails or even a boiler to catch us."

Daniel coldly looked at him and said, "I know, we found the equipment a while ago."

Looking in the distance, the Fresh Start was only a speck. "I don't understand. What happened?"

"I'm not sure." Even through his binoculars all he could see is the Flesh Start's crow's nest. "They just turned around and started heading back."

"But they could have caught us?"

"Maybe, but then what?"

Chapter Seven

Patrick steered the Fresh Start close to shore and told Nick to lower its anchor. As Nick exited the cabin, Simon stepped forward and stood beside Patrick. Patrick turned and looked at him. "It takes a lot of feed to raise meat that tender. Even its organs were unblemished and full of flavour. Select a couple men and find out where it came from."

After checking the depth of the water the three men climbed over the side. Sinking up to his shoulders, Simon waded ashore with his rifle and pack held above his head. Seeing one of the men help Simon ashore Patrick ordered the anchor to be lifted. With his crew manning the pedals, Patrick slowly followed the shoreline towards town noting several dozen inlets capable of hiding a ship.

Spotting the ship, two men ran to the pier and waited for the Fresh Start to get closer to the dock. After catching and tying the aft dock line, one man yelled out, "How was the hunt?"

Nick answered him, "We got a few days supply of meat."

Donning his red coat and feathered hat, Patrick walked to the side of the ship. The two men looked at each other. "Where is the captain?"

Patrick looked down at them and replied, "Meat."

Nick and a few other members of the crew climbed off the bow of the side hull and blocked the dockworkers exit. As the pair drew their knives in defiance, Nick smiled and gazed up at Patrick. "They have some fight in them. Do you want them for crew or meat."

Patrick looked at the two frightened men. "Take off your shirts and let me see how well the mayor fed you."

Confused, the men slowly sheathed their knives and pulled off their shirts. They both had the same long curly blonde hair and square faces. Patrick ordered them to turn around. A few of his crew members began to drool as they eyed the muscular pair. Most of the men and women in town had been whipped so many times their scars were impossible to count. The pair had barely a dozen each. "These two were privileged. Nick, how are their teeth?"

With a bit of brute force, both men reluctantly opened their mouths for Nick to examine. "Much better than mine."

Patrick placed his hands on his waist and looked down at them. "So what do you think?"

Nick piped up, "You can't trust any of the mayor's lackeys." Pointing to the older man, he added, "Him especially. You don't need a crew member that could turn on you."

As the older man grabbed his knife, Patrick yelled out, "Stop if you want to live." With the man's blade pressed against Nick's rib cage, he added, "We can use a man like you. I have seen you around. What is your name?"

The man sliced Nick's shirt as he withdrew his knife. "Most people call me Killy Billy."

"You are the mayor's butcher. I didn't recognized you without your black hood. I've seen you fetch the losers of the meat lottery. You really like your job."

Twirling his hand and knife in a flamboyant figure eight in front of him, the large man declared, "Guilty as charged."

With a curl of Patrick's index finger, the men rushed behind him and grabbed his arms. The younger man raised his hands in the air. Beyond the poor growth of whiskers and small patch of chest hairs, the well defined muscles on young man's chest made Patrick smile. "Take them both aboard and strap their hands and feet to a set of gears. We can decide their fate later."

As the young man climbed on board Patrick asked him, "What's your name?"

"Roger."

"I've heard rumours that Killy Billy had a son. Is he really your father?"

The young man shrugged his shoulders as he was escorted to the port hatch. "How would I know? The way women are passed around, how would anyone know?"

Leaving a few armed men behind to guard the ship, Patrick led the rest of his crew into town. Upon seeing the red coat, the mayor raised his arms in the air and went into the street to meet them. When he realized it was Patrick and not his brother wearing the coat, his hands fell to the butts of the pistols on his belt, "What's going on?"

"The men didn't like the way the ship was being run." Walking straight to him, Patrick added, "And I think this town needs a few changes as well." A large dagger slipped out of his sleeve. Before Charles could pull his pistols from his belt, the blade of Patrick's knife was shoved under his rib cage and into his heart. As the mayor gasped in shock, he heard Patrick whisper in his ear, "We are taking over."

Patrick extracted his knife and Charles fell to his knees. Grant and nine other armed men ran to his aid. While the others stood back, Grant knelt beside Charles. The mayor looked at him. "Remember, we had a deal. Save as many as you can and wipe the rest from your mind."

Not sure what Charles was talking about, Grant said, "The town will survive."

Unable to speak, the mayor shook his head and keeled over. Grant looked up at Patrick. "Why did you have to kill him?"

"We killed his brother. It was him or us." As both sides shouldered their rifles Patrick used his coat to wipe the blood off his knife. "We need meat and fuel. You can have the mayor's body if you want, but we are not leaving without the supplies we need."

Grant pointed his musket at Patrick's head. "Why should we give you anything?"

Patrick looked around as the men on both sides were vying for position in case any shooting started. "We could kill each other and the survivors could feast on the dead, but what good would that do? This town has almost consumed itself as it is. Like us, travellers are getting fewer and fewer. We both know that the ship is the town's best hope of finding the meat the town needs. "

Most of Grant's face was shaded by the brim of his hat as he growled, "The sea harvesters are finding edible creatures amongst the seaweed. Charles was overseeing the construction of better boats for them to use."

A large smile grew on Patrick's face. "Good, but right now people are starving."

After licking his lips, Grant looked up and grinned, "Those sailors did taste pretty good."

"So did the ground dweller we caught last year." Patrick's smile disappeared as he added, "And how many lives were lost getting him. Most of the meat we harvested was from our own dead. The people on those ships had lived above ground. If we can find where they came from, we wouldn't have to waste lives digging them out."

"You have a point." Grant halted his advance and lowered his musket. "The problem is that even if we stock your ship, we have no guarantee you will return. Once you discover their home what's stopping you from staying."

"Numbers. Finding the place is one thing. Conquering it maybe another. We might need a lot of men to do that."

Grant rubbed his chin and glanced at the men pointing muskets at each other. "How many sacrifices do you think you will need for this venture?"

"It might be a long voyage." Making wide gestures with his arms, Patrick replied, "A lot, especially if we expand our crew. You and some of your men are welcome to join us."

Grant stepped back. "How do we knew that you don't want us for fresh meat incase you run out?"

"I'll need men that know how to fight." While looking around at the remains of the town Patrick added, "By feeding the weak you are depriving the healthy. Why not have a good culling and give the rest a better chance of survival."

"That's not how we do things. We have laws."

"And you and your men get the best cuts of meat for enforcing them." With a wide grin, Patrick added, "Why not accept the fact that you have less than five hundred people in town and only a couple hundred worth feeding." Patrick raised his left arm and slowly lowered it. As his arm fell, so did the muzzles of his men's muskets.

Grant's narrow eyes told Patrick that he was still leery. His men had been together a long time. They had no control over the boats and never trusted the men working the docks. One of them yelled out, "No sea harvester if going to tell us what to do in our town."

Ignoring the outburst, Patrick told Grant, "You are now the new mayor. While my crew is searching for better hunting grounds, you have some serious decisions to make."

"Maybe?" Without looking away from Patrick, Grant hollered, "Lower your weapons."

Patrick smiled. "So we have an understanding."

"Maybe?"

"Everybody still where you are. Me and the new mayor need to talk over a few details." Putting his hand on Grant's shoulder, he said, "I have something to show you."

As Patrick and Grant began to stroll back to the ship, the deputies dragged Charles' body into a nearby shack. Nick and two crew members followed them but were blocked by several deputies. "I thought we were to share the meat?"

While pointing a long knife at Nick's chest, a tall scrawny deputy sneered. "Your captain said that we could have him."

Looking up into the man's eyes, Nick calmly stated, "Have him. Compared to the succulent meal we had this morning eating him would be a huge disappointment."

******

Aboard the ship, Patrick led Grant into the pilot house. Suspended from its ceiling was a tightly fastened net containing several long tubes. Reaching up, Patrick took one down and extracted a large, thick, rolled up paper from it. "Do you know what this is?"

"It's an old map. They are useless."

"Not completely." Patrick used his finger to follow lines on the map. "The landscape maybe somewhat tilted but they can still be used as a guide. Look closer at the rings. The basic contours remain the same. Despite all the changes they are still useful."

Grant studied the map. Someone had drawn in the coastline along with placing circles, stars and X's on numerous spots. "Maybe they might be of some use."

"As long as we stay away from the boxes on the map we should be alright. We don't know what kind of buildings they were or how tall they were."

After going over all the maps Grant realised that there were large gaps. "The maps don't overlap. They are like a checkerboard."

"I think they divided them between the two ships." Patrick was surprised to see Grant grinning ear to ear. "What's up with you?"

"You may not need them all. Killy Billy got a couple of women to talk. I guess they weren't used to seeing their children being slowly skinned alive in front of them. Anyways they both told Charles the exact same story before he agreed to grant them mercy. Between the maps they drew and these, you should be able to retrace the path the ships took."

"And reap all the meat and sun grown plants we can eat."

Grant studied Patrick's face. "When you find this place you may need every man you can muster to overtake it. We know they have weapons."

Patrick put his hand on Grant's shoulder and added, "We need to work together. If we don't, we are both doomed."

"But killing off over half the town's population."

"What's worse, harvesting them while they still have some flesh on their bones or letting them die from hunger and be left with nothing but soup bones? Either way they are dead."

Grant looked out at the sea. "You will need more than just food. Plus we'll need men, boats, gunpowder and weapons in order to launch an invasion. That will take both time and manpower." Placing both hands on the doorframe he gave out a sigh before adding, "There has to be another way."

Patrick looked at the empty crows nest and thought for a couple seconds before answering, "There is. You could route out the earth dwellers. Their meat would more than make up for the sacrifices needed for our initial voyage. Plus their weapons could help arm the men we'll need for an assault."

Grant turned around, looked at him and shook his head. "How? We have been trying to capture them for years."

Patrick cheerfully smiled, "I think I may have found their lair. If I am right, all you will have to do is rout them out."

"That would be costly."

"So what. If done right, it would be a good way of eliminating the weak without the backlash of a massive lottery."

Grant looked out the window as people cautiously poked their heads out of their meagre homes to see what's happening. "So you want me to let the earth dwellers do the culling for me." With a slight chuckle he added, "I could lose over a hundred men and still be hailed a hero."

"I'm guessing that you'll need Killy Billy back."

"He can be a heartless creature, but sometimes you need someone like him to do the jobs no one else wants."

"And take the fall if things go wrong."

Grant glared at Patrick. "What about his apprentice?"

Patrick smiled at Grant. "As I said before, we need some more crew members. Roger is strong lad that knows how to take orders. He's mine."

Chapter Eight

Two days later, it was almost nightfall before the New Hope approached the mouth of the channel in front of the cavern. They had fought the wind all the way back. With one arm wrapped around the mast, David stood on the top spar and peered through his father's binoculars. Spotting the nose of their sister ship in the channel, he yelled out, "It's a trap!"

David then noticed three men walking along the shore towards the cavern. "They are searching for the water inlet."

Beth looked up at him and yelled, "Come on down. Up there you are an easy target."

The tide was at its lowest, making the channel extremely hazardous to navigate. Daniel yelled to Josh, "Drop anchor gently, but don't give it any slack." As soon as Daniel felt it touch bottom he twirled the steering wheel and let the wind flip the ship almost completely around.

Under full sail a person would have to be blind not to spot the ship. From the crow's nest of their sister ship a call rang out, "They're back."

With his ship facing forty-five degrees to the wind Daniel yelled out, "Mary help Josh raise the anchor. Beth tighten up the jib we are heading back to sea. I guess the rest the rest of the volunteers will have to stay behind. We can't risk another trip back."

******

Joe had aimed one of the cannons at the ship as it cruised by the cavern. Afraid of giving away their location, he had held his fire. He noticed that the name on the ship was disfigured. The 'T' at the end was removed and the first 'R' was hammered into a "L". In addition to the two cannons at its bow, the Flesh Star had one on each side and two smaller ones facing the rear. Joe turned to Jake who was manning the cannon across from him, "I hope they didn't spot the opening."

"I hope not." looking back at Joe, he said, "I also hope they got away safely."

Staring towards the end of the cannel, Joe told him, "Me too." Shaking his head he added, "If they don't make it back, all our efforts and sacrifices would have been for nothing."

******

As the Flesh Star crept away from the cavern, two of the men on shore ran into the water and swam to it. Standing on a outcrop, Simon stared back at a small stream of water coming out of a cavern and trickling back into the channel. The yelling aboard the ship shook him from his concentration. Realizing he was alone, he dove into the water. The ship didn't stop. Instead, lines were thrown into the water for him to grab. He managed to grab one. As the ship started to gain speed, several men hauled him out of the water.

"I could've drowned." Simon coughed up some water, got up and stormed into the pilot house. "What was the hurry?"

"That." Patrick pointed straight ahead of them. The sails of the New Hope were disappearing into the waves. "They must have spotted us." Patrick turned to Simon and grinned, "So was I right? Is that where the ground dwellers are hiding?"

Still trying to catch his breath, Simon forced out, "It sure looks like it. We could attack them now."

Patrick smiled and gave out a slight sigh. "Why waste good men when you have dregs that you can sacrifice instead."

In the distance, dark skies formed behind the New Hope's silhouette. Within a half an hour, only the ship's top sails could be seen above the foaming crests of the waves. "We are not going after them either?"

Wrapping his arm around Simon, Patrick replied, "I already know where they are going." Rubbing Simon's head, he added, "The same place we will be heading, as soon as we tell Grant the location of the earth dweller's lair."

******

The winds intensified as the New Hope sailed into a storm. The waves poured over the deck and splashed against the front window of the pilot house obscuring Daniel's vision. As the ship was tossed around, Josh and David cranked up and secured the top and bottom sails, leaving only the jib, aft and mid sails to help steer the ship through the storm. Water poured through the cracks around the hatches. Below deck, Mary, Beth and Sarah manned the bilge pumps in the three hulls and tried to keep everything dry.

After helping Josh secure the last of the top sails, David worked his way along the railing towards the pilot house. "They are still behind us. If it wasn't for a bolt of lightning striking the water we would never have spotted them." As he shut the hatch, David continued, "We can't outrun them in this weather."

The rain started to pour down. Without looking away from the window, Daniel asked him, "How far behind are they?"

"Not far." David looked back as another lightning strike hit the water. "I just can't figure out how they found us."

Josh put his hand on David's shoulder. "They won't do anything in this weather. If they use their cannons they risk sinking the ship. Our best bet is to try to lose them in the storm."

Glancing back at them, Daniel yelled above the storm, "I've got a better idea." Turning to David, he added, "Take the wheel and try to keep the bow of the ship pointing directly into the oncoming waves."

David watched as his father worked his way along the guard rail towards the forward mast. As the water poured off the deck, Daniel dashed over to the mast. He grabbed the lever that locked the bottom sail in place and gave it a yank. As the ship's bow hit a wave the unfurling sail struck his face and chest. The blow knocked him off his feet. An onslaught of knee high water slid him across the deck. Somehow he managed to grasp the railing and hang on. Both David and Josh cringed as they watched him from a cabin window. Josh exited the cabin and quickly secured the door after them. Knowing what had to be done he worked his way along the railing opposite Daniel and secured the flapping sail.

After his side was finally secured, Daniel yelled over to Josh, "loosen the jib and get ready for a quick turnabout."

The waves were cresting a metre above the nose of the ship. Using the large sail in the middle of the ship as a focal point, at the top of a swell, Daniel cranked the aft sail to the side. With Josh's help they let the wind spin the ship around before the next wave hit. "You can't do this using only a rudder."

Leaving Josh to secure the jib, Daniel crawled to the pilot house. With the two ships racing towards each other, he grabbed the wheel. "I'll take over the helm." The wind pushed the ship over the waves, while the jib and aft sails gently veered them to the side of the oncoming vessel.

******

Patrick watched as the New Hope abruptly swung around in front of him. As he tried to turn and cut them off, a huge wave hit the side of his ship. The starboard hull was tossed into the air nearly capsized the ship. At the top of his lungs, he yelled out, "Give me everything you got."

By the time he had finally regained control of the ship, the New Hope had disappeared into the dark stormy night. The ship's sails were masked by the huge white crested waves.

While Patrick tried to get back on course, Nick told him, "They are running scared. By the time we finally catch them, there will be no fight left in them."

"Not yet." Patrick snickered. "The fools let us get ahead of them, and their luck is about to run out."

******

Out of sight of the Flesh Star, Daniel ordered, "We lost them, now lets get the ship back on course." With Josh and David manning the sails, they did another abrupt about face. As they cranked the large middle sail back up, Daniel muttered to himself, "Now, we just ride out the storm."

After a couple hours of relative silence, Josh spoke up, "I think the storm is dying down."

An hour later, Daniel told David and Mary to unfurl the sails. Josh and Beth went around and secured them in place. Handling each rope was like a tug of war. A gust of wind caught the sail Beth was securing and tossed her against the railing. Her tight grip on the rope saved her from flipping over it and into the water. Josh crawled across the deck. While she limped to the pilot house, he finished securing the sail.

Daniel lashed the wheel and helped Beth through to door. "Are you all right?"

Sitting on a fold down stool at the rear of the cabin, she rubbed her leg and told him, "Yeah, I just smashed my back against the railing and banged my bad leg against a post. Good thing I had my brace on."

After all the sails were secured, David, Josh and Mary migrated to the cabin. David squeezed in and knelt beside his mother as the other two clung to the doorframe. Beth smiled at him. "I'm fine. I'll have a lot of bruises in the morning that's all."

Relieved but still worried, David asked, "Are you sure you are all right?"

Beth gasped her son's hands. "Absolutely. Now get your wet clothes off before you get sick. We are under manned. We can't afford anyone getting sick."

As David, Josh and Mary worked their way to the main cabin, Beth lowered her head to her knees. Daniel passed her his tunic. "It's your turn. You can't get sick either."

Clenching her teeth, she forced out, "Thanks, but I'll need a bit longer. My leg is starting to throb."

"At least strip down to the waist and keep your chest warm."

Daniel candidly watched her pull off her wet top before putting on his dry tunic. "I'm better equipped for that kind of work then you are. You should be the one behind the wheel and I should be doing the heavy work."

Beth held up her head, "I can't anticipate the ship's movements like you can. Without you behind that wheel, we would've been meat by now."

Starring out the window, he replied, "Maybe." Glancing back at her, he added, "Can you stand."

"Sure."

"Then take the wheel while I get you some dry clothes."

With Beth leaning against the wheel, Daniel ran across the deck to the main cabin and came back with some dry clothes under his arm. "These are the best I could find. Everybody else is huddled under blankets waiting for their clothes to dry."

Daniel grabbed the wheel as Beth took off her pants and brace. Still wearing his tunic, Beth slipped on the dry pants and asked, "What are we going to do now?"

"Make it through the night." Glancing back at her, he added, "This is a big sea. During the day a person can see a ship twenty kilometres away. On a clear night half that, but under these conditions only a few kilometres. Even under full sail we should be safe."

For the rest of the night Daniel and Beth took turns manning the helm. Beth slouched behind the wheel as the sun broke over their starboard side. A gentle breeze effortlessly pushed the ship over the calm sea. After spotting some debris sticking out of the water she glanced at the map on the bench beside her. She searched for circled square dots indicating they had been sighted before. They were no groupings like the ones in front of her. Unsure of what to do she yelled out, "Daniel I need your help."

Sleeping in the engine room below her, Sarah woke up and yelled, "What's wrong?"

"There is some debris sticking out of the water on the port side. I'm not sure where we are on the map nor which way I should be steering."

Sarah thought for a moment. "Are there four piles of them in a straight line?"

"Yes."

Sarah thought for another moment. "They might not be on the map you are using. There was only one set of maps so both captains had to share them."

Anxious Beth yelled out, "So you saw them before."

"No, but I remember hearing some of the others talking about them. What side did you say they were on?"

"Port."

"This isn't right. It should have taken longer to get here." Still half asleep, Sarah fidgeted with her hands to figure out the various directions before answering. "Sail parallel to the piles until I get up there." Pulling herself up the ladder, she knocked on the hatch door. "I need some help."

Beth tied off the steering wheel and helped Sarah onto the fold-up seat. As she regained control of the wheel, she asked, "Does anything look familiar?"

Sarah looked around. "No, when we passed through this debris field I was below pedalling. The captain thought sailing though it would be to dangerous."

After making sure the Flesh Star was no where in sight, Beth dug the rag out of the ships bell and rang it. Before it stopped echoing,

Daniel swung the cabin door open. With two mugs of hot tea in one hand, he ran to the pilot house. As he rushed in he spilled some of the tea on Sarah and anxiously asked, "What's wrong?"

Beth pointed to the piles of debris. "According to Sarah we are about to enter a large debris field. It's not on any of our maps."

Daniel turned to Sarah and asked, "How did you get through it?"

While holding her tea soaked pant legs away from her skin, she answered, "The captain stripped the sails and ordered everyone to petal through it. Needless to say, I was below deck."

"I guess that would be safer. You never know when a sudden gust could come and push us off course." As the rest climbed out of the cabin, Daniel yelled out, "Drop anchor and wind up the sails."

Josh piped up, "We are in the middle of the sea, the anchor won't hold."

"We are in a debris field. Surely it'll catch on something." After thinking about what he had just said, he added, "Lets hope it is not to close to the surface."

Daniel took out his binoculars and studied the surface of the water around him. At the bottom of a few undulating waves he noticed more debris lying several metres under the surface. Feeling a small jolt as the anchor latched onto something, he turned to Sarah, "Do you remember anything that could help us get through this mess?"

"I remember someone saying that the field was circular shaped with corridors like the spokes of a wheel." Sarah bit her lip and thought for a while before continuing. "I also remember that the elders tied ropes with weights on to long poles and used them to keep within the channels. A bell attached to the tip would ring if the weight struck anything."

Daniel glanced over the ship's deck. "Where did they get the poles from?"

With the tea cooled off, Sarah wrung out her pants. "They removed the guide rails and even a couple of the beams from the lower sails." Looking up at him, she added, "They had plenty of time to set them up. We had to wait two days for the weather to die down. The captain didn't want to take any chances."

Daniel looked at the sails. "I don't think we need to dismantle any sails."

Beth piped up, "Why didn't he just go around the debris field?"

"Because of its size. It stretches out a long way. It would have added two or three weeks to the voyage."

As the ship bounced around in the water, Beth tried to keep it steady. "What do you want me to do?"

"We need to get a couple more anchors down. Until then, just try to keep the ship as steady as you can."

An uneasy feeling came over Beth. "What if they spot us. There wouldn't be enough time to raise multiple anchors and unfurl our sail. We would be meat."

After placing a mug of tea in Beth's hand Daniel took a deep breath. "I think I know why they keep finding us. They are also trying to find Sarah's homeland. Unfortunately, they probably have the map of the debris field."

They both went quiet. Behind them, Sarah broke the silence. "What will happen if they find it?"

With a blank look on his face, Daniel looked at her and said, "They will turn it into their new hunting ground."

After the sails were secured and addition anchors were in place, Mary joined Beth and Sarah in the pilot house. As the men took apart the rails, the three girls sat down with some tea. While massaging their sore legs Sarah and Beth thought about the gruelling chore of pedalling their way through the debris field. Mary watched them and blurted out, "We should've made another attempt to pick up the others that wanted to join us."

Beth starred at her sore leg. "The townies were scouring the coast line looking for a way in. If they are attacked, those volunteers might be needed to defend the colony."

Mary looked at her, "But if we don't get the nutrients it needs, the colony is doomed."

Shaking her head, Beth replied, "Aboard that ship is the town's strongest and healthiest members. The majority of the rest are barely clinging to life. If we can keep their elite away from the tunnels, our clan has a good chance of fending the townies off until we get back."

"So you want to play hide and seek with them until then?"

Beth saw the colour fade from Mary's face. "If we have to."

"What if our luck runs out?"

A tear ran down Beth's face as she said, "Then it's over."

With both hands wrapped around her steaming mug of tea Sarah looked out of the rear window. "They could be waiting for us on the island. At least out here you can see them coming. In the bilge there are some iron plates with rope holes in them. The elders told us to tie them around our waists and jump overboard if the ship was ever captured. They never intended any of us to become someone's meal."

The wind died and the sinking sunlight shimmered off the rolling waves. With the anchors holding firm, Daniel walked over to the pilot house and poked his head in. "It is too late in the day to attempt crossing the field without a map. The sky is clear and it looks like it should be nice day tomorrow. I say we rest up. We have a long, gruelling day ahead of us."

Sitting on top of the lowest spar left on the front mast, Sarah could see the tiny bells on the tips of all of the extended poles. As the weights attached to them struck submerged debris, the bells rang out. From her vantage point she saw which pole rang and pointed at it. Beth reacted to her signals and steered the ship accordingly. Despite a cool breeze sweat poured off Sarah's brow as she nervously concentrated on the poles.

Inside of the pilot house Beth knuckles were white. The corridor they were travelling through was lined by mounds of debris and intersecting pathways. Some of the mounds spread over half way into the channel and others barely broke the surface. By the time Sarah spotted the hub in the middle of the debris field, the steering wheel was covered in sweat.

Sticking out of the water at the hub was a large bronze hand holding a dagger. Beth rang the bell inside the pilot house. Josh crawled out of the port side tube and yanked the lever that released the anchor. After tying the steering wheel in place Beth rushed out and yelled, "Sarah are you sure there is no debris here?"

Sarah yelled back, "None, as long as we don't hit the statue we should be safe."

Anchored next to the statue, a steady current pushed the ship away from it. This allowed everyone some time to relax. With sore legs David and Beth hobbled over to the forward mast and looked up at Sarah. In anticipation of being hoisted down, she rechecked her harness and took a final look around the debris field. Far down the pathway that they were heading, she saw a glimmer of light. It repeated itself every few seconds. Not wanting to yell, Sarah waved her arms. Something was wrong.

******

Standing on the highest spar, Simon saw the New Hope's masts. With his arm wrapped around the mast he scratched a note on a piece of plastic and dropped it down to Patrick. 'They are anchored next to the statue.'

The sun glistened off the edge of Nick's knife as he sharpened it. The surf polished glass that was lodged in a nearby piles of debris reflected the light. Turning around he saw the wide grin on Patrick's face.

Looking up from the message, Patrick said, "Tell the men below to quietly switch. We need fresh legs on the pedals if we want to harvest them before nightfall."

Nick sheathed his knife as he stood up. "I'll make sure they don't make a sound."

Gazing in the direction of the New Hope, Patrick said, "Remind them that there are women aboard. The thought of playing with their food before eating it may give them some extra energy."

Chapter Nine

In two overloaded skiffs, Grant led fourteen men along the edge of the water. Guided by Simon's hand drawn map they dropped sail and began to row as they entered the narrow the canal. At low tide the water trickling out of the hidden dam was easy to spot. With ropes tied around their waists two newly recruited members peered inside the cavern. As one of them turned and gave a thumbs up, a musket ball blow off part of the skull of the second man.

Grant bellowed out, "Haul him back."

As some men hauled the dead man away from the entrance, Grant studied the huge mound above the cavern. "That hole is too small to attack. There has to be another way in."

Without being told, the men hacked apart the dead man and divided his carcass between the two boats. For the new recruits it was a huge feast. For Grant's men it was just another meal. With strips of flesh hanging over their shoulders two men approached Grant and gave him his share. Deep in thought he nodded his head in thanks. After taking a bite he placed the thinly sliced meat over his shoulders. He needed a little time to plan his next move.

******

John ran through the dimly lit tunnels to warn the others. He bumped into Joe and almost knock him off his feet. "They found us. Jake shot one but another one got away. From the reflection off the glass, there were two loads of them."

Joe grabbed the frantic man's shoulders. "Are the cannons and guns primed?"

"Yes, Jake is manning them as we speak."

Joe turned to his wife. "Karen, go back and tell the others to prepare for an assault. Tell those that can't fight to help lay traps and build retaining walls."

While the men rolled boulders and jammed slabs of concrete in front of the main opening, several women primed the three fixed cannons and mobile multi-barrelled gun aimed at the narrow corridor. All the other entrances were just small crawl spaces. Most of the air shafts were virtually impassable by anyone larger than a young child.

Before blocking the lookout shaft on top of the mound, John crawled out and looked around. He spotted a half dozen townies scouring the front of the mound. Placing an air rifle with a silencer on the ground beside him, he got a slab of concrete ready to flop over and cover up the tunnel. After making sure that he wasn't spotted, he lay down and pressed the rifle against his shoulder.

A towny climbed onto a narrow ledge barely five metres below him. John waited until the large man bent over to help another man up before firing. The almost silent bullet struck the man's between his shoulder blades. He lunged forward and grabbed the man he was helping. Unable to keep their balance, the pair of shrieking men tumbled down the side of the mound.

Seeing the large man awkwardly flip over a ledge, Grant yelled out, "What happened?"

Someone yelled back, "We don't know."

Grant raced toward the bodies. Two men beat him there and started to strip them. "Stop, I want to find out what happened to them before you hack them apart." The new recruit's fragile body was bent backwards over a steel girder. Despite the fact that the man was still swishing his knife around, the scavengers had already pulled his pants off his lifeless legs. "Take mercy on him and at least slit his throat first."

The larger man's head was twisted awkwardly to the side. Grant turned him over and noticed the round hole in his coat. Kneeling beside him, he pulled out his knife and cut open the back of his coat. Pieces of the shattered bullet were lodged in the multiple layers of leather that were wrapped around the man's chest for extra protection. "The fall may have broken his neck but he was shot first."

The man standing next to him used the sleeve of his leather jacket to hone the edge of his knife. After shaving a swath of hair off the back of his hand, he impatiently asked, "Can we harvest them yet?"

Grant had worked alongside the dead man for most of his life. After patting his dead friend's shoulder, he turned away and said, "Do what you must."

It didn't take long before a crowd formed around the two dead men. A man scampered over the debris and gazed over the side. "Save some for the rest of us".

The man stood up and rubbed his head. Seeing the back corner of the man's head, John squeezed off another bullet. A splash of blood exited the man's head as he tumbled sideways. The two men standing beneath him were caught by surprise. Seeing a piece of steel sticking out of the debris, one man rolled behind it. The dead man's body deflected off the side of the girder and struck the other man. Losing his footing, he began sliding feet first down the side. As he grasped for anything he could get a hold of, one of his feet struck something solid and twisted him sideways onto a concrete slab.

The dead body bounced and slid down the steep mound. Grant walked over and saw the bullet hole. With his hands pressed against his cheeks, he yelled, "The gunman is right above you. Climb up and get him."

With a half dozen men racing up the mound, John slipped into the narrow tunnel and dislodged the bar that was holding up a concrete slab. As it fell forward it pushed and rolled boulders into the tunnel's funnel shaped opening. When the dust cleared, the slab covered the sealed opening and left little evidence of it behind.

With four men dead, Grant reassessed the situation. "If we can't find a way in, we will just have to create our own." Taking two of is loyal men aside, he told them, "Take one of the boats and come back with as many men as you can. We may have to dig them out. Anyone that refuses to volunteer will be taken off the food dispensing list and put on the to-be-culled list."

While shaking his head one of them said, "They won't like that. What about the sea harvesters? We need to eat."

Grant glared at him. "Leave only enough to man the pontoon boats." Grant turned and looked at the mound. "A lot people are going to die before this is over. That means plenty of meat to go around."

"At least that will give them some incentive."

"Tell Killy Billy to round up any strays. If we don't harvest them, the poachers will."

The other man spoke up. "Some of them have barely any meat on them."

Grant smirked. "That's why we should harvest them now. If we wait any longer all that will be left is soup bones and leather."

******

Beyond several mounds of debris, Daniel noticed the oscillating tip of the Flesh Star's tall middle mast. "Josh hoist the anchor. David get in the harness, we need you on the mast. Mary, help Sarah start up the engine. Beth, man the helm."

Beth poked her head out of the pilot house and looked at him. "Which way are we heading?"

After briefly studying the various corridors exiting the circle, he pointed his arm ninety degrees away from the approaching ship. "That way. It looks the widest." Running to the forward mast, he handed David his binoculars and grabbed the rope. As he hauled David up, he told him, "We have to move fast. Give your mother as much notice as possible of any obstacles you spot. Even if you don't think it's vital, let her know anyway."

David looked down at his father and said, "I'll do my best."

His father smiled back at him, "I know you will."

Daniel saw the tip of the Flesh Star's mast. It was getting closer. The channel they were in was about to intersect theirs. The debris field was cris-crossed like a tangled spider's web. In it, the person holding the map had the advantage. Their only chance of escape was to crank up the steam and hope Beth could steer the ship around the debris.

As the New Hope gained speed, David's chatter became endless. At first the wide corridor had only a few obstacles protruding from the sides. The faster they went, the harder it was to spot the steadily increasing volume of debris. David didn't notice the masts getting closer as he concentrated on the water hazards in front of them.

Looking down the long barrel of his sniper rifle, Daniel focussed on the Flesh Star's masts. Its oversized chamber was almost twice as thick as their regular rifles. He held it against the forward mast to steady it. He carefully tried to adjust his aim to the rocking rhythm of both ships. With the lookout perched on the top of their forward mast in his sight, he fired. After the cloud of black smoke blew away, he saw his target draped over the top spar. Thinking of David, he looked up and yelled, "Get down from there."

As the ship was about to cross the intersection a loud explosion echoed through the debris field and the front of the ship was lifted into the air. As it came down a second explosion lifted up the stern and nearly pushed the bow beneath the water. With his rifle slung over his shoulder Josh hung onto the front railing as the bow popped out of the water. Daniel held onto the forward mast and stared at David's dangling body.

******

Patrick glanced up at Simon and watch him hang onto the spar with only one arm. Some of the crew became more interested in him than what they were doing. "Hang on, we'll get you down from there."

As the New Hope made its way though the intersection, Patrick bellowed out, "We are going too fast." Pulling on a level, he disengaged the pedals. Patrick tried to turn into the channel after them. Between the ship's speed and the wind pushing against the side hull, the ship's stern started to drift. By the time Patrick regained control of the ship it had made a complete circle. Heading down the same channel that they had been on, they were lucky the ship wasn't damaged.

All the swinging had loosened Simon's rope. With his legs wrapped around the mast he tried to hang on. Patrick turned to Nick, "Get him down and bring him to me."

As the ship began to slow down, Nick ran out of the pilot house and grabbed the rope attached to Simon. With the aid of a couple other crew members, Simon was lowered to the deck. Seeing Simon's blood covered shirt, Nick bent down and pulled out his knife. Simon grabbed his wrist and told him, "I'm not dead yet."

Nick eased back and said, "You have been shot. We don't have a doctor. How about you end it now and forgo the agony. Even Patrick would agree to that."

Simon grabbed Roger's arm and looked up at him. "Don't listen to him. Take me to Patrick."

After putting his knife back into its sheath, Nick patted Simon's belly. "If you can't work, you don't eat. Between that bullet and your growling gut, you will regret your decision."

Trying to the suppress the pain, Simon blared back, "I don't think so."

Unable to leave the helm, Patrick could only watch what transpired on deck. Furious, he screamed out, "I said bring him to me."

Roger wrapped Simon's arm around his neck and semi dragged him to the pilothouse. Shaking his head Nick followed them. "It's a crime to watch that juicy young meat go to waste."

As Roger helped Simon into the pilot house Nick felt it odd that Patrick cared so much about him. Nick stuck his head in and said, "He's shot and will probably be dead within a week. If it was anyone else he would be meat by now. You can't keep him all to yourself."

Roger looked down at Simon and then at Patrick. "What should I do with him?"

Patrick bit his lower lip as the colour left Simon's skin. Disregarding the smirk on Nick's face, he said, "Nick take over the wheel while I see to Simon."

Shocked, Nick blared out, "But they are getting away?"

Patrick grabbed Nick's jaw and pulled it towards his. "Then you better tell the men below to start back pedalling and get us into the right channel."

Roger opened the hatch to the engine room. After the man controlling the boiler crawled out and exited the pilothouse, Roger climbed down the ladder. Patrick picked up Simon by the arm pits and eased him through the opening. There was only one way out of the boiler room. Sensing the tension between Patrick and Nick, Roger spoke up. "Captain, I'm really good with a knife. I could cut the bullet out of Simon if you want me to?"

Patrick looked at a nervous youngster. Holding his tongue, he gazed at the disillusioned faces of the men peering into the pilothouse's windows. "Do it, you are the closest thing to a doctor the ship has, but if anything happens to him I will be holding you responsible." After Patrick tossed down the first aid pouch, Patrick closed the hatch door and glared at Nick. "Have you ordered the crew to start back pedalling yet?"

Dazed, Nick stammered, "I was waiting for the ship to come to a halt." Nick looked into Patrick's enraged, glaring eyes. "I'll do it right now."

******

After getting David out of his harness, Daniel looked back and saw that Beth was having trouble steering the ship. Going to the aft of the ship, he noticed that the port rudder was out of sync with the others.

"I hope we don't have to do any sharp starboard turns."

David followed his father inside the pilot house. "Why is the ship moving so erratically?"

His father told him, "Something is wrong with the port side rudder."

Beth spotted a couple dozen huge mounds of debris off to the starboard side. "Look to the right. We could hide behind those mounds until the Flesh Star leaves the area."

David looked at the mounds. "They are high enough to conceal our masts."

Daniel looked around. There was no sign of the Flesh Star. "When they last saw us, we were under full steam. Hopefully, they might think we outran them or veered off in another direction."

Beth turned to him and asked, "But how are we going to make a sharp starboard turn?"

"By cutting the engine and manning the port pedals."

After Daniel disengaged the starboard propeller, he joined Mary and Josh in the port hull. With David clinging to the mast signalling directions, Beth slowly turned the ship a hundred and thirty degrees into the channel behind the large group of mounds.

******

The rattling of pedals echoed from both side hulls as Roger opened up the first aid kit. Killy Billy had taught him how fragile and resilient the human body could be. Knowing the balance between life and death was vital when torturing captives. Shutting out their screams had also taught him how to drown out background noises while concentrating on his work.

Sweat beaded on Simon's forehead as Roger tossed the blood soaked jacket aside. "It'll be all right. As I told the captain, I'm very good with a blade."

Roger took a closer look at Simon's wound. The bullet nicked the top of the leather strips that were wrapped around his chest. "Your padding didn't help you this time."

As Roger untied and began to unwrapping the leather strips, Simon yelled, "Stop."

Confused, Roger put up his hands and said, "What's wrong?"

"Nothing, just leave the strips on."

Roger shook his head. "Do you want me to get the bullet out or not?" As one side of the leather armour slipped down, he discovered the reason for her strange behaviour. Sitting up he looked at Simon and announced, "You not one of us, you are a girl!"

Simon sat up and revealed the knife she was holding. "I'm Patrick's sister. If you say anything to anyone, he'll introduce you to more pain than your mentor ever dreamt of."

With the tip of Simon's knife touching his nose, he put his hands in the air, "Your secret is safe. I won't even whisper a word."

With her secret out Roger removed the top portion of Simon's wrap. Knowing her blade was at the ready, Roger gingerly feel around for the bullet. The slug had cracked one of her ribs and lodged itself under the pectoral muscle beneath her shoulder.

While Roger searched through the first aid pouch, Simon turned away from him and removed the remainder of her leather wrap. As she winced in pain, she told him, "You have no idea how good it feels to breath again."

Roger looked at her. The tiny wrinkles in the pale skin that was hidden under the leather wrap started to expand. "Enjoy it while you can. This is going to hurt."

As Simon used her shirt to cover her breasts, she replied, "I'm used to pain."

While Roger sterilized his knife, a pair of long nosed pliers and a needle in the boiler's fire pot, Simon prepared herself. As Roger pushed the needle nose pliers into the bullet hole she bit on a rolled up piece of leather.

Using his fingers to guide the pliers, he ignored her groans. He wiggled the claws over the slug. As he tugged to get the bullet out, the claws slipped to the side of the slug. Instead of pulling out the slug, out came the wad of material that the bullet had cut out of Simon's jacket.

"You are lucky. If that had stayed inside of you, it would have caused an infection and you would be dead within a week."

As Roger pushed the pliers back into the wound Simon pounded the floor with the pommel of her knife. By the time he finally removed the slug Simon had passed out. After he was confident that he had cleaned out the wound, he stitched it closed.

The golden slug was oddly shaped. It wasn't like the round musket balls that he was familiar with. Instead it had a cylinder shape to it with grooves down its sides. "It would require a lot of powder to force that down a rifled barrel. She's lucky the shot was from so far away and had lost most of its momentum."

Exhausted he rested against the side of the tube and stared at Simon. She was only the third living teenage girl he had ever seen. He had barely got a glimpse of the other two before they were bartered away. Most women he saw were disfigured by either torture, or years of abuse.

Tugging Simon's shirt away from her chest, Roger was mesmerized by her smooth skin as it reflected the flickering light radiating from the furnace. There wasn't a lash or even scar on it. "Your brother really did protect you."

Above him, he heard Patrick angrily scream out, "Were did they go? They can't just disappear." He stormed out of the Pilothouse and slammed the hatch behind him. After glancing at Simon's limp body, Roger grabbed a piece of pipe and jammed it against the lever that opened the hatch.

Chapter Ten

With Nick at the helm, Patrick stood on top of the pilothouse and looked for any signs of smoke or the New Hope's masts. "We need a spotter." Glancing over the crew, he pointed at the smallest man he saw. "Strap him into the harness and haul him up the mast."

The scrawny man struggled as the harness was strapped on him. "I'm afraid of heights."

Patrick looked at him and grinned, "So don't pass out. It's a long way down."

The man glared at him. "That's not what I meant. Whoever shot Simon was a terrific shot. You can't just offer me up as his next target."

The small man screamed as he was hauled up the mast. Before he could even lashed himself in place, Patrick was yelling at him, "Can you see them?"

Hugging the mast he glanced over the debris field. "Nothing. I can't see nothing at all."

"Not even their smoke?"

The scared man glance down at Patrick. "When I say nothing, I mean nothing. Can I come down now?"

Patrick shook his head as he returned to the pilothouse. "Not yet. You just got up there."

******

From the top of a huge mound, David hid behind an old, rusty girder as the Flesh Star slowly cruised down a nearby channel. Using poles and ropes the rest of them hauled the ship around the tall mound to keep its masts out of sight of the Flesh Star's lookout.

By nightfall, he could barely see the Flesh Star's masts as it ventured further and further away from them. Crawling down the side of the mound he noticed a dim light coming from an adjacent mound. The moon was not strong enough to cause such a bright reflection. Feeling they were being watched, David yelled over the crashing waves, "How long before the rudder's fixed?"

Mary looked at him and yelled back, "We are still not sure what is wrong with it."

Pointing to the light, David told them, "I don't think we are alone."

As Josh popped out of the water, he called out, "Help me up."

Mary and Daniel hauled him aboard. As he gasped for air, he told them, "The cannon ball must have hit it. We can't fix it in the water. It needs to come off."

Daniel scratched his head, "Are you sure that there is no way to fix it in the water?"

"It's to thick. I'll need to soften it over a hot fire in order to straighten it."

Daniel thought for a moment before suggesting, "It would be awkward but we could steer the ship with only two rudders and repair it later."

Beth piped up, "A large fire could warp the deck. We would have to do it on land. The hammering would be like ringing a dinner bell."

******

A soft woman's voice echoed down a dark tunnel. "Does anyone know what's going on outside?"

Joe looked towards the vague outline of the frightened woman as she tried to quiet her whimpering young child by bouncing him on her hip. "With all the exits sealed, we have no way of finding out what they are doing. We know that they are still out there. We can hear them digging and chipping away at the slabs we used to block the entrance."

The woman glanced over at Karen, "To them this mound is like an egg and we are the meat inside of it. It is only a matter of time before they find a way to crack it open."

Karen gazed at Joe and told him, "She's right. We have to prepare for a mass evacuation."

"Without a place to go to, we will be offering ourselves to the cannibals."

Karen looked at the different families that were huddled together along the edges of the tunnel. Reaching for Joe's hand, she told him, "If they break in, I know that this is where you are needed. I could lead a search for another place for us to start over."

"That could take months. We may not have that much time." Shaking his head, Joe reluctantly told her, "We will have to return to the mine. It's the only place we can go."

"There was a reason why our parents left. It can only support so many mouths. What if it is still over occupied?"

"If we can't negotiate a truce, we will have no choice but to fight. We are not the same feeble creatures that fled from it."

Karen went to the storage room and dug out an old map. "Everything has changed. We need another map." She turned to Joe. "Someone will have to go out and plan an escape route." Putting her head on Joe's shoulder, she added, "And it can't be you. You are needed here."

Joe wrapped his arms around her and kissed her forehead. "The cavern is the only way in or out and they will be watching it. Your best chance will be during high tide."

The townies had set up a series of torches in front of the cavern.

Using a crossbow, John fired a grappling hook out of the opening. As it hit the water he could hear a pair of shots fired. While hauling in the line the hook got snagged on some debris. With the line tightly secured, they waited for the tide to come in.

As the water filled the opening Karen secured her pack and musket tightly to her body. She couldn't afford to loose anything in the surf or have it see by the guards. After a long hug and exchange of half-hearted smiles she turned and crawled into the water. With no words said, Joe watched his wife wrap her body around the rope and use it to stop any of their limbs from bobbing to surface. John got into the water and followed her. Kneeling beside the opening he waited to hear if any shots were fired. Luckily there were none.

The extra weight tied to their waists held them under while they walked and crawled under the surface of the water. All the guards saw were the small plastic balls that kept their breathed tubes afloat.

******

Killy Billy sharpened his knife as the procession of rag covered men along with several woman left town. Their carts were full of the digging tools and supplies. From the shadows behind him, a raspy voice proclaimed, "We will soon have the entire town to ourselves."

Without looking away from the exodus, he put down his knife and replied, "Now they will find out who really runs this town."

In a half giggle, a half naked woman pulled a rope off her neck. "That they will."

Confused by the remark, he turned and faced the woman as she thrust a dagger into his chest. While grasping her knife hand to prevent it from going in to far, he wrapping the fingers of his other hand around her neck. "I should have twisted that rope a bit tighter and broke your neck instead of just your voice."

While punching his head, she flailing her neck back and forth trying to get some air. After getting a breath, she coughed out, "Then you would have to rape a corpse." Raising her foot against his stomach she pushed herself away from him. "Then again you never did care if the women you were screwing were dead or alive?"

After bracing his back against his counter, he pulled the dagger out and tossed it on the floor. With blood dripping from the corners of his mouth, he told her. "Without me you would have been harvested a long time ago. I even let you poach what ever your lot needed to stay alive."

Kneeling in front of him, Tara shook her head as she tried to catch her breath. "You mean to keep your future offspring alive." Feeling the scars on her neck she added, "As soon as they are old enough to be taken, we are treated like meat."

Shaking his head, he told her, "You just don't arouse me as much as you used to."

Tara snapped back, "That's hard to do when you are strapped across a table."

Ignoring her comment, a faint smile grew on his face as he told her, "When I put that rope around your neck, I thought of Roger. He was perfect." Gazing at her weathered skin, he added, "Why is it that you can conceive a perfectly healthy child while most cannot?"

"Like you I'm very picky about what I eat." She thought of Roger as she picked up her knife. "Before you turned me into your private whore, I was raped almost every time I left my shelter and never got pregnant."

He smiled as he collapsing to one knee. "It takes two healthy adults to conceive a child."

Glancing at his chest Tara knew that the wound wasn't fatal. She snatched the dagger from the floor and extending it in front of her. "So what is stopping me from harvesting you right now?"

"My men are out there searching for stragglers. If they come back and find me dead, I can't keep them from discovering you and that band of worn out vaginas you hang out with."

******

While attaching a series of pullies to a pair of girders sticking out of the side of a mound of concrete, Beth and David felt that they could handle the weight of the twisted rudder. On the ship Mary tugged on a rope attached to the rudder and tried to help Josh and Daniel pry it free.

Sitting in a sling near the top of middle mast, Sarah noticed two more lights coming from the surrounding mounds of debris. "I think we better hurry up. There may be more out there then we thought."

The men's loud hammers rang out above the rolling surf. As the rudder broke free from its mangled supports the ship heaved up and down. Mary did her best to control the dangling rudder as it swung back and forth banging against the ship's stern. Despite being cold and exhausted, Josh and Daniel climbed aboard the ship and ran to Mary's aid.

As they pushed the ship away from the loose rudder, Beth and David hauled it up. Using grappling hooks and poles, Josh and Daniel positioned an open area of the ship under the dangling rudder. Each time the waves lifted the ship, the suspended piece of twisted metal banged against the deck. Fortunately, the ends of the twisted rudder were facing upwards and didn't dig into the hull. With Sarah relaying Mary's messages, Beth and David began to slowly lower it onto the deck.

While retrieving the rope and pulleys off the make-shift boom, Beth noticed some objects in the water coming towards them. "We got visitors."

In the moonlight Sarah counted five small vessels in the water. "This can't be good." Looking down at Daniel, she yelled, "I think we overstayed our welcome."

Not waiting for David and Beth, Josh began hauling up the anchor while Mary lit the boiler. After Beth slid down the rope attached to the boom, David hack off the pullies with his knife and leaped onto the top of the rear mast. With rope and pullies cascading down onto the deck Beth looked up and yelled, "Are you all right?"

David looked at Sarah dangling on the mast and smiled, "Why wouldn't I be."

As Josh cut the ship's tether, the current flowing through the debris field pushed them away from the large mound. Daniel used the current to help steer the ship towards the nearest channel.

The moonlight shining behind the small fleet obscured most of their features. The five crudely constructed rafts had single square sails of varying sizes. David slid down the mast and ran to retrieve his musket. As the engine began to turn the main propeller, Beth saw a dark figure stand up at the front of the lead raft. As the tip of a mound temporarily blocked out the moonlight, she got a better look at him. Without looking away from them, she told Daniel, "I think he is wearing the same type of coat that Sarah's father had."

"They could be the some of the cannibals that overran Sarah's island." Daniel glanced up at Sarah as she pointed to the bells that were triggered by the submerged debris. "I am glad she is to busy to see them. Right now we need her mind to be focussed."

As the ship gained speed, the surf made the yells and screams from the small fleet unrecognizable. Having primed his musket below deck, David walked up to his parents. "I wonder why they never fired a shot?"

******

Anchored behind a large mound at the outer edge of the debris field, Patrick woke from a brief nap and yelled to the small man lashed to the mast. "Can you see anything?"

"Nothing."

With the glowing sun rising, Patrick saw the lookout's head fall forward. "Stay awake up there. If they escape because you fell asleep, you're meat."

A sudden downpour of puke hit the corner of Patrick's hat. As he jumped back the sick man spoke up. "If I have to stay up here much longer, there won't be enough meat left on my bones to make soup."

"Then you better hope that Simon has a quick recovery." While walking back to the pilothouse Patrick glanced over the open water. All he saw was the odd white crested wave. As he entered and kneeled next to the hatch leading to the engine room Nick barely glanced at him.

Patrick tapped on the hatch door. "Has Simon woken up yet?"

Roger opened the hatch. In a low soft voice, he whispered, "Not yet. By the way the sweat is pouring out of her, I would say that she has a fever or maybe even some infection. We need to either turn off the boiler or take her somewhere where it is a bit cooler."

Despite the waves splashing against the hulls of the ship and Patrick's body covering the entrance, the muffled word 'Her' caught Nick's attention. He shook his head as he turned and looked at Patrick. *'Did I hear what I thought I heard.'* Thinking of Simon's smooth, whisker free face, he started to smile. *'Most boys that age have at least a few hairs above their lips.'* Looking away incase Patrick glanced over, he hid the smirk on his face while he desperately tried to make out what was being said.

In a low harsh voice, Patrick told Roger, "He is not to be moved. He will just have to sweat it out. The boiler has to remain hot in case we spot the other ship."

Feeling a bit bewildered Roger stared at Patrick before he could respond. "She."

Patrick stopped him from uttering another syllable. "*He* is your responsibility. We need *him* up on that mast as soon as possible. If anything happens to *him*, it will be your flesh on the line."

Glancing back at Simon he realised why Patrick was so gruff. If the others knew the truth, Patrick would not be able to protect her. After the crew got tired of raping her, she would be butchered. A freshly killed young woman's flesh is far more tender and much tastier than jerky made from withered old men. "Nothing will happen to him, I promise. I'll have him up that mast by tomorrow, the next day at the absolute latest."

"Good." After closing the hatch Patrick looked at Nick. Even though he was slumped over the wheel, Patrick wasn't sure what he had overheard. Standing up, he told him, "Roger told me that Simon should be able to go back to work by tomorrow."

Nick turned and nodded his head. As Patrick left, Nick tried to comprehend what he had heard. *Maybe I should go down there and find out the truth for myself.'*

After a while, Nick lashed the wheel and opened the hatch. As he stuck his head down, he heard the hammer of Roger's pistol. With the muzzle pressed against Nick's forehead, Roger asked, "What do you want"

"Nothing, just wanting to know how you were doing."

Roger pushed Nick's head out with the end of his pistol and slammed the hatch shut.

******

As the New Hope sailed out of the debris field the sun came up behind it. David helped Sarah onto the fold down seat in the pilothouse and got her a mug of tea before taking over the watch. Feeling the warm sun shining through the door's window, Sarah told Beth, "I never saw the sun rise over the stern or the bow of the ship. You may have to dig out some more charts because I think you are heading towards the open sea."

Beth glanced back at her. "Don't worry, we'll swing back towards the coast when we are sure nobody is out to ambush us."

Spending the entire night strapped to the mast listening to bells had taken its toll on Sarah. At least David had rigged up a seat for her to sit on to give her a small degree of comfort. The thick waterproof blanket that was wrapped around her body and legs had kept her from freezing, but did little to warm her arms and head. "I think I'll crawl into the boiler room and warmup."

With a smile on her face, Beth said, "Try to get some sleep while you can."

From the open crow's nest David could see into the pilot house. After Sarah slithered down the hatch he muttered, "Get some rest. We don't know what the day is going to being us."

Under full sail the engine room turned cold. Sarah couldn't stop shivering. She wrapped every blanket in the storage compartment around her. Mere seconds after she curled into her cocoon, she fell asleep. She had no idea how much time had passed before a wave tossed her against the side of the hull. After fighting to get out of the blankets she looked out a porthole and saw the raging storm.

Crawling up the ladder she opened the hatch and saw Beth struggling with the wheel. A lightning strike lit up the sky and revealed that David was no long sitting on the mast. As she held her breath, Daniel rushed into the pilothouse. "Without the port rudder we can't correct the direction the ship is pointing fast enough between the swells. We have to change course."

Beth glanced at the map. "That will send us into uncharted waters."

"It is either that or risk capsizing the ship."

Chapter Eleven

Standing under a canopy made from rusted sheets of metal, Grant watched his men search for a way into the fortified mound. Believing the pouring rain would help loosen the debris, he order his men to hammer and pry their way in.

The earth shook as a bolt of lightning hit a steel beam sticking out of a neighbouring mound of debris. Pieces of rubble were shot into the air. Grant went out into the rain to investigate. He noticed the small crater the lightning left behind. "That's what we need to do. We need to crack their fortress open."

Without any thought of their safety, he ordered a dozen of his new recruits to hammer steel rods into the top of the mound. Two of them briefly stared at him before picking up their hammers. To defy him meant certain death. Their odds of being killed by lightning were much better. For added height, Grant instructed them to strap long pieces of copper pipe to each rod.

******

The strong wind and violent waves accompanying the storm lifted the New Hope's starboard hull out of the water. Using ropes and pulleys, Daniel and Josh hauled the damaged rudder over to the starboard side of the deck hoping its weight could help hold it down, while Mary and David adjusted the sails. Using the jib and mid sails for thrust and the aft to help steer with, they fought the raging storm the best they could.

Below deck Sarah listened to the chaos above her. The boiler had run out of fuel. Above the raging storm and the squealing beasts, she heard Josh shout at the top of his lungs. "This can't go on much longer."

******

The heavy rain made climbing the fortified mound extremely hazardous. The feeble recruits were forced to claw their way up on their hands and knees, dragging rods, pipes and hammers behind them over the slippery debris. Flakes of rust and shards of glass sliced through their wet leather clothing and the toes of their shoes. Streams of water poured over the concrete slabs in every direction. With bloody hands, knees, and feet, every move they made was risky.

As thunder shook the mound causing a man to slid down a large slab. The others paid no attention to his misfortune. The man let loose a terrifying scream as his legs were impaled by the twisted mass of rebar that was curled around the end of a slab of concrete.

Clinging to the edge of a crevice, a man tried to ignore the screams as he attempted to dislodge his wedged hammer from a crack. As he yanked it free the sudden jolt caused him to loose his grip. A piece of rusty steel slit open his side as he tumbled past the impaled man and fell to his death. Only eight of the ten men made it to the summit.

As two men held a rod two others took turns hammering it into a crack in the mound. After securing the copper pipe to four rods, the men sat down and took a brief break. Grant saw them sitting down and yelled up, "What are you doing? This storm won't wait for you."

One of the men used a copper pipe to help him stand up. Grasping one of the secured rods with the other hand he tried to shout over the thunder. "We need a few minutes to rest up."

In the pouring rain, Grant was unable to make out his words. "I'll turn you into meat if you don't get back to work right now."

Hoisting a piece of copper pipe in the air the man yelled back, "We are". His sentence was cut short by a bolt of lightning. As it travelled from one rod to the other, his arms broke away from his illuminated chest. The man's burnt body crumbled to the ground as the bolt jumped to the other three rods. Four more men were jolted into the air. The combined blast strew debris everywhere killing the rest.

******

Joe watched the electricity from the lightning bolt melt the wires along the tunnel and blow apart several strings of light bulbs. In the generating room Jake jumped away from the generator as sparks fused the coiled wires inside of it. By the time the lightning grounded itself in the tidal pool the entire colony was dark.

Groping around in the dark family members gathered their things together. The tremor caused by the lightning strike had collapsed sections of a few tunnels and left some members stranded. Joe felt his way though the corridors telling everyone he met to gather their things and go to the main hall. As word spread, the colonists got together and a head count was taken.

Two, three member search parties were formed to find the rest. The others tended to the injured and children. As Joe was about to depart with one of the search parties, he instructed two of the elders to take an inventory of their supplies.

With streams of water flowing down the tunnels, small pools were formed in front of piles of debris. The first place Joe went was the gardens. After hauling up the two gardeners one of them told him, "The plants can survive a couple days without light. After that, they will start to rot."

Joe placed his hands on the young girl's shoulders. "We'll need to harvest everything we can before that happens. If I send you some help, how long do you think that what take?"

"A full day maybe longer, depending on how many are helping us. If you want to harvest all the inedible parts that we normally give to the beasts, a couple more."

After thinking for a moment, Joe told the young girl, "Give the beasts whatever is above ground. Leave the roots for the magic fingers. They don't need the light to multiply. We can harvest them later."

******

In the distance Karen stood on top of a tall cliff and gazed at the lighting strike through her small telescope. From her vantage point she could see the pouring rain working its way over the mound. "They may only have another hour of rain. Then the townies will regroup."

John looked at her. "Will the colony be all right?"

"From what I can see, the strike only damaged the top of the mound. They should be fine until we get back." Looking behind her, she surveyed the route ahead of them and added, "And that could take us a few weeks."

******

After the storm had moved on, Grant led a party of men to the top of the mound. Looking at the dead bodies, he turned to a short, thin man and blurted out, "Get Killy."

The thin, short man standing next to him was confused. "We don't need him. We are capable of butchering a few corpses."

While slapping Eric across his face, he growled, "That's not why I need him."

With his long, straggly blonde hair covering most of his face, Eric got to his knees and looked up at him. "Killy Billy won't like this. He doesn't like to leave town."

A swarm of men began to crawl up the mound. A dozen of them dug out the bodies and collected the severed parts. Under Grants orders, others rummaged through the debris looking for how the ground dweller that shot the two men had disappeared. As their smiling comrades carried away the body parts, several of others stopped their search, stood up and watched them leave.

Grumbling under their breath, a couple dozen men used steel rods and narrow shovels to pry apart and dig around the edges of the shattered concrete slabs. Unable to lift his shovel, a frail man wearing only a cloth wrapped around his waist mumbled, "It's just like before. Only the chosen few get any meat."

The man beside him wiggled his long pry bar and replied, "At least here you still have a chance. I heard that Killy Billy's shop was full of hanging corpses. Apparently anyone that didn't volunteer, was considered free for the taking."

******

Feeling his way through the upper tunnel, Jake heard the ringing of steel against steel as the sound vibrated its way through the steel reinforced concrete. As he led his two comrades closer to its source small pieces of gravel rattled down the walls. Looking up he saw a small beam of light. The end of a steel rod had wiggled out of the upper corner of the wall leaving behind a second small hole. "They are chiselling their way in. We have to go back and prepare for an attack."

Back at the hall Jake told everyone what he had encountered. Joe's first question was, "Did you see any of the rods break through."

"No, they were on a angle and hit the wall."

"Good, that means they may not know about the upper tunnel yet."

Jake reached for Joe's shoulder and asked, "What about the shaft going up to the lookout?"

As a couple women lit an oil lamp, mirrors bounced its soft light around the hall, Joe looked around at the huddled families. Turning back to Jake, he said, "The shaft drops down into the upper tunnel. Even if it was filled with rubble, they will eventually find it. It is just a matter of time before the tunnel is breached."

"Both the shaft and tunnel are narrow. With a couple of the repeating airguns a gunman and loader could hold them off."

"As long as they don't run out of bottles of air or bullets." Gazing into Jake's eyes, Joe added, "Or get killed."

******

The water being pumped out of the bilge holes on the sides of the hulls began to slow down. Nick turned to Patrick. "They should have made their way through the field by now."

With a crooked grin on his face, Patrick looked at Nick and said, "Maybe they spotted us and are trying to wait us out. Maybe the storm tossed them into some debris. For all we know they may be shipwrecked."

Licking his lips, Nick replied, "If that's the case, maybe we should go back in and see if we can find them."

"I agree." Screaming loud enough that even the men below deck could hear, Patrick bellowed out, "Man the propellers, we're going back in."

Glancing down at the hatch, Nick asked, "Why not fire up the boiler?"

Pointing at the chimney, Patrick added, "Because we don't want them to see our smoke and sneak away."

As a precaution Patrick stationed two armed men on a small pile of debris. With them, he left enough oil and tar to produce a plume of smoke that could be seen even at night. "We will pick you up when the hunt is over. Now remember, if you see them trying to escape, use the hot flash from one of the muzzles of your rifles to ignite the oil. Don't use a ball, it'll blow your fire apart."

******

While manning the bilge pump, Josh heard Mary climb down the ladder. Not wanting to lose any suction, he continued to pump with one hand as she offered him a mug of tea. "I'm glad the storm is over. Water was pouring in around the rivets that attach the port rudder's bracket to the ship. The way the ship was leaning, if a single rogue wave could have sunk us."

In the pilothouse Daniel and Beth combed over the charts trying to figure out where they were. Shaking her head, Beth looked out the window. "The wind had shifted again. With the sun hiding behind the clouds we are completely lost. No matter where I look, all I can see is water. We don't have any landmarks to go by."

"We still have the sun, moon and stars." As he wrapped his arms around his wife, he kissed the back of her head. "Hopefully, the clouds will break up overnight and let the moon and a few stars shine through. I'll fasten a line and bell to the front of the ship just incase we come across any sunken debris. Hopefully we should be back on course before morning."

Chapter Twelve

Patrick slowly twisted the ship up, down and around the debris field looking for any sign of their sister ship. Switching their boiler from crude oil to the methane collected in the ship's sewage digester made the Flesh Star's exhaust much harder to see at night. From behind him, he could hear Nick snore loud enough that he woke himself up. "I must have dozed off."

Patrick shook his head. "Only for about an hour. How about going below and getting a few more zzz's before your shift."

"If anything happens, you will need me to alert the others."

"Right now I can't hear anything above your snoring. You will be doing everyone a favour by crawling into your bunk."

After yawning and vigorously shaking his head, Nick listened to the racket the crew was making below deck. "I couldn't be worse than that lot?"

Patrick started to chuckle. "I heard people being tortured to death that were quieter then you."

Grabbing the door handle, Nick growled, "Fine, I'll see you in a few hours."

Below deck most of the crew slept with their feet strapped to the pedals. Through a tube, Patrick softly said, "Roger, Simon, the coast is clear."

Roger help Simon up the ladder. As she poked her head out of the hatch, she breathed in the fresh air. Patrick look at her. Wearing only her shirt, she was drenched in sweat. As the cold air cooled her off her nipples began to poke out. It had been a long time since he had seen her true figure. She was no longer a child.

Patrick took off his coat and hand it to her. Simon smiled at him. "No thanks, I want to cool off some more before I go back into that sauna."

Patrick noticed the way Roger stared at her chest. "You haven't abused her have you?"

Straightening his back, Roger snapped back, "No sir!"

"Good, you know what I would do if you had."

From up in the crows nest the short, thin man peered into the dark pilothouse. As Simon leaned back and ran her hands through her wet hair the moonlight broke through the clouds. Her protruding breasts stuck out of her revealing silhouette. Without realizing it the lookout cried out, "The rumours are true. Simon is a girl." After taking a long look at her, his jaw dropped as he muttered, "She's no girl, she's a full fledged woman."

Patrick looking up at the lookout and waved his arm. "Roger, get her below and secure the hatch."

Roger glared through the window. "It's to late. When the rest of the crew finds out, we will be meat and Simon will become their new toy."

The lookout tried to hide behind the mast as Patrick let go of the wheel and grabbed a harpoon. With the rope tied to it loosely dangling on one arm , he stormed out of the pilothouse and threw the harpoon at the man. The tangled rope caused it to fall short.

As Patrick shook the rope off his arm, the man started to scream, "Help, the captain's gone insane." He watched Patrick retrieve the harpoon as he loosened his harness. Twisting his body behind the mast, he cried out, "You can't hide a woman from us. You told the crew that everything should be shared equally."

As he tossed the harpoon as hard as he could, Patrick muttered, "Not my sister."

The harpoon struck the man's left thigh. Patrick jumped and grabbed the end of the knotted rope and began to tug on it as the men below began to clamour about. With the harpoon's barbed tip hooked on the man's leg, Patrick's second massive tug twisted the man off his perch. With blood pulsated out of leg, he dangled upside down in his loosely fastened harness.

Covered in blood, Patrick turned around and saw Nick exiting the cabin. Pulling out his knife he growled, "Nobody touches her."

Weakened from lack of blood, the small man slipped out of his harness and fell to the deck along with the harpoon and line. As more crew members emerged from the side hulls and cabin, the bow of the ship drifted into a partially submerged pile of debris. Still half asleep the jolt knocked the crew onto the deck. With no one at the helm, Simon and Roger watched the steering wheel twirl around. They were tossed against the wall as the ship started to spin around.

With his legs spread far apart, Patrick struggled to stay on his feet. Seeing that the ship was about to crash into a large mound of debris he lurched towards the pilothouse.

Simon grabbed the door latch. Wearing her brother's coat, she yelled out, "We have to jump for it."

Roger exited the pilothouse with two weapon belts over his shoulder and a rifle in his hand. As the ship's aft struck a mound, he was knocked overboard. He landed on a pile of rubble. The collision bounced Patrick off the front of pilothouse and slide Simon against the railing. While the rest of the crew tried to get their footing, Patrick scrambled over to Simon. Wrapping his arm around her, he told her, "Hang on."

As Nick pulled out his pistol, the couple leap into the water. "Get

them."

As the waves continued to twirl the ship around, its bow struck another mound of debris. By the time Nick got into the pilothouse and regained control of the helm, he had only a faint idea where Patrick and the others were. Not knowing what to do next, Nick yelled to a pair of men, "Drop anchor."

As one man grabbed the lever attached to the anchor crank, the other man glanced at Nick. "Good idea. Then we need time to straighten this mess out."

"All right Jeff. We'll do that."

******

After helping Simon onto a slab of concrete, Patrick stood up and looked around. He saw Roger lying on a pile of weatherbeaten debris on the neighbouring mound. His right leg was awkwardly twisted to the side. Wading through chest high water the pair gingerly made their way over to him.

As Patrick felt Roger's broken leg, Simon gently wiped the hair off his face. His mouth started to tremble as she placed her hand on the side of his face. Turning to Patrick, she said, "Without his help I would be dead. We have to give him a chance."

Patrick saw the way she caressed Roger's face. "He is not your savour. Keep in mind that he is Killy Billy's apprentice. I gave him no choice but to look after you."

Glancing at the knife in her brother hand, she shook her head and growled, "I know what you want to do. We are not starving."

Under his breath, Patrick muttered, "Not yet."

******

As the sun came up, the Flesh Star's crew gathered in front of the pilothouse. Standing in front of them Nick blared out, "Patrick betrayed us. He was keeping a woman all to himself." While looking over the crowd he added, "Yes, Simon was a good lookout, but she was a woman." While pointing at the dying lookout he said, "He treated us like meat. Why shouldn't we treat him and his young colleagues the same way."

From the middle of the crowd Jeff yelled out, "We went around in so many circles I got dizzy. There are hundreds if not thousands of mounds in this debris field. Shouldn't we be focussed on our mission instead of three bodies."

Nick snapped back, "We have only travelled a couple kilometres at the absolute most. That means that there are less than fifty mounds to search." Looking around at the crew, he added, "It may take a couple days, but harvesting a woman and two prime carcasses would be worth it."

******

Sitting in the crow's nest, David put his hand above his eyes to protect them from the bright rays of sunlight peeking through the clouds. As the light reflected off the still water, he noticed a wide assortment of colours glistening off a patch of oily film in the distance. Peering through a pair of binoculars, he saw the film drifting towards a half dozen objects sticking out of the water.

Occasionally after strong storms, oil slicks had made their way into the generator cavern. The odour permeated the entire tunnel system. Even after it floated away, the lingering odour was hard to get rid of. "The Rainbow Sea can't be that far away from here."

The calm water made it easy to sleep. Daniel woke up and saw David trying to creep down the stairs. "Is it dawn?"

"The sun isn't completely up but a few rays are trying to break through the clouds." David walked over to his father and quietly added, "I didn't mean to wake you."

"That's all right, it's time I relieved your mother anyway. She must be getting tired."

While watching his father stretch, David told him, "I think the storm pushed us back towards the debris field. I noticed some mounds in the distance."

As he yawned Daniel forced out, "Any signs of the other ship?"

"None."

After vigorously shaking his head, Daniel slowly replied, "Good, maybe they left the area." As he started up the stairs, he glanced back and added, "Get some sleep while you can. We don't know what this day has in store for us."

The sleeping quarters were simple. There were three rows of hammocks on each side of the hull. The upper rows were two deep while the mid and bottom rows were three deep. Along with filling the excess bunks with supplies, the upper bunks were stuffed with plant matter to feed to the beasts. Even their mattresses were stuffed with dried out stems and roots. With the beasts occupying the front compartment of the hull, it made it easier for Mary to feed and look after them before taking her turn as lookout.

David nestled into the hammock above Sarah and his mother crawled in across from them. While at sea, no one got a full sleep. After a few hours Beth heard Sarah stir. She was about to say something when David's arm flopped over the edge of the hammock. After flexing his hand a few times, Sarah reached over and squeezed it. "Good morning."

While yawning David got out, "How are your legs this morning?"

Sarah scratched her head before saying, "They are always stiff when I wake up. I hope that means they are mending, cause I don't want to end up a cripple. I'm going to ask your mother to take a look at

them."

Beth used her arm to prop her head up. "I could look at them now if you want?"

David turned his head and looked at his mother, "I'm sorry mom, we didn't mean to wake you."

Beth dangled her legs out from under her blankets, "That's all right." She slid out of her hammock and bent down in front of Sarah. After a couple yawns, she shook her head and began examining Sarah's bitten leg, "I won't be able to do much for you beyond checking for infections. It should be able to hold your weight soon. Then you will be able to at least walk with a cane." Glancing over at the other leg, she rocked her head back and forth while pinching and examining Sarah's feet. "It looks like the cast has kept your leg straight. I can't see any signs of any lasting damage."

"But it still hurts."

Beth looked into Sarah's eyes. "It will. That's your leg telling you to stay off it while it heals. Having it suspended while you are on lookout is probably the best thing for it."

Sarah watched Beth crawl back into her hammock. Her foot accidentally knocked some leaves out of the hammock below her. Sarah watched them soak up the water lying on the floor. Seeing the firm foliage go limp caused Sarah to cry. David stuck his head out and asked her, "What's wrong?"

Pointing to the bottom hammock across from her, Sarah replied, "That was where Rebecca slept. She was such a sweet young child. Those savages treated her like she was nothing more then a tasty snack."

David climbed down and started to massage her shoulder, "To them, that's all she was."

Sarah swatted his hand away. She wrapped her arm over her face and started to cry some more. Josh crawled out of his hammock and went over to David. "Leave her. She still needs to work out a few things in her head. Remember, she lost everyone she cared about."

Beth crawled out of her bunk and led David up onto the deck. Once outside she told him, "To her, we are cannibals. She came from a different world. Deep inside, she still believes that we are no better then the townies."

David looked down at the deck and shrugged his shoulders. "I know that you are right, but when I look at her, all I see is a scared young girl who needs a friend."

"You mean, a lonely, attractive young woman. I've seen the way you look at her."

She saw the shocked look on David's face as she raised her eyebrows and added, "Be careful. Be very careful."

From the crows nest Mary screamed out, "We have been spotted!"

Looking in the direction that Mary was pointing, both David and his mother could see a large plume of black smoke rise above a large mound at the edge of the debris field. Beth looked at her son and said, "That's a signal fire."

Chapter Thirteen

The black plume caught the attention of two men as they exiting the Flesh Star's cabin. Nick saw them staring at the sky and stormed out of the pilot house screaming, "Those slabs of meat are not hovering in the sky. Get to the railing and keep your eyes open for a clue to where their hiding."

One of the men pointed to the black plume. "They must have spotted the ship."

As he glanced off the port side and saw the cloud, Nick smiled, "On second thought, we have a much richer prize to go after. Patrick and his tasty friends are not going anywhere."

In the shadows of a dark, shallow tunnel Patrick saw two men running back onto the ship. One of the men stopped, turned and inquisitively looked at the entrance. Patrick held his breath. Behind him Simon tried to look over his shoulder in vain. As her brother's body froze, she whispered, "What's happening?"

The other man grabbed the first man's arm. "Do you want the ship to leave without us?"

"But I thought I heard something."

"Probably just the wind playing tricks on you."

"We better mark this spot just in case." The two men picked up pieces of rusty steel and scraped an 'X' into the concrete beside the opening before running back to the ship. "There, that'll do."

After he was sure that they were gone, Patrick told Simon, "For some reason they are leaving." Sneaking outside he saw the large 'X'. The embedded rust in the freshly scraped concrete made it hard to cover up. "We will need to find another place to hide."

As he helped Simon get out, Patrick saw a flash of light coming from the adjacent mound. With a smile on his face he told Simon, "We are not alone."

Simon gazed toward the nearby mound. "Do you think they are a threat?"

As they dragged Roger out by his arms, Patrick said, "If they were, they wouldn't be hiding from us."

After pulling a couple pieces of plastic pipe out of the debris, Simon placed them beside Roger's injured leg and sharply said, "Take off your shirt. I need it to secure your leg in place."

Surprised by Simon's tone, Roger snapped back, "What good is saving my leg if I'm to die from exposure? It gets mighty cold at night."

"Would you prefer my brother hack it off instead? I'm sure he would obligate you." Watching Roger's face go pale, she added, "He might even slice it up and give you some of it."

Roger closed his eyes and cocked his head back as far as it could go. "Now I know you're kidding. He would not waste a scrap of meat on a dead man."

Simon took a deep breath and calmly told him, "We need to find another hiding place. If you want, we could leave you here until we find one?"

While stripping off his shirt, he announced, "Fine, tear my clothes to shreds. Maybe we will find a warm, dry place to stay while my leg mends. That should only take a few months, unfortunately I will be dead by then."

After the gruelling ordeal of straightening and securing Roger's leg in place, Patrick searched through the debris for anything that could keep him afloat. With chunks of foam stuffed under his coat, his arms could barely move as he walked back to the others. "Simon, I spotted some foam attached to some steel just to the right of the tall upright girder. If you stuff it under your tunic we could use the current to float to another mound and tow Roger behind us."

With the rolled up remnants of a long gown filled with foam stuffed under Roger's arms, the pair kicked their way across the channel. Even with the supplies he had tossed overboard tied to his chest the insulation kept Roger afloat. The current carried them over a half kilometre before allowing them to come ashore. Tired and cold, they barely pulled Roger out of the water before collapsing from exhaustion.

Patrick was lying on his stomach when he heard footsteps walking towards him. Rolling over he saw a man with an air powered gun standing next to him and a woman kneeling next to Roger. Grabbing the man's ankle, he reached for his knife.

The man quickly stepped on Patrick's wrist and pointed his gun at his face. "It's all right. We just wanted to make sure you were all alive. We had heard that a group of cannibals were searching the area."

Roger opened his eyes and looked at the woman. He instantly recognized that she was dressed the same as ones that arrived on the ships. "Are you here by yourselves?"

The woman smiled back, "No we have two young children with us."

Simon saw Roger's face almost glow as he pulled his knife from his belt. The light reflecting off the edge of the knife caught the man's attention. As he turned his wife fell to the side and blocked his line of fire. "Get back!"

The man ran to his wife's aid. As he bent down to grab her, Roger rolled over and thrust his knife into the man's stomach. With a quick upward twist the long sharp blade tore apart one of the man's lungs. As the woman crawled backwards, Patrick grabbed the barrel of the man's airgun with one hand and stuck his knife into the man's back with the other. Looking down at Roger he shook his head in disgust. "You fool, we don't need more enemies. They might've even helped us."

While the woman cried over her husband's body, Roger collapsed. "Ahhhhh." He clenched his teeth and tried to mask his pain as he said, "They are. He's supper and she's our slave. Now you won't need to harvest me in order to stay alive."

Simon watched the agony on Roger's face turn into a smile. She turned and whispered to herself, "Patrick was right. Roger is no different from the rest of the crew. If it wasn't for his constant threats, Roger would have treated me as just another piece of female flesh."

******

By the time the Flesh Star emerged from the debris field, they saw the New Hope sailing off in the distance. With the crew looking at the men on the smoky mound, then to the pilothouse and back again, Nick bit his lip. He knew he had no choice but pick them up. As the ship approached the mound he yelled out, "Drop anchor and stand by to hoist it back up."

Several lines with buoys tied to the ends were tossed ashore. As soon as the second man grabbed one of them, Nick barked out, "Hoist anchor."

With the both men still dangling in the water, he blurted out, "Every available man to the pedals. We got to catch that ship before it gets away."

******

While staring at the black plume of smoke coming out of the Flesh Star's stack, Mary yelled down from the crow's nest, "They are using everything they got to catch us."

After tightening up the jib, Josh barked out, "The wind is against us. We can't cut through it any faster."

Mary looked down at him, "Even if we turn the boiler up to full blast and manned the pedals, we don't have the fuel or manpower to out run them."

Seeing the frustrated pair, Daniel yelled out, "We have no choice. We have to go back into the debris field. At least there, we can hide among the tall mounds."

As a strong gust of wind brushed against the ship and swung the bow fifteen degrees Josh ran to readjust the aft sail. Glancing out the rear window, Daniel saw the Flesh Star closing in on them. Seeing David open the cabin door, he blurted out, "Josh tighten the aft sail and help David twist the rest around." The ship almost came to a halt as he twirled the wheel and pointed the ship towards the debris field. "We

will need all the wind we can get."
******

Nick smiled when he saw the New Hope turn. As he spun the wheel to cut them off, he cried out, "We got them!"

His revelry was short lived as the New Hope's sails puffed out and it picked up speed. The angle where he figured he could cut them off was steadily growing. Scared of having the waves hit the side of the ship, he nudged the wheel slightly before blasting out, "I need you to give all you got."

From the boiler room a man yelled back, "The furnace is already red hot. If I give it any more fuel it could burst."

As the New Hope sliced across their bow several crew members fired a quick volley of shots. Out of frustration, Nick yelled at one of the gunmen, "Tell the men below to pedal harder. They are getting away."

Within a half a minute, the man returned and relayed the message. "It's no use. Their legs are beginning to cramp up."

The veins on Nick's forehead popped out as he screamed, "Then tell your friends to put down their guns and take their place."

I took time for the tired men to crawl out and the fresh ones to strap in. Enough time for the New Hope to glide into the debris field and disappear behind some mounds. The tired men that were sprawled about the deck stared at the vast field. One of the men turned to the pilothouse and shook his head, "What now?"
******

With the rope tied around the woman's neck and wrists, Patrick led her up the steep mound to a small triangular opening under two slabs of concrete. Her scraped elbows rubbed against the rubble as she fought to stay on her feet. As he put his head into the entrance he heard the faint whimpers of two scared children. "They sound young." Looking down at her swollen breasts he saw two wet spots where her nipples rubbed against her tunic. "You are still producing breast milk."

The woman snapped back, "Why should that matter?"

With a large grin on his face, he told her, "It means you can provide us with more than just your cooking skills."

Knowing what he implied, she fired back, "What about my children?"

Patrick laughed. "I suppose they will have to learn to share."

Simon had heard everything. As she followed them into the shelter something inside of her snapped. "Look how skinny she is. Her body can barely produce enough for her kids."

Patrick looked at the woman's physique and answered, "She's not that bad off." He grabbed the toddler's shirt as it tried to get to his mother. He smiled as its tiny fists pounded his arm. "This one's got some fight in him. I suppose this one will keep for a while."

As he left to retrieve Roger, Simon pulled the woman to the side of the shelter and forced her to sit down. "You better stay close to me."

The crying child climbed up on his mother's lap and squeezed her neck so tight that she could barely force out, "Thank you. I'm Nancy. This is Tom and the baby's name is Gail."

Simon wasn't sure how to react to the introduction. Getting close to food was something she had never done. Reluctantly she answered, "I'm Simon. That was Patrick and the injured man is Roger. He is the one you really have to be careful around."

Nancy looked at her filthy cloths, face and hands, "So what are you, their slave?"

"No, a survivor."

******

As the bow of the Flesh Star turned around a mound, a young girl peeked out of a dark cavern. She immediately ran towards the edge of the water waving her arms. "Over here, over here."

Her father ran out and grabbed her. While pushing her to the ground he covered her mouth and said, "Stay down, we don't know who they are."

It was too late. The small man sitting in the crow's nest had spotted the pair. Full of excitement, he twisted his torso so fast that his right leg broke the strap that secured it in place. While awkwardly dangling on top of the mast, he pointed at them and yelled, "There, on shore."

Not knowing what to look for, five crew members ran to the port side and scanned the mound he pointed at. Despite remaining still, a slight breeze caught the young girl's hair and lifted the ends of it above the debris they were hiding behind. Two crew members spotted it and yelled out almost in unison, "I see them."

Nick looked out the pilothouse window. "I don't see anything."

Taking things upon himself, Jeff released the anchor. As the ship jolted to a stop, it began to spin around. In the confusion the man and young girl crawled away from the shoreline and hid behind a slab of concrete.

The men below immediately stopped pedalling and began to unstrap their feet. As they crawled onto the deck, one of them screamed out, "What the hell is going on? If my leg had hit the shaft between the pedalling stations any harder, it would have broken."

Another man cried out, "You are lucky, I think I cracked a few of my ribs."

Nick walked over to Jeff and punched him in the face. Blood gushed from his lower lip and sprayed Nick's cheek as he yelled, "Did I tell you to drop anchor?"

Jeff grabbed Nick's jacket. His curly black hair and dark complexion made the white in his eyes pop out. With his nose almost touching Nick's, he barked out, "Who made you captain? I don't remember any vote."

Nick glared into Jeff's eyes and said, "I'm second in command. The moment Patrick jumped overboard, I became the captain."

A man holding his bleeding arm shouted out, "There still should have been a vote."

Nick pushed himself away from Jeff and grabbed his knife. As he backed away from the growing crowd, he blurted out, "Without me you would be aimlessly drifting around the sea."

After using his sleeve to wipe the blood off his chin, Jeff said, "No, you're not the only one that can handle the wheel. The old captain had trusted me along with a few others to take the odd shift behind it. Besides, you could not even get us close enough the New Hope to gaff her. You knew what they would do and still let them slip away."

As the men squabbled beneath him the lookout readjusted his straps and harness. Feeling secure, he got his bearings and surveyed the mound where he had spotted the pair. "Where did they get to?" By the time the words got out of his mouth, he noticed the top of the man's head as he snuck a peek at the ship. Looking down at Nick and Jeff he bellowed out, "If anyone cares, I spotted some fresh meat."

Three of the men standing under the mast yelled out, "Where?!"

The lookout pointed at a sloped slab of concrete. "Behind that large slab. The one with the slanted 'T' shaped crack in it."

Over half the crew ran to the side of the ship. Both Nick and Jeff sheathed their knives and ran over to the railing. Jeff spoke up, "We need to send out a hunting party."

Nick looked down and saw Jeff's hand resting on the hilt of his knife. "Who's going to lead it. I remember what happened the last time the crew split up."

Jeff smiled back. "Yeah, the Captain got himself butchered."

Nick thought for a moment. "So I guess we should both go. That way we can keep an eye on each other."

"Agreed. But when the hunt is over, we will still need to have a vote."

Feeling like he had dodged a bullet, Nick went to the pilothouse and grabbed his rifle. His underhanded association with the old captain had left multiple scars on the backs of several crew members. To them, it was a lingering reminder of his past deceit. He had to figure out a way to swing the crew his way. As he left the pilothouse, he walked over to Jeff and said loud enough for the crew to hear, "Lets put our differences aside and work together."

"Agreed."

While handing him his rifle, Nick suggested, "You take this. I've seen you shoot. You are a better shot than I am. I'll take the first group ashore and flush them out. You can oversee the riflemen aboard ship."

Jeff looked around at the others standing around them and smiled. "Agreed. That way you can't kill me by accident."

"So if I'm shot, it would not be by accident." Nick watched the smile leave Jeff's face before adding, "I'm placing my life in your hands. We are no longer living under the old captain's tyranny."

The man with the cracked ribs piped up, "We have all done things we are not proud of." Pointing at the shore, his voice got louder, "Why are we standing around yakking while there is fresh meat within our grasp?"

As the crew armed themselves, Nick walked over to the injured man. "I'm sorry for turning you in. The old captain wasn't easy to work under."

Jerry shook his head. "No he wasn't. I'm sorry I lied about you helping me steal some meat. It was just payback for the lashes the captain gave me."

Nick froze. After a couple seconds, he softly said, "We all did things we regret."

Jerry was one of the four crew members that slipped into the water and followed Nick ashore. As they walked towards the slanted slab, the frightened couple tried to crawl away. With the lookout yelling out their every move, the landing party quickened their pace. As Nick closed in on them he felt something smack him on his shoulder. Dropping to his knees he saw blood seeping out of a small round hole in his multi layered leather vest. "I've been shot." His thick vest had stopped most of the bullet's impact. After removing it, he saw that the slug was lodged just under his skin. Using his forefinger and thumb he barely flinched as he squeezed it out.

The rest of his party took cover and looked around. A slug ricocheted off a piece of metal beside Jerry and sprayed flakes of rust over his left upper arm. "There are more of them." Gazing in Nick's general direction, he added, "The rifles they are using seem to be more powerful then the ones we previously encountered."

Nick snapped back, "No kidding."

The lookout yelled down to Jeff and pointed at a dark hole, "Half way up the right side of that giant vertical slab. Next to the pile of steel leaning against it."

Jeff caught a flash from something shiny a few metres to the left of the slab. "There are more of them than we figured." He rested his rifle on the safety rail and waited. As a ray of sunlight broke through the cloud, he saw another flash. After squeezing the trigger he waved away the smoke and looked for any movement. "Did I hit anyone?"

The lookout yelled down, "I couldn't tell."

Jeff eyes focussed on the pile of steel as he pulled back the left handed rifle's bolt and inserted a lead ball and pre-made gunpowder pack. After cocking back the hammer he briefly looked down at his rifle as he primed the flash pan on the right side of the chamber. A bullet ricocheted off a pile of debris near the shore and barely missed his head. "Where did that come from?"

The lookout bellowed down, "I think it came from the next mound."

"There are more of them?!"

As he looked around the nearby mounds, the lookout saw a lot of movement. "They seem to be everywhere."

Jeff smiled. "All the more to harvest."

******

As he carried the dead man's body to the cavern, Patrick gazed in the direction of the gunfire. In the gap between a couple mounds he could barely make out the tip of the Flesh Star's rear mast. Hearing Simon coming out to see what was going on, he glanced back and told her, "We may have to go into hiding for a bit longer than I thought."

Chapter Fourteen

The sound of gunfire caught David's attention. While lying on top of a large mound he saw the flash and smoke of Jeff's rifle. Several pings from the airgun's bullets rang off the ship's metal hulls. After sliding down a large slab of concrete, he ran to the ship. "The people they are hunting are armed with airguns."

Sarah looked down from the crow's nest. "Did you see any of them?"

As his mother helped him board the ship David looked up at Sarah and answered, "No, they were all hiding in the shadows."

Daniel left the pilothouse and looked up at Sarah. "You said that your people only had two ships?"

"That was all I knew about. They could be the cannibals that invaded our island."

"I don't think so. They would be much more aggressive." Daniel gazed at Beth. "Sarah's people could have slapped a few boats together in a hurry. Maybe this was as far as they got." Looking at David he added, "It could have been an act of pure desperation."

Taking the medallion from his pocket, David though of his brother. "Steve knew how desperate the colony was. He died trying to find the plants on this medal."

Beth squeezed David's hand between hers. As the medal sunk into his palm, tears flowed from both of them. "He was a dreamer. He wasn't prepared for such an undertaking."

Sarah saw the trio holding hands below her and thought of her family. They were all killed along with a bunch of people she grew up with. As more gunfire echoed through the debris field she become overwhelmed with grief. "They don't stand a chance."

Mary exited the cabin. "I heard gunfire. Have they found us?" Seeing the tears in everyone's eyes, she added, "What's happening?"

Josh slung his rifle over his shoulder and walked over to her. "We think that some of Sarah's people were shipwrecked here and the townies found them."

"So they are now hunting them instead of us." One of Sarah's tears fell on Mary shoulder and splashed her neck. As she looked up at Sarah her brief feeling of relief was replaced with sorrow. "At least this time they are fighting back."

David squeezed his father's hand. "Can't we help them?"

A blast from one of the Flesh Star's cannons echoed off the nearby mounds. Daniel watched the cloud of smoke dissipate as another volley of muskets rang out. Turning to his son, he said, "I won't risk the life of anyone aboard this vessel. The colony is relying on us to retrieve the nutrients it needs."

Josh took a few steps toward Daniel and stopped. "If we are not going to help them, why not use this opportunity to escape."

After Daniel studied everyone's reaction and rested his gaze at Sarah. "I'm sorry. The colony comes first." Without looking away from her, he bellowed out, "Prepare to set sail."

Josh piped up, "Where to?"

"The quickest and safest path out of here."

******

John waved for Karen to climb down from the ledge she was sketching on. It took her five minutes it get to the edge of the vast stretch of barren land that he was standing in front of. "What did you see?"

John pointed to the barren land. "Did you noticed that line cutting across the surface."

"Sure."

"Could you tell what it is?"

"I assume it was from a trail somebody was using."

"It's more than that." John looked at her and pointed to a gap in the cliff she had just climbed down. "It came from over there."

"So what's so important about the path that someone had taken?"

"I have to show you."

Karen followed John towards the gap. As they got closer, she saw the deep gouges that were left behind. "Who could pull a cart that heavy?"

The gap was littered with cart and footprints. Despite being months old, the rain hadn't erased everything. John pointed at the trail that they had come from. "That trail takes you towards the town." Pointing to the barren land, he added, "There are no footprints leading away from here."

Karen got on one knee and studied John findings. "I would have dismissed it as a cart trail. I wonder what else I missed by sticking to the cliffs."

******

Roger stared at Nancy as she breastfeed Gail. "She has had enough. It's my turn."

Simon saw Roger grab Nancy's arm and pull her on top of him, with the screaming young child pressed between them. Patrick grabbed Nancy's shoulder and yanked her away from Roger. "Do you want to give our position away?"

Defiantly, Roger blurted out, "I only wanted some of her milk."

Patrick picked Gail up by her shirt and handed her to her mother. Turning to Roger, he said, "You wanted more than that. I saw the way you looked at her. It wasn't just her milk you were lusting for."

Simon stood up and walked over to Roger. Kneeling beside him, she shook her head. "I thought you were better than that." With a lump in her throat she added, "Did you ever really care about me?"

Roger propped his torso up with one arm and extended his other hand towards Simon. "I did and still do care about you."

Pointing to Nancy, Simon sharply blurted out, "Then what just happened?"

"I was just playing with the food." Glancing over at Nancy while she clung to both of her children, he grinned and said, "What's the harm? Besides, her milk will soon dry up."

Patrick stood over them and coldly told Simon, "He's right. She won't eat any of her husband's flesh. Her breasts will soon dry up and her children will starve. Why not harvest them now?"

Hearing this, Nancy reached toward the suspended metal rod that her husband's flesh was drying on. After ripping off a piece, she bit off a chuck and cried out, "I'll eat!" As they stared at her, she sobbed and forced out, "You can't butcher my children!"

Patrick watched her stuff the rest of meat into her mouth and smiled, "There may be hope for her yet."

With tears running down her face, she looked up at the ceiling and muttered, "I'm sorry Colin, I love you but they gave me no choice. Please forgive me."

******

Nick circled the mound and snuck behind the leaning pile of steel. He bent down and peered through a wide gap near the bottom of it. The three people inside were obscured by a cloud of dust. Near the back of the hideout, two men were pumping air into the butts of long rifles while a tall woman took aim at the men on the ship. Turning away, he muttered, "I was right. They are using a different style of rifle."

A bullet ricocheted off the metal inside the pile of steel and struck one of the men in the leg. Without a whimper, he clenched his teeth and continued pumping. Stepping back, Nick pulled a small pistol from his belt and primed its flash pan. After waving Jerry over to him, he whispered, "There are only three of them inside. They are not like the ones that sailed into town."

Inquisitively Jerry asked, "Who do you think they are?"

Nick shook his head. "Maybe their guard?"

Jerry bit his lower lip. "Or maybe the cannibals that drove them off their island."

"Maybe."

"In any case, what's your plan?"

Nick answered him, "If I shoot at them through the cracks, it will draw their attention away from the opening in the front. That should give you enough time to rush in. Their long muzzled rifles are no good in a confined space. You should have no problem hacking them apart.”

As the small group of men began to manoeuver around the pile, Nick took the last man's pistol. “I'll have a better chance of hitting one of them than you will.”

The man grabbed his hand and than slowly released it. “You maybe right. A blade is better in close quarters.” His cold eyes stared into Nicks as he added, “But I want it back when this is over.”

“You will.”

Jerry heard the pinging of bullets ricocheting off the ship. He saw the lookout being lowered to the deck by a pair of crew members. After pulling out his knife he leaned over and prepared himself for the mad dash into the dusty hideout.

As one of the men exchanged rifles with the woman, Nick wiggled one pistol on top of the other inside a crack. When the man turned around Nick fired the top pistol and then the other. Before the man collapsed, Nick pulled out the pistols and ducked for cover.

Inside, the woman swung the long barrelled rifle around and shot at the crack Nick had fired from. Jerry rushed into the dark shelter and shoved his knife into her back. As the woman collapsed to her knees, Jerry pushed her aside. In her last seconds of life she grabbed his ankle and caused him to fall on top of the man Nick had killed. As the next man rushed in he was met with a flurry of bullets from a short airgun.

Nick saw the gunman back up to the wall. After pulling out his knife, he shoved it between the two steel beams he had fired through and sliced the man's upper arm. As the man turned around, the man behind Jerry jumped on top of him. Before he could slice the man's neck, Nicked yelled out, “Stop! We need him alive.”

The man glared at Nick and clenched his teeth. “What for?”

“Information.”

The townie hit the side of the man's head with the pummel of his knife. As the others pulled out the dead bodies, Jerry yanked the defiant prisoner to his feet and pushed him ahead of him. Blood drizzled down the man's arm. With a stiff kick to the centre of the prisoner's back, Jerry knocked him to the ground. Stepping on the man's wounded arm, he yelled above the man's screams, “How many of you are there?”

By the time Nick circled around to the entrance the people on the other mounds were peppering the area with bullets. “We have to get him to the ship alive.”

Nick barely stopped talking when a large projectile slammed into the pile of steel. Shattered and broken pieces of metal were strewn everywhere. The men extracting the dead man and woman were instantly killed. Nick was flung over the edge of a slab of concrete and scrambled on all fours to get to safety. Lying on top of the prisoner,

Jerry had a couple pieces of steel protruding from his side.

Nicked looked around. There was no smoke. In fact, he couldn't remember hearing a blast. Seeing their captive trying to wiggle himself free, Nick got up, went over to him and kicked him in the head.

Jerry gingerly ran his fingers over his injuries. Looking up at Nick, he said, "Don't harvest me yet. I can make it."

"No, not yet." With a semi grin on his face Nick looked at the prisoner. "These guys must have an air powered cannon. This guy has a lot of questions to answer."

******

In the distance, Patrick saw a large mast-less, double-hulled catamaran slowly cruise around a mound. At the front of each hull was a black powder cannon. In the centre of its deck was an extremely long barrel with several oval canisters attached to it's base. Next to the canisters, several men were frantically pedalling compressed air into them. Another team of men were loading a large sphere into the cannon's breech.

Patrick glanced behind him and saw Nancy standing there holding a child in each arm. Seeing her face turn pale, Patrick felt compelled to ask her, "Who are they?"

Squeezing her children tightly, she answered, "They call themselves Reapers. They are the ones that invaded our island. The Reapers had captured all of our cannons when they took over our compound." Looking down at her kids, she continued. "The elders sent out a couple ships to find somewhere safer to live." Looking up at Patrick, she added, "Yours was one of them. When neither ship returned, we were forced to surrender. After that things got worse."

Patrick followed Nancy inside. As she sat down, she looked up at Patrick and said, "At first they sent out marauding parties to randomly butcher us. Colin's child was skinned and butchered in front of me as I was being raped. The children and elderly were considered food. Skilled workers and young women like me were turned into slaves."

Patrick studied Nancy's face. "Your people refuse to eat each other, yet you still managed to keep your children alive. How?"

"Neither one of these children are Colin's. They impregnated me. After Gail was born and I started producing milk, they gave me Tom to look after. Along with being a prostitute, I was also a wet nurse." Glancing over at the kids she added, "They gave me enough food to feed their children and nothing more. Colin was lucky. While most of the men were castrated, he had escaped that fate. They needed his skills to forge the metal parts of the ships they were constructing."

Patrick knelt beside her. "So how did you get away?"

Nancy rose her head. In a stern voice she said, "We poisoned their water. It killed a few of them. Most of them just got sick. That gave us enough time to steal whatever boats were still afloat. To bad none of us knew how to navigate or even operate them."

Nancy wiped her hands against her legs. "They will never leave. I heard one of them say that it was the only place they had ever found that could be farmed."

Puzzled, Patrick asked, "Then why are they here?"

Nancy glared at him, "To get us back. They need our knowledge and skills. Without us, it could take them years to learn the skills needed to harvest food from the ground and master the technology we had harnessed."

******

After a couple crew members helped Nick drag his prisoner to the ship, he glanced at Jeff. "Jerry is still up there with a couple pieces of steel in his side. The rest are dead."

As the large catamaran came into view, the newly replaced lookout bellowed out, "We have to get out of here."

Jeff looked down the channel and yelled, "Hoist anchor and load the rear cannons."

Nick barely had time to comprehend what was going on before a cannonball clipped off the top third of the ship's rear mast. As it fell to the deck along with a half dozen ropes, the crew members fired their muskets at the approaching ship. The return fire pinging off the hulls and cabin. Without wasting the time to reload, most of the riflemen retreated to the side hulls and strapped their feet to the pedals.

Lying on the deck, Nick yelled to the men manning the cannons, "Fire at will."

Before they could fire, the catamaran's front cannons lashed out. One ball hit one of the Flesh Star's rear cannons and the other glanced off the side of the main cabin. The shell from the Flesh Star's remaining rear cannon fell short. Jeff crawled over to it. "Don't you know how to aim a cannon?"

With Nick at the helm, Jeff helped right and shore up the struck cannon. Trying to dodge the catamaran's large cannon, Nick twisted and turned the ship at every opportunity. As Jeff ran and took refuge in the pilothouse. "I got a good look at the ship. It is made strictly for attacking. It has no aft or side cannons. If we could get behind it, we would have a huge advantage."

Nick saw a half hidden side channel and cranked the steering wheel to starboard. The ship began to slide sideways as it went around a small corner mound. The back end of the port hull scraped against a pile of rubble. Behind them, the helmsman of the catamaran felt they were travelling too fast to attempt to follow them. As the catamaran passed the channel its crew blasted the Flesh Star with musket fire.

It was Nick's first good look at the catamaran. Pointing to it, he told Jeff, "You are right. It is an open sea fighter. If they cruise by either our aft or bow, we'll have a clear shot at them."

Jeff smiled at Nick. "And as they pass by us, we can slip behind them and attack them from the rear."

As they patiently waited for the catamaran, a loud shrilling scream echoed through the mounds. Nick's first thought was of Jerry. "It couldn't be him. He is too far away."

******

On top of the mound a man held his hand over his daughter's mouth. The sound of Victoria's voice made him curl up in a ball. He whispered to his daughter, "We have to stay really, really quiet. Remember what they did to your mother."

******

Kneeling beside Jerry, Victoria slowly twisted the second piece of steel as she extracted it from his side. Two men held a large megaphone to his mouth to amplify his screams to the point it shook chunks of concrete off a nearby steel beam. "Now tell me where did you come from and how many were with you.?"

Jerry screamed out, "We came from town."

While digging her small finger into his wound, she clenched her teeth and asked, "And where is this town?"

"Along the shore. Don't ask me where it is. I don't know. I was strapped in the hull pedalling most of time."

Victoria pulled out her finger and licked off the blood. Standing up she rested her foot on Jerry's injured side and twisted her heel against his largest wound. "What direction were you travelling when you were allowed outside?"

Jerry screamed out, "Into the morning sun."

His quick response brought a smile to Victoria's face. "You know that your friends are not even going to try to rescue you, don't you?"

Clenching his teeth, he recognized the two skinned faces that draped over her chest as his dead comrades. Glancing towards the pile of steel he saw a man pick up one of their legs.

Their fresh, bloody faces stood out from the rest. Her entire scale like bodysuit was covered with them. A couple of the reapers had barely enough faces to form vests, while others only had enough to use as shoulder pads and chest pieces.

In a low voice Jerry reluctantly replied, "Why would anyone risk their lives to rescue an injured man unless they wanted to harvest them."

Victoria shoved to the men holding megaphone to the side. "I bet if you were on that ship right now, your throat would be slit within half a second."

******

As another reaper cauterized Jerry's wounds with pieces of red hot steel, his screams were broadcasted through the megaphone. After the echos stopped ringing, Jeff looked at Nick and said, "How much does Jerry know about us?"

"Not much." Turning away from the wheel, Nick looked at Jeff and shook his head. "That is why a captain must make his decisions in private. As the old captain once told me, under torture no one cares about the next guy."

Jeff rubbed his shoulder and felt the scars the old captain had given him. "So when you betrayed me, it wasn't just about getting a larger ration."

The blood started to leave Nick's face as he tried to form a reply. Fortunately, he didn't have to. The catamaran's bow was slowly crossing the channel behind them. He caught Jeff off guard as he yelled out, "Man the rear cannons."

His yelling caused a few men aboard the catamaran to open fire. As Nick yelled, "Fire", a man that was about to light one of the cannons was struck in the arm. He twisted around and fell against the cannon. The cannonball from the other cannon blasted a hole into the catamaran's port hull.

The injured man picked up the torch he had dropped. On his knees, he reached up and lit the cannon. The shell sailed over the catamaran's huge port hull and hit one of the large cannon's air tanks.

A cloud of compressed air spewed out of the ruptured tank and flung the ship against the mound on the far side of the channel. A long steel beam sticking out of the mound, pierced the bow of the ship's starboard hull. Two of the half dozen men that were thrown overboard swam to the ship. The rest swam ashore and crawled onto the small mound at the head of the narrow channel.

With only the knives in their belts, the four men flung pieces of concrete at the Flesh Star as it hoisted anchor and pedalled toward the adjacent channel. Looking back at his damaged ship a man donning a face laced vest muttered, "Victoria will have me butchered for this."

******

As the Flesh Star snuck out of the debris field, Jeff noticed a strange gigantic floating mass. It was surrounded by over a dozen vessels. "What is that? It's too big to be a ship."

Nick looked out of the side window and saw the floating island. "There could be hundreds of men living on it." He saw a few vessels breaking away from the island and start heading straight towards them. After pulling out the leather baffles shielding the tubes connected to the pedalling chambers, he yelled into them, "Pedal as if your life depends on it, because it does!"

Behind him, Jeff opened the hatch to the boiler room and declared as he crawled down, "I'm no captain, you can have the job."

"If you can get that contraption down there to go any faster, I'd be thrilled to have you as a second."

"I'll do my best."

Chapter Fifteen

Eric ran down to the bottom section of the besieged mound and barged in on Grant and Killy Billy as they discussed alternative ways to breech the fortified mound. "They done it."

Grant turned to Eric and asked, "Done what?"

Eric bent over and placed his hands on his knees. As he tried to catch his breath, he forced out, "They found one of their tunnels."

Gunfire echoed from the cone shaped hole they had dug on the top of the mound. Killy turned to Grant, "In a small tunnel like that they could kill two, three or even more of our men for every one we pull out." Shaking his head, he added, "That's a lot of butchering. When the rest see their comrades meat hanging out to cure, you might have a revolt on your hands."

Grant looked at Killy and asked, "So what's your answer?"

Killy gazed at the massive mound as he answered, "Let the earth dwellers think we are focussing on that hole, while we search for another opening. When we find it, one well placed explosion will allow us to enter their tunnel system in mass."

After he started to breath properly, Eric stood up and shook his head, "You are getting ahead of yourselves. The tunnel is only big enough for a single man to crawl through. One dead body could clog it."

Grant thought for a moment. "What if we made the men shields. If they push them ahead of them, they might be able to make it into a main tunnel." Turning towards Eric, he said, "Go and tell the diggers to widen the hole while we plan our attack."

As Eric slowly climbed back up the mound, Killy looked at Grant, "What's going on in your head?"

"We could send in two at a time. If the first man is killed, the second man could drag him out. That way we will know what went wrong."

******

After a few large rocks rattled down the cramped tunnel, Joe knew what was coming next. Hearing some grunting coming from the tunnel, he used a string to fire a battery of pre-positioned rifles into the tunnel. The bullets rang off something metallic.

After pulling the rifle stand to the side, he used a rod and mirror to peek into the tunnel. The man crawling down the tunnel had a metal disc attached to the barrel of his rifle with a narrow slit in it to see through.

Combing his hair with his fingers, Joe looked around for a

solution. He saw a lit oil lamp and tossed it as hard as he could into the tunnel. Its clay oil reservoir broke apart and caused a ball of fire to travel up the tunnel. As the first man's charred lungs succumbed to the flames, his rifle fired and jolted his head and shoulder to the side. His rifle and shield became lodged sideways in the tunnel.

As the lead man's oil soaked leather coat fed the flames, the second man dropped his rifle and tried to scramble backwards up the tunnel. The burning rope attaching the two men together held long enough for him to also succumb to the smoke. His rifle slid next to the dead man's legs. A flame ignited the powder inside it. The bullet struck the shield attached to the first man's weapon, allowing it slide past the lit oil.

Using his mirror Joe saw that the tunnel was blocked. The modified rifle was only a few metres from the opening. After tying a rock to the end of a rope, he swung his arm in front of the tunnel and tossed it in. It only rattled back out. His third toss got past the shield. He could only pull the rifle a metre before the rock rolled free. It only took him a couple more attempts to get it out. After smothering the burning oil with dirt, he studied the way the thick metal was lashed to the barrel. Although it made the rifle to awkward to shoot, it served the purpose it was intended for.

******

The smell of smoke and charred flesh rose from the tunnel. Eric shook his head, "This isn't good." Turning around he saw Grant and Killy standing behind him. "What now?"

Grant watched the smoke coming out of the tunnel as he replied, "We pull out their bodies and try again."

******

Joe heard someone crawling through in the tunnel. Behind him, a couple women approached with a few buckets of the crude oil that had occasionally washed ashore. He reached over the barricade that they had set up and took one of the buckets. He poured it into a metal dish near the opening. When he lit it, the thick black smoke was sucked up into the tunnel. Within seconds, a man let go of one of the dead men and began gasping for air.

Joe could hear him yell, "Get me out." He coughed a few times and choked out, "I can't breath."

A woman climbed over the barricade and set down another bucket for him to use, "A child could stop them from using this tunnel."

Joe glanced at her and then at the young child sitting on the wall behind her. "It will take a while before they can plan their next move. In the mean time, maybe you two could can take over my watch. I haven't slept for almost two days."

The woman put her hand on his shoulder. "I'll wake you if

anything happens."

******

Grant grabbed the closest man, knocked him to his knees and tied the end of a rope to his ankles. "I hope you can hold your breath long enough to get you back out." As he pushed the scrawny man into the tunnel, he told him, "Grab a hold of whatever you can and don't let go."

A second after the rope went slack, Grant ordered, "Pull him up and keep on pulling. We want to clear this tunnel not fill it with inedible bodies."

Killy grinned, "That would be a waste of good meat."

As the unconscious man was extracted from the tunnel with nothing in his hands, Grant shook his head. "That won't work." He grabbed a bucket of drinking water and dumped it down the tunnel. "We have to put that fire out."

******

Joe had barely got to sleep before bucket after bucket of saltwater was poured down the tunnel. The splashing water rocked the oil pan over causing the burning oil to spread over the ground. Joe peeked over the pile of debris and yelled out, "Get those pails of oil away from the flames."

******

Outside, a line of townies extended from the inland sea to the top of the mound. They passed hand to hand anything that could hold water. Grant took delight in being the one that poured it into the tunnel.

******

The deluge washed the badly charred dead man out. As he plopped spread eagle over the fire, the woman screamed out, "What should we do?"

"Grab your rifle and get behind the barricade." When the second body was dislodged, he yelled, "Prime all the rifles and get out of the line of fire."

While she primed and lined up five rifles, Joe dumped oil over the dead men. The oil soak into their water repellent clothes. Before he could light them, he heard a man sliding down the tunnel.

Joe stepped to the side as the man landed feet first beside him. The water pouring in after him crumbled up the thin sheet of plastic he was sliding on and pushed it to the side. As the man got to one knee and raised his pistol, the woman shot him in the chest.

A second man's feet landed on the first man's back and began to run towards the barricade with his long knife pointing straight ahead of him. Before the woman could cock another rifle, Jacob had arrived and shot him in the forehead with a airgun. Without looking away from the opening, the woman said, "I'm glad you showed up."

By the time the third man made it down, Joe had lit a rag and thrown it on the oil drenched men. The man landed as the flames began to spread. With his leg on fire, the man rolled to the side. Joe pulled out his knife and slashed the man's neck as he tried to retrieve his pistol.

The fourth man saw the flames and tried to brace his legs against the sides of the tunnel. It was to late. Pushed by the man behind him, he slid forward and landed on his back. The man behind him used him to hop away from the flames. Jacob targeted the free man as Joe chopped his knife into the fallen man's throat.

With black smoke billowing through the narrow tunnel, the men inside it tried to scramble back up. Hampered by the water being poured in, one by one they slid into the muddy tunnel below. Before they could clear the smoke and flames, they were confronted by bullets and Joe's knife. Two brave children ran up and tossed oil over the growing pile of bodies.

******

As the men were trying to claw their way back up the tunnel, Grant tried to force another man into it. Holding a knife to the man's chest, he growled, "Get in there or I'll butcher you right here."

The continuous stream of water being pour into the tunnel made matters worse. Fallen victim to the smoke and water, the bodies of four men were stuck in the middle of the tunnel. Not able to go down, they began to climb out. As Grant was about to slit the throat of a man exiting the tunnel he glanced over the men circling them. Frustrated, he pushed the man to the ground. As he sheathed his knife, he screamed out, "There has to be another way into this giant pile of rubble. Now get out there and find it."

******

There was barely a cloud in the sky as Karen gazed toward the sea. Even though they were over twenty kilometres away, the lingering cloud of black smoke was hard to miss. "They must have found an opening."

It wasn't until John had finished climbing to the top of the massive cliff and stood beside her, that he noticed the cloud. "It's probably only a small breach."

Karen turned and looked at him. "Someone inside must have lit some black goo to force them back out."

John noticed her hand tremble. "Joe knows what he is doing. Don't worry, he'll stop them."

Karen squatted down. "After we map out an escape route, it's going to be hard to sneak back in."

John gazed at the surrounding mounds and rocky cliffs. Spotting a twinkling of green coming from a distant gully, he said, "I wonder what that is?"

Glancing at it, Karen replied, "Probably an optical illusion, maybe a pile of copper."

"What if it isn't? It could be moss. That means nutrients."

After using her binoculars to further scrutinise it, she soberly told him, "It might be worth a peek. It is not that far out of our way."

Seeing the maze of rocky outcrops and piles of debris in front of them, John glanced at her and said, "As long as we don't get lost."

After taking a piece of leather and a crude pencil from her pack, Karen sat down and began to sketch all of the terrain around them. "That is why I've been drawing a map. By using the black cloud as a reference point, from this elevation I can highlight every major obstacle between the colony and the old path we had found."

"So I guess this view was worth the climb."

******

With the tunnel almost plugged solid, the smoke from the burning goo began to filter through the adjoining tunnels. The smoke forced everyone out of the upper tunnel. As the smoke wiggled through the cracks, it left black soot behind. This highlighted every airway and vent in the upper tunnel.

Using grappling hooks, Eric supervised the removal of the bodies from the tunnel. Grant oversaw multiple teams of men as they hammered away at the larger soot covered cracks. It was as if the men had found a boost of energy. With everyone focussed solely on their work, Killy Billy snuck away from camp unnoticed.

As he approach town, one of his men ran out to meet him. "Sorry boss, we searched the entire town and she's not here. The men are searching the surrounding areas now."

With his hand resting on where he was stabbed, he told the man, "Search the rocky outcrops about ten the fifteen kilometres behind town." Rubbing his chin, he added, "I want those whores back, especially Tara. I want her alive and in one piece."

"What about the others?"

"Try to take them alive." Looking at the men walking up to Dennis, he added, "Tell the men that they are allowed to have some fun with them, but not kill them. Maybe that will make them a bit less blood thirsty."

Glancing toward the path leading to town, Dennis asked, "And the rest of the town's population?"

"Harvest them all. If they are too weak to work, why prolong their agony. Why should we let them wither away and leave us with only soup bones to gnaw on."

******

Knowing that the upper tunnel was in danger of being breached, Joe helped Jacob set up a network of snares, spring loaded traps and lethal barriers to help funnel any intruders into the open. In front of the shaft leading to the lower tunnels, Jake and a couple of women constructed a firing station out of rocks and slabs of concrete. The cracks in the chest high wall were filled with moistened ground concrete to help solidify it.

Joe took a quick glance at Jacob and asked, "Where did you get all these devices?"

After he finished connecting the trigger of a swing trap suspended from the ceiling, he answered, "I had to do something with all the pieces of rebar that John and Jake kept piling into my shop."

******

As Karen neared the area where she saw the green patch, she heard someone talking. John kneeled down next to her and asked, "Why did you stop?"

"Shhhhhh." With her forefinger pressed against her lips, she whispered, "Listen."

The pair stayed perfectly still for over five minutes. John finally broke the silence and whispered, "What did you hear?"

"Voices."

She barely finished saying it before they heard a piece of rubble rolling down the side of a rocky outcrop to the left of them. Karen pulled out her binoculars and closely scrutinized every stone, crack and boulder until she saw something move. It was only a small shift in a rock along the top. Putting down her binoculars, she tightly gripped her rifle and said, "They must have heard us."

"I don't think so." John pointed to a ledge near the top of a cliff. "I think they are doing the same thing we are."

Karen saw a townie leaning against a boulder while pointing his rifle towards the hidden patch of green. Not far away from him another man appeared and did the same thing. When the first volley of shots were fired, she heard feminine screams radiating from the nearby gorge. "What is going on? We have to get a better look."

John grabbed her shoulder. "Why? It's not our concern."

Karen glared at him. "How many healthy women have you seen in town?"

John thought about the women he had seen in town. The few he saw were either old or in poor health. "Hardly any."

"Those screams came from women with strong healthy lungs." Judging from the gun fire, Karen estimated that they were only four or five shooters. Only two shots answered the initial volley. "We have to do something."

John looked at the cliff to his right and saw a pair of legs dangling behind a boulder. While gazing at the non-expecting target, he whispered back, "I'm not oppose to killing a few townies."

"We'll have to act fast. Gunfire travels quite a distance." Karen watched John slither around the boulders and silently slit the man's throat while he was reloading his rifle. John glanced at her and began jabbing his arm in front of him. Karen realized that he had seen someone on her left side.

Without hesitation, she slung her rifle over her shoulder and crawled around to the back of the rocky outcrop. She easily spotted a fresh trail leading to the top of a massive nearby boulder. She was three quarters of the way up before she got a glimpse her prey's head. Despite being caked in filth, the healthy sheen in the teenager's hair made her tremble. *'That's not normal.'* Regardless how conflicted she felt, she knew he was still the enemy.

She pulled out her knife and crept behind him. A sharp stone clung to her shoe. The boy heard the faint 'click' as she put her foot down. He turned and faced Karen as she lunged towards him. Stepping backwards he slipped and fell over the edge.

His screams drew the attention of another hunter. As he pointed his rifle at Karen, John's bullet struck his shoulder. Before Karen could shoulder her rifle, John had picked up the dead man's rifle and shot the wounded man in the forehead. "So much for being bystanders."

They both knew that there were more hunters lurking in the surrounding rock formations. Lying on the ground, Karen pulled out her binoculars and gazed at the strange vegetation growing in the valley. Below her, she heard a woman sobbing, "Why, why did you have to be one of them?"

As Karen tried to peek over the side, a bullet whizzed by her head. "Why are you shooting at me?"

The grieving woman yelled back, "You killed my son. I would rather be harvested knowing that he was still alive, then see him bleed to death in my arms."

John saw the woman pick up her dead son's rifle and raise it towards her shoulder. Taking careful aim, his bullet grazed the woman's arm. "That was a warning. My next bullet won't be."

Karen looked at John and saw something moving behind him. "Behind you." As a man stood up and ran towards him, she quickly fired her rifle. She missed. The man hesitated for a split second before he raised a long, thick knife over his head and charged towards John. The delay gave John time to pull out his knife and steady himself as the man leaped into the air. The man swung his knife in mid-air. John ducked from the blade's path as a bullet stuck the man's chest.

The oversized knife rattled down the side of the cliff as a tall woman stood up and yelled, "Now we are even." As a gunshot rang out from the far side of the valley, Karen saw the woman drop to her knees and slowly crumble to the ground.

While reloading, Karen tried to see where the shot came from. On the adjacent formation, John yelled out, "They don't want our help, so lets go."

Karen heard the faint ringing of metal striking metal. "Did you hear that?" She quickly climbed to a better vantage point and took out her binoculars. A group of armed men were coming their way. "They must have heard the gunfire." Scared of being spotted, she crawled down and took out her map.

Carrying everything he could salvage from the dead men, John had barely squatted down before Karen informed him, "We are cut off. Unless we want to risk being spotted climbing over top of one of these cliffs, our only escape route is through that valley."

John packed his loot, slung the dead man's rifle over his shoulder and led the way down. They squeezed into a sloping crevice and gingerly worked their way down the rocky cliff. As the vegetation came in sight, they felt like they were about to venture into another world. Along with the ankle high moss that covered the ground, there were also waist high bushes. John turned to Karen and asked, "How is this possible?"

Two women rose from behind some nearby bushes. As the dead boy's mother raised her rifle, she cried out, "By fertilizing it with the bodies of our dead children."

******

Upon hearing the shots, Killy Billy smiled. As Grant approached him, it disappeared. Turning to Grant, he said, "I think I know where the shots came from. Stay and help Eric dig the earth dwellers out. I'll handle it."

Grant looked at him and cocked his head, "How do you know where they came from?"

Knowing that Grant knew something was up, Killy pulled him aside. When he was sure no one else could hear him, he whispered, "The whores needed a place to mourn for their lost offspring so I steered the hunters away from them. In return, they gave me whatever I wanted."

Grant grabbed Killy's collar with both hands. "So you are telling me that you knew where the poachers were hiding all this time?"

"More or less. As long as they thought I knew, they did my bidding."

"So who is shooting who?"

Killy grabbed Grants wrists and forced his hands away from his collar. "I wanted to renegotiate our agreement, so I gave my men a rough idea where to look for them."

Grant looked at the men working on the mound. "By the sounds of it, they are putting up a fight. If you can capture a few of them, maybe a little entertainment would improve the men's morale. Hopefully enough to smash a hole through that pile of rubble."

******

A large boned woman with a small pot belly walked in front of the bereaved woman. "Put your rifle down and check on Tara. If this pair wanted to harvest us, they would have waited and killed the victor."

Karen looked at the young woman's face as they all knelt behind some bushes next to the opening of the sloped crevice . Outside the two scars that ran down the left side of her face and several smaller ones across the right, she appeared to be healthy. "How have you avoided getting sick like the others?"

Jose tossed back her long, dirty blonde hair and barked out, "By keeping to ourselves and not acting like animals."

Half hidden behind a boulder at the mouth of the crevice, John spoke up, "So you must be the poachers we heard about."

The grieving mother heard him. She turned and stood up. "We did whatever we had to in order to survive." She suddenly fell forward with part of her forehead missing. The shot that killed her echoed throughout the valley.

As a young dark haired woman dragged Tara into a small dugout, Jose yelled out, "Stay under cover." With her back to Karen and John, she shook her head and said, "You have two choices, go back from where you came, or fight with us."

John cocked his head and cautiously replied, "I thought your group was women only?"

Jose turned, grabbed his shoulder and pushed him against the boulder. "You got two rifles. For now I'll consider them your breasts."

Karen spoke up, "You can't stay here. You will be picked off one by one."

John looked at Karen and then Jose. "She's right. There are at least two snipers out there and reinforcements are less then a hour away."

Struck with terror, Jose placed her hand on her stomach and mumbled, "If they take over the valley, how would we survive?"

"The same way we have." Karen put her hand on Jose's shoulder. "If we get the snipers before the others arrive, there is still a chance for everyone to escape."

As Jose crawled back to the others, Karen told John, "These women appear to be clean. I wish we had the time to find out what made this place so special. I bet it is the soil."

John looked up the crevice. "The colony is under attack. We can't waste any more time. We need to find the old mine."

Karen reached out and put her hand on his shoulder. "You know Joe. He'll find a way to fend them off until we get back."

John glanced back and saw a tear in her eye. While putting down his pack, he said, "No one can leave this place until the snipers are killed. We need to flush them out."

"You mean we need bait?"

John slung both of his rifles over his shoulder. "If they want me to risk my life for them, they should be prepared to do the same."

Karen looked at the cliffs surrounding the green valley. "They could be hiding anywhere. Even if we get some volunteers to play peek-a-boo, the snipers won't be stupid enough to reveal themselves unless it's a kill shot. They know we are trying to scope them out."

Within two minutes, Karen was back with a woman carrying a rifle. "John, this is Kelsey. She'll be helping us."

John gazed at the young muscular woman as she finished priming her cradled rifle. "I need targets, not more people clamouring around the rocks and scaring them off."

Kelsey used her fingers to brush a clump of long black hair away from her eyes. A long scar ran down the left side of her face. "You will have your bait." Looking down at her rifle, she added, "Next to Tara, I'm the best shot here."

John looked at Kelsey's battered rifle. "Does it still work?"

Before he finished talking, Kelsey had the muzzle of her cocked rifle pressed against his forehead. "It has never failed me yet."

Karen pushed it away and said, "He's not the enemy. We have no time to waste."

While women dashed from one hiding spot to another along the edges of the valley, the three marksmen crawled about the rocky outcrops to get a vantage point. Staying within sight of one another they communicated through hand signals.

Time passed without any sign of a single sniper. John looked over at Kelsey and saw her lying on top of a cliff facing the cloud of black smoke. Seeing her dangling feet, he knew that she was watching the column of hunters. Gazing toward Karen, he muttered, "The reinforcements must be getting close."

The three converged on top of the cliff. Karen pulled out her binoculars and studied the terrain. The approaching column was now heading straight towards them. John knelt beside her and said, "One of them must have snuck out to meet them. They won't be long now."

Karen turned and looked at him. "They left a couple behind to keep us from leaving."

Finally, John saw a man running from one boulder to another. He was out of rifle range. Putting down his rifle, he cursed, "Damn it. He is too far away."

Kelsey looked up at him with disgust. "Why can't you men just leave us alone?"

Chapter Sixteen

Kelsey knelt beside Tara and wept. "They found our valley. A few dozen of them will be here shortly. I'm sorry. I failed you and every woman here."

Stripped to the waist, Tara layed on her stomach. Her back and sides were covered in blood. Jose stopped probing for the slug as Tara began coughing up blood.

Biting on a piece of leather, Tara mumbled, "You did your best. Now tell the others to pack everything they can." She took a few shallow breaths before continuing. "The best way of saving this valley is to leave it. Men are only interested in our bodies and meat. They don't care what this place has to offer."

Kelsey ran outside to spread the news. From their vantage point John and Karen could see the women scurrying about. A couple shots were heard, but the sniper had disappeared before the smoke had cleared.

Extracting the bullet was the easy part. The gruelling task of digging out the bone shards from Tara's shattered rib was much harder. Jose had to widen the hole in her back to get to a large piece that was cutting into her lungs. Her muffled screams were confined to the large cave that the women called home. By the time she finished cleaning and cauterizing Tara's wound, the leather strap she was biting on had been chewed in half.

As Karen scanned the cliffs for any signs of intruders, John knelt next to her with his rifle in hand. "You know that this place could be overrun soon."

With her binoculars pressed against her eyes, Karen reminded him, "Remember, there is only one safe way out of here. If they are setting up an ambush, I want to know it before hand."

A dozen and a half women worked their way along the edge of the green valley towards a narrow gap between two large rocky outcrops. Staying in the shadows, Karen and John watched them enter the gap. Over a few of their shoulders were some of the airguns taken from Sarah's clan members.

A rock rolled down a cliff near the exit. The trail of dust it left behind caught Karen's attention. A few metres above the cloud, she noticed a man trying to get a better look at the band of women. "Do you see him?"

"I only saw the dust."

"He is behind the rock directly above it."

John borrowed Karen's binoculars. "I can't hit him from this distance." After taking a better look at the cliff, he passed the binoculars back to Karen. "But I might be able to force him into the open." Before Karen could reply, he had shouldered his rifle and fired. His bullet struck an overhanging rock and caused a small landslide. As the man crawled out of the way, a bullet ricocheted off the boulder John was leaning against and landed on the ground in front of Karen.

Karen look at it. "They know what they are doing."

About fifty metres away, a puff of black smoke highlighted the shooter's position. Hidden behind a sloped boulder on the side of a cliff the shooter had nowhere to escape to without being seen. After exchanging rifles, John lay on the ground and pressed its butt against his shoulder. With the weight of the rifle being supported by a rock, he aimed midway down the sloped side of the boulder and waited. Behind him, Karen quickly loaded his other rifle and rested it beside him. "I'm going to try to scout around and see if I can spot any more of them."

At the far end of the valley, a half dozen small dust clouds sprang up around the second sniper as he tried to crawl back up the cliff. While he released a howl, his back straightened. Losing his grip, the man slid and tumbled backwards over a small ledge.

John had to force himself to focus on his own target. The man's screams enticed the other gunman to poke his head out to see what happened. A mere second was all the time John needed to readjust his aim and fire. After the rifle smoke cleared, he saw blood splattered on the boulder behind the shooters position.

After a couple minutes Karen put down her binoculars, adjusted the straps on her backpack and picked up her rifle. On her return she told John, "I didn't see anyone else."

As they briskly walked towards the gap, they both gazed at the cliffs around them. Suddenly they heard gunfire and saw half the women frantically running back into the valley. Not knowing what to do, the pair sunk to the ground and hid within the greenery. As the women disappeared in the surrounding rocks, Karen saw hunters cautiously enter the valley. As more men rushed in, explosions on both sides of the gap caused a landslide. The gap was full of rock and coarse gravel.

Inside the valley, the women were outnumbered. With dust obscuring their view, the men tried to get their bearings. There was no sign of the women, it was like they had simply vanished. The feeling of vegetation rubbing against their legs and moss getting tangled in their sandals was new to them. Dennis knelt in the ankle high mud and felt the long smooth leaves. After ripping one off, he bit it. The sharp bitter juice that leaked out of it had a strong metallic taste to it. He spit it out and declared, "This stuff is poisonous, don't try to eat anything here."

As the dust cleared, a hail of bullets rained down on the men from the surrounding cliffs. A man buckled over. "It's a trap."

As the men scambled to get to the nearest rocky outcrop, they were being picked off by the women hiding in the cliffs. While leaning over a ledge, Kelsey fired, slid her rifle to the side and was handed a pre-loaded one. In a small cave behind her, two women reloaded the rifles as fast as they could.

The cloud of smoke around her, made her a target. As the men returned fire, ricochets and rock chips made them duck for cover. Inside the small cave, the bullets bounced off the ceiling and were scattered in every direction. While standing against the wall, one of the women was struck in her thigh. The downward angle of a second bullet sliced a hole in her side and tore through her intestines. She looked down and saw it resting under the skin a few centimetres below her belly button. Looking at Kelsey, she started to cry. "Harvest me. You will need meat to live on."

Kelsey looked back at her. After seeing her wounds she told her, "If there's time. If not, do what you must."

As Jose helped Tara out of a cave, she looked around and saw the men firing on Kelsey's position. "We are still outnumbered."

While sitting outside of the mouth of the cave, Tara told her, "If Kelsey can keep them occupied, we still have a chance."

Jose looked at all the dust and smoke surrounding the small cave. "They are getting hammered. We can't just leave them?"

Tara reached out and grabbed her hand. "They knew the risks when they volunteered. In order for our colony to survive we must stick to the plan."

Karen noticed a small group of women midway up the side of a rocky outcrop on the opposite side of the valley. Below them, she saw a couple more dash towards a large crack in the rock face. As they slowly climbed up one at a time, even more women gathered around the bottom of the crevice. With a pile of boulders blocking the men's view, the frightened women hid while they waited their turn.

One of the women stepped on the side of a rock. It broke off and rattled down the rock face. Through her binoculars, Karen saw her regain her footing. The women below had to get out of the way of the mini landslide. As one of them stepped backwards a couple of the men spotted her. Karen saw several men race towards the wall of boulders. "The women are in trouble."

John rested his rifle on a boulder and fired at the lead man. Besides warning the women of the men's approach, his shot invoked return fire.

With a break from the constant bombardment of bullets and debris, Kelsey had more time to aim before pulling the trigger. Poking her rifle through the small opening between the three large rocks she used as a shield ten seconds felt like an hour. It was worth it. A man had stood up and tried to go around the wall of boulders. Her bullet slammed into his back and knocked him to the ground. The men's response was almost instantaneous. The bullets hitting the flat rock on top of her improvised gun port cracked it in half.

While extracting her rifle from the rocks, Kelsey broke its front sight off. "Put this gun aside."

The wounded woman spoke up. "I'll use it. That way they can't use it against you."

Kelsey could see the colour leave her colleague's face. "I hope it doesn't come to that."

Under the protection of John and Kelsey's fire, the women made their way along the ridge above the men. It wasn't until a few of the men got around the wall of boulders that they realized the women had escaped. John turned to Karen and told her, "It's time."

While John loaded his rifles, Karen poured small piles of gunpowder and lit different lengths of fuses in each of them. As the first one went off they snuck away behind the dark cloud of smoke. The slight breeze drifted the smoke over their path and masked their retreat while concentrating the mens' gunfire on the ledge they had been using. From the crest they saw another group of men racing towards the rocky outcrop that protected the valley. Karen turned to John. "If we can see them, they can see us. Our best chance is to stay on the valley side of the ridge and try to avoid being spotted by the men inside."

After twenty minutes of crawling they heard a 'ting'. Something metal had hit a rock. Freezing behind a boulder, they waited. They could hear the shuffling of arms, feet and bodies making their way along the same path they were on. With no way out John cocked his rifle and jumped into the open. Kelsey's face was less than a metre away from the muzzle of his rifle. "Oh, it's you."

Behind Kelsey the badly wounded woman held her gut in place while clinging to the other woman. Kelsey slipped the rifles off her shoulder and removed her backpack. "You are heading in the wrong direction."

Karen revealed herself. "We have to get back to our colony."

Kelsey looked at the distant cloud of black smoke. "You mean that hell hole?"

"Our colony is under attack. We can't abandon them."

"What possible help could you be to them? If you try to get near that place, they will skin you alive."

Karen notice the blood dripping from the wounded woman. "It won't take them long to find your trail, or was that your plan?"

Kelsey glanced at the blood running down the woman's leg. "If we can get them to follow us, the others may be spared."

******

With crude bandages wrapped around his torso, Jerry stood up and looked around the huge floating island that he was chained to. It was nothing more than a floating platform of garbage. Anything that floated was collected, wrapped in salvaged pieces of netting and lashed together with ropes. The houses on the outer edges were short and people had to crawl inside them. As they got closer to the middle, their size increased. Dozens of tethered boats along with an assortment of sails hauled the island wherever Victoria wanted.

As he gazed at the shoreline Victoria walked up to him and asked, "Does anything look familiar?"

Beyond the fleet of both sail and row boats, he pointed at the rusty skeleton of a cargo ship. "Yes, I recognize that shipwreck. We are almost a third of the way there."

Victoria smiled and put her arm around his neck, "Good, my men should have the rest of the islanders rounded up by the time we get there. They might even have time to help us harvest the remnants of your so-called town."

Jerry had a hard time breathing and it wasn't because of his injuries or the smell of the withering faces that Victoria was wearing. The people in town were his only family. Betraying them meant having no one. He would be alone. In an attempt to hide his emotions from her, he put his hand over his wound. The sudden pain dropped him to his knees. "I think I over did it."

After bending over and kissing Jerry's clammy forehead, Victoria smiled and whispered in his ear, "Now ain't you glad that you picked the right team to be on. It's much better than being processed."

******

With his ear pressed to the amplifying cone attached to the wall, Joe listened to the picks, shovels, hammers and pry bars as the townies chipped their way deeper into the mound. "There aren't as many as there were before."

Jake put his hand on the wall and felt it vibrate. "Maybe it's the weather?"

Joe closed his eyes. "You know better than that. Something or somebody has drawn their interest away from us. Why work for something if you can simply snatch something else."

******

Karen look at the sun. "It will be dark in a couple hours. That will make it harder for them to spot. We should be able to slip past their lookouts."

Kelsey gave her a cross look. "So you still feel bound to help your comrades."

Glancing at John as he repositioned his rifles on his shoulder, Karen answered, "We have no choice. We have to."

After looking at the other two women, Kelsey gazed toward the cliffs on the far side of the valley. "That will certainly lead them away from the others."

The injured woman looked up and studied everyone's faces. "You know I can't make it. If we are forced to fight or need to run, I would be nothing but a hindrance."

Kelsey stretched her hand towards her and said, "You know your options."

The woman raised her head and stretch her neck as high as it would go. "When it is time, I'll take the poison. If they try to harvest me they will die like the others."

Kelsey turned to Karen. "That's why the hunters have never tried to harvest us. They think our bodies are toxic."

Karen extended her hand and helped the injured woman to her feet. With her arm wrapped around her, she said, "Still, we can't just leave her to die."

Kelsey coldly informed her, "Her wounds are beyond our help. She knows that they will slowly fester, and she will die. She has accepted it."

The woman looked down as Karen turned to her. "I haven't and she's coming with us."

John took the lead as they continued their journey towards the embattled mound. In the rear Kelsey did nothing to hide the drops of blood from the injured woman. Under her breath she told herself, "At least the others will be safe."

Hearing it, Karen turned her head around and said, "So we will both get what we want."

******

As the sun set, David looked down at his mother as she stood in front of the pilothouse. "I see a lot of black smoke in the distance."

Beth answered back, "We must be getting close to the source of the black goo." After looking at the sky, she added, "Any sign of the Flesh Star or the Reapers?"

David double checked the waters behind them before yelling down, "None, it is as if they gave up looking for us."

As the ship entered an oil slick, Beth coughed before replying, "Or maybe it was the direction we took. After all, who in their right mind would sail into the Rainbow Sea." Turning to Daniel in the pilothouse, she yelled out, "Kill the boiler. The fumes are getting stronger. One loose spark could cause the gooey slick we are in to erupt."

As the hulls of the New Hope cut through an oily film, David peered through the binoculars. Beneath the black clouds, he saw dozens of fires stretched along the distant shoreline. Their plumes leaped into the air like erupting volcanos. Even at night their glow allowed him to see sections of the scorched barren shore. "I can't see anything worth going after." After putting down the binoculars, he yelled down at Josh as he brought some tea to Daniel, "The fires seem to be popping up everywhere."

While taking a sip of tea Daniel noticed a corner of a piece of paper. Curious, he tied the wheel and lifted a loose panel in the wall in front of the steering wheel and pulled out a map. After studying it for a while, he turned to Josh, he said, "Takeover, I need to talk to Sarah."

As soon as he reached the bottom step the light chatter between Beth and Sarah stopped. Daniel saw Sarah lying on the cold floor with both legs exposed. "What's going on?"

Beth turned to Daniel, "Her legs were bothering her. Since neither one of us could sleep, I figured that now was a good time to check her over." Running her fingers down Sarah's broken leg, she added, "The moisture coming up from the bilge was destroying her cast. When the sun is up, it's like a sauna down here. After her skin drys, I'll make another one."

In a stern voice he asked, "How long will it take?"

"It will be an hour or two before the cast is set."

"At least we are no longer being pursued." Daniel took a deep breath. "I won't stop you. I just need to talk with her."

Beth knew that he was worried about Sarah but didn't want to show it. Daniel knelt next to them. "Sarah, someone put stars and X's on a hidden chart. Do you know what they were for?"

Sarah propped herself up with her elbows. "No, I only glanced at it a few times. Sometimes the captain would spread it out on the deck for the elders to look at."

"Can you remember the places where the ship stopped?"

"Sure. Like everyone else I was on the deck whenever we anchored."

"What about a place surrounded by oil slicks and fires erupting everywhere?"

"So that's what I'm smelling. Some men went ashore to collected some thick goo. The captain said they needed it to smear over the larger gears and bushings on the ship. They also came back with some thinner oil to lubricate the smaller gears and bushings."

"So they didn't stay long?"

"Some of the crew stayed on shore overnight. By morning, the forward compartments of both ships' centre hulls were full of the smelly stuff. The fumes from some of the barrels would give you a headache. We had to keep the door shut. The townies must have taken them."

Daniel walked back to the pilothouse. He knew that the noxious fumes Sarah described was from refined oil.

He spread the hidden hand drawn map over the table next to the steering wheel. Despite being crude and disproportional, it tried to include as much as possible. It didn't take long to figure out where they were on the map. Beyond the star on the shoreline, someone had drawn an inland elevated area followed by a line with a star at the edge of the paper. "They didn't have time to even separate that much goo." Turning to Josh, he added, "They needed help. There must be people on shore refining it."

Josh tapped his finger on the map. "That's why there is a star here."

Shaking his head, Daniel agreed with him, "I wonder where these captains came from and what kind of people they were trading with?"

Exiting the oil slick, Daniel saw that the oily film on the ship's hulls was being slowly dispersed over the water. Daniel looked up at David as he sat on top of the mast. "Can you see anyone?"

"Still nothing."

"Then I will have to let them know where we are. I can't have them joining the attack on the colony. We have to take whatever pressure we can off them."

While waiting for the oily film to drift away from the ship, he cut a hole in the top of an empty container. After filling it with oil and stuffing the opening with rags, he lowered it into the water.

A stream of open water finally separated them from the oily film. Daniel lit the container and used a pole to push it toward the film. The sides of the plastic container melted and the oil inside poured out. As the two oil slicks joined together, the flames spread. As they sailed further away, a floating sheet of flames lit up the night sky behind them. "Even if they can't see the fires on land, they should at least be able to see a wall of flames in the middle of the sea."

******

The lookout in the crow's nest of the Flesh Star saw a faint red glowing line running across the water. Yelling down, he proclaimed, "I think I found them."

An armed guard looked up at him and asked, "Who?"

The angry lookout yelled back, "It has to be the earth dwellers aboard the New Hope. The Reapers are all behind us."

"I'll wake up Nick."

Chapter Seventeen

Daniel compared the map to the charts, and searched for the next landmass. He didn't look up as Beth entered the pilothouse and told Josh. "Go and try to get some sleep. I'll take the wheel."

Behind them, Daniel mumbled, "In order to get to the next landmass we'll be sailing into the wind. It will take us forever to cris-cross our way there. We'll have to ration our supplies."

Beth stared out the window at the wall of frames. "You lit an oil slick to help draw the townies away from the colony. Why not go ashore and gather some oil to burn in the boiler. If you want them to follow us, why not leave a trail of black smoke for them to follow."

After looking at the fires on shore and the height of the moon, Daniel said, "You might be right. We still have plenty of time. Hidden behind those flames, it could be a day or more before they even spot our masts."

******

On top of the same cliff that she had drawn her map, Karen leaned against a boulder and watched the red glow in the distance. "It is too early for the sun to be coming up."

Sitting down she crossed her knees and spread out the map on the ground. She slightly twisted her body to allow the moonlight to shine on the map. "It's coming from the sea. One of the oil slicks must have caught on fire. If it washes up on shore, we'll have no way in or out."

Standing outside of a small cave, John looked up at her. "If it does, the smoke could travel through the tunnels and suffocate them."

The cave was nothing more than a slanted flat bottomed boulder held up by a pile of rocks. Kelsey crawled out of it and stood beside John. "I told you that it was a bad idea for you to return to your colony. Now get down from there before you are spotted."

A gust of wind flapped her unfolded map. As she used stones to pin the map to the ground, a bullet whizzed through the corner of it and nearly struck her head. "Too late." While ducking down she asked, "Did anyone see where it came from?"

After the echos stopped, John looked up at her, "The boulder is in our way. Can you see any smoke?"

Lying on top of the boulder, Karen looked around. It was to dark for her to see anything. "They had to have been within shooting range or they wouldn't have wasted a shot."

Kelsey piped up, "Maybe with the map fluttering in the wind, they thought they had more than one target. If you shoot into a crowd, you are sure to hit someone."

As she rolled up the map, Karen said, "Hopefully it was just a scout."

"We'll check it out." Using a rope, John and Kelsey climbed down the side of the cliff. A third of the way down, they crawled along a ledge and looked down. Near the base, they saw three men darting from one boulder to the next. Turning to Kelsey, John asked, "How good are you with a knife?"

Kelsey shook her head. "I'm much better with a rifle."

"In that case, stay here and make sure they don't sneak up behind me."

As she attached a long knife to the end of her rifle, she told him, "I'll do my best."

After leaving both of his rifles with Kelsey, he quickly slithered another third of the way down the steep rocky cliff. Pressing his back against a boulder, he waited for the men to climb past him.

Hearing the clink of a loose stone, he turned his head and saw the shadows of the first two men. He held his breath and froze. Focussed on finding solid footing and hand holds in the loosely packed rock formations in front of them, neither one of them looked his way.

Hearing the last man approach, John crept around the boulder and snuck behind him. The man stopped. Thinking he heard something, he held his breath while listening for anything strange. Twisting his head around he barely saw the moonlight reflect off the edge of John's knife before it sliced through his throat. With his knife lodged in the man's neck, John jumped on top of him. He pinned the flailing man against the side of the cliff. Using both hands he wiggled his knife until it dug into the man's spinal column.

One of the other men looked back. Amidst the rocks and shadows, all he could see was a man on his hands and knees. John simply waved them on. As the man turned away, John stabbed his knife sideways into the dying man's rib cage. With a quick figure eight motion, he sliced through the man's heart and both of his lungs. Under his breath he muttered, "That should keep you still."

With the other two almost half way up the side of the rocky hill, John had to hurry. Without being weighed down by a rifle and kit bag, he could climb much faster than the men he was pursuing. Believing he was their comrade, they made no effort to conceal themselves from him.

Within a couple minutes he was only a few metres away from the trailing man. As the first man was about to climb onto a shelf, Kelsey ran her bayonet through the top of his skull. Seeing him sliding downward, the second man grabbed the man's arm. By the time he realized that his comrade was already dead, John had climbed beside him. Seeing him, the man released his comrade and reached for his knife. John lunged his knife into the side of the man's chest.

While John tried to extract his knife, the man grabbed him. In the struggle, they both lost their footing. As they slid down the cliff they started a small landside. John slashed the man's arm. After breaking free of him, John's legs slid around a jagged rock. The sudden stop took his breath away. He wanted to scream in agony but nothing came out. The pain from his crushed testicles made him want to faint. He bit down and tried to breath. Above him, Kelsey tossed down a rope. As he looked up at her, he noticed the smile on her face. "You enjoy seeing me in pain don't you?"

In a soft giddy voice, she answered, "It's not just you. I would enjoy seeing any man get his balls crushed."

Sitting on the shelf, they watched the sunrise. John looked down and only saw the hand of one man and the foot of another. "No one will find them until their rotting corpses begin to stink up the place."

Kelsey glanced over the side. "We should go down and collect what we can from them. You never know what we might need."

They gathered everything they could and returned to the shelf. As they took a breather, they heard a flurry of shots coming from the top of the hill. With a steep rock wall between them and the others they felt trapped. Kelsey glanced at the rope she used to climb down. "If they see it, they've got us."

Dennis had carefully orchestrated the stealthy attack. Distracted by the red glow and the men climbing up the side, the women didn't spot them until they were only a dozen metres away. Hiding behind large boulders, they never gave the women any soft targets to aim at. As the women reloaded their rifles, the men rushed in. Karen barely had time to grab her knife before three men piled on top of her. The weight of their bodies prevented her from fighting back. The same with the other women.

Seeing the scars down the right side of injured woman's face, Dennis smiled, "Do what you want to this one. She was one of the old mayor's whores. Just drag her body back when you are done with her."

One of the men that had her pinned down yelled out, "But she's nearly dead."

Dennis yelled back, "I've seen what you can do to a corpse. At least she's still warm."

With three men on top of her, Dennis stepped on Karen's wrist and twisted his foot back and forth until she released her knife. After kicking the knife away, he grabbed her hair and lifted her head. "What do we have here." While running his fingers up and down her smooth face, he added, "Killy is going to really like you."

Karen spat in his face. "You are all dead men walking. You are just to blind to see it."

Dennis grinned as he looked at the men pinning her to the ground.

"But we will still live longer then you."

Dennis wedged an unloaded rifle between Karen's back and inner elbows. After lashing her hands in front of her to press the rifle into her back, he nudged her along the gruelling trail down the steep incline. The strain on her wrists made the tips of her fingers go numb.

In front of her, the other woman slipped and slid several metres before tumbling into a boulder. A man grabbed the barrel of the rifle she was lashed to and pulled her to her feet. They both knew that even if they got away, there was no escape. Between the rugged terrain and the length of the rifles they wouldn't be able to run fast enough.

Kelsey clutched her rifle and pressed her body against the wall as John climbed up the rope and peeked over the edge. He heard moaning coming from a small cave near the top of the cliff. He crawled over the top of the wall and pulled out his knife. While creeping along the top of the gully, he discovered that the sounds were coming from more then one person.

From behind a boulder, John pulled a shiny piece of metal from his pocket and held it close to the edge. Using it as a mirror, he saw three men hovering over the dying woman. No one was facing him. John quietly crept behind the men and pulled a thin, double edged dagger from his belt with his left hand.

As one man pulled down his pants, the other two grabbed an arm and leg, and held the injured woman's almost naked body face down over a boulder. With each thrust the man ground the sharp edges of the stone deeper into dying woman's chest and abdomen. Unable to scream, her gasping moans were barely audible over the men's babbling.

The grinding cut through the bandages holding her intestines in place. Blood ran down her leg and made one of the men released the woman long enough to wiped off his hands. "I hope her blood's not poisonous."

The man holding the other side of her answered, "Nah, just don't drink it."

As he said it, he saw John and reached for his knife. John lunged forward and plunged his dagger into the man's chest. While giving it a twist, he swung his large knife around the back of the sexually engaged man's thighs and slashed the neck of the man holding the woman's bloody leg.

Caught up in organismic relief, the third man barely released the woman's waist before John yanked out his dagger, reached up and sliced his neck. While the bleeding men struggled to retrieve their weapons, John frantically hacked, slashed and stabbed their chests and throats. He didn't stop until he was sure they were dead. It was only then that he checked the injured woman.

He turned her over and saw what was left of her front. He had to look away. The scraping against the stone had peeled sections of skin off her stomach and breasts. With some of her ribs exposed, he knew that there was nothing he could do for her.

Picking up her shirt, he was about to cover her as Kelsey walked up behind him. Grabbing his arm, she took the shirt. While taking a small clay vial from its pocket, she said, "For her, it's finally over."

The woman could not even open her swollen eyes as she faintly said, "Don't let them harvest me."

Kelsey knelt beside her. "John made them pay for what they had done." After putting the clay vial in her mouth, she told her, "Now bite down and drink the nectar of eternal sleep."

After the woman used her tongue to removed some of the clay shards, she said, "Thank you. At least now I can die with some dignity."

******

Josh used bailing buckets to collect the thick goo from the oil saturated shore and place it into topless plastic barrels. After the brackish water separated, he skimmed the oil off the top and put it into the secured containers onboard their makeshift raft. When the three containers on the raft were full, he pulled on a rope that was wrapped around pulleys attached to both the ship and shore.

The inlet that they landed in was surrounded by rocky, black, soot covered hills. On the tallest two, Daniel and David stood on guard. David saw that Josh was having trouble getting the raft away from shore and started to climb down to aid him. Seeing his father gesturing for him to come to him instead, he stopped. His confusion turned to fear when he saw his father lay on the ground and suddenly disappear behind a boulder. *'We are not alone'*.

Unable to see Josh, Mary watched the rope travel around the pulley. She immediately wrapped the rope around the retrieving winch and began pedalling. After Beth adjusted the multi-geared winch to make it easier to pedal, she looked up at Sarah. "Do you see anything?"

Strapped in a harness, Sarah twisted herself around the mast and carefully examined every visible piece of debris floating on the water. Putting down her binoculars, she finally answered, "Still nothing."

"It has been over six hours." Beth looked at the fires on shore. "Signal the men and let them know that we are still safe."

Sarah reached for the long hose that David had attached to the methane tank. After cracking open the lever next to the mast, she grabbed the head of the hose and rapidly squeezed the trigger until a spark ignited the methane. With one hand on the lever she pulsated the flames and made four huge puffs of smoke. "That should do it."

On shore, despite being surrounded by smoke Daniel saw the last two bursts and counted the clouds above the ship. "They are all right, but I wish we could signal back to them know that we may not be."

In the valley beneath Daniel, a half dozen men pulling three handcarts had emerged from behind a thick wall of smoke. With large bulky masks covering their heads they quicky got to work. While a couple men inspected a maze of pipes, two others removed and welded a patch on an elbow. On a cart, the fifth man shifted his weight from one large air bellows to another, in order to maintain the constant flow of air they needed to weld. While he pushed down on one, an overhanging set of ropes and pulleys pulled up the other. A sixth man did the same on another cart, but instead of air, his cart was attached to long hose connected to a pipe in the ground.

Daniel turned and whispered to David, "They had built a small refinery." Seeing that his son had no idea what he was talking about, he added, "The equipment down there converts the thick goo into a thin, very volatile liquid. It's the kind of stuff Jacob uses to loosen pieces of rusty metal. When I was a kid, the townies had something simular to it, but not as complex."

Lying next to his father, David whispered back, "Maybe they have a piston motor that still functions? I've heard rumours that a few of them survived."

"I heard the same rumours, but I doubt it. I think they are using the stuff for barter. The ships' captains may have even been involved. That is why they didn't want any of the Islanders to go ashore. They didn't want them to know what was really going on."

"I thought that they just needed fuel for their ships and some lubricating oil?"

"No, crude oil spews out dark smoke. That would attract the Reapers." Daniel turned to his son. "But the refined stuff produces a lot less smoke."

Confused, David glanced at the shore and then at the ship. "I wonder how they got all the barrels onboard without waking everyone?"

Daniel looked at the men below them. "I think they had help."

David watched the men hammer the red hot edges of the metal and weld them in place. The constant fires that flamed up around them were quickly smothered in dirt. "So where is all the refined oil?"

With his binoculars, Daniel studied the shore. "If they are loading it onto ships, there must be a stock pile somewhere near the shore. We just have to find it."

As David watched the men work, one of them caught on fire. As the others ran over to put him out, David turned to his father and asked, "I wonder what the captains could have used for trade. Those men are risking their lives down there. They wouldn't just give the fuel away."

"That is why I think there is more to it. I know Sarah said that the barrels they took ashore were empty, but she won't have been privy to everything that went on. Maybe even the elders didn't know what was going on?"

******

Gunfire echoed throughout the debris field. Simon peered outside and saw a group of men fan out across the adjacent mound. A few mounds away, a group of shackled islanders were being escorted onto a waiting ship. After slinking back inside, she looked at Patrick and said, "They are getting closer. They will be here soon."

Patrick glared at the entrance and told her, "They don't need to take any of us alive. We are not tradesmen. To them we are nothing but meat."

Roger looked at Patrick and growled, "They won't be harvesting me without a fight. I'll take more than a few of them with me."

Patrick glanced at Simon and then at Roger. "You mean we will." Gazing at his bad leg, he added, "That will hamper you in an attack, but it shouldn't impede your shot. You can keep them busy while we thin them out."

Nancy heard every word they said. Huddled in a dark crevice with her sleeping children, she told them, "You don't stand a chance."

Simon went over and knelt beside her. "They don't need you either. They needed you for leverage over your husband. He is dead. You will be harvested along side us."

As tears flowed down her face she muttered, "But over their loud speakers they said that if we surrender, we will live."

Patrick looked at her and chuckled. "We would tell our prey the same thing. It gave us some free labour until we had time to properly harvested them."

After Patrick and Simon crawled out, Roger tried to help Nancy conceal the entrance the best he could. While leaning against the wall to catch his breath, he told her, "Don't worry, as long as you do as you are told, I won't harm you."

Nancy glared at him. "And what is stopping me from slitting your throat?"

Roger chuckled, "Do that and you and your kids are stew meat." As his face went cold he added, "Now pass me the rifles, I have to make sure they are primed and ready."

From the top of the mound, Patrick counted every Reaper he saw. *'Fifteen, there is probably double that plus a few more.'* As Simon crawled up and lay next to him, he told her, "There are fewer than I thought. I estimate that the islanders outnumber them almost three to one. If only we could get them to fight back. They are surrendering after the first volley."

Simon put her hand on his shoulder. "They are not fighters. Half the men we killed outside of town were castrated. They are simply not capable of fighting back."

"That's it!" Patrick slapped Simon's shoulder. "The Reapers would not expect any kind of pre-emptive assault. We could turn everything around on them."

It was only a half an hour before the first Reaper set foot on the mound. Not far behind him four more waded ashore. The riflemen aboard the ship were semi-preoccupied with managing captives. The Reapers scattered over the other mounds were solely focussed on their own searches.

Seeing the tip of a rifle barrel sticking out from behind a pile of rocks, the scout signalled to the rest to get down before he snuck behind a boulder. With all five Reapers out of sight of the riflemen aboard the ship, Patrick smiled as he came out of hiding and crept behind them. "Let the fun begin."

As a man peeked around a large boulder, Patrick jumped up and rolled over the top of it. His knees almost cracked the man's spine as he fell on his back. After wrapping his arm around the man's face to muffle his screams, he slit the man's throat from ear to ear. The man's attempts to scream sounded like a pieces of metal being scraped against a rock as it gurgled out of his throat.

Simon saw a small mirror being extended in the air. As the Reaper tried to figure out what was going on, Simon crawled behind her on her fingers and toes. She managed to carefully pull the Reaper's rifle away from her. Realizing her rifle was no longer lying on the ground beside her, the woman turned around. Simon jabbed her knife under the woman's jaw and with a bit of a twist forced it up into her brain. After a few violent convulsions the woman's body went limp.

Staring at the woman's long braided hair, Simon smiled as she extracted her knife. She quickly stripped the woman and exchanged clothing. The woman's vest only had four faces sewn on it, two over her shoulders and two fleshly skinned faces covering her breasts. She quickly dressed the dead woman and used her knife to cut across the woman's forehead. After cutting around her hairline, she carefully peeled off the woman's scalp. Using dirt to conceal the blood, she put it on, stood up and looked around.

Within seconds she heard a man mutter, "Get down you fool."

Simon smiled to herself as she repositioned the woman's body. After concealing the dead woman's missing scalp by plastering the top of her head with sandy debris, she grunted, "Help". Within seconds, she heard the man scamper his way towards her. As she bent over the dead woman she could hear the man pull out his knife. The soft whooshing sound of metal rubbing against leather was unique. As he came up behind her, he gave out a sigh of relief, "I thought it was you calling for help."

"It was." As she turned and sliced her knife across the man's belly, she added, "I needed help turning you into meat."

The man began to fall backwards and then lunged forward. While yelling, "You bitch", at the top of his lungs, he fell towards Simon knife first.

She tried to roll out of the way but his knife struck the side of her rib cage. "Not again!" The man tried to pull it out but she held onto it. Using her knee, she tried to pry him off her. The man's intestines began to ooze out of his gut. Simon smashed the hilt of her knife against the man's temple. As the man rolled off her, she shouted, "Die you piece of meat, just die!"

Patrick heard her and knew that the others probably did to. As they rushed to help, Patrick ran up behind them. He simply stabbed the nearest man in the back, pulled out his pistol and shot the last man in back of his head. The shot attracted the attention of the Reapers on the adjacent mound.

Amidst the gunfire, Patrick worked his way to his sister. Kneeling beside her, he carefully extracted the knife, took off his shirt and used it as a bandage. "You are always getting yourself injured. You are lucky it didn't nick any organs." He pushed the scalp off her head and ran his fingers through her blood soaked hair. "What would happen to you if I wasn't around to look after you?"

As two bullets sprayed them with rock fragments, Simon gazed up at him. "Die and become someone's stew."

Picking up the woman's rifle, he fired back at one of the shooters on the adjacent mound. Patrick handed Simon the empty gun and scrambled to collect the other dead Reapers' weapons. To his surprise, two of them had airguns. "Now these could be useful."

In the distance he noticed a pair of small vessels sneaking around the neighbouring mound. He ran back to Simon and gave her one of the airguns along with the muskets he collected. "These should give you something to shoot. It appears they are planning to land on the far side of the mound and try to swarm us."

Simon handed him the woman's rifle. "Here, I reloaded it. Take it. I have Roger to take some of their attention away from me."

With an airgun and a large sack over his shoulder, Patrick circled around the mound. To distract the Reapers Simon fired at the men on the ship as fast as she could reload the black powder rifles that Patrick left behind.

After circling around to the far side of the mound, Patrick opened his sack and removed the heads of three of the Reapers they had killed. He placed them between boulders and stuck long pieces of metal debris next to them. "That should distract them for a while."

Putting down their oars, the first boat glided along the shore and several of the men hopped out. As they secured the boat, a man in the boat saw the heads and cried out, "Get down, Snipers!"

Over a dozen men rolled over the gunwales and crawled ashore. While the rest stayed along the shoreline, four men crawl towards a shallow ravine that led to the far side of the staged heads. When they turned a corner all four men were travelling in a straight line. Hidden in the shadows at the end of the gully, Patrick took aim at the lead man. As the man peeked over the side to get a better look at the heads Patrick squeezed the trigger. The impact of the smokeless shot echoed inside the ravine as the man's body slid back into the gully.

Not knowing where the shot came from, the others ducked for cover. From the shadows Patrick emptied the airgun's magazine before the last man realized that he was firing in a kneeling position only a few metres away. While his friends suffered fatal shots to their heads, he was shot in the arm and across the neck. Despite the blood spewing from his neck, he pointed his rifle towards Patrick and fired. The bullet went wild.

The man dropped his rifle and ran down the ravine. Keeping his head down, Patrick pulled out his pistol and ran after him. As he looked around the corner he smiled. The man had only got a couple more metres before collapsing. He dropped to one knee and yanked out his knife. While slitting the man's throat he muttered, "And that makes nine."

On shore, the men didn't know what was happening. While collecting their weapons, Patrick saw another man scampering down the ravine. With the men's bodies stewn about by his vigorous search, he knew the direction of his attack was unclear to anyone that came upon them. Grinning, he crept back into the crevice and waited. As soon as the nervous man spotted the carnage, he turned around and started to head back.

With his bloody knife in one hand and his pistol in the other, Patrick leaped out of the shadows and ran after him. In his chase, the man's rifle slipped off his shoulder. Instead of grabbing it, he drew his long knife and turned to face his pursuer. As the two blades collided, Patrick lunged forward and clubbed him with the barrel of his pistol.

As the man sprawled on the ground, Patrick struck him a few more times. Looking at the unconscious man, he decided to send the Reapers a message. Patrick went and got a long metal pole that he had spotted while looking for something to imitate rifles. He flipped the man onto his belly and sliced open the crutch of his pants. The man regained consciousness as Patrick shoved the end of the pole into his anus. Echoing screams radiated from the ravine as Patrick twisted and shoved the pole in even further. After anchoring the other end of the pole between two boulders, he hoisted the man into the air and leaned the pole against the side of the ravine.

The more the man struggled, the deeper the pole penetrated his body. His curdling screams drew the attention of every man on shore. A volley of bullets silenced him. His riddled body began to lean forward as the battered pole started to bend.

Patrick looked at the lifeless man. "And that makes ten. This has been a good hunt. I wonder how many more I'll have to harvest before they get the message."

On shore the eight remaining men came together and tried to figure out what to do. "There must be a small army of them up there."

A man wearing a well adorned vest looked at the disillusioned man . "We have recaptured most of the Islanders already. There can't be that many left."

The white faced man looked up at his superior. "We lost a quarter of our men already. How many more should we sacrifice for a few scraps of meat. I say leave them to rot."

Gazing towards the top of the mound the highly adorned man knew that his subordinate was right. "There are plenty more on the other mounds. If these vermin want to stay and starve to death on this heap of garbage, I say let them."

Chapter Eighteen

In the upper tunnel, Joe used a large cone to listen to the noise radiating from a copper pipe wedged in the wall. Most of what he heard was incomprehensible garble. The odd time, when the hammering had stopped, he could almost make out what they were saying. Suddenly, they dropped their tools and made their way down the side of the mound. "Something's up. They've stopped digging."

Sitting beside him, Jake piped up, "I wonder what happened?"

"I'm not sure, but they sound pretty excited."

Jake put his hand on Joe's shoulder and said, "That could only mean fresh meat."

Joe turned away from the cone and walked to the other side of the tunnel. "I know."

Outside the mound, one of the men told the others, "The hunters are bringing in a couple female prisoners."

The only word they could make out was 'female'. Jake stared at Joe. "That doesn't mean that they caught Karen. There are other women out there."

Glaring at him, Joe snapped back, "But Karen is the only one that would have any reason to venture anywhere near this place."

Jacob came running down the tunnel. "The sentries outside the cavern have abandoned their posts. We finally have a chance to escape."

Jake walked over to Joe and placed his hands on his shoulder. "We may never get another opportunity like this."

Joe looked up at him. "How about you making the call for me. I'm afraid that my judgement might be slightly clouded."

Jake slid his hands down to Joe's clenched fists. "You maybe right. This is not the time to pick a fight we can not win. Lets leave while we can, regroup and pick the battles that we at least have a chance to win instead."

Joe turned to Jacob. "Tell the others to pack and inform them that Jake will be in charge of the exodus."

Jacob looked at him. "What about you?"

With his hand behind his head, Joe looked up at the ceiling and replied, "Don't worry about me. I'll be fine. I just need some time to myself."

******

Killy and Grant walked up to Dennis as he paraded the two women around the camp. Both of them were transfixed by Karen. Grant pulled Killy away as he went to grab her. "You have had your share of fresh blood. This one is mine."

Killy squeezed Grant shoulder. As Grant forced his hand away, Killy smirked, "Look at the men. They are animals. These women are not private property. The moment your back is turned, one of them will take her. By the time they are through passing her around, you won't even recognise what is left of her."

Grant looked at the men as they stood in awe. "You might be right. Things are more in the open here." Glancing at Eric, he said, "But the men need to know who is in charge. Take her to my tent and strap her to the bed. When I'm tired of her, I will turn her over to the others myself."

As a dozen men swarmed around the other woman, Killy blared out, "Get off her." Dennis helped him pulling them away. By the time they reached her, she was stripped naked. Even the bracelet he had given her was snatched by one of the men.

Despite her penned up hatred toward Killy, she reached up and took his hand. "Please don't harvest me. I had alway done what you asked of me. This time I'm asking you..."

Shaking his head, Killy interrupted her. "It is too late. This is not like town. There are too many eyes here and no dark corridors to sneak you in and out of." Glancing at the crowd, he added, "The men want to see blood and soon they will be demanding their share of fresh meat. If we don't offer them any, they could turn on us."

She shook her head. "Why me? Why not the earth dweller?"

"Because you are more expendable."

As Karen's high pitched screams rang through the camp, Dennis, Eric and two others tied Killy's ex concubine's arms and legs to two metal girders that were sticking out from the top of a mound of debris. With her naked body stretched into an 'X' for all to see, the men formed a large circle around the small mound. After the four men left, Killy whispered into her ear, "Sorry it had to end this way. You were one of my favourites."

She softly whimpered back, "Could you at least kill me first."

Shaking his head, he told her, "That would deprive the men of a full harvest ceremony. However I will sever some of your nerves so you don't feel as much pain."

She spit at him and said, "You just don't want me to pass out from the pain."

Killy grabbed her hair and yanked her head back. Dennis passed him a tube and held open her mouth while Killy shoved it down her throat. After opening a sealed jar of blood clotting agents mixed with pain numbing drugs, he poured it into the tube. The lethal mixture was designed to keep her alive during the ceremony. As he pulled out the tube, he told her, "The men need a good harvest. I'm just sorry it's you."

While waiting for the drugs to kick in, the men listened to the screams coming from Grant's tent. Killy tried to remain calm as he sharpened the knives used in the harvest ceremony. He knew that it would require all of his attention and skill. If he is too slow or mishandles his knife, she could die prematurely. Seeing the colour leave the woman's lips he knew it was time. Putting his emotions aside, Killy kissed her forehead, turned, raised his knife into the air and announced, "Let the harvest being."

He cut the skin around her ankles and ran his knife up the underside of her legs all the way up to her groin. Despite the mind numbing ingredients in the concoction he had given her, her screams drowned out Karen's. Next he circled her wrists making sure he didn't nick any veins. After slicing the skin up both of her arms, he went across her upper chest and down to her groin. As his fingers rubbed against the lining of her stomach, he felt something move. Placing his hand under her skin, he smiled. Within a few seconds a gush of liquid drained out of what was left of her groin and a small creature began to squirm on the ground. Killy looked up at the woman's face. "You should have said something."

The delirious woman tried to raise her head but couldn't. "It wouldn't have mattered."

Killy cut another line down the left side of her face. "I know that you were both clean and fertile. Now the others will to."

He picked up the embryo and shoved it into his pocket. Then he stood back and looked over the crowd. "I need four volunteers." The same four men that had tied her came forth. Each of them grabbed the same hand or foot that they had tied. "Let the flesh of this harvest be seen by all." Each man peeled the skin away from their assigned limb. After Killy pulled the skin away from her chest and abdomen, the four men stood behind her and yanked it off her back. All that was left was for Killy to slice the skin away from the back of the woman's neck.

The clotting agents had turned her blood into a thin jelly. With both her brain and facial muscles deprived of oxygen, the woman was unable to shut her eyes. She watched the men wrap her skin around Killy's shoulders like a bloody robe. The weight from her attached breasts kept it from slipping off. Killy bent over and looked up at her face. "You made a good harvest." Turning to the men behind him, he added, "What say you?"

With joyful cries ringing out, Killy placed a large bowl beneath her and said, "Now I can fulfill your wish and let you die." She never felt the metal tube being inserted into her heart. Running his free left hand down the fresh cut on her face he choke up slightly and added, "I'm sorry it came to this." Before his final words were said, her lifeless head flopped into his hand.

Only a small amount of a dark pudding like liquid dripped into the bowl. After dipping two of his fingers into it, he licked them clean. Turning to the crowd, he raised the bowl into the air and proclaimed, "I am still alive, therefore the harvest is clean and safe for everyone to enjoy."

******

Killy's announcements were loud enough that Joe could make them out. He put the cone down. Sitting against the wall, he rested his head on his folded arms and wept. "Oh Karen, I hope that wasn't you."

It was low tide and there was hardly any water dribbling out of the tunnel. A half dozen members waited inside as Jake stepped into the escaping water, crouched down and began to crawl into the small tunnel. Behind him, a salt and pepper haired woman inquired, "It's broad daylight. Shouldn't we wait til dark?"

Jake glared at Gloria. In the dim light she appeared small and frail, but he knew that beneath her wrinkled leathery skin were strong sinew like muscles capable of doing anything she demanded from them. As the eldest member of the colony, the others looked to her for guidance. Glancing at the others, Jake answered, "We don't have a choice."

With the aid of a long pole with a large hinged mirror attached to it, Jake peered out. He couldn't see any guards. Using wires to adjust the angle of the mirror, he carefully checked every vantage point that the guards had been spotted. No one. "They must all be at the harvest festival. They probably felt we would never risk a daylight escape during low tide."

As Jacob helped him remove the pole, he said, "I think you are right. It is now or never. We may not get another opportunity like this."

Jacob led the colony along the shore towards a crack in the seawall. Joe was the last to leave. As he poked his head through the tunnel and began to crawl out, he saw the bow of the Flesh Star turn into the channel. He found himself to stunned to talk.

Perched on the mast, Jeff bellowed out, "They are escaping."

Nick saw them race along the shore and blared out, "Get your rifles. I don't want any of them to get away."

A couple of the men fired their muskets before they were in range. A mother holding her child looked back and saw the ship. "It's the cannibals."

Joe finally yelled out, "Get off the beach."

A handful of the men, women and children turned back and raced toward the tunnel. The rest sprinted towards the small gap in the seawall. With bullets peppering the shore, they dropped most of their belongings and ran, limped and crawled towards safety.

Joe shot at the ship in vain. As bullets struck the shore and whizzed by him, he crawled back into the tunnel in order to reload.

They had to get off the beach. Several were shot while trying to help the wounded. Several women were shot as they tried to save their bewildered children. As the odd wave splashed against the shore, everything was stained with the blood from the dead, dying and wounded. Their meagre possessions, weapons and supplies were strewn everywhere.

The gunfire from the ship shook the festive townies back to reality. After grabbing their weapons they made their way towards the shore as fast as they could. While some crawled up the mound others took a longer but easier path to the shore. Before any of them saw the water, the gunfire had stopped. The next thing they heard was the roar of one of the ship's cannons and the thundering impact its ball had on a pile of concrete next to the shore.

The dust from the impact was still floating in the air as most of the ship's crew jumped into the water and waded to shore. As they rushed to claim the bodies of the dead and wounded earth dwellers, hordes of Townies scrambled down a pathway to beat them to it.

From the top of the mound, Grant yelled to the ship, "How many escaped? Did you get them all?"

From the mast, Jeff used a cone to amplify his voice, "I don't know. I think we got most of them. I'm not sure."

After looking down at the bodies littering the shore, Grant yelled out, "What happened to the rest?"

Pointing to what was left of the gap, Jeff replied, "Most of them went through a small gap between a couple slabs of concrete. Our gunners hit it with a cannonball. There are probably several bodies buried in the rubble."

"And the others?"

"They went back inside."

With the anchor dropped, Nick came out of the wheelhouse. Seeing some of his men on the shore, he yelled out, "How many did we get?"

A crew member yelled back, "I've counted three dead and a half dozen injured so far."

Two others spotted an injured woman trying to crawling over a dead body next to the tunnel. Joe reached out and grabbed her extended bloody right hand and began pulling her inside. As the Townies tugged at her ankles, he lost his grip. Before they dragged her half a metre, he lunged forward and wrapped both of his hands around her left wrist. With his knees dug into the sides of the tunnel he quickly leaned back and yanked her head and arms into the tunnel.

Screaming was of no use. Feeling like her arm was being pulled apart she clenched her teeth and wrapped her right arm around Joe's thigh. Despite being pulled from both directions, she felt a small relief. Pumped full of adrenaline, she tried to kick her legs free. Aided by another man, Joe managed to wiggle his legs and got his feet next to the walls. With the man's arms wrapped around his shoulders, they pulled her torso inside.

Joe's planted his feet firmly against the wall of the tunnel. A young girl handed one of the steel rods that were leaning against Jacob's bench to the man helping him. "Get them off my mom."

The woman was lying face down between Joe's legs. The man crawled over them and jabbed the rod into the tunnel. He stabbed the back of one of the men's wrists. The woman immediately used her free leg to kick at the other man's hands. Afraid of spearing her legs, the man dropped the rod and grabbed her arm pits. As they tried to pull the woman in further, a young girl crawled between them and slashed the Townie's hand with her knife.

Outside of the tunnel, the two men watched the woman's feet disappear. While shaking off their injuries, they confronted several townies who were trying to drag away the bodies outside of the tunnel. With blood pouring from his cut hand, the sailor pulled out his knife and stabbed one of them in the back of his left shoulder. "That will teach you not to steal my meat."

Behind them Killy fired a shot in the air. The blast made them turn and face him as he blared out, "What do you think you are doing?"

As the man removed his knife, he answered, "Teaching the thief a lesson."

Killy looked at the sturdy man and then at the frail man he stabbed. He could see his ribs sticking out of his sides. "While you have been eating your fill, back here everyone has been starving. There is more meat on one of your legs than there is on that man's entire body. Maybe if I chopped one of them off to teach you a lesson on sharing."

The man walked backwards away from Killy. "He's near his end. To take one of my legs would render me useless. That would be like killing both of us."

Killy smiled as he walked toward him. "I wouldn't want to waste a healthy body like yours just to prove a point, but if you cross me again, I'll take both of them."

Grant approached the anchored ship and noticed a naked man lashed to the railing. The man's face didn't look familiar. Nick stroked the back of the captive's head as he looked down at Grant, "We need to talk. There is trouble coming our way."

Refusing to be silenced, the battered prisoner belted out, "You will all be sliced meat within a week. From what I see, none of you are even worth turning into slaves."

With the tide coming in, the men on the shrinking shore stood still as the stranger's words echoed off the steep banks. The frail man with the bleeding shoulder stared at him and said, "At least we'll be the ones eating tonight."

******

The prisoner's muffled words made their way into the tunnel and also to the sentry that was standing behind the collapsed gap. The injured captives' screams rang out between the rushing waves of the incoming tide. She had to cover her ears as a third of her clan was being harvested.

Gloria's nimble slight frame made her the ideal lookout. Strains of her dust covered streaked hair concealing her face, making it blend in with the rubble. She slowly stretched out her arm and laid it on the debris in front of her. Using a mirror, she saw the townies drag away the dead and injured members of her clan, along with the supplies they were forced to leave behind.

With the surf coming in, Killy began chopping off the limbs of the wounded while they were still alive. Their screams echoed above the crashing surf. Twisting her wrist, she saw a group of Townies brave the surf as they began to ascend the steep pile of rubble that sealed the gap. As loose pieces of concrete gave way, the lead pair slipped into the water. Turning her head she told Jacob, "This pile won't hold them off for very long."

Jake looked around at the surviving members of his clan. Including himself there were only five men, three women and two children left. If Jake hadn't dragged his mother through the gap, Gloria would have been among the dead.

Jacob looked up at her, "Do you need help down?"

Gloria glared at him, "Of course I need a hand."

With one hand on her thigh and another on her side, Jacob lowered her to the ground. "We have no time to waste. They will have us surrounded in no time."

Gloria thought for a moment, "Did you hear what the prisoner on the ship said?"

"I couldn't make it out."

"He said something about others coming. He gave the Townies only a week."

Jake looked at her, "Some people will say anything to stay alive." Standing still, he looked at Jacob. "The question is, why is he still alive? Once they interrogate a prisoner, they normally butcher them."

Chapter Nineteen

With the camp almost empty, Dennis peeked into Grant's tent. Karen was lying face down with her arms and legs lashed to the four corners of the bed. He smiled as he took off his pants. With his hand pushing her face into the mattress he rammed his penis into her bloody anus. As his other hand felt her soft skin, he shook his head. Despite all of the bruises, cuts and dried blood, he knew something was different. He pulled his penis out and slowly inserted it into her swollen vagina. He could barely remember the last time he had penetrated a live woman.

With a smile on his face Dennis began to pulsate back and forth. He shut his eyes to revel in the moment. The flap of the tent flung opened. Before he could turn his head to see who it was, John used both of his hands to hack his long curved knife into Dennis's neck. The blow nearly severed his head.

"Karen, we gotta go."

Kelsey had cut three of her limbs free before Karen could comprehend what had transpired. "Why John? I'm done for. You could be caught."

As he helped put one of Patrick's shirts on Karen, John replied, "It's alright. The camp is almost empty. As long as we are quiet we should be fine. We were going to wait till dark, but when everyone suddenly ran to the shore, we decided that it was now or never."

Rocking her head back and forth in a daze, Karen said, "That means that the others are in trouble."

John took her hands and tried to comfort her. "We couldn't do anything about that, however we saw the opportunity to save you and we took it."

Kelsey bent over and peeked out of the bottom of the tent's flap. She noticed her friend's skin staked to the ground to be cured. After taking a deep breath, she poked her head out and looked around. Seeing nobody looking their way, she whispered, "It's clear."

Even with John supporting most of her weight, Karen could barely stand. Her legs were like rubber. With his arm wrapped around her waist, anyone seeing her could still tell that she was a woman. They skirted around the large tent and passed a dozen smaller ones. Behind a small pile of debris John put Karen down and rested. While he uncovered their stash of weapons and supplies, Karen looked around. "Where's Kelsey?"

Rifle in hand, John peered over the top of the small mound. After a few seconds, he noticed her hunched over body. She was carrying something. He watched her sneak pass a couple rows of tents. "Where is she going?"

After she tossed her friend's skin under the pot of a cooking fire, she briefly stood up and watched it burn. John spotted a Townie reaching for his rifle. Before the man could even take aim at Kelsey, John fired and blew off the top corner of his skull.

Kelsey dropped to the ground, and grabbed the side of a nearby tent. Pulling with all her might, she tore it from the ground and drag it across the edge of the fire. The oil soaked leather lit up like a torch. Trying to outrun the flames she tossed it from side to side as she ran through the camp. Leaving a wake of burning tents behind her, all the Townies saw was a wall of flames. Their random shots tore off chunks of inflamed leather. The wind caused the fire to spread.

Protected by a wall of black smoke, John and Karen went ahead, while Kelsey made sure nobody was following them. Gazing at the fire, she told herself, "No one is going to wear the skin of any of my friends."

******

Grant and Killy held their rifles above their heads as they waded to the ship. As they heard shots coming from the camp, Grant smiled at Killy. "Maybe they spotted the escaping earth dwellers."

Once aboard the Flesh Star, Killy went over to the prisoner and examined his body. Despite the injuries he obtained by being continuously raped by the crew members and whipped for information, the man appeared healthy. Turning to Nick, he asked, "Where did he come from?"

"He's an islander. We found him hiding in a large debris field. He wasn't alone." Facing Grant, Nick added, "They were being pursued by another group. According to him, they are hundreds of so called Reapers heading our way."

Grant crouched down and studied the prisoner's face. "Are they all as healthy as this man?"

"Yes, and none of the Reapers we saw were under fed."

Grant glared at Nick, "What do they know about us?"

Nick took a half step back and scratched his head, "They nabbed Jerry. I don't know what he could have told them."

Grant looked at Killy, "Jerry's a spineless coward. He would tell them whatever could keep him alive the longest."

Killy ran his hand up the prisoner's spine and across his muscular shoulders. "I might be able to persuade him to talk. We need to know everything we can about these Reapers."

"And what is so valuable about the islanders." Nick put his hand on Grant's shoulder. "They wanted to capture them alive. It was not their meat that they were after."

Grant watched the way Killy grinned as he felt the man's body. "Do you honestly think you can extract anything more from him?"

Killy wiggled the tip of his finger into the deep gash in the man's arm. The prisoner's wild scream brought a wide grin to Killy's face. "He is not used to pain." After licking some sweat off the back of prisoner's neck, he smiled at Grant. "I don't think I'll have any problem jogging his memory."

Nick took his hand off Grant's shoulder. "We will need to prepare the town for their arrival."

Sitting in the privacy of the pilothouse, Nick showed Grant the garb that was taken off a dead Reaper. "Along with their weapons and overwhelming numbers, they use fear tactics to help subdue their opponents. That alone means they sometimes give them the opportunity to negociate their fate."

Grant began to chuckle. "They try to avoid any bloodshed whenever possible. There lies their weakness." Gazing at the prisoner he added, "Even the name Reaper implies that they want to harvest without minimal use of their own resources. They want to sit back and reap the bounty of others. They are lazy. That's another weakness."

"So you think they are no real threat?"

While rocking his head back and forth, Grant licked his lips. "Just look at that prime meat. Forget the earth dwellers. If we play our cards right, this could be the biggest and best harvest ever."

Nick glared at Grant. With a puzzled look on his face, he asked, "The question is, what do we have that they would be willing to go to war over?"

Looking out the window, Grant answered, "I am sure Killy will soon be able to tell us." His eyes were quickly diverted to the large cloud of black smoke rising from the far side of the mound. "It is coming from the camp."

Nick stood beside him and said, "I hope the gunpowder is safe."

******

From his vantage point on top of the mound, Simon saw a group of Reapers land on the adjacent mound. He had previously seen activity on the mound and knew that there were islanders on it. As the Reapers approached a dark cavern, Simon fired a shot at them. She missed. The invaders scrambled for cover.

As the Reapers attempted another assault, Patrick and Simon steadied their rifles. Despite ascending the far side of the mound, they still had to come around and travel through a wide open area below the islander's hideout. This time they were in Roger's view. Not waiting for Roger to shoot, Nancy shouldered a rifle and fired it at them. With their position revealed, Roger opened fire. At that distance, all they could hope for was a lucky shot or ricochet. Patrick's large rifle was the only weapon they had that was capable of placing a bullet anywhere near the target.

With Roger lying at the mouth of their shelter, Nancy knelt beside him and followed his instructions. "If they were anyone other than my clansmen, I would not be doing this."

"I bet if I was out there, you would take a shot."

Nancy lowered the rifle she was carrying and looked down at him. "If I wanted to kill you, I could do it right now."

Roger snorted and told her, "Not with an empty rifle. Now pass me a loaded one."

From within the shadows, the emboldened islanders used airguns to spray the open area in front of their hideout. The advancing Reapers retreated leaving two of their members lying in front of the entranceway. As they attempted a second assault, Patrick steadied his rifle. When their highly adorned leader stood up and waved for his reserves to rush the hideout, a bullet spun him to the ground. Instead of attacking, the reserves dragged him behind a pile of concrete.

Not knowing what had gone wrong, the man leading the assault stopped and turned around. In less then a second the tide had turned. Separated by less than a dozen metres, several islanders charged out of the cavern shooting their airguns. Behind them, others wielding knives and sharpened metal rods joined the skirmish.

With their leader spewing more blood than words out of his mouth, a couple Reapers grabbed his arms and dragged him away. Looking through his binoculars, the lookout of a nearby ship relayed the outcome of the attack. After hearing the news, the redheaded captain yelled out, "Prepare to depart." Turning to his second in command, he added, "We already have enough captives onboard to satisfy Victoria. Why should we risk anymore lives."

"What about the others?"

"They will see our aft and get the message. By the sound of it, they won't have many captives to weigh them down. They should be able to catch up to us in no time."

The retreating Reapers compelled the islanders to pursue them to the far side of the mound. After hearing a volley of gunfire, Patrick and Simon saw them run, limp and crawl back to the cavern. Seeing the mast of a departing ship getting further and further away, Patrick slung is rifles over his shoulder. "That maybe our only way out of here."

"What are you talking about?"

Almost hidden behind the adjacent mound, the tip of a mast gently rocked with the current. Pointing to it, Patrick said, "There is another ship. If the islanders can keep its crew occupied, we might be able to capture it."

"How, I can't go into salt water with an open wound?"

While laying his guns on the ground next to Simon, he said, "You won't have to. Just keep them occupied while I swim over there."

After securing a pair of knives to his belt, Patrick lowered himself into the water and swam to the besieged mound. With Roger's and Simon's gunfire distracting the Reapers, he made it ashore unseen. He slowly worked his way around the shore with barely his head above the water. Not wanting to get needlessly injured, the jagged debris took longer to navigate through then he expected. A half hour later, he spotted the ship's gunwales. After taking a deep breath, he swam underwater away from the shore.

With the ship's guards exchanging fire with the defiant islanders, no one noticed him come up for air. After scooting along the canal side of the ship, Patrick climbed onto the ship's starboard rudder. Hearing another round of gunfire, he took the opportunity to glance over the deck. To his amazement he only saw two guards leaning against the railing.

While loading their rifles the guards chattered about what was happening on shore. As they aimlessly fired, Patrick hoisted himself aboard and crept alongside the pilothouse. With his long, bent knife in this right hand and a short dagger-like one in the left, he waited for the right moment. As time passed, his bent legs started to get cramped. Hiding under the pilothouse's side window, he flexed them the best he could.

As the mound erupted with shouts and screams, the two men were mesmerized by the attack. Seizing the opportunity Patrick dashed out and ran across the deck. With a wide swinging blow his blade sliced through the unprotected area between the nearest man's helmet and shoulder armour. With his knife semi stuck in the man's upper neck, he lunged his dagger into the side of the second man. Its long thin blade pierced the leather armour, but didn't penetrate very far. As the first man collapsed, Patrick yanked his long knife free and withdrew his dagger. The guard stepped back and used his rifle to block Patrick's blow. The heavy blade slid down the barrel and broke off its rear sight.

The musket accidentally discharged and the barrel was blown away from the man's left hand. The bullet cracked the front window of the pilothouse, waking the man inside.

Patrick's next blow slashed the guard's face from his right eye, across his nose and down to the left side of his chin. A slug from the woken man's pistol grazed the top of Patrick's shoulder and etched his chin. With the second guard reeling in agony, Patrick dropped and rolled behind the dead guard's body. The third man raced toward him wielding an oversized blade over his head with both hands.

Patrick threw his dagger at the man's chest. It barely penetrated the man's body armour. He swiped it off with one hand. That extra second allowed Patrick to yank the pistol from the dead man's belt. The quick shot caught the man's shoulder and spun him around. By the time the man regained his composure, Patrick had used both legs to push away from the dead man and slide across the deck behind him. While Patrick sliced the back of the man's knees with his dagger, the man's oversized blade narrowly missed Patrick's thigh. As he collapsed to his knees, Patrick shoved him against the ship's railing. Unable to stand, he swung his blade from side to side in front of him.

With the second man flailing about, Patrick stood up and looked around. The sporadic gunfire had masked the ruckus aboard the ship. He walked over, picked up the dead man's unfired rifle and put a bullet into the third man's forehead. As the second man pulled himself to one knee, Patrick kicked him to the deck. While he used both hands to lift himself up, Patrick pounded the butt of the rifle into his mangled face.

The man's flattened nose and smashed mouth left him unable to breath. Leaving him to die, Patrick ran to the pilothouse. It was empty. He grabbed the pistol that was lying on top of a chart on the captain's desk. Through the tubes going to the side hulls, he heard chains rattle.

The ship had the same design as the Flesh Star. After opening the hatch to the boiler room, he stepped back. Looking down the pistol barrel, he finally took a quick peek inside. In the dark he could barely see the bottom of the stairway. He used a sparker to light the oil lamp that was hanging in the pilothouse. Patrick lowered the lantern into the boiler room. Nothing happened. He then poked his head inside. There was no one in the boiler room.

Going over to the starboard tube, he opened the hatch and yelled down, "Come into the light and I might spare you."

Several voices blared out, "We can't." "We are all chained to our stations." "Free us."

Patrick slowly stepped forward. "Are there any Reapers among you?"

In the dark voices yelled over the rattling chains, "No", "None", "Nope", and "Why would there be?", came all at the same time.

As he climbed down he saw a set of keys hanging on a hook behind the ladder. After handing them to the man in the rear station, he said, "Release your friends."

By the time the men in both tubes were released, the only gunfire Patrick heard was coming from Simon and Roger. The surrendering Islanders were cautiously exiting their hideout. The battle left none of them unscathed.

Patrick shook his head. Turning to the men standing beside him, he added, "If they could have held on for a bit longer, we could have mounted a counter strike."

The parade of demoralized islanders hobbled along at a crawl. Two had to be carried. Others couldn't walk without assistance. Despite several Reapers being wounded, only one needed assistance.

Focussing on their prisoners and treacherous terrain, they hardly glanced at the ship.

As they circled around the mound and slowly started toward the ship, Patrick mumbled, "If they thought something was wrong, they wouldn't be still coming." Looking around, he pointed to a group of men and said, "I need three of you to dress up as Reapers."

A bald older man snapped back, "But this guy is still alive?"

Patrick knelt down and stabbed his dagger through the man's broken nose and into his brain. "Not any more. Now strip him and get dressed." Looking around at the bewildered men, he added, "I'll need at least half of you down below. Once we raise the anchor, we'll need to get away from this jagged shoreline."

While some of the confused Islanders went below, most of them silently hid behind the pilothouse and watched them strip the dead men and drag their bodies to the far side of the cabin. After he got into the dead Reaper's garb, the confused older man looked at Patrick, "Now what?"

"Pick up one of those rifles, load it and try to act like one of them."

As the strung out parade walked around the large piles of debris that littered the side of the mound, Patrick counted nine survivors including two juveniles. There were only six Reapers guarding them. A few of the men standing next to him gazed at the prisoners with open jaws. They all began whispering to one another.

Patrick heard their dishearten chatter. With fewer Reapers then he expected, he proclaimed, "Change of plans."

Pointing to the two closest men, he added, "Search this ship for anything that can be used as a weapon." Pointing to another man, he said, "Tell the men below to get top side. We will need everyone on deck in order to save your comrades."

The men's vigour surprised Patrick. Within a minute and a half a man emerged from the main cabin with a few rifles. "That's it, there aren't any more down there."

Looking at the men standing around him, Patrick said, "Grab whatever you can. I only counted six of them and we have six rifles and two pistols. If we catch them by surprise and get off a good first volley, we should be able to easily overtake them."

Leaving the three armed men in Reaper garb behind, Patrick led the rest ashore. He stationed two riflemen next to piles of debris near the ship, one rifleman on one side of a narrow gap where the column will be passing through and a man armed with the last pistol on the other side. The rest of the men hid along the side of the path.

Patrick quickly scampered up the mound and made his way to the end of the slow moving column. At the rear, a Reaper with a bleeding arm was helping a colleague with a wounded leg. Their muskets were slung over their shoulders and pistols pointed at the ground.

With a grin on his face Patrick snuck up behind the wounded pair. He jabbed his dagger under the hobbled man's arm, through his exposed armpit and into his chest. As he pulled his dagger out of the screaming man's chest, the other man felt his knife scape across his back. Releasing the dying man he quickly turned around. Nobody was there.

The man yelled out, "There are more of them out here. One of them just got Hank."

Confusion overcame the column. The Islanders were ordered to lay down on the ground. Two Reapers ran to see what was going on. One of the Islanders on shore fired his pistol at one of the running men. He missed.

The lucky Reaper yelled out, "Get down. They must be after the prisoners."

The men aboard the ship yelled back, "Hurry up and get onboard."

As two Reapers led a small group of women to the ship, they looked back to see if anyone was behind them. The men aboard the ship took the opportunity to raise their rifles and fire. One of the Reapers fell backwards while the other was merely spun around. A bullet had penetrated his shoulder armour. The man those chest armour had withstood the other two bullets, grabbed his rifle and fired back. One of the men aboard ship collapsed. Standing four metres away, one of the Islanders on shore stepped out in the open and put a bullet into the side of the gunman's head.

The man with the injured shoulder dropped his rifle and grabbed his pistol. The other armed Islander on shore fired and hit the side of his armour. As the man spun around, he squeezed the pistol's trigger and sent a bullet across the shooter's cheek. Two of the captured women got off the ground and tackled the wounded Reaper. The third woman got to her knees. Despite her head wound and bleeding calf, she picked up a piece of concrete and smashed it against the man's head. Her first blow knocked off his helmet. She continued pounding his head until she had smashed his jaw and his body had stopped twitching.

In the middle of the column, two confused Reapers fended off the armed Islanders while trying to maintain control over their captives. The unarmed male islanders screamed, threw stones and tossed ropes for the women to grab a hold of. Through distraction, they managed to drag the injured women free of their captures one at a time.

The two Reapers found themselves with no human shield to hide behind. On the trail in front of them was a sled carrying their dead leader along with all the Islanders' weapons.

At the tail end, the third remaining Reaper slowly made his way towards his comrades brandishing two pistols. Over his good shoulder were both his and his dead partners rifles. The two fresh faces tied around his neck told Patrick that he had been second in command. Patrick knew that if he made it to the others, the Reapers might form a counterstrike.

The male Islanders helped the women onboard the ship. A couple gunmen remained on shore and guarded the ship. While trying to link up with them, Patrick got an idea. Stopping several metres from the pinned pair, he hid behind a pile of concrete and waited for the third Reaper to arrive. As the man was turning the last bend, Patrick gave out blood curdling yell. The pair heard the rifles rattle and saw a shadow. They both turned and fired as the Reaper came into the open. One bullet struck their comrade's chest and the other his jaw.

Before either one of them could grab another rifle, Patrick dashed out and dragged the thrashing man out of their line of sight. He dropped the man and rammed his dagger through the his open mouth and into his brain. The man froze then turned into putty.

Patrick now had a pair of pistols and two rifles. He hid behind a pile of rubble and checked them over. Not hearing anyone pursuing him, he climbed to the top of a large slab of concrete.

Gazing toward the ship he saw the last of the Islanders board it. "Damn it. They're leaving without me."

Not long after that, he noticed the two remaining Reaper running toward the ship. As he grabbed a rifle, he cursed again, "Damn them right to hell and back." As he took carefully aim, he muttered, "Those cowards don't deserve my help."

His shot ricocheted off a piece of rusty metal causing the two Reapers to duck for cover. It also alerted the Islanders of their location. To Patrick's surprise, a volley of gunfire rang out from the ship. He slid down the slab and ran to the shore. While he waved at the Islanders aboard ship, the bald headed man fired a warning shot into the water. Putting his arms down, Patrick turned towards where the last two Reapers were hiding. "So this is what I get for rescuing a you."

From the shore of the adjacent mound Nancy and her two children waved at the emerging ship. As it dropped anchor to let them board Roger hobbled out from behind a pile of rubble. The old bald man yelled down to them, "Who is he? I have never seen him before."

Nancy yelled back, "One of the group that helped free you."

"Are there any more of us left?"

After glancing at Roger, Nancy answered, "Us three, plus the three nomads that helped rescue you."

The bald man shook his head, "We don't want any cannibals on board this ship."

Nancy glared at him. "So you never ate anything while you were held captive?"

The frustrated man blared back, "That doesn't make me a cannibal. I ate to survive."

No one noticed Simon climbing up the far rudder and pulling herself onto the deck. With blood dripping down her side, she pressed the blade of her knife against the throat of the man inside the pilothouse. As the bald man finished his rant, Simon yelled out, "Yes it does. Now help my friends aboard and pick up the man you left behind or I'll slit this man's throat and burn a hole through the bottom of the ship. I know where both the boiler's pilot light is and where the all the oil is stored. I would rather turn myself into a pile of flaming ash than starve to death. If we can't leave this place, you don't either."

Three young men went over to the old man and tried to reason with him. He tried to push them away. As one of them glanced at Simon, he bit his lip. Suddenly, he turned and punched the side of the old man's head. "They helped us escape and this is how you repay them?"

Turning to the others, the bronze haired man said, "He doesn't make the rules here. We are no longer on the island." Pointing towards Nancy, he added, "Help them aboard."

After seeing that Nancy, her kids and Roger got aboard with all their weapons, the man walked into the pilothouse. He saw the blood seeping down Simon's side. "Now will you put down your knife. One elder does not make a council. He does not speak for all of us." While poking his finger into the wheelman's forehead, he added, "But we were overruled weren't we?"

The scared man muttered, "I was only following orders."

The two Reapers had Patrick pinned down near the shore. While lying on top of the pilothouse, Roger opened fire along with half a dozen men and women lying along the deck. As the Reapers ducked for cover, Patrick left the guns behind, dove into the water and swam to the ship.

Once onboard he noticed all the young women. All the Islanders that had been chained below deck were men. After Simon hobbled over and gave him a hug, he looked down at the battered women. "It's no wonder they fought back. They are too young to be highly skilled workers. They knew the Reapers would either treat them as party toys or grind them into meat."

Simon looked at the men. "Too bad the men didn't have any backbone." Spotting the bronze haired man, she smiled, "Well maybe not all of them."

As he bent over and hugged the woman with the head and calf injuries Simon stopped smiling. "Maybe they needed some incentive."

The woman looked up at her tentative spouse. "I am sorry Mike. I lost our baby."

Simon watched the tears flowing down his cheek as he caressed her face. A tear formed in the corner of to her eye. "Those people are soft. Maybe that's why the Reapers want them. They can be easily manipulated."

Patrick stood beside Simon and told her, "Mark this spot in your mind. If we ever get back this way, I bet we'll find two skeletons huddled beside a cache of weapons. We might need them someday."

Chapter Twenty

Daniel noticed four oil covered men rolling barrels into a crude structure a half dozen metres from shore. Without seeing the men, they would have overlooked the small warehouse. Tilted slabs of concrete formed its slanted walls and overlapping pieces of bent sheet metal covered the gaps in the roof. Covered in a thick layer of soot, it mimicked the surrounding mounds.

After the men left, David and Daniel acted as lookouts as Josh approached the shelter. He slipped on an oil covered rock and fell. From their vantage points, neither David nor Daniel saw what happened. They looked around for any sign of trouble. After a few seconds, Josh got up and gave them a wave.

Josh placed a coned shaped piece of metal between his ear and a flat piece of steel that filled in a gap on the outside wall. Through it, he heard two men talking inside. "We are almost out of empty barrels."

The second man piped up, "First they tell us to increase production, and than they abandon us. They should have returned weeks ago."

"What if something happened? We both heard rumours about a war being fought. Maybe it spread?"

The second man tried to calm his friend down. "And maybe they got enough fuel to last them for a while. They will back soon."

"All I knew is that I haven't eaten in days."

After hearing this, Josh made his way up the slippery, soot covered cliff where Daniel was stationed. Daniel grabbed his arm and helped him over the edge. "What did you find out?"

"We were right. They are trading the refined goo for food." Josh smiled as he added, "They haven't eaten for days. They are weak and vulnerable. We could take them."

Daniel considered his options before answering, "No, there's another way. Mary won't like what I am to about to propose, but I think it might be our best option."

Josh instantly knew what he had in mind and shook his head. "We can't sacrifice the sacred beasts. We could kill the guards and steal whatever fuel we need."

Daniel looked through the smoke. He could barely see the ship. "Our colony will die if we don't succeed. We don't need the sacred beasts to tell us that the soil on Sarah's island is clean."

Josh bowed his head. "What if they won't trade?"

With an emotionless face, Daniel looked at the makeshift shelter and replied, "Than we do it your way."

The pair exited the shelter and met two men walking toward it. A couple metres away, Daniel stood up. A clump of concrete concealed most of his body from view. His oily soot covered clothes and face were hidden behind a cloud of black smoke. In the dark gloomy terrain, only the white in his eyes were clearly visible.

He stood and watched them sharing their thoughts about what was going on. It wasn't until he said, "Hello gentlemen.", that they realized that there was a rifle pointed at them.

There were only two airguns amongst the four men. As one of them was about to take his off his shoulder, Josh stepped out of the black haze and stuck the barrel of his rifle between the man's shoulder blades. "I wouldn't do that if I was you."

Without letting go of the airgun, the man extended his hands away from his sides. "If you wanted our meat you would have killed us. So what do you want from us?

With his rifle aimed at the other armed man, Daniel smiled and said, "A simple trade. Some of our food for some of your refined fuel."

All four men put out a sigh of relief. A thin, long bearded man commented, "Is that it?"

Daniel refused to lower his guard. "Yes, so who should I be negotiating with?"

The thin man looked at his three companions before replying, "I guess me. I don't think the others would mind as long as they get their share."

Daniel found that dealing with starving men was easier than he expected. During the negotiations he found out that the fifteen men stationed there had only a handful of weapons. They originally argued that a barrel of refined fuel was worth either a days ration for all of the men or half a days ration plus a rifle and ammo. Daniel talked them into trading six full barrels for one sacred beast, three quarters of the beasts' stored roots and two pistols. He clinched the deal by added that they might return with more food to trade.

Using rope and tackle, they hauled an empty barrel followed by a dozen half full barrels to the ship. Daniel hauled the empty barrel onboard and placed it where it was staying. After running a hose from the deck to the forward storage compartment, the oil workers provide a hand pump to transfer the fuel from the barrels in the water. After Josh got tired of pumping, David took a turn. "No wonder Sarah and the other islanders didn't wake up, once the emptied barrels are in place, it is relatively quiet."

It took a few hours to transfer the fuel. As the last barrel was emptied, Daniel passed the transfer pump down to the long bearded man. On his return trip, the sacred beast squealed at the top of its lungs. With the empty barrels in tow, two men rowed while he examined one of the bags of forage. After chewing on a piece, he said, "These roots will boil up nicely. The men back in camp won't believe that such a plump, meaty creature like this even exists. Together they will make a great stew. We are going to feast tonight."

Daniel turned around and saw Josh hugging Mary near the ship's centre bow. Her hands were covering her ears as the squealing beast drove her to tears. Daniel went over to her, "You know that we did what was best. We can't wage war on every clan we meet. You never know when we might need allies."

******

Jacob noticed drops of blood on the trail they were taking. As he led his clansmen up a tall outcrop attached to a long ridge, the blood became more evident. He looked at Jake. "This is the highest point around. It makes sense that people would fight over it."

Jacob ran and climbed on top of the boulders at the furthest end of its ascending crest. He pulled out his binoculars. Instead of seeing a massive horde chasing them, he only noticed a few scattered groups of hunters. Slipping down from his lookout, he announced to the remnants of his clan, "It looks like half the camp had packed up and moved back to town. I saw a few hunting parties, but no one coming our way."

Jake piped up, "Good, that means that we can finally rest and take inventory of our supplies."

Gloria poked her head out of the small blood stained cave. "That won't take long."

A small girl poked at something that had slid under the edge of a rock. Gloria bent down and used her knife to remove it. It was Karen's knife. She looked at the girl's mother. "There's no blood on it. They must have taken her by surprise."

Their complete inventory was finished within two minutes. They had four rifles, three pistols, a dozen knives and barely enough food and water for a week. Jake shook his head. "We don't even have a sacred beast to tell us what is safe to eat."

Jacob spoke up. "They were in the backpacks. The Townies probably have them."

Gloria suddenly stood up and went over to the edge of the cliff. Jake saw her and asked, "What are you doing?"

"I thought I heard one of the beasts. It was faint. Probably a ways away."

"Their squeals can be heard a long ways away. Maybe it was from their camp?"

As she climbed up to where Jacob was perched, she said, "No, closer than that."

Jacob took a closer look at what the hunters were doing. After a few gunshots were fired, he saw a pattern to their movement. "They let one of the beasts go. By taunting it they are making it seek help. The creature is leading them right to us."

Gloria shook her head. "And why won't it. We are the ones that fed and looked after it. We need to kill it before they find us."

Jake heard the entire conversation. While slowly rocking his head back and forth, he looked up at them and said, "They are hunters. With or without the beast, they will eventually find us. Right now we have the high ground. We need to shore up our perimeter and prepare our defences."

As the beast got tired the groups of hunters came together and formed a wide line. At times they had to stop to let the beast catch its breath. They didn't want it to have a heart attack before it lead them to their prey.

Counting the children, it was ten against seventeen hunters. Their only advantage was the steep cliff that wrapped around the outcrop. Behind them the ridge sloped gently into an inverted 'T' shape that blended into the sides of the adjoining outcrops. There weren't many places for an attacker to hide. Jake bobbed his head. "We need to turn this place into a fortress."

As Gloria helped roll a boulder to the makeshift wall protecting their rear, she told Jake, "You know that they could starve us to death."

"That would mean less meat on our bones." Jake stopped and pointed towards the largely dismantled camp. "The prisoner on the Flesh Star had convinced them to change course. We are no longer their main prey. That might work to our advantage."

Gloria stopped and gazed above the rocky outcrop that blocked the town from view. Her jaw dropped as she saw countless plumes of black smoke rise above it. "They are definitely expecting company. Judging from the amount of fuel they are wasting, they definitely want to lure them into town."

The squealing beast made Gloria turn away and glance over the side of the cliff. In the distance she saw it zig-zagging up the moderate slope that joined their outcrop to the ridge. Behind it were a couple of hunters with knives attached to the ends of their rifles. As the tired beast tried to get away, they poked it just enough to spur it on. The rest of the hunters followed behind them in single file.

After steadying their rifles in the cracks between large rocks they had piled in front of the cave, the four riflemen took careful aim at the slow moving column of hunters. There was barely half a second between the first and last shot. Three of the four riflemen hit their targets. Jacob's had made a fatal head shot. The other two hit their upper armour and only dazed their targets. As the hunters fired back, their upward angled bullets fell short. After quickly reloading and trying to make every bullet count, the four riflemen forced the hunters down the side of the ridge to regroup.

Feeling relieved, one of the riflemen turned to Jake and said, "It is nice shooting at someone that can't hit you."

With only one hunter killed and another shot in the hip, Jacob shook his head. "I was hoping for at least five kills. We used up thirteen bullets. At this rate, we might run out of ammunition."

The man looked at his rifle. "It's hard to judge where the bullet will land when you are shooting that distance at such a low angle."

Jacob turned to them. "You have to readjust your sights. The bullet arcs differently at these heights. Even the wind blowing up the side of the cliff has to be factored in."

While Jacob showed the other two riflemen how to adjust their sights, Jake took out his binoculars and tried to figure out the hunters' next move. As the beast's squeals came to an abrupt end, he knew that no attack was imminent. Within a half an hour, the intoxicating aroma of roasting meat rose up the side of the ridge. As their empty stomachs grumbled and drool dripped from the corners of their mouths, they stared with envy at the hunter's fire. "What's their hurry? They know that we can't escape without them knowing about it."

******

After watching the Townies dismantle most of their camp, John crawled over the seawall. Looking up and down the canal, he saw two pairs of guards stationed on the rocks above the flooded beach. It was high tide and the guards appeared nervous. It was the best time for someone to slip into the water and escape.

Reporting back to Karen and Kelsey, John said, "I couldn't see any boats in the canal. It's the same as before. A pair of guards are posted in each lookout."

Kelsey spoke up, "You both heard the shooting." Pointing to the distant ridge, she added, "They are out there. Is checking your old home worth the time and risk we would be taking?"

Karen looked at her and calmly said, "We don't know how many escaped. If there are any survivors inside, they will need my map."

Kelsey snuck behind one pair of guards while John made his way towards the other. As she waited for Karen's signal, she slipped the knives strapped to her thigh partially out, to make them easier to withdraw. A wave crashed against the seawall. All four guards looked over the edge to watch the retreating water. Seeing that John was in position, Karen waved her arm.

John's reaction was swift. Kelsey's was more stealthful. With the heads of both guards tilted forward, John ran and stabbed his dagger under the nearest guard's helmet. The force of the rush pushed the guard sideways into his colleague. The hilt of his dagger mashed the man's ear as the tip of the blade hit the far side of the man's skull.

The second guard stumbled and tripped over a boulder. As he

went down his head glanced off a rock.

John shoved the first guard aside. With his dagger embedded in his brain, he became a limp mass of bones and jelly. Before the second man could comprehend what had happened, John dropped his knife and jumped on top of him. He grabbed the man's head and pulled it back as far as it would go. With his knee pressing the winded man's back into almost a 'V' shape, he snapped the man's neck three quarters around. A loud crack rang from the man's back.

The crack diverted the other pair's focus, derailing Kelsey's attack. One of the men turned and caught a glimpse of her before her knife slashed his throat. The second man stepped back and wildly fired his rifle. He immediately dropped it and reached for his knife. Kelsey leaped on top of him and rammed the blade of her knife under his jaw. She twisted her wrist and worked it upwards into his brain. Behind her, the other man held his throat in one hand and got to one knee. As he pulled out his pistol, Kelsey tossed a handful of gravel into his face. Unable to see her, he waved the pistol from side to side. She rolled to the side, got to her feet and kicked the pistol out of his hand. She smiled as she slowly walked back and forth in front of the defenceless man. With a violent calculated kick to the forehead, the man's neck snapped backwards and his entire body began to twitch.

Hearing the gunshot Karen knew that they didn't have much time. Despite her badly battered body, she dove into the water. As she waded towards the tunnel, she saw a mirror dangling on a pole. She held her breath and crawled into the submerged tunnel. Two pairs of hands grabbed her arms and shoulders and dragged her onto the dry shelf inside. As she flipped over and looked up, a candle was lit. Joe stood up and placed his hands behind his head. With his eyes almost popping out of his head, he cried out, "I thought you were harvested."

It took a while for her eyes to get use to the dim light. As Joe dropped down and wrapped his arms around her neck she screamed in pain. His sudden release brought tears to her eyes. With his face only a blur, she declared, "I miss you but my body is bruised from head to foot." Reaching into her pocket she pulled out the map she had made. "I don't know how much time we have, but here's the map you wanted. John had managed to keep it safe."

Despite being soaked, the faint lines on the map were still legible. After only a quick glance, Joe asked, "How do you know this is the path back to the mine?"

Karen rolled over on her side and used her arm to prop up her head. "Notice the 'X'?"

"Yes."

"That is where I spotted the tracks. They appeared to be a few months old. They were unlike anything I have ever seen before. The grooves were dug into the ground by something heavy with wide steel tires with deep, arced treads fastened to them.

"What about footprints?"

"That's the problem. Up to that point they was lots of evidence of foot and a cart traffic along a narrow trail. They end where the strange tracks begin."

"Any idea where the foot-trail leads to?"

"Town." Karen shifted her body and got on her knees. "We followed the strange tracks for a little ways and discovered that it intersected another path with fresh tracks on it. Nothing seems to be pulling them. There are no footprints at all."

Joe smiled. "Do you know what this means?"

Karen smiled back. "Some of the miners have survived. They are the only people I've heard of that could forge a self-propelled vehicle. The Townies can't."

"Not only that, but they have taken control of part of the surface."

Chapter Twenty-One

Eric heard the shot. He noticed that his men had stopped packing up the carts. "Don't worry about it. It was probably just another shadow under the water. If it was someone trying to escape we would have heard a lot more shots fired." After thinking about it, he pointed to a small group of men. "But just in case maybe a few of you should go and check it out."

One of the men Eric elected to go asked, "What if it's the Reapers and they are trying to save their ammunition. That could have been just a warning shot."

"Go but don't be seen. If you spot anything rush right back and let us know."

******

Standing on top of a tripod over a dozen metres above the waterline, Victoria gazed through a massive set of binoculars that had been salvaged from a shipwreck. The lookout she was on was only one of a series stationed around the perimeter of the floating island. She saw the black smoke rising from the crumbling buildings. After telling the man with her to lookout for anything unusual, she slid down one of the poles.

She walked over to Jerry. "I have some questions and you better answer them."

Tied in the open with no shade from the sun nor any protection from the cold wind, Jerry sat there with his arms around his head. "What questions? I have told you everything I know."

Kicking his injured side, Victoria yelled out, "Look at me when I'm talking to you!"

Dropping his arms to his side, Jerry looked up at her. "What possible questions could you have that I haven't already answered."

Victoria paced around him. Stopping in front of him, she pointed towards town. "That town of yours appears to be deserted and several of the buildings have been set on fire. What is going on?"

Jerry's head bounced from side to side trying to keep up to Victoria pacing. "They must have found out that you are heading their way. They are laying a trap."

Victoria lashed out "We'll see", as she walked away.

Two small boats sailed towards the docks. Out of rifle range from shore, the smaller boat dropped anchor. The other pulled up to the middle dock. Six armed men jumped onto the pier while the seventh man secured and guarded the boat. After doing a swift visual check of the piers and adjacent buildings, a well decorated man put both of his arms straight into the air. That signalled that the dock was clear.

Onboard the small boat, the two men pointed the bow of the anchored boat into the wind. They raised and lowered the main sail three times, signalling that the men got safely on shore.

Travelling in pairs, the men tried to systematically cover as much of the town as possible within the time they were allotted. Avoiding the burning building, they searched everywhere that they thought someone would hide. As the sand in the hour glass stopped flowing, the man guarding the boat blew a horn. It was time for them to return to the dock. Standing at the outer edge of town one pair shrugged off the call and gazed upon a wide path of both foot and cart tracks. They were leading inland away from the large cluster of collapsed and crumbling buildings.

After seeing the men on shore raise their rifles above their heads, the men on the small boat pulled up anchor. The man controlling the tiller told his partner, "They are holding their rifles with only one hand. The place must be deserted."

The small boat sailed closer to shore. After the men walked to the end of the pier, the man with the most faces on his vest waved and yelled out, "The town is clear. Tell Victoria that there is a large path leading inland. They could be on the run."

It only took a half hour to get an additional seventy men to shore. From her lookout, Victoria nervously watched the boats being tied to the piers two abreast. As fifty-five Reapers were led through the town towards the path, fifteen continued to search through the town and the remaining seven guarded the boats.

Inside the charred ruins of the freshly burned down buildings, Townies peered out from the underground tunnels and cellars. The cracking fire and crumbling debris concealed any noise they made. When an all clear was given, armed men began to pour out. Throughout the town dozens more men climbed out of secret hiding places and prepared for the awaiting battle.

As the odd gunshot was heard, the main force of Reapers shrugged it off as diehard hold outs. Unknown to them, the Reapers searching the town were being lured away from one another by fleeting shadows and strange noises. A flash from a mirror, a tossed stone, a shoe scuffing the floor, the gentle tapping of a knife against a rifle barrel, were all subtle ways to distract the intruders.

Once out of sight of their partners, they were choked, muffled, dragged away and sliced open. As their partners searched for them, they met the same fate. The Townies knew every piece of debris in their town. Anything shifted out of place was marked as a possible hiding spot or lookout for a Reaper.

A pair of Reapers found a feeble, half-starved Townie hiding under a pile of rusted sheet metal. They dragged him back to the wharf and tied him to the lamppost. After cutting off his clothes, a well decorated woman cut a deep gash into his upper forearm. "How many are still in town?"

Wanting a swift death, the man tried to smile. "More than you can handle."

His wish wasn't answered, instead two other Reapers began to tie tourniquets around his upper arms. The first Reaper smiled at the man. "For each time you fail to answer me, you will lose a limb. Look at my men. They are starving."

The man looked at the beefy men and defiantly told them, "I am nothing but grizzle. I have nothing to offer you."

One of the men withdrew a machete from his belt and with a single swing hacked off one of the man's arms. "Now tell us how many Townies are there left in town."

The man screamed out, "Enough to harvest you!" Looking at the man wielding the machete, he added, "I hope they use you for their harvest ceremony."

In a rage he gripped his machete with both hands and chopped off the man's head. Standing behind him, the woman yelled out, "What did you do that for."

The angry man screamed back, "Because he wasn't going to tell us anything useful."

With all the Reapers on the dock circled around the lamppost, scores of townies swarmed in. Taking shooting positions within the nearby buildings, they waited for Killy to fire first. A moment after his bullet blasted a hole through the woman's forehead, a barrage of bullets tore apart the other Reapers' armour. As they sprawled around the ground searching for their weapons, two dozen Townies charged with makeshift bayonets fastened to their rifles. They shot and stabbed the Reapers' hands and arms, rendering them helpless. Within minutes poles were being pounded into the ground. The limbs of the wounded Reapers were lashed to them.

Only two managed to escape. After leaping into the water and crawling onto a boat, they cut the dock line, ducked down and drifted away unnoticed.

******

The gunfire had alerted the main body of Reapers. As they raced towards town, the buildings along its edge became covered in smoke as scores of riflemen released their first volley. Caught in the open, as they returned fire, all the Reapers could do was get on the ground and become as small a target as possible. As they began to spread out, they triggered several large landmines. The trip lines pulled back and released repurposed musket hammers to ignite the gunpowder inside. The blasts sent pieces of scrap metal and kiln-dried clay a half dozen metres in every direction.

The Reapers had no other option but to stay on the path leading to the cliffs. As they crawled toward the boulders at the bottom of the cliff, dozens of gunmen popped up and forced them back into the open. In the centre of the valley, they found themselves out of reach of the Townies' guns. While some Reapers dug a hole to crawl into, others fired at anything that moved. Grant ordered the cannons to be aimed towards the centre of the valley in order to push the Reapers back to within rifle range. Staying clear of the landmines the half starved Townies crawled towards the edges of the Reapers entrenchment. They hurled matted balls of flaming oil soaked leather into their ranks. Hiding behind the black smoke they used lassos, knives, and pistols to whittle away their numbers.

******

From her lookout, Victoria watched as the first man was stripped and skinned alive. Scores of men and women lined the edge of the island. Many were speechless as they watched a Townie parade up and down the wharf wearing the man's skin like a robe. Victoria yelled down, "Get us within cannon range!"

With four helpers, it took Killy only fifteen minutes to skin the two men. He had saved a young teenage boy and the woman for last. Taking great care, he even offered them his numbing concoction to drink. This made their prolonged harvest more enjoyable for his men. At the same time it infuriated Victoria and the Reapers that were lined up along the edge of the island.

The small fleet of boats pulled the island closer to shore. By the time Victoria finished sliding down the pole she was surrounded by her well decorated officers. One of them angrily asked, "What do you want us to do about this atrocity?"

"Prepare the boats and arm our reserves."

Victoria went up to Jerry and punched the side of his head. "Those skeletons on shore are obviously quite clever. How about we slice you up for them to watch?"

Jerry began to chuckle. "They would sit down and enjoy the show."

Victoria punched him again. "Why should I keep you alive?"

Shaking off her last blow, he said, "Because I can get your men safely on shore."

After leaving Jerry, Victoria marched over to her officers. "There is a beach a few kilometres outside of town. You should be able to safely land there." While beating her chest with her fists, she screamed out, "I want every one of those animals butchered!"

******

By the time dusk arrived, there were less than two dozen Reapers left alive in the blood soaked valley. Fires were lit and large pieces of reflective metal were placed behind them. The Reapers' eyes were easy targets for the riflemen. Their only reprisal was to shoot into the dark and hope for a lucky shot. When the shooting stopped, the Townies pulled out their knives and stormed the encampment. After placing the metal plates over the fires, they used them to fry the freshly butchered pieces of meat.

As everyone got their fill, no one paid attention to three Reapers that were completely covered in the dirt and debris spewed from a landmine. When a Townie walked by dragging one of their comrades, they fought the temptation to jump up and slit his throat. Surrounded, they knew they had to be patient.

******

To the men going ashore the welcoming beach appeared to have a gentle sloping mound of debris followed by a small rock formation. Unfortunately it was an optical illusion. A small mound hid a large inland salt lake with vertical cliffs on the far side of it. Anyone gazing at it from the sea would only see the gentle mound topped by what looked like a small secondary set of cliffs.

It took until dusk to carry a boat over the mound, paddle it across the lake and survey the terrain. During the same time a messenger sailed back to the floating island and told Victoria their progress. As the gunfire stopped, she gazed towards the fires along the wharf. Within a half an hour, more captives were tied to the stakes. "They are too late."

******

The hunters had used the night and echoing blasts to their advantage. On the gentle sloping corners of the outcrop, their bodies were mere shadows with nothing concrete to aim at. It wasn't until they reached the top that they became vulnerable. Knowing this, they waited until the moon disappeared behind the clouds before climbing the last few metres. Pumped full of adrenaline, they tucked their heads down and raced towards the summit.

The terrain had changed from the last time they had been there. The knee high boulders that had littered the slope had been all moved to the sides. The earth dwellers had created a corridor in the middle that they would have to travel through.

Carefully placed flat stones were littered with round, hand picked pebbles. The lead hunter stepped on one, lost his footing and slipped backwards. His fall was cushioned by the hunter behind him. As they grabbed each other for support, they both stepped on the marble like stones and twisted sideways onto the loose rocks along the edges. The rocks gave way. As one slipped over the side, he held onto the other man and took him with him. Behind them, another hunter slipped and fell to his knees.

The screams coming from the men tumbling down the side of the cliff alerted the sleepy guards. They had worked all day on their defences and had little time to rest. As Jake aimed his rifle at the approaching shadows, he told the other guard, "Wake the others."

There was no need. By the time he got to the small cave they were all armed and prepared for a fight.

Jake rested his rifle in the gap between two boulders and fired about chest high into fleeting shadows of the approaching horde. As he reloaded he reminded the bewildered man, "In the dark, by the time you have a clean kill shot, you wouldn't have time to reload before they are on you."

As the hunters returned fire, the flames coming out of their rifle barrels gave away their position. The three riflemen pointed their rifles at them and fired back. The women lobbed fist sized stones over the makeshift wall, while the two children used slingshots to litter handfuls of round peddles in front of the advancing hunters.

When the shadows passed a tall boulder, Jacob grabbed a rope and gave it a tug. It was tied to the tall boulder on the other side. As he pulled and released it, it caught the ankle of the lead hunter. As he scrambled to get up, he grabbed the leg of another hunter. The riflemen took aim at the flailing targets. Two of the four shots were lethal. One head shot and the other ripped through a hunter's neck.

As the moon came out from behind the cloud, the hunters could see what was lying ahead of them. With over a dozen metres of foot traps and trip hazards to go, the hunters knew they couldn't charge forward. As one hunter retreated, he complained, "Meat isn't any good if you are not alive to enjoy it."

Knowing that they had to conserve their ammunition, Jake and the others watched the dark shadows carry off the dead and injured. The only one they left behind was the dead man that had his ankle entangled in the rope. "At least they no longer outnumber us."

Jake patted the back of the man crouched beside him. The man didn't respond. Rolling him onto his side, he discovered that the left side of his face was covered in blood. A bullet had broken off a chunk of rock and was wedged into the man's skull.

His wife raced over to him and felt his neck for a pulse. "He's still alive."

Jacob walked over and looked at his wound. "Beth is the only person I know of that could possibly save him, and she isn't here. As soon as the shard is taken out, his wound will have to be completely cleaned out and the blood vessels cauterised before his skin can be stitched together." Gazing into the man's wife's tear fulled eyes, he said, "He doesn't look good. He may not survive the procedure."

The weeping woman begged Jacob, "You are the only one here that has even seen it done. You have to at least try to save him."

As the hunters worked their way down the side of the ridge, they noticed the light coming from the small cave on the outcrop's summit. One of them stopped and told the man behind him, "We left them meat. That means that they could last for weeks up there."

The hunter shook his head. "They won't eat him. They think our meat is contaminated or something." After readjusting the position of the dead man on his shoulder, he added, "It will only be a matter of days before they are too weak to fight back."

Gloria helped one of the men pull the dead hunter and his rifle behind the wall. After stripping him, they sorted through his belongings. A rifle, pistol, two knives, some ammunition, leather clothes, helmet and body armour was all he had. Jake walked over and looked at the pile. As he pulled out his knife, he said, "He has more to offer us than that."

In the cave, Jacob sterilized a small sharp knife over a small flame. Outside the entrance, the two children used the backs of knives to rub the oil and fat from the underside of a hunk of the dead hunter's skin. After trading some fresh skin for the oil the children had collected, Jake dipped a rag into it and lit the edge that laid over the side of the concaved stone.

The extra light gave Jacob the encouragement he needed to start the delicate operation. As he removed the stone shard, the man screamed at the top of his lungs.

With Gloria and the man's wife holding his head steady Jacob pulled out the small pieces of bone, stone and hairs. Using the lamp to keep the tip of his dagger hot, he cauterized all the bleeding blood vessels he could find. Afterwards he gently placed his hand over the gapping hole in the man's skull. Turning to Jake, he said, "I'll need something to cover the hole. You saw how big it is."

"I know exactly what you can use." Jake looked at Gloria. "Where is the shiny spoon you use to stir with."

Gloria rummaged through her pack and handed it to him. "I hope it works."

Jake placed the spoon over a rock and tapped it with the hilt of his knife, trying to curl its edges and flatten it a little. Afterwards, he rested its blade across the spoon's handle and hit the backside of his knife with a rock. He looked at the score it made. Feeling satisfied, he began bending the spoon back and forth until the handle broke off.

After using a rock to grind off the rest of the handle, he presented it to Jacob. Jacob looked at it. "That will work, but it needs to have some barbs in order for it to cling to the bone."

Using his knife and the pliers he used to repair the guns with, Jake nicked, bent and formed five barbs along it edges. Once Jacob was satisfied with the results, he cleaned and sterilized the metal plate.

Gloria placed a hunk of leather into the man's mouth. "Better bite down cause this is going to hurt."

Jacob scraped tiny gouges into the man's skull where the barbs were to be inserted. The man pound his fist against a rock. He clinched his eyes together and tried to think about his throbbing hand instead of the painful surgery Jake was performing on his head. Every time he twitched, Gloria tightened the leather straps holding his head still.

After setting the crude plate in place, Jake tapped each barb in as flush as possible. When he was satisfied it was secure, he pulled the skin over it and sewed it together. By the time he tied his last stitch, his hands began to shake. He had to sit down. His head began to spin. Even when he faced his own possible death, nothing matched the terror of having a friends life in your trembling hands.

He shut his eyes and tried to breathe normally. Something touched his shoulder. He jumped up as the man's wife stepped back and said, "I just wanted to say thank-you."

"Don't thank me yet. He still may not make it through the night." Seeing the weeping woman turn away, he said, "I can forge metal into anything we want. I'm a blacksmith not a healer. I don't know anything about saving lives."

The woman shook her head. "You are more then that. You know what has to be done, and you do it, regardless what it may cost you." Staring at him, she added, "That is why everyone looks up to you."

Twenty-Two

As dawn broke, the Townies that fell asleep around the fires packed up and headed back to town. The three remaining Reapers waited until they were out of sight before lifting their heads out of the dirt. They saw one another and didn't say a word. With some of the Townies wearing Reaper vests, they felt an uncomfortable ease. Crawling out of their holes, they took off their vests and tucked them under their arms. With their rifles slung over their shoulders they trailed behind the slow moving parade. To anyone seeing them, they were just three lazy stragglers.

At the outskirts of town they veered away from the otheres and hid between two abandoned structures. "What do we do now?"

"While coming ashore I noticed a beach not far from here. Even if Victoria wanted to leave, it takes time to move the island. We could signal for help."

With no other options, the three men made their way to the cliffs next to town. After they climbed to the top, they noticed the first group of Reapers that scaled the cliffs. Over the rocky terrain it took a while to reach them. As the Reapers secured ropes for others to climb, one of them turned to the trio and asked, "Where are the rest of you."

"We are all that's left. The rest were either butchered or taken to be slaughtered later."

Getting down on their knees, they drew lines on the ground and went over the layout of the town and surrounding area. "They are cunning. They faked a withdrawal and trapped us in the open. We didn't know that we were being led into a meat grinder."

"But most of them are nothing but skin and bones."

"That makes them more dangerous. A starving man has nothing to lose." Glancing towards the pier, he added , "Human harvests are not as plentiful as they once were."

As others began their ascent, the Reaper shook his head. "So how did you escape?"

"A blast from a landmine rendered me unconscious. When I woke, everyone was dead. I never saw any reason to stand up and yell, 'Here I am, eat me'."

From the top of a nearby cliff, a lookout saw the growing mass of Reapers. He primed and fired a small cannon loaded with oil laced debris. It lit up the sky and showed everyone where to look. The blast even caught Grant's attention.

As the Reapers watched the flaming debris fall to the ground around them, the vocal survivor said, "I told you that those cannibals were not to be taken lightly."

It took all day for the invading force to scale the almost vertical cliff. Looking over the ledge, one of the leaders saw groups of Townies moving cannons into firing positions. "It is getting dark. We should attack while they can't see us."

A well adorned man walked over to him. "It doesn't matter if it is night or day. Those cannons will light up the sky." Looking back at his men, he added, "They need a rest. Any attack we make will have to be thoroughly planned out."

That night, Killy ordered his men to take the boats the Reapers landed in and anchor them in a cove a half kilometre from town. With over seventy bodies to feast on, Grant was in no hurry to waste gunpowder. Instead, he turned to Killy and said, "We should let Eric keep those morons on the cliff at bay while we finish planning how to cut their throats."

Throughout the still night, the fires along the bottom of the cliff gave off a choking cloud of black soot. The men on top of the cliff were forced to bury their heads under their blankets in order to breathe. The soot also covered the side of the cliff with a slippery film.

As dawn broke, gunfire erupted on the left side of town, Victoria ordered her artillerymen to fire their cannons. The smoke from the cannons drifted towards the dock. The cloud prevented the artillerymen on both sides from seeing their targets. Using their cannons last settings, both sides continued the onslaught.

Eight two-manned cannons were used to defend the town. Four were aimed at the cliffs and the other four at the island. The smoke they created drifted with the morning breeze across the wharf and obscured the shore on the right side of town.

Hidden from view, Nick guided the Flesh Star to the rear of the floating island. As its port side rubbed against it, Grant was the first of the thirty men lying on the deck to get up and jump off. Before the ship departed, a few members of Nick's crew decided to joined them.

Armed mainly with long knives, they kept their pistols on their belts while they ran from dwelling to dwelling. Most of the people they met were nursing women, young children and their caregivers. They were hacked to death without mercy. Few were spared. They considered the caged and shackled slaves not worth the time nor effort to kill. As a growing number of screaming women tried to outrun them, they fanned out across the floating island. They had nearly covered a quarter of it before they hit any resistance.

At the front of the island, the roar of the cannons masked the exchange of gunfire. Under Victoria's command, the frantic men were oblivious of the carnage behind them. Each cannon ball that hit the island spewed watertight plastic containers and foam everywhere. Men and women fought to keep the lookouts upright and cannon platforms from sinking. Others patched holes and lashed together the tears and gaps, preventing the island from coming apart.

As word travelled, more and more men left their assigned tasks, grabbed their rifles and rushed back to halt the invading cannibals' brutal rampage. When Victoria heard the news, she ordered the cannon fire to halt. As the smoke began to clear, she saw the Flesh Star's masts. "They are treating us like fools. Arm yourselves. We have got to defend the island." Turning to a nearby battery of cannons she yelled out, "Not you! I want you to destroy that ship!"

After dropping off a second wave of men, the Flesh Star was returning to the cove. Behind it was a string of boats filled with dead bodies. Any prisoners they took were shackled to the pedals below deck. Those that refused to pedal were taken out and butchered. A cannonball slashed water into trailing boats.

Despite having almost sixty men on the island, Grant figured it might be too risky. They had taken over half of it. Before beginning their retreat, they fired a couple captured cannons at the approaching Reapers then cut the platform behind it. As the cannon slid into the opening, one of its wheels got caught on some netting and dragged a Townie into the gap. Unable to free his ankle from the net, he was left behind.

Outside a large hut, a Townie unscrewed the top of a barrel of lamp oil and tipped it over. Hiding behind the structure, he lit a lantern and tossed it at the oil spill. The flame was just starting to spread as a Reaper stepped in the oil. Flames ran up his leg as he slipped and tried to roll away from the spill. Covered in oil, he turned into a screaming, flaming banshee. The melting petroleum based debris that kept the island afloat created a wall of black smoke.

Between the smoke and newly formed holes in the platform, the Reapers' advance was stymied. Seeing them stop to fight the spreading fire, Grant looked at the men around him. "We are using the wrong weapons. Light anything that burns. Cut apart anything that doesn't. Lets rip this island apart."

The fumes from the choking smoke forced the Reapers to retreat. Held by anchors, bit by bit the rear quarter of the island began to separate from it. As newly captured slaves hauled dead bodies and looted supplies to the boats, Grant's men ran around burning and slashing everything they could.

As the anchors on the right side of the island held, it twisted the front of the island around. A burning section of the left side of the island broke off and collided into the dock. As the smoke filtered through the town, Eric and his remaining men retreated into their pre-dug hideouts.

With the fires out of control and their main storage sheds sinking into the water, the Reapers had no choice but to abandon their floating platform. Semi-surprised by the lack of resistance, they grabbed what they could and hauled it ashore. Unopposed, the Reapers on the cliff repelled down and joined them. Despite their massive losses they were still the dominant force.

Victoria surveyed the damage. Until her cannon boats returned, all she had left were seven small boats. "We can't even pull what is left of the island away from shore with those." Seeing Jerry still tied to a post, she took out her knife and ran it through the left side of his chest. With the tip of the blade protruding out of his back, she had to twist it in order to work it out of his rib cage. She barely nicked his heart. "Why are you people so hard to kill?"

With blood pouring out of his mouth, he spit in her face. "We don't like being harvested. Every drop of energy we use means less can be extracted, and turned against our clan."

"So why were you so eager to help us?"

"I got you here didn't I? Your meat will lift my clan out of starvation." With a bloody grin on his face, he added, "They will bottle your people up and let starvation takes the fight out of them. In the end, we always win."

Victoria gazed at the town and the surrounding cliffs. "So this town is nothing more than a prison guarded by cliffs."

Jerry pressed his chin over the gash in his chest and tried to stop the blood and air from escaping. "Normally, a few prisoners are selected to oversee the meat lotteries." After coughing up more blood, Jerry mumbled, "The weak and stubborn are sliced into stew meat. The cooperative ones are allowed to live and maybe even join us. That is how we retain their numbers."

Bewildered, Victoria looked at him. "So the lottery is rigged. Is that how you joined their ranks."

As the weight of his head became heavier and heavier, he uttered, "I was given the choice between slicing my mother's throat or watch her being skinned alive." With his last breath, Jerry whispered, "I still remember how her liver tasted."

******

At the first sight of the ships' masts, the Reapers controlling the island forcibly confined the Islanders to either their workshops or living quarters. Once shackled, only a few guards were required to oversee them.

After the ships were secured to the dock, the captives were herded ashore. On the wharf they were lined up for the governing chief to decide their fate. He remembered most of their faces from before. As a quarter of them were pulled aside, the others screamed out their virtues, "She can cook." "He can farm." "She can sew." "She can clean." "He can ..." Their pleas were brushed aside as the culled members were escorted to a large fortified building at the edge of the complex.

The chief stepped on top of a stainless steel barrel and looked over the remaining captives. "You thought you could escape us, but here you are. Since your departure, we have made steps to insure no future escape attempts will be possible. By imprisoning the ones dearest to you, I will retain your loyalty. If anyone gets out of line, their loved ones will be publicly flogged. In severe cases, they will be butchered, sliced into jerky and be replaced by another."

******

As the distant cannon fire began to dwindle, Kelsey perched on top of the mound. Inside the labyrinth of tunnels, Joe and John searched through every room, for anything they might need to take with them. With a few scraps of food and a handful of weapons, they ventured out.

The surf pushed Karen into the seawall as she waded along the shore. Keeping his rifle and pack above his head, John was the first to climb out. Half swimming the young girl was the second. The couple helped Karen out of the water before returning to the tunnel for more supplies. Behind them, Joe carried the last bag of supplies and ammo out of the tunnel. With an airgun and primed musket over his head, he stood in the surf and listened for any sign of danger.

Hearing only the surf and distant canon bursts, Joe looked up at the sky and then back at the tunnel. "I guess this is it. There is no turning back."

******

While acting as lookout, Gloria heard the hunters climb the side of the outcrop. The sound from falling grains of sand and loose gravel got closer. With only a knife to protect her, she waited until she could smell their rank body odour. Then she told herself, "*Now.*"

One by one, she rolled boulders over the edge. They struck the side of the outcrop and bounced into the air. The small landslide they caused did little to impede the pairs advance. A rock glanced off one of the hunters and made him tumble a few metres before he regained his hold and resumed climbing. The commotion alerted the others.

Jake rushed to the edge. There was nothing else they could do. As he rolled a boulder towards the edge, he spotted the main force of hunters ascend the sloped corner. This time they were carrying large shields over their backs. "It's a distraction." Pointing to the far end of the ledge, he added, "Look."

They watched the hunters make their way onto the long, narrow corridor that lead up to the peak. Protected behind oversized leather shields, they knew better than to waste their remaining bullets on them. Even though a bullet could easily penetrate the shields, it wouldn't penetrate their body armour. All they could do was wait for something to aim at.

As a wall of shields made its way along the ridge, the anxious riflemen waited. They knew that the wall had to be shifted once it reached the maze of boulders that they had laid out. To their amazement, instead of twisting them around the boulders, the hunters stopped and slowly slid their shields over them before continuing on.

It wasn't until Jacob noticed their feet that they realized their weakest link. His well placed shot struck one of the hunter's ankles. The man twisted his shield as he collapsed. Seeing the side of the hunter's face, Jake fired. Despite missing its target the bullet ricocheted and hit another man in the arm. This caused the line of hunters to drop their shields and charge at them.

With the hunters only a half dozen metres away, there was only time for one volley to be fired. After dropping their rifles, they fired their pistols and drew their knives. By the time the men could brace themselves, a barrage of rifle fire erupted behind the charging hunters. Several hunters fell and others turned around to face their unseen foe. As the four shocked men waited for the delayed attack, the women and children bombarded the hunters with rocks. The two hunters that were climbing up the side, peered over it and saw the wild band of women on the ridge. They quickly sunk from view and began their retreat.

Confused, Jake lowered his knife as the band of screeching women used theirs' to hack the heads off both the dead and wounded hunters on the ridge. As they collected the blood pouring from the men's necks, Jose stood up and approached him. Like a statue, Jake stood there with his knife at the ready.

Extending her bloody hand, Jose introduced herself, "I am Jose. You must be what is left of Karen's clan."

Confused by her forced smile, Jake switched his knife from his right hand to his left before extending his arm. Her strong, rough hand told him all he needed to know about her. "Karen was a member of our clan, but hopefully we are not all that remains of it."

After a woman passed a bowl of blood to Jose, she took a drink and offered some to Jake, "Drink, some of your bullets had hit their marks. This was a joint victory."

Jake looked at the blood and than at Jose, "How do you know if it is safe to drink?"

Jose chuckled while answering, "Unlike the rest of the Townies, the hunters eat only the best. Look at them. They hide beneath their filthy clothes and crud they smeared over their skin to conceal their health from the rest of the Townies. The crud is what fools your beasts. It is their way of denying you their bodies nourishment."

A woman handed Jose a piece of a hunter's liver. Jose studied it before saying, "The liver can tell you everything you need to know about a man. Look at its colour and texture. That's not the liver of a sick man."

******

The gunfire spurred Joe into quickening his pace. Seeing the cliff where the hunters had captured her, Karen halted. The young girl looked back and waved her on. Walking beside John, Kelsey clenched her fist and struck it against her chest. With a musket and fully charged air tank in her airgun, she ran and caught up to Joe.

After reaching the abandoned hunters' camp, Kelsey took the lead. The men followed close behind her. With only a small pack over her shoulder, the girl cradled an airgun in her arms and jogged ahead of her mother and Karen.

At the base of the cliff, Kelsey saw what looked like women peering over the side along with a man. They were to far away to identify. As she got closer, she waved at them to get their attention. By the circular way they waved back, she was sure that they were really who she thought they were. She returned the strange, open handed, circular wave, but did it in the opposite direction.

They met on top of 'T' intersection. After giving Jacob a hug, Joe looked back and saw Karen plopping down next to a boulder. "Karen knows how to find the mine. According to her, the Miners now control a large section of the surface."

Overhearing the two men, Jose walked over to them and asked, "Is that mine you are talking about in the wasteland beyond the far ridge?"

Karen pointed to her right and began rolling her hand. "It's way back over that way."

"That's dangerous territory. Even the hunters don't go there."

"It's where our clan originally came from. It's the only place we can go."

Two women put Tara's stretcher down next to the small group. "Did I hear that you plan to go into the faceless territory?"

Joe turned as said, "Faceless? What do you mean?"

"The people there are faceless. They wear masks that cover their entire heads."

Joe turned to Jacob. "Their eyes and skin can't take the sun. That means that they had only recently immerged. They could even be first generation."

Tara looked at them and asked, "Will they even take you back?"

"We don't know. Right now it doesn't matter. We have no where else to go."

Tara glanced over the remaining women. "What about us? Like you, we no longer have a home to go back to." Seeing the young girl sling an airgun over her shoulder, she added, "One thing I know is, the more women you have the better your chances."

A bit puzzled, Joe looked at her and asked, "What do you mean?"

Tara sternly told him, "Men need women. I imagine that the miners are no different. Plus, in a fight we know what is really at stake."

"And what is that?"

"Men think about today, women think about the future. That's why we are the ones that have the children."

At the bottom of the cliff, the two surviving hunters watched a group of women disassemble their camp and portable solar still. They didn't even leave so much as a blanket behind. One of them looked up the cliff and saw glimpses of the women hack apart their friends and colleagues. "Killy isn't going to be happy about this."

Chapter Twenty - Three

As the New Hope got closer to the island, Daniel followed Sarah's directions and made a broad circle around the island. He knew that they couldn't afford to be spotted by either the Reapers or the Islanders. In order to survive, people have a tendency to switch loyalties.

He sailed the ship into a hidden boot shaped bay. After travelling around a mound of coral, the ship entered a quiet saltwater bog that was invisible from the sea. The bay was part of a long heaved up ridge of crumbling coral that had once thrived deep beneath the waves. With the ship protected from the wind and surf, Josh tied a rope around his waist and climbed over the side. Holding his rifle and kit over his head, he waded through the chest high muck towards shore. The others slid a crude raft made from four empty barrels overboard.

After Josh secured the rope around a boulder, David, Sarah and Daniel got onto the raft and used the tether to pull themselves and some supplies through the bog. Josh picked up Sarah and carried her through the thick, knee high muck onto dry land.

Using her crutch, she made her way to the top of the coral and looked around. They were over a dozen kilometres from the nearest house. The only building in the area was a shed housing a large wind powered mill that the Islanders used to grind the coral to enrich the soil.

As Daniel made a return trip with Beth and Mary aboard, Sarah wrapped her arm around David's shoulder and pointed to where the shed was. Within half an hour they rounded a rocky outcrop and there it was. Made from sheets of metal fastened to a curved metal frame, the arc shaped structure had a wide opening at one end and sloped into the ground at the other.

Daniel noticed cart tracks in front of the structure mixed with footprints of various sizes. He bent down to examine them closer. "They all come from the direction we are heading." Turning to Josh, he said, "We can't let them knew were to find the ship. Go back and brush away and footprints we left behind."

David noticed a cart with a broken wheel off to the side of the shed. After helping his father repair it, they lifted Sarah on to it along with their backpacks and extra firearms. By the time Josh caught up to them, David was beat and gladly let him take a turn pulling the cart.

About every kilometre they switched. It was Daniel's turn to relieve Josh. Josh ran ahead and joined Beth on point. In the hot sun, they stripped off everything they could except their chest armour. With rifles in hand the pair carefully looked for any sign of danger. As the sound of a rolling pebble caught Beth's ear, she raised her hand and the procession halted.

Mary ran to find out what was going on as the pair were hit with a barrage of bullets. Mary fell to the ground and rolled to the side of the narrow path. Partially hidden behind a few boulders and a patch of small shrubs, she saw Josh try to crawl to safety. Bullets from the semi-automatic airguns tore blood and tissue from Josh's legs and arms. Folded over, Beth's lifeless body was being struck by random shots.

David grabbed Sarah and placed her down beside the cart. Without any smoke it was hard to spot where the bullets were coming from. The angle they were hitting Beth was their only clue. Mary aimed at where she thought they would most likely be hiding.

David joined his father and circled around the shooters. By the time it took them to get into position, Sarah had limped towards Mary and yelled at the shooters, "Stop firing, we are not Reapers." As a bullet whizzed by her head, she continued to yell, "Don't you recognize me? I'm Sarah, Fred's daughter. We had a house and garden near the metal pile next to the dock."

As a bullet hit the side of Sarah's chest armour and spun her to the ground, a woman yelled out, "How do we know you are who you say you are?"

Daniel watched the woman stand up and peer over the hedge in front of a well placed wall of boulders. The three women with her were busy replacing their air cylinders and magazines. With his rifle aimed at her head, he bellowed out, "Because she's telling you the truth."

As the women turned around, they saw a pair of rifles sticking out from behind some rocks. With their backs pressed against the wall, they all turned pale. The vocal woman was the first to lay down her rifle. "Who are you?"

"A man that is having a hard time fighting off the urge kill you. Now who are you?"

The woman was at a loss for words. Quaking from fear, she dropped to her knees and began to stutter, "Iiiiiiif yyyou are nnnnnnot Rrrrrreappppers, wwwho are you?"

Daniel screamed back, "I asked you first. If I have to ask again, one of you WILL die."

Before she could answer, the crackling of rocks and pebbles colliding together announced Patrick's arrival. With six armed men at his side, he waited at the edge of the small clearing. "The woman asked you, who are you?"

Daniel turned and pointed his rifle at Patrick. "You know who I am and I certainly know you. So this is your new hunting ground?"

Patrick took a few cleansing breaths as he looked at the two lifeless bodies lying on the path. Walking over to the vocal woman he slapped her across the face. "Within an hour, every Reaper on this island will know we are here. Who told you to open fire on them?"

As the woman babbled her apology, Patrick turned to Daniel, "I want the same thing as you want. We all need a place to live and this island is the only place I know of that can grow food."

"And I hear that it is full of Reapers."

Patrick stepped forward and said, "That's why I need you. These islanders don't know how to fight. You saw for yourself how badly they lack discipline."

The vocal woman cried out, "I'm sorry. I didn't know."

David darted forward and sliced off a piece of her ear. With his dagger pressed against her throat and his knife across Nancy's neck, he spat in her face. "That was my mother you just killed." He shook the tears away from his eyes. "Give me a reason not to kill both of you."

Nancy closed her eyes. With David's blade pressed against her throat all she could do is mumble. "Because we are both mothers."

As David stood up, he etched the skin of both women. "That's a reminder. Do anything to cross us, I'll kill you and your children."

Daniel looked at the men behind him. They barely knew how to hold a gun. "How do I know that we can trust you?"

Patrick looked at the two dead bodies and replied, "With our past, I don't think you ever truly will." Glancing at the skittish Islanders around him, he said, "Lower your guns. Enough damage has been done."

With the muzzle of Daniel's rifle still pointed at his head, Patrick walked up to him and quietly said. "These people know that I eat human flesh. I'm aware of your ritual of honouring your dead. To them, that makes us both cannibals. We may be enemies, but on this island, if we work together we might have a chance to survive and maybe even thrive."

Daniel stared into his eyes. "We don't intend to be staying here very long. We are only here to collect nutrients for our underground gardens."

"There are only three of you left. How do you expect to run a ship?" Patrick glanced at the dead bodies and then back at him. "Besides, the rest of your clan has probably been harvested by now. You have nowhere else to go."

"You don't know what are you talking about. They are a lot more resilient than you give them credit for. Your people have been after them for countless years and have always failed."

Patrick nudged Daniel's muzzle away from his face and answered, "Your colony was under siege when I left. The Flesh Star was heading back there and the Reapers were not far behind them. If my kinsmen haven't butchered them by now, the Reapers have."

Daniel turned and saw David walking towards his dead mother.

Without saying a word, he looked back at Patrick and shook his head.

Simon limped forward and stood next to Patrick. Patrick looked at her. "You know that we were not always so-called Townies. Before I was forced to join them, my family had search all over for a place like this. The Reapers saw it as a source of food and slave labour. After exploring this place I believe it is worth fighting for. It might even be man's last bastion of hope."

Daniel had a hard time comprehending everything that Patrick said. Looking at the Islanders around him, Daniel finally lowered his rifle. This huge gruff, fire haired man had somehow earned their respect. "You are not like any Townie I've encountered."

Patrick lowered his head. "No, I don't imagine I am." As he glanced at Simon, he added, "Maybe protecting my sister has made me think of others as something more than just meat." Looking back at Daniel, he said, "However, no one can live without something in their belly."

Sarah cried as she saw Mary drag Josh's dead body to the cart. She became numb at the sight of David weeping next to his dead mother. As she hobbled towards the other Islanders, Nancy stood up. "Sarah, is that really you?"

Sarah looked at her. Nancy had always been the neatest and tidiest person she had ever known. In her ratty hair and ripped dingy clothes she was barely recognizable. As Nancy ran up to her, Sarah lost her balance. Nancy caught her and gave her a hug. "I thought I would never see you again."

Daniel and David left Sarah with the other Islanders and placed Beth's body into the cart. Mary knelt beside her dead husband. "What can we do with them. We can't celebrate their death, not here. Not under their guns."

After they set Josh's body down, Daniel stood up and looked around. Glancing over the group of Islanders, he rested his eyes on Patrick and decided, "We can not let their lives go to waste. Lets build a fire. We will take them with us."

Sarah, Nancy and the other Islanders watched them butcher and place Beth and Josh's flesh next to the fire to dry. While Mary braided Beth's hair together, Daniel took the bones out of the fire and ground them into a course powder. Daniel looked at Mary. "You know that we have no choice but to help Patrick."

Mary shook her head. "You sailed with only three before. We can manage."

"What if he is right? What if we have nowhere to go?" Daniel looked at the crushed remains of Beth's skull. "It would be nice to have somewhere as backup, just in case."

"There has to be two or three dozen Reapers on the island. We are outnumbered."

Daniel cocked his head to the side. "All we have to do is kill off enough so that they can no longer control the Islanders. Maybe a third of them. With the element of surprise on our side, that is doable."

A group of women watched the top of the two bobbing heads beyond the cart. Unable to hold in her rage, the woman with the cut ear grabbed her rifle and told the others, "Lets just kill the cannibals and be done with them."

Sarah reach over and grabbed the muzzle of the woman's rifle. "Don't be stupid."

'Click', a few metres to the side of them, David stood up and finished releasing the hammer of his musket. "She just saved your life." With two pistols in his belt and a long knife hanging from his side, he took a step forward. "We won't be ambushed a second time. There may only be three of us, but we will take most of you with us. Remember my promise."

Daniel and Mary had disappeared. Under the cart a line of primed rifles were waiting. In the shadows, only the slight waver of two of the muzzles was visible.

Patrick appeared on the other side of the women with a pair of pistols in his hands. "As I told you, we need them." He turned and looked at the bald elder. "You can't rely on your men to protect you. You know that they are nothing but a bunch of castrated cowards."

After Daniel and Mary put the remains into bags and placed them into the cart, Patrick took Daniel aside. "Me and a few of the Islanders had scouted around the buildings surrounding the port. As far as we can tell, there are only a couple dozen Reapers on the island."

"Good. If we can retain the element of surprise, we can over take them."

"There is a problem. The Reapers had taken hostages to keep the others in line. If there is any kind of trouble, they will be publicly butchered. The Islanders are terrified that if we do anything, the hostages will be killed. We will need them to be on our side."

"So they won't help." Daniel looked at David. He was standing over Sarah as she chatted with another girl that was close to her age. '*If the others are dead, what kind of future does he have to look forward to. At least here, he has a chance.*' "These Islanders are weak. They would rather die a slow death than fight. We both know that in battle people die. When it is over, they will thank us."

"They don't know about us yet. If we delay, we will be the ones being hunted. You can't win a war while hiding in a cave."

Nancy, two women and one man had volunteered to join Patrick, Daniel, and David, as they headed towards the port. Despite being weighed down with extra weapons and digging equipment they maintained a brisk pace. The cluster of solid, chiselled stone buildings looked like a fort. The walls that ran from building to building had three large gates for the farm workers to push their carts through. Each was manned by two armed Reapers. The rest of the Reapers were all inside. Like a prison, all their attention was focussed inward. They were not prepared for an attack from the outside.

The first step of their plan was simple, dig under the wall of the building where the hostages were kept and get them out. With the hostages safe, the Islanders shouldn't fear an attack.

The loud ringing of hammered steel and the clunking of bellows fanning the furnaces, drowned out the sounds the men made with their picks, chisels and shovels. Luckily, the building was made to hold in the heat. Once the outer crust was breached, the thick porous walls were easy to dig though.

From on top of a nearby hill, a handful of men watched them dig. The bald elder came up behind them. "It's foolish. They are going to get them killed. Those outsiders don't care how many of us are butchered. All they care about is themselves, and their next meal."

Walking back the bald elder spotted the cart and the bags of remains. He clenched his teeth and took his airgun off his shoulder. Pointing it at Mary, he said, "We don't need any help from your kind."

Mary circled to the far side of the cart. "Stay back. I don't want to hurt you."

"Don't you mean eat me?" He poked the bags of remains with the muzzle of his gun. "I suppose you have been secretly munching those remains, haven't ya?"

As some of the remains fell out of the hole the front sight of his muzzle made, Mary pulled out her knife and yelled, "Get back. If you touch those bags again, I will kill you."

The grinning egotist began to laugh, "You are living proof that your kind can't live a day without eating someone."

A crowd began to form around them. Mike called out, "Put that gun down and leave her alone. Do you want to give us away?"

******

Nancy's slim figure made her the ideal person to crawl through the hole. Inside, the hostages lined the perimeter. Each one had one of their legs shackled. The chain attached to their legs were squeezed through two steel beams and attached to steel hooks near the centre of the building. As the others enlarged the hole, she unhooked the chains as fast as she could.

Dragging their chains behind them, the hostages began to crawl out. A musket shot echoed from the hills outside of the compound. It was too late for the hostages to think. It was escape or die. Fearing for her life, Nancy pushed her way to the hole and crawled through it.

Carrying their chains, the escaping hostages limped away. The hidden male Islanders finally built up the courage to run to their aid.

A half dozen Reapers, stormed out of a nearby gate. Both Patrick and Daniel made their shots count. Without armour, the bullets blew holes through the men's chests. David's shot had only winged its target's shoulder. Along with the ill fired shots the others made, the Reapers began to retreat.

******

The bullet the bald elder had squeezed off whizzed by Mary's ear and tore a few hairs off her scalp. Before he could fire a second shot, a musket ball from Sarah's rifle had gone through his hand and cracked the side of the airgun. A stream of leaking air launched the gun into the air and caused it to spin in circles as it hit the ground.

The man turned and screamed at Sarah, "Look what you have done."

The distant gunfire amplified the consequences of the elder's rage. Mike jumped between them. With one of his hands stretched out towards both of them, he blared out, "Stop it. All this has done is ruin any chances of them freeing the hostages."

Sarah put down the empty rifle and lifted a pistol. "Nobody harms my friends. Right now they are risking their lives for a group of strangers and this is how they are treated?"

The elder glared at her. "And how much human flesh have you eaten?"

"None." Sarah pointed the pistol at his head as Mary stood up and raised her knife above her head. "Mary, he's not worth it. Look at his hand. He can't work. When the Reapers find him, all they will see is meat."

Mary flipped the knife around and slammed its hilt against the side of his forehead. As he fell to the ground, several Islanders pointed their guns at her. Mike waved his arms in front of them. "He had that coming. It's over." Looking towards the compound, he added, "We need to find out what damage all this had caused. Your friends are in that compound. Don't you want to free them?"

Two men stayed with the kneeling elder and tried to help him to his feet. The rest of the Islanders picked up their weapons and ran towards the compound. Halfway there, they met two men helping three limping hostages. The hostages dropped to their knees. Between the lack of food, the heavy chains draped over their shoulders, and their raw swollen ankles, they could barely stand let alone walk. One of the men helping them spoke up, "Some more hostages have escaped, but these are the only ones that can walk. The rest will have to be carried."

Mike hugged one of the freed hostages. "The Reapers are not just cannibals, they are monsters."

******

Rushing into the breeched building, the Reapers shot at anything that moved. The remaining hostages dropped to the ground and froze. The leader grabbed the nearest hostage and dragged her into the courtyard. Turning to three of his men, he bellowed out, "Tie her to the posts and make an example out of her."

A crowd formed as the young girl was stripped and her ankles tied to ropes looped through rings attached to the top of two poles. As the ropes were pulled, she was lifted upside down into the air facing the crowd with her legs spread apart. After slicing her throat, the butcher anxiously began gutting her before she bled out.

It took a while for the girl's father to recognize who it was. When his daughter was taken hostage she was a beautiful healthy girl. The stick figure that was being butchered was barely recognizable. Even her fledgeling breasts had disappeared. "You told us that they would be kept alive. You were starving them."

From the balcony behind them, the leader yelled out, "You knew the rules. If someone doesn't work, they don't get fed."

The entire crowd began to converse. The murmurs quickly grew into discontent. One man yelled out, "So you hid them in order to keep the truth from us."

A woman yelled out, "They weren't hostages. You never intended to free them."

The leader rocked his head slowly back and forth. "If you got the ships repaired faster, there was a chance they would still be alive."

The Reapers standing watch over the crowd rested the butts of their rifles against their shoulders. Staring down their barrels, they focussed on the more vocal members of the crowd.

As the butcher hacked through the girl's pelvis and down her backbone, it took two Reapers to hold her father back. Using the butts of their rifles they knock him unconscious. Several Islanders dragged him to safety as the various pieces his daughter's beheaded and butchered remains were placed on a table for others to process her remaining flesh into thin strips for drying. As the large Reaper sharpened his long, thick knife another screaming hostage was dragged out.

As the crowd got more and more defiant, the Reapers began to shoot anyone that tried to interfere with the killings. The yelling and screaming coming from the courtyard almost drowned out the gunfire.

Patrick heard the commotion and knew that now was not the time to fall back. Gripping Daniel's shoulder, Patrick told him, "They don't know how many of us are out here. They are not going to leave the compound and risk coming into the open. Now is the time to strike."

"They maybe expecting it."

"I don't think so. I think they believe that if we had had the manpower to attack the compound, we would have."

David stayed with the man and two armed women. Hidden amongst the rocks, they shot at anyone trying to exit the hole they dug and the nearby gate.

Dressed as Islanders, Patrick and Daniel circled the compound and crept as close as they dared to the furthest gate. After climbing on Daniel's shoulders, Patrick peered over the wall. To their surprise there was only one guard and he was standing a few metres inside the gate. With his rifle pointed at the crowd, the guard barely glanced at the gate.

The pair ran to the gate. Patrick placed his foot on Daniel's locked fingers and stepped onto his shoulders. Then Daniel grabbed the bottom of his feet and boosted him over the three metre gate. The 'Thud' Patrick made as his feet hit the ground made the guard turn around. Patrick jumped up and drove his knife into the man's throat before he could speak. He glanced at the crowd. Everyone was focussed on the butchered hostages, the crowd or the wounded.

After unlatching the gate and letting Daniel through, Patrick looked around and spotted what he was after. "There." Pointing at group of men standing on a balcony, he added, "If we take out their leaders, the rest should scatter."

Daniel looked to the far side of the compound. "If you can work your way up there, I could take out their main leader. If I can get behind those barrels, I should be able to make the shot." After studying Patrick's reaction, he added, "When they come for me, you can do what you do best."

Knowing the risk Daniel would be taking, Patrick said, "Good luck." Patrick grinned as he wiped the blood off his knife. "I think I will be able to take some of the pressure off you."

Patrick hooked the eye holes of the two faces attacked to the shoulders of dead Reaper's vest over the pin of one of the gate's hinges. With the guard held upright, the pair went their separate ways.

Daniel looked over his shoulder and saw Patrick wrap his arm around a Reaper's neck and haul him into a building. The more enraged the crowd grew, the more brutal the Reapers became. Daniel used his legs and torso to conceal his rifle as he skirted around the compound.

A Reaper looked back and saw him. As he waved for him to join the confined rabble, he shook his head. The irrate man pulled out his long knife and charged at him. Daniel stepped to the side and rolled on the ground. The Reaper swung his blade and narrowly missed him. Turning back he saw Daniel's rifle. He grabbed his pistol but its front sight got caught in his belt. A quick second yank freed it.

Daniel threw his dagger at the Reaper's head. The blade glanced off the man's hard leather helmet. Before he could refocus, Daniel swung the blade of his long knife upward and caught the man's groin. With both his knife and pistol in hand, the man dropped to his knees. Daniel slid the blade of his knife up the man's gut, twirled it around his head and slashed the man's throat.

After removing the man's vest and helmet, Daniel put them on. With a bit of dirt kicked over the guards pants, from a distance, he could easily pass for a dead Islander. He rolled him onto his side, got down, and rested his knife on top of him. Using the dead body to prop up his rifle, he pointed his rifle at the three men on the balcony. As one of them took off his helmet and waved it in the air, Daniel took his shot.

Before the smoke cleared, Daniel pushed the rifle in front of the corpse and grabbed his knife. As he stabbed the dead man a screaming group of nearby Islanders broke ranks and ran towards him screaming. Thinking Daniel had killed the shooter, three Reapers quickly corralled the Islanders. With their backs toward him, Daniel drew out his pistol.

As the men on the balcony aided their shot leader, Patrick took out his pistols. He shot one man in the back of the neck and the second in the forehead as he turned to face him. Several Reapers in the courtyard saw the attack. Patrick ducked for cover as a barrage of bullets ricocheted off the wall behind him.

As if it was an echo, in the courtyard Daniel shot one of the Reapers in the back of his neck. Only the closest one to him saw the smoke coming from his pistol. Daniel tossed his dagger at the man's head. The blade struck his cheek as he tried to duck. Daniel ran over and yanked it out. Its blade had cut though the man's tongue and left him choking from his own blood.

Patrick rolled the leader's body over the balcony. The compound went quiet. With the bodies of four butchered hostages spread in front of them, when the silence broke, the Islanders went crazy. The reapers had no time to reload. With magazines half to three-quarters empty, they began to fall back. As the Islanders that were spearheading the revolt were shot, the others hesitated.

The Reapers used that time wisely. With reloaded weapons, they advanced a couple steps. Still enraged, the Islanders at the back pushed the scared ones at the front forward. As they fell to the ground to escape the bullets, a wall of flailing bodies began to form. With renewed confidence, the Reapers ordered them back.

From the balcony, Patrick shot the man that gave the order. The Reapers glanced at one another and realized that their numbers had dwindled. The dead Reaper fell off the gate as Mike led six armed Islanders inside. By the time each side recognized the other, they both fired at the same time. Feeling overwhelmed the Reapers retreated to the water front. The Islanders picked up their fallen weapons and chased after them. The ones trapped in the building where the hostages had been kept opened fire.

Nancy was the first to rush the breach. She shot over the remaining hostages at the three Reapers standing near the doorway. Before they could turn around, David shot one of them in the hip. The man crumbled to the ground. A hostage grabbed a Reaper's ankle and pulled him to the ground as a group of Islanders rushed inside. Armed with wrenches and hammers, they smashed the Reapers' skulls and dragged them outside.

Amidst scattered gunfire the remaining Reapers ran to a ship in dry dock. As they climbed aboard the large, nearly refurbished catamaran, they took turns returning fire. After shooting the cables attached to the two sets of trolleys, the ship slid into the water. Protected behind the metal hulls, they pedalled out to sea.

Back in the courtyard, the Islanders came to grips with the cost of their newly found freedom. Four butchered, seven killed and dozens of islanders wounded.

Daniel saw no sense of relief on the Islander's faces, only dismay. Feeling uneasy, he walked backwards towards the gate. Patrick saw him, stopped for a moment and looked around. This was not the joyous victory he was hoping for.

Chapter Twenty - Four

The two surviving hunters made their way to town. They met up with the Townies guarding the entrance between the town and the valley filled with the giant mounds of debris. After hearing all about the Reapers, they were given directions to where Killy was staying. Camped on a ledge near the top of the cliff, Killy could pin point most of the Reapers' movements.

Killy was in the process of moving stones to adjust their updated positions on a map as the two men entered his tent. "Sorry Killy. The women attacked our rear as we were about to overtake the earth dwellers. We are the only survivors."

It took time for Killy to digest the fact that most of his elite force were butchered. After pacing back and forth and flailing his arms, he looked at the two men. "I got a very secret job for you two."

Wearing Reaper garb, the pair waited til after dark to climb down and sneak into the hidden tunnels beneath the town. Under the unmarked trap door in the floor of Killy's torture room, they listened to the snores of three Reapers. When they were sure the only creaking they heard was coming from the tired bodies rolling from side to side, the pair peered inside.

Fighting the urge to slit the snoring Reapers' throats, they tip-toed passed them. The cracks around the door gave them a good view of the buildings along the waterfront. The sea had wreaked havoc on the floating island. Pushed against the shore, pieces of it were heaved onto the wharf by the pounding surf. Most of its inhabitants had come ashore. A couple brave souls still manned one of the two remaining watch towers.

Opening the door, they threw up their arms and stretched. From the rocking perch on the island, they looked like two restless men that couldn't sleep.

The hunters slowly strolled down the middle of the road. As the two lookouts turned around and gazed over the ruined island, they dashed under the floor boards of the remnants of a large porch. When the lookouts stopped searching for where they were and returned to assessing their ruined island, the hunters made a dash to the front door of what was once the mayor's home.

After slipping inside, they quietly looked around. They saw a dozen or more Reapers asleep in the various rooms on the main floor. Using a ladder instead of the badly damaged stairs, they climbed through a hole in the ceiling. They spotted Victoria in the large room facing the waterfront. After retrieving a carefully wrapped clay vial, one of the hunters broke off the tip of it, poured it on to a rag. While one man held her down, the other man placed the rag over Victoria's nose and mouth.

Victoria opened her eyes and punched the stealthy hunter on the side of his face. Before succumbing to the potion, she kneed the man that was holding her down. The Reaper sleeping only an arms length from her, barely stirred. The hunters carried Victoria's limp body out of the room and slid her body down the slanted ladder. With her arms around their necks, they held up her head and guided her footsteps outside and down the waterfront. With her body concealed between theirs the lookouts could not tell who she was. They only saw three chatty colleagues taking a midnight stroll.

At the outskirts of town, Killy helped carry Victoria up the side of the cliff. She was lying on his bed for nearly an hour before her eyes opened. After finding that her wrists and ankles were lashed to his bed, she started to scream. The two hunters shoved a long, leather wrapped piece of copper pipe in her mouth. The more she fought, the more force they used to keep it in place. Killy stood next to the bed. "Before they break your jaw, I should tell you that I only brought you here to talk. You can return to your men after you hear me out."

It was almost morning before Victoria wandered into town. Looking around she saw the predicament she was in. She had over a hundred fighters, plus workers, women and children under her care. She had been given an ultimatum. She had to decide who should live and who's names should be entered into the weekly meat lottery.

On a cliff on the far side of town, Grant took out his binoculars and watched a group of bound men and women being led out of town. "What's going on?" He saw Killy standing on the ledge as a small group of Reapers were handed over to his men. "It's too early. We have enough meat. I told him to give her a month."

A few minutes later Eric appeared. "Grant, the men are talking. They think Killy has made a deal with the Reapers and he is cutting us out."

Grant turned and told Eric, "Get one of your men to go over there and find out what is going on."

******

Word that some men and women were bound and handed over to the cannibals caused a stir. Within minutes, a crowd formed in front of where Victoria was standing. Surrounded by her elite soldiers, She walked out and addressed the crowd. "We are running out of food. It hasn't rained since we got here and our water supply is almost depleted. I agreed to a truce and gave them a few of our slaves as a peace offering. Every time we attempt to repair the island, their canons tear it apart. With our cannons on the sea floor, we are utterly defenceless."

"Those slaves were suppose to be meat for our bellies."

Another man in the crowd yelled out, "We still have our knives and rifles. We are not cowards. Lets show them who we are."

Victoria raised her hands in the air. "You can not protect yourselves from their canons. They are out of range of our rifles. Any attack would be a futile and a waste of lives."

"We have to try to fight our way out while we still have the energy. If we wait, we will be to weak to fight. I would rather die fighting and take some of them with me, then be tied and led to their butcher's block."

The crowd cheered at the man's short speech. The ranting crowd dispersed, armed themselves and reunited near the narrow valley. As scores tried to climb the sides of the cliff to disarm the sharpshooters above, a couple canons released porous balls that broke apart on impact. If the earth quaking impact didn't knock the nearby climbers off, the shrapnel did.

After ordering her elite guards to stay back, Victoria said, "What a tragic waste, and all over a few slaves."

The men and women that entered the narrow gorge were mowed down by two dozen concealed sharpshooters. Not knowing their fate, others continued to pour in. As the bodies began to pile the mob began to lose its vigour.

Killy's men had strict orders to fire only on those that were attempting to advance. As the Reapers halted, the gorge grew quiet. Stepping back, they saw the price of their folly.

******

The massacre was over by the time Eric's man approached Killy's campsite. He noticed a stranger standing out side of his tent. Sensing that something was wrong, he hid behind a boulder and watched what was going on. After a brief conversation with the stranger, Killy told four men to help the man haul sacks of meat. An hour later the four men returned. Despite not knowing what was said, he muttered, "That whole thing was staged. They must have formed an alliance."

Returning to Eric and Grant, he relayed what he saw. Wanting to give Killy a chance, Grant said, "They just got a lot of meat. Lets give them some time. It might take a day or two for them to transport some of it to us." Turning to Eric, he added, "In the meantime, tell the men to be on guard. Tonight, I want the canons moved and kept hidden from their view."

That night, as Grant's men were moving the canons, they noticed some commotion going on below. They knew that climbing the steep cliffs at night was suicidal. Eric tossed a flaming oil rag into the air. As it fluttered down, he saw what was happening. They were using brightly coloured rags to mark the canons' new positions.

Upon hearing what Eric saw Grant knew what was happening. "Victoria sacrificed some of her people and now Killy is wanting to sacrifice us."

"Why? What for? That doesn't make any sense."

Grant cocked his head to the side and grinned. "You must have heard the rumours about Killy's elite hunters being killed?"

"Sure."

"He used those men to control the town's meat market." Shaking his head, he added, "Right now, my men are better trained than his. He is afraid I'll take over. An alliance with Victoria is his only chance on retaining his position."

"What's in it for her?"

"She stays in power and let's Killy be the big bad harvester. In a sense, she becomes the new mayor."

Grant ordered his men to retreat into the hills. They took everything they could carry or pull. Tying two canons on sleds, they pulled them over the rocky terrain. On smoother ground, they reattached their wheels. A couple blasts from Killy's canons announced the attack on the abandoned cliff. Looking back, Grant told Eric, "They will be at least a half day behind us. Luckily, they have no idea where we are heading."

A few hours after sunup they made it off the rocky cliffs and down to the vast flat ground. Ahead of them were kilometres upon kilometres of nothing except the odd hill and mound of rocks. Using his binoculars, Grant spotted a manmade trail. It only took them fifteen minutes to reach it.

The set of deeply gouged tracks had reminded him what Charles said before he died. 'Remember, we had a deal. Save as many as you can and wipe the rest from your mind.' Looking at the tracks, he figured out what the old mayor had meant. When Charles had handed the ships' captains and Islanders over to the faceless ones, they made a pact. *But that deal died when Killy's men ran amuck and took over the Fresh Start and the others fled.'*

After gazing up and down the cliff and over the wasteland, he told Eric, "We might have a place to go. That is if the faceless ones are willing to finetune their deal."

Eric shook his head, "What do you mean?"

Grant just smiled as he led his men along the trail. He noticed a bunch of assorted footprints on it. They kept to a narrow path. That made it hard for him to guess how many there were. He knew that the faceless ones never walked anywhere. "They must be the ones that slaughtered Killy's hunters. Lets keep them a safe distance ahead of us. That way, if there is any trouble ahead, they will get the brunt of it and not us."

Chapter Twenty - Five

The Reapers banishment left the Islanders bewildered. Their once homogeneous society had been disembowelled and they had to start anew.

With scores of wounded to tend to, they had little time to think about their future.   Some armed themselves and manned the lookouts while others were too distraught to do anything. Mike and Nancy took it upon themselves to take inventory of the remaining food and supplies.

They both knew that the catamaran the Reapers escaped on had no supplies onboard. Nancy turned to Mike. "They will be coming back. They can't go out to sea without any food and water."

Mike looked towards the dock and said, "I know"

From the roof of the tallest building, David watched the Islanders feed a large fire in the middle of the courtyard. They wrapped and tossed their dead onto the hot coals. The deaths of some of the more seriously wounded men and women added to the death toll. Favouring his bandaged hand the bald elder told them to let the fire die out on the fourth day. He looked up and saw David in the lookout tower. "Those cannibals did this. They are the ones responsible for all the deaths."

Sarah looked up from the injured woman she was tending. "How dare you say that. If you didn't cause that ruckus, this would never had happened."

The bitter man snapped back, "That is a lie."

"Those so-called cannibals could have freed the hostages without a single shot fired. They had a plan and you ruined it."

"They had no plan."

"They had a plan and you turned it into a bloodbath." Glancing up at David, she added, "Patrick was right. The men on this island are nothing but a bunch of castrated cowards."

A women tending to her husband stood up and screamed, "How dare you say that. My husband took on armed men wielding only a wrench."

Sarah snapped back, "Only after he was given no choice."

The woman shook her head. "You have been with the cannibals too long. Maybe you should leave with them."

Sarah looked up at David than back at the woman. "At least I will know that I have someone I can trust watching out for me."

David watched the Islanders collect the ashes from the fire and haul them to the gardens beyond the walls. As several of them spread and raked the ashes into the soil, he muttered, "How can you call us cannibals when you eat your dead through the plants you grow, just like we do."

******

Grey smoke bellowed from the New Hope's stack as Patrick helped Daniel guide the New Hope into the harbour. On the deck of a salvaged Reaper ship, Mary stood watch as Simon checked on Roger's leg. "We can't stay here."

Roger pulled himself up and leaned against the cabin. With his hand gripped around the stock of his rifle, he said, "She's right. We can't stay where we are not welcome. If we lower our guard for even one night, they could slit our throats."

Mary turned and told him, "I should have killed that elder. He's the one that is stirring them up."

The bald elder stood at the gateway leading into the compound and watched the two ships lash their hulls to each other. Turning to the two men beside him, he said, "We can't trust them. How can any of us sleep at night knowing that we could be taken from their beds and butchered. Once a cannibal, always a cannibal."

Mike overheard them. Seeing them lead a crowd of people towards the dock, he yelled out so all could hear. "Every man on that ship ate the human flesh that the Reapers gave us. So we are no better then they are."

The elder yelled back, "We were given no choice."

"We all had a choice. It was eat and live, or starve to death." Pointing to the ship, Mike yelled out, "And what choices have they had?"

******

Outside the compound, the two men that had been fertilizing the garden put their tools inside the carts and started hauling them back to the gate. Their tools rattled around as the carts bounced over the furrows.

The distracted lookouts were gazing at the dock when the rattling stopped. One of them looked back as saw the workers on the ground beneath several Reapers. One of them saw him. Before the lookout could swing his rifle around the Reapers lifted the workers out of the dirt and ducked behind them. Not wanting to hit them, the guard fired a shot over their heads.

After ropes were wedged into the workers mouths and secured at the back of their necks, the Reapers used them as human shields. All the lookouts could do was fire warning shots as the Reapers walked backward towards a cluster of boulders.

Men and women grabbed their weapons and rushed out of the gate. Caught in the open field outside the compound, a volley of bullets halted their advance. Amongst the shallow furrows, the only protection they had were the rocks they used to mark the rows. Dragging their wounded behind them, they ran back to the compound and latched the gate.

Surmising what had happened, Patrick left Simon and Roger behind and jumped onto the New Hope. By the time he had cut the lines binding the ships together, Mary was releasing the sails. With Daniel at the helm, David finished cranking up the anchor.

The Reapers' ship left a nearby bay and headed straight out to sea. Patrick pinged two shots off their starboard hull before it cruised out of range. Looking up at the limp sails, he said, "If only we had more fuel."

As the bald elder went into the compound to inspect the wounded, Mike met the New Hope as it pulled up to the dock. Patrick tossed him a line. While tying the ship to the dock, Mike said, "Why should they leave. They have us to hunt."

Patrick answered, "You will have to make them."

Before Mike could reply, Daniel butt in. "If you give us the fuel we need and a safe place to come back to, we can keep them away from you."

Mike looked up at them and shook his head. "I can't offer you a safe home. Some of the people here fear you more than they do the Reapers."

Hearing the men talk, Mary came over to the railing and asked, "What if we anchor our ships in the bay at the far end of the island. We could grind all the coral you need along with fending off the Reapers."

After thinking for a moment, he replied, "I'll have to talk to the others."

******

The elder saw Mike enter the courtyard. While rubbing his injured hand, he said, "I heard that you were talking to the cannibals. What do they want from us?"

Looking around at the wounded men and women, he said. "They offered their services. In return they want a safe place to moor their ships and come ashore."

"Where?"

"The muddy bay at the far end of the island was mentioned."

"That's near the coral reserves." The elder glared at Mike. "We need those reserves."

"They offered to grind it for us and use it as trade."

The bald man rubbed his hands over his head. As one of the wounded men being stitched up screamed at the top of his lungs, the pair looked towards the port. "We lost two more men and have more wounded than upright. We can't fight them off."

Mike looked around the courtyard. "There was a reason why they castrated so many of the men. They needed to make sure we couldn't put up any resistance." Spotting a pregnant woman, he added, "Plus they wanted to make secure their legacy."

The bald elder rubbed the inside of his groin with his good hand. "I am still a man."

Mike slowly rocked his head back and forth. "But nothing like the man you used to be. You've changed."

The elder sat on the ground and looked at the scores of wounded lying in the courtyard. "If we can't tend and defend our gardens, we will starve. What's our guarantee that the cannibals won't start hunting us for meat?"

"Only their word."

Mary and Daniel saw the unarmed procession walk up to the ship. The elder looked at Mary and then at Daniel. "I have a proposition for you. If you vanquish the remaining Reapers, we will grant you a safe harbour."

Patrick walk over to the railing and said, "You mean kill them."

After rubbing his head with his good hand, the elder yelled out, "Yes, kill them." Taking a couple deep breaths, he lowered his voice and added, "Sometimes you have to do what you must, to survive. Even if it goes against everything you believe in."

Daniel piped up, "Have all the people behind you agreed to this?"

The elder looked at Mike and answered, "Yes, I promise that none of us will cause you any harm, unless you harm us first."

Patrick spoke up, "That's fair. We can live with that."

While pumping methane into both ships, the Islanders used a hoist to fix the New Hope's rudder plus mounted a cannon on it. Under full sail it took from dawn until dusk to navigate around the island. Not wanting to be predictable, each morning they flipped a marked stone and went in the direction its markings indicated.

With a young girl trailing behind with her children, Nancy helped Sarah up the ship's ladder. From the crows nest David looked down and waved to her. Her wide smile took the chill out of the cold breeze. The stone landed on its edge. Patrick looked at Daniel, "Lets toss it again."

Daniel shook his head. "No, it is telling us to go halfway and then circle back."

As Nancy checked on Roger, Sarah sat on the pier and played with Tom. With the New Hope out of sight, the sea looked peaceful. From the crows nest, Simon noticed something bobbing in the water. The way it moved with the waves told her that it was the mast of the Reaper's ship. "Did the catamaran have a mast?"

Nancy looked up at her and answered, "No, but I heard people talk about mounting a bracket to attach a pole to."

Overhearing the conversation, Sarah butt in, "With four cables, they could use it to erect a crows nest."

Simon gazed at the bobbing object. "In that case, I think I spotted the Reapers."

Nancy dashed to the railing and jumped down onto the dock. Grabbing Tom on the way, she ran into the compound screaming, "They're coming. The Reapers are coming."

Mike grabbed his gun and led six others to the pier. "I don't see anything. Where are they?"

Simon yelled down, "They are still quite a distance away. I guess they were waiting for the New Hope to leave before coming ashore."

A couple men saw the ship's canon and climbed aboard. By the time it was loaded, they could clearly see the catamaran's mast above the waves. Roger dragged himself to the front of the ship. Looking back at the two men, he yelled out, "What are you waiting for. Fire the cannon. We have to let the New Hope know where they are."

Roger covered his ears as the canon fired. Looking back at the compound he saw two men shut the gate and a half dozen more scurry about.

Upon hearing the blast, Patrick swung the New Hope's steering wheel and the others ran to readjust the sails. "Those sneaky cowards."

By the time the New Hope returned to port, the catamaran's watchtower had vanished. After tying the ship to the dock, Daniel walked over to Sarah. "If we are to catch them, we will need someone in the boiler room that knows how to run it."

Sarah looked at Nancy and than up at David. Sarah picked up Gail and passed her to Nancy before answering Daniel, "Sure, I'll join you."

Patrick stood beside Daniel. "I would like to take Simon and Roger with us too."

Daniel turned to him and said, "Roger is nothing but a hot headed cripple."

Patrick cocked his head. "That may be, but he is loyal and we can use him as a lookout." With raised eyebrows, he added, "That would free up both Simon and David."

With Mike and a few Islanders' help, they started loading the ship for a prolonged voyage. That was when Mike discovered that most of their gunpowder had vanished along with the cannon balls for the catamaran's air cannon. When he told Patrick, he shook his head. "So that's why they stayed out at sea. The ship sighting was nothing more than a distraction."

Both Patrick and Daniel followed the short trail the Reapers left behind the storage shed. It headed to a small dock at the end of the pier. "Wasn't there an old boat tied up here?"

"Yes." Mike looked around the shoreline. "It's gone."

Hearing the news, Roger told them, "I thought I saw some commotion going on along the shore."

Looking at the New Hope, Mary said, "We have to arm it with everything we can."

Simon spoke up, "What about using the other ship. It is already fitted with cannons."

"It doesn't have any sails and we don't have the manpower to pedal it."

Sarah cocked her head and said, "We could always fuel up in the Rainbow Sea."

David looked at her. "But we know the New Hope. We don't know the other ship handles. I think we should stick to what we know."

While using the other ship to patrol the sea in front of the compound, the Islanders used the cranes in dry dock to mount seven cannons onto the New hope. There were two gunpowder cannons placed on both sides plus the stern, along with an air cannon on the centre bow. The weight of the cannon lying on the side of the forward mast and jib was countered by the air tanks and pump on the other side. It was smaller than the one on the Reaper's catamaran but it could be reloaded in less than a third of the time.

Daniel was amazed at how fast the Islanders could cast the cannon supports and manipulate the cranes that placed the cannons and tanks into position. Turning to Patrick, he said, "It is no wonder the Reapers spared them. They can do anything with metal."

In the middle of the night, Nancy looked up and waved to Roger as they set sail. From the crows nest, he couldn't make out Tom and Gail's small faces but knew who they were. Simon saw Mike and had to look away.

As the sun broke over the horizon, the compound was a speck on the distant shoreline. With the sails cranked tightly against the spars the ship was harder to spot. In the rolling waves, Roger rocked back and forth in the crows nest for two more hours before spotting the tip of a ship's mast. "I see it. It's on the port side and a touch to the bow."

With Patrick at the wheel, Daniel directed how to set the sails. "Lets chase her out to sea. It can't have a lot of fuel left. After their legs get tired the ship should be ours."

Patrick looked at him. "Unless their cannon sinks us. It has a far better range than ours."

******

Jose and another woman scouted ahead. The wasteland was a sea of barren knolls. Lying on the top of one of them, she took out a pair of binoculars. A long, grey cloud of smoke poured out of a large, rusty, metal contraption. "Go back and tell the others to hide. The metal beast is coming back."

"Where?" After spotting the beast, she added, "We got nothing to hide behind."

"Than tell them to start digging."

******

Eric ran back to Grant. "They've stopped. For some reason they are digging trenches to hide in."

Grant saw the long grey cloud of smoke. After glancing at his men, he turned to Eric. "Enlist a volunteer to go back and find out how far Killy is behind us."

"So far, none of our scouts have heard or seen any sign of them." Eric shrugged his shoulders. "They may not have even begun hunting for us."

"They will." Grant stared at the column of smoke. "And I don't want us to be trapped."

"What are you talking about?"

Grant pointed at the smoke. "That metal beast has the firepower to kill all of us."

Eric gazed at the smoke. "What do you want us to do?"

"Dig three trenches. The first two should be about three metres apart and a metre and a half deep. Have the men toss the dirt in front of the trenches. The main trench should be at least two dozen metres behind the two wheel traps. That is where we'll be hiding. We can position our cannons at both ends of the trench."

"Couldn't the beast go around the wheel traps?"

"It won't." Grant grinned and told him, "The faceless ones have too much faith in their machinery. Their pride won't let them go around."

******

The metal beast stopped about thirty metres from Jose. Down the centre of it, the steam powered engine spun a large heavy flywheel. Inside, levers and gearboxes controlled the wheels, steering, fans and a strange centrifuge mounted on top of the machine.

A man wearing gloves and a bag over his head with dark eye holes plus slits to breath through, appeared out of a hatch. Every centimetre of his skin was covered in cloth. Taking out his binoculars, he looked around. A gust of wind lifted a clump of Jose's hair slightly above the small knoll she was hiding behind.

The unusual movement caught the man's attention. Taking no chances, he got behind the centrifuge and pointed the pipe coming out of it at the knoll. As he squeezed a trigger metal balls were injected into it. When they spun to the top they shot out through the pipe at a staggering speed. The man held the trigger in and air pushed the balls out of a reservoir and into the centrifuge. Within seconds, over a hundred steel balls tore the knoll apart.

Behind it, Jose rolled over. Her right arm, thigh and cheek had been hit. As soon as the firing stopped, Kelsey popped up from behind another knoll and shot the man's shoulder.

The man tried to adjust the centrifuge but couldn't. He needed both arms to control it. He slipped through the hatch and another man appeared. Kelsey was nowhere in sight. In a horrifying minute, over a thousand balls spewed out of the pipe and riddled the area. Dirt was strewn over Kelsey's shallow trench.

As the beast rolled ahead to examine Jose, John watched it from afar. The man on top peered over the side at Jose's blood drenched body. After looking around, he poked his head into the hatch and said, "She's dressed like a hunter." Glancing at his partner's arm, he added, "I think they got the message, plus we left them some meat. Let's get you some medical aid."

Seeing the metal beast leaving, Jacob, John and a couple women rushed to see what happened. John rolled Jose over and checked her vitals. She was still alive. Jacob and the women searched for Kelsey. A woman stepped on her leg while calling out her name. Kelsey's arm shot up from across her face and sprayed dirt everywhere. Gasping for air, she shook the dirt away from her face before opening her eyes. "You didn't need to step on me."

By the time Joe and the others reached them, John had already started stitching up Jose's arm and face the best he could. The two stretcher bearers set Tara down beside her. "What about the leg? Can you remove the bullet?"

John looked at her. "Sure, with some help."

"She has lost a lot of blood." Glancing at one of the women, she said, "Make sure she gets plenty of broth to drink."

Joe and Jacob walked over to Karen. Joe hung his head low as he said, "This is not a good start. We shot one of them. The next time they see us they will shoot first. They may not give us a chance to talk to them and reach a truce."

Karen drew circles in the sand as she answered, "It will take days to get to the mine. That should give us some time to figure something out."

******

After seeing them pick up three stretchers and carry their injured comrades away, Eric put down his binoculars. Biting his lip, he mumbled to himself, "Why would they do that? Dried meat is much lighter and easier to carry."

Chapter Twenty-Six

The next day, Killy walked up to the unfinished trenches. He surmised from the way the two fortified pits were constructed that Grant had two cannons with him. The man standing beside him nudged his shoulder and pointed to a series of small, distant puffs of black smoke. "We've been spotted."

As they proceeded Killy examined the nearly flattened knolls. Next to a darkened section of gravel, he noticed a cluster of blood covered steel balls and small wads of leather. He rubbed his head. "Maybe Grant knows something we don't. There has to be a logical reason for them to venture into Faceless territory."

******

Through a series of lookouts and runners, it was almost dark before Grant was told, "They are about a day behind us."

Grant thanked the runner and turned to Eric. "At our present pace, that means that they might catch up to us in maybe three."

******

Before sunrise, the women spread their blankets and anything else that would soak up the morning dew. The women preferred using leather, as it gave the wrung out water more flavour. After appointing sentries, the earth dwellers huddled together and the women formed a circle around Tara. One of the women asked, "Why are we doing this? No one travels through Faceless territory and lives to tell anyone."

Kelsey spoke up, "That we know of. What if they found something better and didn't want to leave."

Tara listened to the two banter. "Do you think I agreed to this without thinking about it first? We have no home to go back to and very few options."

"Surely they are other places we could go."

"Sure, but nothing with a renewable food source. Without it we can't survive."

"How do we know if the people inside the mine will even accept us?"

"We don't." Gazing toward Joe and the others, Tara said, "They believe there is something there that is worth risking their lives for. They are not cowards. They could have stayed in their underground maze and fought, but they chose not to. It was a fluke that they got caught in the open and were nearly wiped out. I'm hoping we can benefit from their misfortune."

Without knowing all the facts, none of the women knew what to say. They once thought of the earth dwellers as a cunning and almost mystical foe. In fact, most of the women had envied them. Now their mystique is gone. They had found out that they bleed and die just like they do.

After feeling the scars on her face, Jose used her rifle to help her stand up. "I for one feel that they are not telling us everything they know. We are travelling together but are still divided. We have two camps. Maybe if we unite them, they will open up to us. Maybe then we will get some answers."

******

After avoiding the miners' metal beasts for two days, Grant's scouts stood next to a vast crater. It was over six kilometres across.

In the middle of the converted strip mine was a deep shaft. It lead down to the honeycomb of tunnels that were once used to extract the rich ore below. The miners had fortified the entrance with a tall five metre thick wall of concrete slabs, rocks, and dirt. On top of the wall were several enclosed centrifuges. Within the crater there was nowhere for anyone to hide. Its smooth sides allowed someone to tumble down, but offered little to grip to climb out. The only visible way in or out of the crater was a long, sloped road that circled over a quarter of the way around it.

One of the scouts led Grant to where the metal beasts went in and out of the crater. He was amazed by the massive, fortified structure within it. "Who would be foolish enough to risk going down there."

A runner had to stop to catch his breath before walking up and kneeling beside him. "Killy will catch up to us by mid-afternoon tomorrow. Maybe even sooner, if they travel through the night."

"He wouldn't risk it. He knows that my men do their best hunting at night." Grant stood up and noticed their footprints next to the deep tracks. "If we get caught in the middle, we're meat. We can not stay here."

As he lifted his binoculars to take another look at the fortress, the sunset reflected off the lenses. Gloria saw the flash of light. After verifying who it was, she reported it to Joe. Joe immediately went to Tara, "We are not alone. Some of Grant's men are only a half a kilometre away. We can't set up any type of dialogue with the miners tonight. If we don't move our camp now we will be trapped."

Gloria stood beside Joe. "Too bad we can't leave them a note."

With Grant's men circling the crater to the right, they went to the left. Just knowing that there were Townies close by made both Joe and Tara on edge. Without being burdened with cannons and carts, they finally set up camp almost straight across from the mouth of the narrow road. Grant's men only travelled a quarter of the way around the pit.

An hour after they finally got to sleep, it started to rain. Both groups got up and spread out everything they had to collect the rainwater. With water being tightly rationed, they had to control their thirst. They knew that drinking too much water could make them sick.

The rain loosened the soil and muffled the sounds they made with their digging. By morning, both camps were dug in. The downpour had washed away their footprints and left nothing for anyone to follow.

It was noon before the gates of the fortress opened up and several metal beasts rolled out of it. The lead vehicle rolled back and forth as men walked beside it checking the condition of the ground. The ground had been dry and it soaked up most of the rain. The dirt barely stuck to the treads of the beast's wheels. As they rolled towards the narrow road on the side of the crater, three of Killy's scouts spotted them. Two stayed behind, while the third ran back to report it.

Upon hearing the news, Killy remembered the trenches Grant's men dug. "The first two trenches were nothing but wheel traps. That's why he had placed the cannons so far back." Grinning, he strutted back and forth with delight.

Killy was still smiling when Zack ran up to him. As he tried to catch his breath, he said, "I heard the news. The death machines are coming our way." Looking up, he saw the grin of Killy's face. "Why are you so happy?"

"Because I know how to stop them." Killy dropped the smile. "We have to get to work. From what the scout told me, we have only about half an hour. Remember the three trenches Grant's men dug?"

"Yeah."

"Well tell the men to start digging three more exactly the same."

"How do you expect me to remember their exact dimensions."

Killy threw his arms in the air. "The first two are wheel traps. Make them a little wider than their wheels and just as far apart. That way the machines bottom out and can't move. That will make them easy targets for our cannons. The trench at the rear is for the men."

Knowing the metal beasts were coming, the men worked at a pace that was beyond them. By the time the first machine was about to crawl out the men were exhausted. Several of them had to be dragged to the rear trench.

Killy watched the lead machine roll out of the pit. As it spotted the frightened men race to safety, it adjusted its course and headed straight towards them.

The others travelled behind it in a broken 'V' formation. As the man operating the centrifuge on the lead beast opened fire, its front wheels fell into the first trench. Its rear wheels pushed them out. As both sets of wheels slipped into the two trenches, the metal beast became stuck. Resting on its chassis, its gunner briefly stopped firing and blew on a horn. Hearing it, the other two machines came to a stop.

Despite the lead machine firing at them, Killy ordered all three of his cannons to focus on the two machines in the rear. In response, the machines directed their fire at the men manning the cannons. As one man was hit, he was dragged away and replaced by another and then another.

A cannonball grazed the side of one machine as it circled around the trenches. The other pulled up behind the trapped beast. Amidst rifle fire, the men on the trapped beast crawled out and leaped onto the one behind it. Before the last man jumped, he tossed a lit cannister into the open hatch.

A thick cloud of black smoke spewed from every crack and opening in the beast. As the rear machine retreated behind the wall of smoke, a cannonball smashed the front right wheel of the beast that was trying to cover their escape. The hit threw the gunner over the side. As he scrambled behind the machine, the escaping beast sped to his aid.

The smoke was replaced by bright multi-coloured flames as the black cloud dispersed. With its gunner spraying a constant stream of steel balls up and down the entrenched Townies, the men climbed out of the disabled vehicle. A rolling cloud of dust formed in front of the trench as the balls tore through both dirt and flesh. As the driver of the immobile beast lit a cannister, a cannonball glanced off the side of the metal machine and knocked him off.

As the driver smashed his upper side against a rock, his hood fell off. Killy noticed his golden skin.

The driver grabbed his broken arm, got up and ran alongside the last beast with the rest of his crew. Using the immobile vehicles as cover, the metal beast retreated into the pit.

After seeing them disappear into the crater, Killy turned to Zack. "I need you to take a message back to Victoria. You can take a few men with you if you want."

"It will take a couple weeks to get there and back."

"Don't worry. We are not going anywhere. Not with such a delicious gilded harvest at our fingertips."

******

Despite only spotting the Reapers' ship three times, Patrick knew it was still out at sea. As Daniel was about to relieve him, he secured the wheel and pulled out the charts. Uncertain if the Reapers were heading towards the Rainbow Sea or the debris field, Patrick spoke up. "We haven't seen them for over a day. They could have veered off in either direction."

Daniel straightened his back. "Do they even know about the oil workers in the Rainbow Sea?"

"Probably not."

"Then they probably are heading to the debris field. Maybe they believe that there are more Islanders there to harvest."

Patrick looked at him. "We left a couple Reapers there along with a small arsenal."

Daniel bit his bottom lip. Glancing over the charts spread out throughout the cabin, he proclaimed, "They could get there a half a day before us. That would give them plenty of time to lay out some traps for us."

Patrick nodded his head. "They will be expecting us." Looking up, he added, "What do you propose?"

Daniel gazed out of the cabin's front window. "We loaded extra provisions to use as barter. Lets get as much fuel as we can. It will be days or maybe a week or more before they realize that we are not stupid enough to enter the debris field. We should have plenty of time to get the fuel and lay out our own trap."

******

There was only a little over four kilometres between Killy's and Grant's camp. The only thing that protected them was wave after wave of small rolling knolls. Grant's scouts secretly kept a watch on Killy's men along with the women and earth dwellers. As a scout walked over to him. Grant stood up. "How's our perimeter?"

"I don't think Killy's men know where we are yet. However the others do. We had spotted a woman and a man within gunshot of the camp."

"What are Killy's men doing?"

"Laying more traps for the faceless ones. That narrow road is the only way in or out of the crater. They are digging wheel traps and fortified cannon placements along the top of it to prevent them from using it."

The ringing of metal striking metal rang from Killy's camp. "So what's all that banging?"

"They are taking parts off the burnt beast and attaching them to the other one."

Gazing toward the crater, Grant told the scout, "Maybe we should fortify our position incase they try to turn the machine against us instead of them."

******

Both Grant and Killy had time to collect and haul all the supplies and equipment they needed to take with them. The women and earth dwellers did not. They had plenty of dried meat but not enough water nor the equipment to make it.

They only had two solar water stills. Only one of the women's still survived the exodus. The rest were in need of repair. The other still was the one they stole from the hunters. As they depleted the rainwater, the urine they collected was greater then what the stills could process. Despite the distilled water and the dew they collected each morning, everything drop had to be strictly rationed.

John and Kelsey went directly to Joe's hole as soon as they returned to camp. Using two canes, Tara stood up and joined them. Sitting along the edge, the three of them faced Joe. John turned to Tara and back to Joe. "For the past few days, a four man team showed up at Killy's camp about mid-day with a hand cart full of food, water and supplies. Normally only two return with the cart and two stay behind. For some reason, four left today. One of them was Zack, Killy's new henchman."

"Something must be going on. If we stay here, we will need some supplies." Tara looked at Joe. "We are at least six days from Town. Pulling a cart, probably seven or eight. We could intercept one or maybe even two of them and steal the supplies we need. It could take days before Killy finds out."

Kelsey spoke up, "By that time, we will be gone."

Joe shook his head. "They would find us. We have enough dried meat and Jake is working on the broken stills." He paced a bit before continuing, "We could use some more water to hold us over. Grant's camp is closer to them then ours. We could set it up and implicate them."

Kelsey looked over at where Jose was hidden. "Jose's wounds are clean but she needs a little more time to heal. Your fella can barely stand up and Tara can barely walk. We might be able to hide out for another week. We'll be stronger then."

Joe looked at Tara. "She's right about one thing, we need more time to recuperate."

Tara twisted her lips from side to side. "The problem is, they will also be stronger."

Joe cocked his head. "You are also right. A lot can happen in a week."

******

As the Reapers' ship went slowly up and down the main corridors of the debris field, a man would swim to each mound. Not expecting any resistance, the men were not burdened by armour or any weapons other than their knives. By the time the ship went down the next canal, the men would have searched their assigned mound as they crossed it and be waiting to swim back to the ship.

The ship was in the debris field for a day and a half before one of the previously stranded men saw it. A blast from his musket alerted the ship to their presence. The pair waved their vests above their heads as they ran to the shore to meet it.

After all the weapons, leftover meat and accumulated supplies were loaded on to the ship, the two men shared their tribulations with the others. When they mentioned overhearing that the floating island had gone to a populated town, the crew began to mumble. One of its members yelled out, "So that's why it isn't here!"

The most talkative of the pair spoke up. "Your leaders would have been told. I'm sure of it."

"Unfortunately they kept it to themselves."

The talkative man shook his head. "I only found that out by eavesdropping on Victoria after she had interrogated a prisoner."

The loud man grabbed his shoulders. "Do you know where this town is?"

Grabbing the man's wrists, the talkative man clenched his teeth. "I believe so. I got a good glimpse of the map they were using."

Releasing him, the loud man stood erect and yelled out, "So what are we doing here? Lets find them."

******

The Rainbow Sea looked the same, but as Daniel and Patrick rowed ashore, Daniel sensed that something had changed. The place was deserted. Barrels of refined oil were left outside unguarded. The path leading to the main camp was covered in soot.

Standing on the path, Daniel looked at Patrick. "No one had travelled down this for a day or maybe two. Whatever happened, just happened."

Armed with airguns, the pair walked down the path. Near the edge of the small compound, they climbed the side of a cliff to get a better look. The oil workers were busy packing the carts they had used to haul barrels. Patrick glanced at Daniel. "They are not packing everything. They are only taking what they believe they need."

Spotting some musket barrels sticking out of a cart, Daniel said, "You can't fire one of those off anywhere near this place."

"The carts are pointed inland. Maybe they are being threatened."

"Maybe we should find out who by?"

Daniel climbed down and walked into the compound with his arms above his head. A thin, long bearded man saw him and ran towards the others. After a bunch of loud banter, a tall man with a beard squared off to his chin, walked towards Daniel. "Are you the one that gave us the weird animal in trade?"

"Yes."

The man extended his arm and smiled. "It was delicious. Got any more?"

"Unfortunately no, but we did bring you more food to trade."

The man dropped his smile. "Give us what you can and take what ever you need. It will be nice to start off our journey on a full stomach."

Daniel looked at a couple men packing a cart. "Where are you going?"

"Home. We just got word that it is under attack."

"By who?"

"The cannibals from that damn town."

Daniel thought for a moment. "Your home, it wouldn't be in an old mining complex?"

"How did you know?"

Daniel straightened his spine and smiled. "Because my clan originated from the same place. The Townies have our home under siege. We have been trying to find yours incase we need to evacuate."

The man looked at Daniel and cocked his head. "So we have a common enemy. If the mine is taken, both of our clans are at risk."

Thinking of the divided crew, he slowly walked back to Patrick. A few of the oil workers agreed to come with them to load and unload the ship. The mood on board was tense. They had been through a lot. After the last barrel was loaded onboard, David gave Sarah a hug. "We have no choice. We have to go."

In tears, Sarah answered, "Don't get yourself eaten. I couldn't bare that."

As Mary made her rounds, Daniel told Patrick, "Protect the island. You have got enough fuel on board that you don't have to worry about the sails. Watch out for their big cannon. I don't want to hear that you sunk my ship."

Patrick grasped Daniel's hand with both of his. "I won't." Looking into his eyes, he added, "You know where the island is. Hopefully, you will find a way to get back there."

With a musket and a air rifle each, Mary and David walked beside the cart full of the provisions from the ship. Daniel placed both his long range rifle and air rifle in the cart and cradled his musket in his arms. The square bearded man walked back to meet him. "We welcome your help." After studying their well used knives and guns, he added, "We are just workers. None of us have fought before. Maybe you can teach us a thing or two on our way."

Thinking about the fight ahead of them, Daniel sharply answered, "Gladly, from what I've seen so far, your men may need all the help they can get."

Chapter Twenty - Seven

Zack walked ahead as the others pulled the cart into town. From the balcony, Victoria saw the empty cart. She heard her men question him as he entered the house. By the time he entered her room, she was fuming. "So what has happened? The carts are all coming back empty. I have yet to see or hear any evidence of the slaughter that Killy had promised me."

Holding a rolled up piece of leather behind him, Zack stepped back and squared off his stance. "He has found another target. An entire mine full of gilded meat."

Victoria stood up and took two steps towards him. "So where is this harvest?"

"It is fortified. Killy said that he will need more men to crack it open."

Victoria turned away and looked towards the sea. "Does he have a plan?"

"Yes." Zack handed her the piece of leather. "He even gave me a map detailing his plan of attack. He wanted to make sure you knew what was at stake."

Victoria studied the map. "What are all these lines of small dots and the bigger dots?"

"The big dots are the range of the cannon placements. The smaller ones are the range of the guns placements."

"Why is he so afraid of their guns?"

"They are mechanical contraptions that can rapidly fire one bullet immediately after the other. He doesn't want our men to be mowed down."

Not being able to grasp the destructive power of the centrifuge guns, Victoria gave them little mind. "He is smarter than he looks. He intends to simply blast his way in and dig out the bodies. Any idea how many they are."

Zack shrugged his shoulders. "An entire underground city capable of making self moving armoured vehicles to protect their base. They had three of them. We already took out two of them."

With a smirk, Victoria chuckled, "They couldn't have been that well made."

"We dug trenches for their wheels to fall into. With the wheels unable to touch the ground the mechanical beasts couldn't move."

Victoria put her hands on her hips and barked out, "So what does he need from me?"

"He needs more cannons and enough skilled men to operate

them."

Victoria faced the balcony. Beyond it lay the remains of her floating island. "As long as he doesn't see my men as worthless sacs of meat."

Zack rocked his head back and forth. "Not at all. He also needs as many men as he can get to cause a diversion. He wants to be able to advance his cannons with the least casualties as possible. He thought that maybe some of your men could help spearhead the more feeble town folk in that endeavour."

"As long as they are his men being slaughtered and not mine."

Along with supplies, every cannon in town was readied for the trek. As the long column began to depart, a lookout mounted on the surviving section of the floating island blew a horn. Victoria noticed the large catamaran approach the harbour. "Halt everything."

It took a few hours for the ship to reach the town. With all the debris from the floating island scattered about, it had to anchor off shore. Victoria climbed aboard the Flesh Star and went out to meet it. Once lashed together, Victoria climbed onboard the catamaran and looked around at all the unfinished repairs. "This was once my prized vessel. What happened to it?"

The loud man spoke up. "It was shot up and went aground."

Nick climbed onboard behind her. The man stared at him. "Who's he?"

Victoria glanced back, "The man that shot up my ship." Seeing the confused man raising his rifle, she stuck out her hand. "Ease up. He is now an ally."

Victoria looked at the two ships and thought of the island. She finally remembered the last time she saw the man. As if someone slapped her face, she bellowed out, "You were on the island. What happened?"

The man began to stutter. "I-I-I-I don't really know. Some strange men appeared and everything fell apart."

"How many?"

The man's face turned pale. "Just a few, but they got the Islanders to join them."

Victoria looked at Nick. "Do you know who they were?"

"From what I just heard, I think one of them was my old captain." Nick grinned as he shook his head. "He is the only person I know of that would disregard the odds, attack, and walk away without a scratch." Turning to the man, Nick asked, "Was he a tall, red haired brute that fought like he was bulletproof?"

"That sounds like the one that tossed the men off the balcony."

Victoria pulled out her knife as she turned and faced the man. "So you let a handful of men steal the island away from us?"

With the blade of her knife pressed against his throat, the man muttered, "Our defences weren't prepared for any attack."

Victoria flicked her wrist and sliced through the man's throat. As the man fell clutching his throat, she said, "I don't need spineless men, I need warriors. Men that can fight." Looking around the vessel she noticed that most of the men appeared sheepish. "You are not warriors. You are nothing but a bunch of fattened guards."

Back on shore Victoria went through her ranks and personally selected the men she wanted to take with her. She left orders that the men that had brought the catamaran to town were to help pull the carts. As her men emptied the town, she watched them leave from the bow of the catamaran. With the Flesh Star trailing her, she walked into the wheelhouse and charted a course back to the island.

******

Onboard the New Hope, Patrick looked at his skeleton crew. Simon and Sarah were both still recovering, and Roger's leg made him a cripple. "If we encounter the Reapers, we'll need a pilot, a lookout, a boiler operator plus a gunner, someone who is capable of both firing and reloading the cannons."

Roger looked at him. "If it wasn't for this leg, I would be your man."

"But your leg is broken. In a battle, you can't move around as quickly as we will need you to."

"So I'm to be stuck up that pole?"

Patrick looked at him. "No, it means I'll have to prop you up somehow and teach you to steer this ship. I'm the only one here fit enough to man the cannons."

Sarah smiled at him, "So you still intend to protect the island?"

"We are outcasts. We have nowhere else to go."

******

Kelsey and John led the raid. Jacob and two women cautiously followed about a dozen metres behind them. While sneaking around Grant's encampment they planned their return path. They needed for any trail that they left behind to implicate Grant's men. The route the carts took was marked by a set of deep gouges.

It was mid-morning when they spotted the empty cart returning to town. With their rifles slung over their shoulders, the two scrawny, sweaty men used both hands to grip the crossbar attached to the cart's tongue.

Kelsey and one of the women popped out from under their earth covered blankets in front of them. The men dropped the tongue and went for their rifles. The momentum of the cart kept rolling it forward. Both men were forced to hop to the sides. Before the two men could shoulder their rifles, the others leaped out from behind some knolls and rushed them. John took three large steps and hacked through one man's windpipe while Jacob's knife chopped through the other man's jaw. He used his dagger to finish the man off.

Kelsey walked over and rolled one of them over. The pockmarks on his face and hands lead her to one conclusion. "They are not even fit to eat."

As a woman was about to cut the genitals off the other man, Kelsey sharply said, "Stop, we don't want anyone to advertize who did this."

John and Jacob began pushing the cart along the path. After spotting the supplied laden cart, they pulled the cart over to the side to let it pass. As the armed men that were walking ahead of the cart approached them, they turned away and reached for some water. One of them piped up, "Hey, do I know you?"

Seeing the men in front of them raise their rifles, the two pushing the cart pulled back on the crossbar and tried to stop it. Kelsey jumped up from the cart. As the wind caught the tarp and flung it to the side, she thrust the bayonet on her rifle into the nearest man's chest. The man behind him turned his rifle on her. Getting a glimpse of the bloodthirsty women rushing the unarmed men pulling the cart, he stepped back. He knew that he would only have one shot.

Seeing John and Jacob pulling air rifles out of the cart, the man began to walk backward. He knew that as long as his musket remained loaded, they won't rush him.

The women hacked the hands and heads off the men pulling the cart. As all five of them began to fan around the last man, his steps got faster. Unable to see behind him, he tripped over a rock. His gun accidentally went off. Jacob rush forward and put two slugs into the side of the man's skull.

******

The gun shot was faintly heard by both Grant's and Killy's scouting parties. Killy's men were the closest and reached the site first. Most of the raiding party's footprints had been brushed away. The cart with the remains of the two butchered men had been left behind.

It was harder to conceal the imprints of the loaded cart. Two of Killy's men trailed it until it took a ninety degree turn. Seeing where it was heading, they went back to tell the others.

All four of Grant's scouts watched them from a distance. As Killy's men pulled the cart along the path, one of Grant's scouts peered through his binoculars and saw a butchered man's genitals. "The earth dwellers don't eat our meat and the women are usually a lot more aggressive. I think we are being setup."

******

Before getting within gunshot of Grant's encampment Jacob

pulled the four dead bodies off the cart. Kelsey saw him and angrily walked towards him. Before she could speak, Jacob told her, "All they are is extra weight. We are not going to eat them."

Kelsey scrunched her lips and shook her head. "A dead body is more than just meat. You are throwing away fat for fuel, plus leather, tendons and bones."

John walked over to the three women. "Cover them in dirt and leave a marker. Right now, we don't have the time nor energy to haul them back to camp."

******

On the way back to the encampment, Grant's scouts stumbled upon the crude rock marker. Studying the tracks, one of them said, "The tracks may be an hour or two old."

While two returned to camp, the other two continued to follow the tracks. They had almost encircled the encampment before they finally spotted the wheelless cart.

To lower their profile, the raiding party had removed the wheels and tied on runners. Pulling the cart on their hands and knees had slowed them down.

One of Grant's scouts shot at the cart. His men rushed to see what was going on. As more shots were fired, Grant rushed to scene.

Outnumbered, Jacob told them to leave the cart. Kelsy nodded and agreed. As they snuck back to their camp, she told one of the women, "It served its main purpose."

Seeing the abandoned cart Grant ordered a cease fire. While gazing at the men around him, he said, "Those thieves are not a threat to us, Killy is. They just made sure that we were trapped in the middle."

******

After seeing the raiding party abandon the cart, two of Killy's scouts raced back to camp. Killy heard they were returning and went to the edge of the camp in order to meet them. A scout saw him and ran over to him. Out of breath, he was semi-buckled over as he forced out, "It was the women. It wasn't Grant's men. We saw a couple of them as they ran away."

Killy grinned and rolled his head. "So the women are here too." After releasing a couple involuntary smirks, he said. "By the time this is over, we will have the harvest of a life time."

The scout asked, "What do you want us to do?"

Killy looked at him. "Nothing, just keep me informed of what is going on."

"Nothing?"

A couple more shots echoed through the field of knolls. Killy looked towards the commotion. "Let them kill each other. That will mean less rifles for us to face."

******

Simon yelled down from the crows nest, "I've spotted something about fifty degrees off the port side. It looks like the top mast of the Flesh Star."

Patrick yelled back, "Do you think they see us?"

"No."

Patrick faced the pilothouse and bellowed out, "Nick doesn't know about our big gun."

As Roger turned the ship towards the Flesh Star, he muttered, "Their ship will be taking on water before we are even in range of their cannons."

Simon heard what sounded like a musket shot just before the starboard side of the ship was lifted out of the water. The shell's massive plume drenched Simon. As she looked around, she barely made out the mast on the low riding catamaran. She wrapped her arms around the mast and tightly held onto it as the side hull of the ship splashed back into the water.

Everyone onboard knew that even without the sails, they couldn't hide the ship's masts. Patrick ran into the pilothouse. With one leg straddled across a tall stool, Roger looked at him. "We are heading straight at them. We should be in firing range in a few minutes."

"You have to start weaving. You can't be predictable. Use my stone if you have to figure out which way to turn next." Patrick passed him a flat stone with an 'X' marked on one side. "We normally used the 'X' for port."

With the wind blowing her hair across her face, Victoria stood next to the mast and used the lookout's extended arm as a guide. As the Flesh Star ploughed through the waves towards the dodging New Hope, the large catamaran twirled back and forth positioning its large air cannon for its next shot.

With the Flesh Star heading straight at them, Roger turned the ship to face them. Patrick adjusted the elevation of the air cannon and fire a round. It landed under its bow and lifted the front of the ship over an oncoming wave. As it twisted to the side, the lookout fell to the deck and rolled to the railing. By the time Patrick could reload the Flesh Star had veered off to starboard side. Patrick ran over to the ship's side cannons and took off the oiled tarps that protected the powder from getting wet. Seeing that the Flesh Star was out of range, he put the tarps back on.

A large cannonball narrowly missed the air tanks and collided with the sloped cabin. The impact tore off the cabin's door and pushed the entire ship to the side. Roger shook his head in disbelief. Twirling the wheel, he aimed the ship directly at the catamaran.

Patrick ran to the air cannon, switched to his reserve tank and cranked its barrel as high as he could. The blast pushed the front of the ship into the water and drenched the bow. As water poured into the open cabin, all eyes were on the cannonball. It was a miss. The catamaran had swerved to its port side.

With the cannon on the catamaran pointing away from them, Roger headed straight for it. Seeing its air cannon being lowered, he swung the steering wheel to starboard and narrowly avoided being hit. The port side was lifted out of the water. Patrick grabbed a hold of an airline and pulled himself back onto the seat of the airpump.

Patrick pedalled air into the cannon's primary tank as fast as he could. As soon as the pressure button popped out, he raised his hand. This told Roger that he was ready. As the catamaran twisted and tried to readjust its sights Roger used a large wave to help flip the New Hope towards it.

Patrick was ready and quickly pulled the lever to fire another cannonball. While it arched high into the air, he ran to the port side and tossed the tarps off the cannons. It was a hit. The cannonball punched a hole into the catamaran's starboard deck.

They were close enough to see the men repositioning a small cannon. It fired and glanced off the New Hope's hull, leaving behind a metre long gash a half metre above the waterline. Patrick fired the first cannon and ran to the second. Instead of aiming at the men huddled around an overturned cannon, he took aim at the air tanks. With musket balls pinging off the hull, he fired and ran for cover. The air tanks exploded as the New Hope sailed passed the catamaran.

The Flesh Star reappeared off to their starboard side. As its forward cannons fired, Roger swerved to avoid them. He yelled down to the engine room, "Put on some smoke."

Sarah flipped a few levers and turned a couple valves. Roger continued to weave as black smoke began to bellow out of the smokestack. A huge thick cloud formed in their wake leaving nothing for Nick's men to aim at.

It took Patrick three quarters of an hour to pump up the air tanks and reload the cannons. After he caught his breath, he walked to the pilothouse. "They are ready."

Sarah turned off the black goo, flushed the lines and piped the refined fuel into the boiler. By the time the Flesh Star's new lookout noticed them off to the side, the New Hope's air cannon was pointed directly at them.

Still partially covered by the evaporating black cloud, Simon told Patrick when to fire. The cannonball blew a hole through the black cloud. The Flesh Star's new lookout saw both it and the New Hope at the same time. The ball punched a hole near the waterline of the Flesh

Star's port hull. Simon watch the men scramble out of the hull. As the Flesh Star began to spin in a circle, Patrick finished reloading another round.

Without a clear target, he simply aimed at the ship and fired. The cannonball glanced off the back of the pilothouse and hit the gearbox that controlled the rudders. Not knowing the damage that was inflicted, the New hope turned away.

Knowing that they had the largest working cannon gave the crew of New Hope some relief. While taking on water from the gash in the side hull and the twisted open cabin, Patrick began pumping water.

As the wind eased and the waves settled down, Roger kept an eye out for the two damaged ships. Even without the large air cannon, they were a threat. Knowing that there was little he could do about the damage to the cabin, Patrick spent his time thinking about how to fix the gash in the side hull.

After melting the edge of a plastic container over a strip of leather doused in oil, Patrick caved it in. He did the same thing to the other upper edge and created a long semi-solid 'T' shaped piece of plastic. After making several more, Patrick melted the ends together to extend its overall length. Harnessing himself to the railing, he climbed over the side and placed the crude plastic plug against the gash. Using his knife, he trimmed off some of the extended plastic until the plug fit into the hole.

With the harness around his torso, Patrick used his feet to stamp the plastic into place. Swinging from the side of the hull, he pounded it in as far as he could. While holding it in place, Simon and Sarah used oil lamps to heat both the steel and plastic. Sarah worked on the lower edge while Simon did the upper. The melted plastic easily curled around the lower edge of the bent steel. Simon had to gently blow on the flame to secure the upper edge. Outside, as the plastic melted, Patrick's weight helped push the section they were working on tightly against the side of the hull. After both the plastic and steel cooled off, they crammed oil soaked leather into the cracks to make it as water tight as they possibly could.

After it was done the three of them rested against the large cannon. Simon turned to Patrick. "What now?"

"Now we find out what condition the other ships are in."

Chapter Twenty - Eight

Grant looked around his camp and noticed a bunch of his men holding their guts and a few others curled up into balls. "What's going on?"

A man reached up to grab his hand. "The women must have poisoned the water in the cart."

With almost half his men sick, Grant returned to his hole and talked to a few of his scouts. "The poison the women use is designed to kill quickly. The fact that the men are not dead means it was diluted beyond its normal use. We don't know how long it will take for the men to either recover, or die."

A scout peered out of the hole and scratched his head. "What can we do? Killy has us boxed in."

"Pretend nothing is wrong. They don't know that we drank the water. If either side knows that we are vulnerable, they might attack."

******

That night, a half dozen metres from the road's exit on the rim of the crater, a small knoll seemed to slowly implode. A periscope appeared. Standing on the ladder of an old air duct, a miner gazed through a series of mirrors and tempered glass. Dark rain clouds rolled in and blocked out most of the moonlight. Only a handful of stars were strong enough to penetrate them. "It's clear."

Three men climbed out. Piece by piece, men hauled up the arched shaped sections of a fake knoll. The distant, rumbling thunder masked any noise they made. It was the lightning bolts that scared them. As they lit up the night sky behind them, the silhouetted men were easy targets.

The team of miners secured all the bent semi triangular pieces of the fake hinged knoll in place with heavy pins, nuts and bolts. After closing it a pair left to scout the area. Inside, hidden from view another group hauled long sections of pipe up the ladder and welded them together. When the welders retreated into the tunnels, a third team of men passed various pieces of a centrifuge gun up the ladder. As the man finished assembling the gun, the rest of his team climbed down into the tunnels.

******

As the storm got closer, Jacob could barely hear the muffled moans coming from Grant's encampment. Using a cane, Jose walked up behind him. "I'm glad the rain held off long enough for them to ingest some of the poison."

Jacob turned around to face her. "What are you doing here? Shouldn't you be in bed?"

Jose gave him a sour look. "It doesn't take two arms or two legs to listen and hear. I can take a turn on watch and give the others a rest."

As Jacob retired, the sharp pains that kept Jose awake also numbed her senses. The approaching storm further concealed the sounds the inquisitive scouts made, sounds that she normally would have easily heard.

The tug of a trip wire woke Kelsey. She untied the thin leather cord from her wrist and rushed to the perimeter. Jose saw her. "What's up, it's not your turn yet?"

Kelsey grabbed her wrist and put her index finger across her lips. Without another word said, the pair studied the terrain around them. A bolt of lightning partially lit up the sky. Jose got a glimpse of a man's foot protruding from the side of a knoll. She reached down, grabbed a braided leather cord and gave it a tug. It dislodged a pole that held up a small platform filled with metal utensils. The calamity was almost muted by the sound of rolling thunder as the storm crept closer.

Kelsey caught a glimpse of the top of the scout's head and fired. It vanished before the bullet got there. Behind her, the entire camp was scrambling for their weapons. Without a drop of blood spilled, the inquisitive scouts retreated.

Kelsey looked at Joe. "Maybe the poison didn't work as well as we planned?"

Joe grinned and said, "It probably did its job. Grant knows that a good offence is a good defence. He is trying to keep us on our toes."

******

As the rain started, Killy crawled out of his hole and looked around. Everyone was scrambling to set up anything they could to collect rainwater. He took a stroll around the camp's perimeter and checked their defences. The rain quickly intensified. Raising his arms in the air, he yelled above the thunder, "This is exactly what we need!"

A call to arms rolled through the camp. Amidst the thunder, lightning, and pouring rain, his men climbed out of their trenches and advanced toward Grant's encampment. From inside the refurbished metal beast, Killy led the way.

Grant's men saw the light from a lightning bolt reflect off the beast as it began circling around their outer trenches. While the beast made its way around the wheel traps, Killy's men began encircling the camp. Staying out of gun shot they waited for the beast to do what it was designed for.

Grant ordered the men manning the cannons to fire at will. A cannonball from the nearest cannon glanced off the side of the beast. A cannon firing from the far side of the camp missed by several metres.

Pushing the beast to its limit, Killy raced to a gap behind several trenches. Grant's men were ordered not to waste any bullets on it. As the hatch opened and the gunner climbed out, two of Grant's scouts crawled out of the nearby trenches and climbed onto its sides. Unable to see them, as the men following them shot at the clinging attackers, the gunner turned the gun around and mistakenly fired at them. Seeing several of their comrades collapse in agony, the rest retreated.

Realizing his mistake, the frazzled gunner redirected his fire at the nearest cannon placement. As steel balls rang off the cannon, a scout reached over the spinning flywheel and slashed the gunner's throat. The second scout climbed behind the gunner and wrapped his knife around the man's neck. Grabbing the back of his knife with his other hand, he quickly yanked it back. With the blade wedged behind the man's jaw, the scout pulled him out of the beast and rolled his flailing body onto the ground.

Killy looked up and saw the scout. By the time he pulled out his pistol, it was to late. The scout had slammed down the hatch.

The other scout stuffed a hunk of leather into the exhaust and jammed it in place with the muzzle of his musket. As smoke began seeping out of every crack, they could hear Killy coughing inside.

As his lips pressed against the driver's narrow view hole, Grant walked over, raised his pistol and fired. Looking up at the scout sitting on the hatch, he said, "Drag his carcass out of there and put him on display. I want everyone to know he is dead and I am still the mayor."

Seeing Grant's men surround the stalled beast, Killy's men lost their fervour and slunk away.

******

It was mid-morning before the rain finally stopped. Joe and Jacob went to the trench Tara was in. Despite all the rain, her elevated stretcher kept her out of the mud. Looking up at them, she said, "What happened last night?"

"Everything." Jacob rocked his head back and forth, while adding, "Grant's men raided our camp. Then Killy's men raided his. Somehow, Grant came out on top. He captured the metal beast Killy had repaired and has taken over."

Tara lowered her head. "So Killy must be dead."

"His skinned body is stretched between two poles beside the cart path leading into the townies' camp. I guess Grant wants everyone to know who is in command."

Tara looked up at them. "Why are we still here? After poisoning his men, I thought he would be out for revenge."

"Almost everyone has been packed up." Joe stood up and looked around. "Kelsey and John have already found another place for us to hide until the fighting is over."

Tara straighten her arms to help her sit up. "What about the man with the bandaged head?"

Joe looked back at her. "He's being carried there as we speak."

Tara's face turned red. "Why am I the last know all this?"

"Because Kelsey wasn't sure that you would like our decision."

******

At noon, a column of Reapers and Townies cautiously pulled cannons and carts past Killy's hoisted remains. As they saw his mostly skeletal remains they slowed to a crawl. His shot face was stitched up and left mostly intact. Stretched between two poles, the butchers had carefully left only enough flesh behind to hold the bones in place.

Surrounded by the men that had remained loyal to him, Grant came out to meet them wearing Killy's skin as a robe. The blackened metal beast was only a few dozen metres away. With a plume of smoke rising from its stack, its gunner was ready in case of trouble. The most decorated Reaper came over to him and nodded his head towards the machine. "What's that?"

"A mobile death machine."

The man thought for a moment. "It can't be that good. You captured it."

"Everything has its flaws." Grant put on a devilish smile and added, "Now that I'm aware of all of its faults, I'm not going to be stupid enough to overlook them."

"You never opened fire on us so you are obviously smart. Much smarter than the man you are wearing." The Reaper gazed at his men and looked back at Grant and smiled. "So what are your plans?"

"The mine." Grant grinned from ear to ear. "But my plan is much better then anything Killy could have ever dreamt of."

******

Roger zig-zagged the New Hope against the prevailing wind and returned to where they last saw the other ships. Simon spotted and pointed to the Flesh Star's tilted mast. "The Flesh Star has barely moved. It looks like it's sinking."

Patrick looked up at her and smiled. "What about the catamaran?"

"It's nowhere in sight."

The Flesh Star's slanted deck made it impossible to fire a cannon. Knowing this, Patrick lowered Simon from the crow's nest and began cranking up the sails. "We don't need the wind whipping us about when we try to board them."

As Roger approach the Flesh Star's semi-submerged port side, a few musket balls pinged off the ship's bow. Patrick held his fire. With its propellers disengaged, Roger turned the ship and slid sideways towards the Flesh Star. Facing the New Hope's side cannons, the men scrambled to the starboard railings. Upon seeing Patrick, some of the men placed their rifles at their feet while others slung them over their shoulders.

Patrick knew most of them, while others looked only vaguely familiar. The ten frail men used the railing to hold themselves up. A scrawny salt and pepper haired man waddled forward. Slipping on the slanted deck, he caught the port side railing and pulled himself up. "You know us. We hold no grudge against you."

Patrick pointed the barrel of his rifle towards Simon. "What about her?"

The man looked at Simon. "A lot has happened between now and then." Looking back at the line of men, he added, "I talk for all of us. We understand why you did what you did. We have no more desires of her."

Patrick looked at the men's parched lips. "So the Reaper Queen chained the best of you to the pedals and left the rest behind to die?"

"She said that we weren't worth the effort it would take to turn us into soup."

Patrick pointed the muzzle of his rifle at the two remaining cannons. "Why did she leave them behind?"

"She said she didn't have any more room on deck for them. She took the other six along with all the powder and cannon balls. All we have is what's loaded inside them along with our muskets."

Sarah tossed a rope over the side. One by one the men climbed onto the New Hope. After they were disarmed, Simon handed them a container of soup and escorted them to the hatches leading to the pedalling chambers. With five men secured in each chamber, Patrick jumped onto the deck of the Flesh Star.

The cabins and hulls had been ransacked. There was not a morsel of food or drop of clean water anywhere. As he was about to climb back onboard the New Hope he heard a 'Thump' behind him.

He slid back down the rope and waited. A half a minute past before he heard another 'Thump'.

"It seemed to be coming from the pilothouse. Knowing that he had already checked it, he tried to not make a sound as he crept toward it. Peeking through the window he saw the hatch leading to the engine room start to rise. Under his breath, he said, "He must've hid in one of the empty barrels."

After sneaking around to the door, he ducked out of sight and waited. Twenty minutes passed before he heard something slide against the wall. Darting through the door, he saw Nick peering out the window.

As Nick turned to face him, Patrick slammed the butt of his rifle into his side. Nick squeezed the trigger of his pistol. The ball ricocheted off the ceiling and out the door. Patrick rammed the barrel of his rifle across Nick's throat. "You traitor."

Nick tried to pull it away. Patrick asserted more pressure. As

Nick collapsed, Patrick whacked the butt of his rifle against the side of his head.

With his rifle slung over his shoulder, Patrick grabbed Nick's feet and dragged him over to the rope dangling from the New Hope's railing. After tying Nick's feet to the rope, he climbed onboard and pulled the lifeless man onto the deck.

With Nick's arms lashed to the railing Patrick splashed salt water over his face. The stinging sensation of the salt entering the bloody gash on the side of his head woke him. While screaming in pain, he looked at Patrick. "What do you want from me. Why don't you just get on with it." Seeing that he was still dressed, he asked. "You intend to butcher me don't you?"

Patrick bent down and stared into his eyes. "That depends on the answers you give me."

Nick nervously shifted his jaw back and forth. "You mean if you like what I tell you?"

"No, I mean if I catch you lying to me, I'll use your skin to keep my cannons dry."

Nick saw Roger's grinning face peering out of the pilothouse. He knew what Killy was capable of, and his son was always there watching. "Keep him away from me and I'll tell you everything I know."

"What happened in town?" Before Nick could say a word, Patrick barked out, "And I mean every detail." Glaring into his eyes, he added, "I'll warn you, I already know enough to tell if you are lying."

Sarah and Simon sat on the deck behind Patrick as Nick recalled both the Reapers' downfall and their comeback under Killy. Using a crutch, Roger came out of the pilothouse and leaned against the front of it. "He would never do that."

Nick glared at him. "He did."

Patrick looked up at the sky. "Killy was always looking out for himself." Turning to Roger, he said, "It fits. It is most likely the truth."

Nick studied everyone's reaction before he said another word. "Killy was still out hunting Grant and his men when word came back about them finding another gilded harvest. Apparently, both Grant and the old mayor knew about them but didn't tell anyone." Everyone was silent as Nick watched Patrick nod. "Did you know about them?"

"I had heard some rumours. As I said, I know if you're lying to me."

"Then you know that Victoria is heading back to the island that you helped liberate."

Sarah drew her knife and limped forward. "She is planning to butcher them all this time isn't she?"

Seeing the hatred in her eyes, Nick's face turned white. "No, she said she still needed them."

Sarah raised the knife above her head and screamed out, "Liar!"

Patrick tried to grab her arm. As a sharp pain ran up Sarah's bad leg, her arm dropped. Her knife sliced diagonally across Nick's chest. The cut was only deep enough to etch groves into his ribs. Patrick glared at her. "He may still be of use to us."

Simon walked over and stared at the blood seeping out of Nick's wound. "I don't think so. From here on, all he is going to tell us is what we want to hear. He is nothing but a con. He always had been and always will be." Turning to Patrick, she added, "Look what he did to you."

Nick looked at Patrick, "You said if I told you the truth that I would live."

As the blood poured out of Nick's wound, Patrick glanced at the two women. "They don't trust you and neither do I."

Roger hobbled over and sat down next to Nick. "Your men are no good to us the way they are. They need to eat."

Nick shook his head. "But, but..."

"But nothing." Roger gave Patrick a quick glance. "It was your fault that they were left to starve. Now you are going to fix it."

Giving Patrick no time to even respond, Roger rammed his knife through Nick's jaw and twisted it up into his brain. "A person should never second guess their decisions."

Sarah watched as Patrick and Roger methodically stripped, skinned, hacked and sliced Nick's flesh into thin strips. Roger took one look at his liver, "He was a bottom eater. His meat is garbage."

Patrick looked at the discoloured blotches in Nick's liver. "But it should be able to keep those men alive for a while longer." Turning towards Roger, he added, "Killy must have taught you that nothing buys loyalty better than a full stomach."

Sarah went over and took a closer look at Nick's dismembered corpse. Patrick handed her a large handful of sliced meat. "Give this meat to the men in the tubes."

She briefly stared at the meat before saying, "Is this all they get? Those men are starving."

"For now. I don't want to make them sick. Their guts have shrunk. Tomorrow, their stomachs might be able to accept a lot more."

Simon watch the Flesh Star drift away. "What about their ship?"

Patrick looked at her. "We don't have the time to worry about it."

Not looking away from the ship, Simon said, "As long as it has two good hulls, it will stay afloat. I guess we could come back for it later."

Chapter Twenty - Nine

With his men divided into groups, Grant ordered the town dregs down the narrow road into the crater. While his scouts checked for wheel traps, he carefully manoeuvred the metal beast around the trenches. Half of his loyal followers walked behind him. The rest, still recovering from the poison, stayed behind.

The mine's entrance was too far from the rim for its cannons to be of any use. Afraid the wheels on the cannons would be to hard to control, the Reapers dragged them down the path on sleds. Behind them, the rest of the Townies crowded around the mouth of the roadway. Eric stayed with the rest of Grant's men to make sure nobody snuck away. Grant needed everyone to play their part in his plan.

******

From the far side of the crater, Daniel watched the procession through his binoculars. Putting them down, he waved for the others to continue their trek. They reached a bunch of recently dug holes and trenches. As they walked through the abandoned camp they found nothing to indicate whose it was.

Behind a knoll on the far side of the camp, Mary spotted a piece of parchment tied to a rock. She untied the knot and handed the note to Daniel. After glancing at it, he gazed towards the crater.

Mary tugged on his sleeve. "I can't read it. What does it say."

Daniel bit his bottom lip and studied the note. "I'm not absolutely sure. It is not very specific. It is obvious that the others didn't read it. That means that they could be safe, taken prisoner or maybe dead."

As the square bearded oil worker walked by him, he glimpsed at the note. "To bad they didn't get it."

Daniel caught up with him and asked, "Do you understand what it says?"

"Sure." Without slowing his pace, he told him, "It says, it doesn't matter who they are, their actions will determine if they live or die. Now lets step up the pace."

"I still don't understand what it is trying to say."

The worker glared at him. "The miners were asking for their help. But, before anyone joins their ranks, they wanted to know if they were willing to fight for it. Sometimes gaining respect and trust can be costly."

As they passed by Grant's abandoned encampment, David went over to investigate it. Daniel didn't see him go. His attention was on a reluctant group of Townies that were lingering near the rim of the crater.

******

From the top of his beast, Grant watched the Reapers reattach the wheels to the cannons. At the bottom of the crater, his men helped orchestrate the way the cannons and men were to be lined up. The dregs were forced to the front to protect the Reapers.

Grant saw the line of men wandering down the narrow road. At the top, he could see a reluctant cluster lingering behind. Knowing that they outnumbered his men, he took mental note of where everyone was.

The gate leading into the mine's entrance opened up and a metal beast rolled out. Beside it, were a couple dozen armed men covered in fabric from head to toe. They ran behind a chest high wall of rocks. The beast rolled to a stop in front of it.

The dregs slowly advanced. Behind them, the Reapers hauled the cannons and ammo carts. They knew that if they could capture the wall, it would make a great placement for the cannons to fire behind. Stopping within cannon range of the wall, they dug ditches and backstops to hold the wheels in place. Once content, the Reapers looked at the scorched beast for a signal from Grant.

The rest of the Reapers waited in reserve near the bottom of the road, and main body of Townies waited on the path above them. Grant parked the beast behind the cannons. Sitting on top next to the centrifuge gun, he yelled out, "Charge!" With bayonets fastened to their rifles, the dregs ran forward. "Fire!"

Cannon balls shot over the dregs as they ran towards the rock wall. Each cannon ball strike added to the growing cloud of dust in front of them. Plumes of smoke floated above the line the cannons. Grant clenched his teeth and gripped the trigger of the centrifuge. As the wheels of the beast began to turn, he squeezed the trigger.

An almost continuous stream of steel balls tore through the artillery men at close range. Grant's loyal men ran along the far side of the beast. As it rolled towards the next cannon, they attacked and hacked apart the bewildered and wounded Reapers behind it.

With the smoke drifting away from one end of the line. The Reapers close to the bottom of the roadway saw what was happening. Irrate, they began to fire at Grant's beast along with his men. Grant's driver adjusted the fuel and a heavy, black cloud crept over the battlefield.

******

Above the crater, Grant's men began to fall back. Confused Townies began to retreat up the road. With a 'Bang', and a puff of smoke, the artificial knoll burst open like a blooming flower. The faceless man operating the centrifuge began shooting a continuous stream of steel balls into the cluster of men.

Grant's men crawled into the trenches and opened fire on the

Townies. "Remember what Grant said, we can't let any of them escape."

******

The square bearded oil worker raced towards the shooting. David saw the others running and leaped over a trench. His foot slipped. As he slid to the bottom, his foot landed on something hard. Jacob saw him and yelled out, "Get off my rifle."

Jacob pulled his earth encrusted head out of the wall and tossed off his dirt covered blanket. "David, is that really you?"

David looked up and down the trench as more muddy faces suddenly appeared. John and Kelsey hopped out of another hole and ran to see what had happen. Seeing Daniel, Mary and the oil workers running towards the gunfire, John cried out, "What's going on?"

Confused, David didn't know which way to look. "The mine is under attack. If we don't save it, we may not have anyplace else to go."

Tara pulled the tarp away from her face. "We are grossly outnumbered. How can we help?"

The square bearded oil worker yelled out. "By keeping them pinned to the road leading down the crater. That will limit the number we have to contend with at any given time."

Joe stood up and walked over to David. "The miners can defend the mine. The problem is that their skin can't take any sunlight. They will need our help with anything in the open."

******

The Townies rolled dead bodies on top of each other and used them to shoot behind. Several more picked up the bodies and used them as shields as they ran towards the trenches.

As the centrifuge gunner was shot, Joe watched the oil workers duck behind knolls and fire on the Townies that were rushing the gun placement. "Grab your weapons. The stranger's right. If we hurry, we can keep them penned up on that road. We might have a chance."

Jose spoke up, "I guess It's better than hiding for the rest of our lives."

Hunched over, they ran toward the road entrance. Using her rifle as a cane, Jose trailed behind them. As the Townies rushed the converted air shaft, they were fired upon by both Grant's men and the oil workers. Daniel and Mary snuck over to look into the crater. Daniel couldn't believe what he was seeing. "What is going on?"

A Townie grabbed the controls of the centrifuge gun. He could hear the clinging of a few steel balls as they entered it, but it was slowing down. The balls barely had enough speed to exit the gun. He pulled out his pistol and used the opening like a fox hole. From somewhere below, a bullet ripped through the flesh on his legs. As he tried to crawl out, the square bearded oil worker shot him in the back.

******

Seeing the blackened metal beast obliterate their ranks as it rolled behind the line of cannons, the artillery men stopped firing. With the cannons planted in the ground, they were hard to move. Instead, the Reapers used them as cover and reached for their rifles.

Without the protection of the cannons, the dregs layed flat on the ground. The miners' beast sprayed the area in front of it with steel balls. The masked miners walked behind it and checked the bodies. As the miners approached the seemingly dead bodies, several dregs rolled away and used their bayonets to cut open the miners suits. Afraid of the sunlight more than them, the miners retreated. Without the protection of a ground force the beast was put in reverse. As it retreated towards the gate, it fired on anything that moved.

As several dregs tried to climb onto the beast the gunner stopped firing. Slashing his knife in every direction, he tried to hold them off. A handful of armed men wearing no protective headgear rushed out of the mine, hopped over the wall and ran to the gunner's aid. One of them shot a man as he tried to reach over the flywheel of the beast. Collapsing onto the flywheel, the man was spun around and thrown over the side. His leg struck another man's face and knocked him off the beast. The others jumped off and ran for cover.

Using long, curved knives, they chopped the heads off any dreg they saw lying on the ground. Confident that everyone behind them was dead they slowly treaded forward. Their courage spurred the miners back into action. As they joined the advance, the dregs got up and ran back towards the line of cannons. Seeing them flee, the beast's gunner mowed them down.

On the side of the crater the Townies watched with disbelief. A few of them cried out, "Has Grant gone mad?" Pushing their way up the narrow road, some of them slipped over the side and tumbled to the bottom.

Above, even as the women and earth dwellers joined up with the oil workers, the flood of escapees outnumbered the combined firepower of the various groups.

Below, both the miners on foot and Grant's men converged on the remaining artillery men. The two beasts turned their attention to the advancing Reapers. As they both opened fire, the Reapers quickly discovered that they had nowhere to hide. They had no choice but to retreat.

The ferocity of the beasts' guns caused the Reapers to push their way up the narrow road on the side of the crater. Sticking to the wall of the crater, they shoved several Townies over the side as they elbowed their way up the road.

With the two metal beasts spraying steel balls back and forth in front of them, the bewildered men at the bottom had no chance of survival. The men protecting the machines made brutally fast and messy work of the dead and wounded.

Seeing the stabbed and hacked apart bodies, the men on the road shot at the butchers instead of the machines. While several of their bullets bounced off the metal beasts, a few hit their target. By the time the machines reached the bottom of the road, their ammunition hoppers had to be refilled. While the beasts stood idle, Grant's men tried to lay down as much cover fire as they could. Behind them, the miners faced a rash of gunfire as they climbed onto the beasts. Several were shot, but only one fatally.

As the machines began their slow ascent up the road, their width gave little room for anyone to pass. Their wheels ground apart the dead and wounded bodies. The men trailing them had little left to do.

On top of the crater, the Townies used the wheel traps to hide in. The over flow crawled through the field of dead bodies towards the encampment. Outnumbered, Grant's men were forced to fall back. Eric yelled out, "We can't let them escape."

A scrawny man looked at the seasoned scout, "What if we can't stop them?"

Eric gave him a glaring look. "Would you rather die in battle or starve to death?"

******

As the fighting intensified, the scattered line took the brunt of the Townies' fire. Half of the men and a third of the women were bleeding. Most had multiple scrapes and flesh wounds. Gloria tried to bandage them the best she could, some while they were still shooting. Behind them, Jose, Tara and the head injured man helped load rifles, pump up air canisters and anything else they could do to help.

Weakened from loss of blood, Jake, two women, and two oil workers collapsed. Gloria ran to her son. He had been shot in the upper arm, side, and across the ear. The long gash along the side of his head bled the most. His other two wounds were more serious. He had restrictive use of his left arm and the bullet in his side had no exit wound.

One of the women succumbed to her head injury. The other forced herself to sit up and started loading rifles for the others. She wouldn't let her injured leg and forearm stop her from helping. Weakened from blood loss and weeks of barely eating, the two wounded oil workers didn't have the energy to move.

Jacob dropped to his knees. A bullet grazed the side of his forehead and cracked open part of his skull. Two women grabbed his shoulders and pulled him behind a knoll. They quickly packed and bandaged his wound before returning to the line. As one of the women picked up her rifle a bullet smacked her in the forehead.

The remaining Reapers made it to the top of the crater and saw the chaos. Ramming their knives into the dead Townies, they used their hilts to lift the carcasses into the air. Using the dead bodies as human shields, they charged the line of fire.

As the Townie's body was push and rolled out of the air duct, steam puffed out of the centrifuge. Grabbing the controls, a miner sprayed steel balls at the rushing Reapers. With blood pouring from their wounds, a couple dozen continued the charge. Joe dropped his spent rifle and pulled out his knife. A Reaper flung the dead Townie aside, extracted his long knife and raised it over his head. Joe lunged forward and chopped through the Reaper's forearm before he could finish his downward swing.

As their chests collided the Reaper was in shock. Joe pushed himself away and slashed the man's throat. Behind him, another Reaper took a swing at his head. He ducked and a clump of hair was all that was cut off. Joe head butted the man's groin and flipped him on his back. John was there to run his knife through the man's collar and into his chest.

The hand to hand combat made it hard to pick a target. Jose and Tara lay over a knoll and did their best. A Reaper circled around Kelsey as she clashed knives with the one in front of her. Jose shot the man's temple as he was about to stab her.

The Reapers' discovered the weakest section of the line. Within a half a minute three of the oil workers had been sliced apart. Screaming wildly, with a dagger in one hand and her long knife in the other, Kelsey led a group of women to their aid. The wounds the centrifuge had administered had finally begun to slow the Reapers down. Unfortunately, the injured women were also beginning to tire.

Each blow, each swing, and each dodge was a streak of luck. The Reapers' body weight gave them an advantage as their blades met. The women's agility and flexibility were their saviour. As the women spurred the men into charging, they would step out of their way and attack them from the rear.

The remaining oil workers became fixed targets for the Reapers' rage, as the women tried to blind side them. An oil worker shot at a Reaper that was about to slice open Kelsey's throat. In the struggle, the bullet sliced off the tip of Kelsey's nose before smashing into the Reaper's left eye.

Turning her head, the blood spurting out of her nose temporarily blinding a charging Reaper. She flung her knife upward and caught his armpit. His knife arm flopped behind him as he twisted sideways. Kelsey fell on him and thrust her dagger into his jugular vein.

Seeing her on the ground, another Reaper ran toward her. Both

Jose and Tara saw him and fired.

John also saw Kelsey and ran to her aid. An escaping Townie's bullet sliced across his eye and broke a piece of bone off the bridge of his nose. The scattered bone pierced his other eye. Blood along with the fluid from his eyes gushed out as he twisted to the ground gasping for air.

******

Eric ordered his men to fall back to a trench on the far side. With the encampment almost free for the taking, the escaping Townies leaped over the wheel traps and ran passed the centrifuge gun towards it. Only a handful risked the centrifuges fire to join the Reapers attack.

******

While David and Mary pulled John to safety, Daniel challenged and fought anyone that got in their way. Karen shot the shoulder of a charging Townie. The muzzle of his rifle slipped from his weakened arm. The bayonet stuck into the ground and tore the rifle from his other hand. Daniel wildly slashed the Townie's good arm. The man jumped back, winced in pain and retreated.

Feeling outnumbered, a few of the remaining Reapers ran towards the encampment. Grant's beast rolled over a filled in section of the wheel traps and blasted the fleeing men. Using pistols, knives and bayonets, his men fought the men hiding in the wheel traps. Grant pressed on to allow the second beast to get over the traps. Behind them were over fifty armed miners.

Knowing they had the advantage, they rushed the half dozen dazed Reapers that wouldn't retreat. With more than two against one they were no match. Body parts were hacked off almost at will. The women and oil workers took pleasure in brutally killing the wounded and dying. The earth dwellers pulled and carried their wounded away from the battlefield. Jose smiled as she rested her head against the side of her smoking rifle. A sharp pain resonated from her stomach. "Not now! Not after all I've gone through."

Gloria saw her. She grabbed her pack and a flask of water and ran over to her. After retrieving some ground up herbs from her pack, she used her hand to funnel it into the flask. With her hand on the back of Jose's neck, she said, "Drink this."

The blood coming from her groin told her it was to late.
Turning to Tara, Jose cried out, "Why now?"

Gloria gazed at the blood soaked ground in front of them. "It was just his time. You are still young. You can have more."

Jose spotted a dead Townie with the same frame as Killy and wiped the tears from her eyes. "Maybe." Seeing some miners checking the dead bodies, she added, "Maybe next time things will be different."

******

With no cannons and most of their ammo spent, the surviving Townies huddled in their holes and trenches. As they reloaded their weapons and prepared themselves for the attack, so did Grant's men along with the miners.

When Karen noticed Grant on top of the beast, she began to shiver. As she aimed her rifle, Joe put his hand on the barrel and lowered it. "Now is not the time."

There were only six oil workers that were still capable of fighting. Ignoring the pain from their bandaged wounds, they walked over to a group of masked miners. While carrying a wounded woman, Joe and Karen watched them hug their comrades. "They don't need us to mop up the remaining Townies."

Karen looked at Joe. "Grant's men are Townies too."

As he positioned the injured woman's torso against the side of a knoll, he said, "Yes, but they must have something that separates them from the rest. They had the time and opportunity to attack our camp, but they didn't even try to."

Karen gazed at the blackened beast and said, "I still don't trust him."

Joe looked at her, "I just wish I knew his connection to the people in the mine." He saw that she was mesmerized by Grant. Seeing him direct his remaining men plus a small group of miners, he mumbled, "I wonder why he turned on the others to help them? With the army he had under his command he could have taken the mine."

Sitting on top of the Blackened beast, Grant gazed over at the earth dwellers. He recognized Karen. While he ran his fingers through his hair, he shook his head and grinned.

Chapter Thirty

Victoria scaled up the quickly erected lookout pole and peered through her binoculars. Beyond the waves she could see the compound. It hadn't changed very much since the last time she saw it. Besides the catamaran sitting in dry dock, the Islanders had a the few small boats tied to the wharf.

The moment Victoria's feet hit the deck, the pole was lowered. Her top men gathered around her. "What did you see?"

"They put the catamaran in dry dock and must have forged some more cannons. I saw some mounted on top of the walls and roofs, along with a few more on the ship." Victoria studied their mixed reactions. "We need to send a scouting party ashore to see if they made any extra modifications to their defences before we attack."

A large man with faces covering his entire vest and down the front of his legs spoke up. "I'll lead it. I need to find out what I'll be sending my men into." Staring at Victoria, he added, "You can keep them busy along the waterfront."

Victoria wasn't used to orders from anyone. She paced back and forth in front of him. "So what makes you think that I don't want to lead the assault?"

"Because lately, you have been underestimating your enemies." As she reached for her knife, he grabbed her arm. "We may only have one shot at recapturing that compound. We may not have the manpower for a second assault."

As several of the other men gathered behind him, she released the hilt of her knife. "All right Paul. You can lead the attack, but I am still in command."

"No one ever said you weren't"

The tension between the men and women standing around the deck relaxed somewhat. They all knew that in order for any attack to succeed, everyone had to work as a single unit.

******

Mary and Karen cut and pulled the shirt off an oil worker in order to get to the wounds on his chest and shoulder. Even the skin under his shirt was covered in crude oil. As they wiped it away, it started to turn red. The man laying beside him pointed to the sun. "He needs shade. Without the crud covering his skin he can't take any direct sunlight. He needs shade."

Joe and a woman quickly constructed a temporary shade over the man. With rocks securing a blanket to the top of a knoll, they stuck the bayonets attached to two muskets into the ground and used them as corner posts.

One of the maskless fighters that spearheaded the miners second charge, slung his rifle over his shoulder and approached the line of injured and disfigured bodies. Joe stood up and walked over to meet him.

As the man studied Joe's face and the colour of his skin, he said, "You look like one of us, but I don't know you. Where did you come from?"

After seeing the thick, wadded paper collar and shoulder armour beneath his ripped open multi pocketed coat, instead of answering, Joe said, "You are not a miner. You are an islander." Shaking his head up and down, he continued, "How did you manage to survive the attack?"

"There wouldn't have been an attack at all if it wasn't for Killy's henchmen." The man twisted his neck and told Joe, "But you are wrong. I am not an islander. I am a sea trader." Turning to face Joe, he asked again, "So, where did you come from?"

"A large underground structure next to the sea."

"You do have that gilded look about you." The man studied Joe's face for any hint of deception. "How do we know we can trust you?"

"The same way that we know we can trust you."

As the man walked back, Joe looked around. There were more wounded on the ground than there were standing. There was only a handful of women fit to fight, and all the able oil workers had joined the rest of the miners.

Karen took the bandage off what was left of Kelsey's nose. In the process, she disrupted the clotted blood vessels. As Kelsey began choking on the blood, Karen plugged her nostrils. After stitching and cauterizing what she could, she pulled out the plugs and stuck tubes in what was left of Kelsey's nostrils. The bullet had blown off most of the flesh and cartilage that had formed her nose but missed her facial bones.

Beside her, Gloria had cleaned the bone and debris out of John's nasal cavity and eyes. After inserting tubes up his nose to keep his airway clear, she sewed his eyes shut. Then she carefully pulled and stretched the skin over the bridge of his nose.

Joe handed her a piece of black moulded plastic. "This is the best I can do with the tools at hand."

Gloria placed the moulded plastic over the bridge of John's nose and cris-crossed a few stitchs over it. "If it stays in place, the bone might heal itself."

John reached over and grabbed Kelsey's hand. Needing his mouth to breath, he could only get out one word at a time. "Ain't... We... Quite... The... Pair."

In nearly the same condition, Kelsey answered, "Yeah... We...

Are."

Although they mostly remained hidden behind knolls, Grant and his men watched the women and earth dwellers every move. It was bad enough that they had to hide any butchering they did from the miners, but watching all the badly wounded bodies go to waste was revolting.

As he drank some of the water brought up to them from the mine, Grant knew that the men in the trenches had less then a five day supply of water. Any attempt to erect a solar still was answered with a volley of bullets. All Grant's men had to do was find a place where they could not be shot at and wait it out.

******

About five kilometres from the compound, Victoria slipped the ship into a bay. Using weighted ropes to judge the depth, she got as close to shore as she could. With the ship spun around to face the open sea, Paul led four more men over the side and into shoulder high water. It would take them less then two hours to get to the compound. Figuring on another hour to scout around and a fast retreat, Victoria pointed to small beach and told him, "We will return in four hours. If I don't see you on that section of beach by those boulders, I will presume that you were either killed or captured."

Paul yelled above the surf, "In either case, you will hear their cannons."

While they were wading ashore, Victoria ordered her men to crank up the anchor and head out to sea. Behind her, a blast that was much louder than a musket's echoed off the cliffs on both sides of the bay. With five men in the water, she order one of her rear cannons to fire at the plume of smoke.

Sitting out of musket range, her men tossed ropes with floats attached to the ends into the water. The men in the water tossed away their rifles and tore off their vests. Two of the five men in the water could barely swim. Paul grab a pair of ropes and handed them to the two struggling men. By the time he made it to the ship, he didn't have the strength to climb onboard. He grabbed the rope and put his feet on the float and let the men on the ship hauled him out of the water.

Victoria stood over him as he lay on the deck gasping for air. "That's why we let others do the scouting for us. You have to learn how to delegate before you can truly lead."

On shore, a frightened young girl buried the signal mortar and crawled into a hole. After rolling a flat rock against the opening, she looked through one of the cracks along the edges. With only a dagger and a pistol to protect her, all she wanted to do is stay alive.

Three men jumped over the side of the catamaran as it rounded the bend of the bay. Using air filled oilskins to keep them afloat, the surf carried them to shore. Victoria looked back at Paul. "This is how you send out a scouting party."

An hour later, the girl heard loose pebbles roll off a boulder above her. Moments later, she saw the legs of someone walking by her hideout. Seconds afterwards she heard a man whisper, "Check this out. It wasn't even a gun."

As the man unearthed the mortar, he whispered to the others, "It is just a buried tube. They must be running short of metal."

The girl took a deep breath as the three men left. *'It's going to be a long time til morning.'* She felt the sacks that were lined up along the side of the hole. *'I have everything I need. I'll be all right. I just have to hold myself together til morning. That's all, just til morning.'*

Knowing that the Islanders might be expecting them, the scouts took a longer but safer route to the compound. They waited til dusk before they got close enough to examine its perimeter. Other than a few cannons mounted on the rooftops, the only visible change was the patch in the outer wall of one of the buildings.

Without the constant fear of being spotted they travelled much quicker in the dark. It only took them a little over an hour to get to the hidden bay. As they raced to the point at the far end where they had been dropped off, one of them slipped on some loose stones. "Ahhhh."

Behind him, another man stepped on the stones and had to catch his balance. "I never noticed any pebbles here earlier. I'm sure I would have taken mental note of them if I had."

With the men only metres away, the young girl froze. Afraid of them hearing her breath, she wrapped her arm around her mouth. With her free hand, she gently rested the tip of the pistol barrow on the top corner of the rock concealing her hideout.

One of the men turned and faced her. "Did you hear that."

Another man whispered back, "I didn't hear anything."

The girl looked down the barrel. She thought her racing heart had given her away. The man turned and said, "We are wasting time. Let's go."

Paralysed, it took several minutes before she could lower and uncock her pistol. At the far point of the bay, she noticed a strange light. It was a signal fire.

Something inside of her snapped. She push the flat stone away and almost leaped out. Within seconds she had unearthed a large mortar and lit the charge. In the dark, the sparkling fuse seemed to linger for hours. It was pre-measured to only take a minute. With her imagination running wild, she grabbed everything she could and darted into the darkness.

For a second, the light from the blast lit up the entire bay. Five kilometres away, the Islanders posted on the wall saw the brief faint light. The following 'Boom', told them what it was. One of the lookouts slid down the rails of the ladder and ran to the main hall. "As you suspected, the ship has returned to the bay."

Mike threw off his covers. "I told you that there wouldn't be any attack. At least we managed to get some sleep." As his scantily dressed wife tried to cover herself, he looked at the men stirring around in their cots. As she pulled her clothes under the blankets, he yelled out, "Don't just lay there, get to the dock."

After hearing the first mortar they knew that something was awry. Almost all of them wore their clothes to bed. Within seconds, almost a dozen men and women ran out of the hall.

Sitting in dry dock the ship gave off the illusion that it was still in need of repair. That was not the case. Not willing to risk it being stolen in a raid, Mike thought it was the safest place for it to be. With everyone working as fast as they could, it only took a half an hour to slip the ship in the water.

******

With the ship anchored in the boggy bay, Victoria climbed overboard and followed her men to shore. Knowing that she needed every man she could get, she had unshackled the Townies she had taken from the Flesh Star. After she pledged that they would be considered as equals if the invasion was successful, given little choice, they wholeheartedly agreed to join them.

Three of the cannons taken from the Flesh Star were loaded on a raft and taken ashore, one at a time. Victoria sent out scouts to plot out their route. During the two hours that the scouts were gone, the men and women prepared themselves and their equipment for the invasion. With her scouts giving her an all clear, Victoria ordered her men onward.

Two of the five remaining men onboard the ship cranked up the anchor. The rest took on the duties as lookout, boiler operator and helmsman.

******

Onboard the Hew Hope, Patrick looked up at Simon. "Did you see any more flashes?"

"With one arm clung around the mast and the other holding a set of binoculars to her eyes, she answered, "Nothing, just the one."

Both the wind and current were pushing against them. Even if they ran the boiler full blast, it would take half a day for the ship to reach the island. As the ship climbed and fell from each wave, Patrick tried to look above their white crests. From the deck he couldn't even see the cliffs that guarded most of the island's shoreline. Looking up at Simon, he screamed above the waves hitting the bow of the ship. "If you see anything, just yell out."

******

After hauling the cannons off the beach, up the steep rocky incline and onto flat ground, the Townies took a break. Victoria glanced at them and then over at Paul. "Let them be. We all need a rest."

"But the sun will be up in a couple hours. We don't have any time to waste."

Victoria shook her head and smiled. "The men can't fight if they're too exhausted to even stand."

"They won't have to fight. All they have to do is look the part." He turned around and looked at his men along with the Townies. "The islanders are cowards. When they see us coming, they will open the gates and attempt to negociate a surrender."

While urinating behind a bunch of short bushes, a Townie turned to the group he was with. "Do you smell something?"

His urine was dispersed all over the bush the young girl was hiding under. Knowing that she was about to be discovered, she dashed out. Two Townies blocked her path. She had no where to go. As she leaped into the air and tried to jump over one of them, he grabbed her ankle. She kick away his hand as she fell to the ground. The other men jumped on top of her.

As the Townies begun to rip off her clothes, Paul yelled out, "Stop, we might be able to use her."

Victoria looked at Paul. "Now you are starting to think like a leader."

Knowing that the Islanders would be expecting them, stealth was no longer required. Instead they broadcasted their arrival by deliberately smacking their weapons against their chests and legs. They wanted them to know who and what they were about to face.

The Islanders on the wall saw a rolling, low riding cloud darken the night sky. The artillerymen on the corner buildings got the best overview of the approaching horde. Despite the invaders being shielded by the rocky terrain, they could tell that the compound was about to be surrounded. With no distinct target to aim at, they held their fire.

The Reapers dragged a cannon to all three inland sides of the compound. Before getting within cannon range, Victoria and Paul surveyed the area and selected where they should be placed. By dawn the compound was under siege.

Keeping her attack force out of sight, Victoria told her artillerymen to "Fire."

Instead of the gates or thick, fortified walls, they targeted at the corner buildings. The Islanders tried to return fire the best they could. After releasing two volleys, the cannons on one of the flat topped corner buildings fell through the weakened roof.

A pair of Reapers' cannons targeted the second corner building.

The Islanders on the other building fired back at an feverish pace as the men below dug out and hauled the fallen cannons onto the walls. As a blast struck the edge of the building, next to the adjacent wall, the Islanders on top could feel the building shake. Fearing they had little time, they quickly re-aimed and lit the fuses of both cannons before retreating to safety.

As the cannons fired the roof gave way and the building succumbed to the Reapers' skilled artillery bombardment. Fortunately one of its cannonballs struck a Reaper's cannon. Along with cracking its barrel the ball ricocheted off and struck a Reaper's hip driving him sideways into a boulder.

See the Reapers were about to advance, the Islander's quickly loaded and fired one of the canons on the wall. Surprised the Reapers hunkered back down. With both sides out of musket range, it was still a cannon battle.

******

The catamaran cruised along the coast. Noticing that the Islander's ship was no longer in dry dock, they aimed and fired their starboard cannons at the compound's gate.

The Islander's ship approached the compound from the opposite direction and fired at the Reaper's catamaran. The Islanders knew they were out gunned. They had only four cannons to the Reapers' eight. As the reapers fired their post side cannons at them, the Islander's ship retreated.

Not wanting to be a stationary target, the Reapers catamaran circled the port in a figure eight. Every time they got close to shore, the gunners would fire their cannons. The ship's erratic movements, along with the surf, made it hard for the two gunners to reload, aim and fire their cannons. With the Islander's ship slipping in and out of cannon range, the lookout was constantly yelling at both the helmsman and the gunners.

Noting which cannons were fired, Nancy spun her ship towards the Reaper's unprotected side. As the two ships danced for position, Nancy knew that despite being outgunned, her six artillerymen could out-shoot theirs. Fortunately for both, as they bounced around in the rough water their shots missed their intended targets.

******

With the corner buildings were reduced to large piles of rumble, Victoria redirected her two remaining cannons toward the gates. After one of the cannons fire its overheated barrel cracked. Its weakened shot still had the power to finish blowing its assigned battered gate off its hinges. A sliver of the hot barrel broke off and sliced through the side of the Reaper standing next to it.

Both back and right side gates were ajar. Paul looked at the piles of rubble that jutted out of the corners of the compound. As he turned towards Victoria, he stated, "Their two remaining cannons are on the far wall. We have to attack while we have the advantage."

Victoria snapped back, "I'll take that under advisement."

Paul noticed the knife in her hand and stepped back. He knew that she was not used to taking orders from anyone. As her face slightly softened, he took a breath. "What are your orders?"

With the young girl's arms tied lengthwise to a rifle, two men paraded her up to the outer edge of the large garden next the compound's wall. After forcing the frightened girl to squat down on her knees, they used her as a shield. Resting their muskets on her shoulders, they began taking turns firing at the men on the wall.

Mike saw her and ordered his men to duck down and not to fire back. Behind him, four men lowered one of the cannons from the far wall. After sliding down a ladder, he ran over to them. "They are probing our defences in preparation for an attack."

******

Under full steam, the helmsman swooped the Reapers' catamaran as close as possible to the shoreline. Its skilled gunners fired its starboard cannons at the stone storage depot next to the wharf. As the ship darted away, clouds of dust from the two holes that were punched through the wall rolled toward the waterfront.

The Islander's lookout brushed the hair off her face as she yelled out, "They never reloaded their port cannons."

Nancy swung the steering wheel and pointed the ship straight towards the Reapers'. The Reapers' helmsman twisted his ship around. Before the Islanders could get off a shot, one of Reapers lit one of their stern cannons.

Nancy instinctively tried to turn away. The cannonball struck the starboard hull along the waterline. As water gushed into the hull, the Islanders fired back. Their cannons punched two holes into the catamaran's port hull. Unfortunately, both were above the waterline.

Driven by fear, Nancy trembled as she pointed the ship away from the Catamaran. One of the gunners ran into the pilothouse. "What are you doing? We could have had them."

Nancy turned and looked at him. "What are you talking about?"

"None of their cannons were loaded. We could have boarded their ship and overpowered them."

Nancy's chin fell to her chest. "I screwed up, didn't I?"

While scratching the back of his head, the man said, "You may have cost us both the ship and the compound."

******

A cannonball blew apart a section of the wall next to the gate. As chunks of stone and dust filled the air Paul led the charge. Floating dust particles blurred the vision of the men on the wall. They fired at the loose formation of hazy forms that were charging towards the opening. As they reloaded, five men rushed over the rubble littering the enlarged gateway. The lowered cannon blasted shrapnel at the men breaching the opening.

Protected behind a speedily constructed wall of rubble in the corner nearest to the wharf, the artillery men reloaded their cannon. As another group of Townies entered through another gateway, the men on the walls tried to hold them off. Shooting through pre-chiselled holes in the wall of the supply depot, several women used mostly airguns to help fend off the attackers as best they could.

Knowing they would be facing mostly empty muskets and maybe a few airguns, Paul waved the Reapers inside. Not trained for close quarter combat, the Islanders scattered. As they Reapers ran after them, the women inside the supply depot continued shooting at them.

Two more cannonballs struck the seaside wall of the depot. Dust filled the air as part of the wall and ceiling began to crumble. Despite this, the women kept firing. Behind them, the children huddled in the corners along with the wounded and frail Islanders.

******

The helmsman watched the Islanders' catamaran tilt to the side. "They are done for." Hearing the attack on the compound, he yelled out, "Drop the anchor."

One of the gunners ran and released the anchor. Both the lookout and boiler operator scrambled to the deck to help man the cannons.

The Islanders' ship drifted in and out of range. With its side hull taking on water, Nancy had trouble steering it. Its leaning deck made firing its cannons almost impossible. After being lit, no one knew where either the cannonball or cannon would end up. A wave hit the corner of the ship and spun a lit cannon to the side. The cannonball rolled along the side of the pilothouse and clipped the housing of the gearbox controlling the rudders.

The Reapers fired at them and hit one of the cables holding up the lookout mast. The mast crashed to deck, bounced in the air and rolled over the railing into the water. With three of its cables still attached to the ship, it acted almost like an anchor.

A blast from the New Hope's air cannon announced its arrival. The shell splashed ten metres short of the anchored catamaran. Even a wide miss was a life saver to the men on the Islanders' ship.

Both the lookout and boiler operator on the Reapers ship quickly returned to their stations. The gunners ran the crank controlling the anchor.

Before the Reapers could crank their anchor off the sea floor, a shell from the New Hope's cannon had struck the side of the pilothouse.

Both gunners were knocked over the railing and into the water. Seeing themselves as sitting targets, the other three leaped overboard and swam to shore.

Eight women ran, walked and limped out of the supply depot to meet them. Most of them had multiple blood soaked bandages covering their wounds. The sneering faces, axes and sharp knives forced the struggling Reapers to their feet.

As the Reapers tried to make it past the slippery rocks and crushing surf, a woman took her airgun off her shoulder and shot them. Before they could escape, the other women overpowered them and continued to hack them apart even after they were dead.

After releasing the sunken mast's cables, the Islanders pointed their ship towards the wharf. The men onboard prepared themselves for the impact. The waves twisted the ship as it crashed into the slip next to main dock. Everyone onboard scrambled to their feet, grabbed their weapons and rushed over the side and into the compound.

******

The surviving Islanders in the courtyard were crammed behind the wall of debris that the artillery men built. In the courtyard, the wounded were being systematically hacked apart. The men manning the cannon on top of the wall along with the sharp-shooters were all dead.

Victoria walked through the gate. Behind her were three men pulling a cannon. As they aimed it at the men in the corner. A woman shot Victoria's right shoulder. She turned to her artillerymen and pointed to the supply depot. "Blast a hole through that wall!"

A flood of fresh rifles poured through the open gate leading to the dock. The unexpected rush of men took the Reapers by surprise. A mere second changed everything.

Victoria's artillery men tried to quickly readjust the lit cannon. The cannonball missed the gateway and bounced off the corner of the supply depot. Along with it, chunks of shattered rocks struck several of the Reapers that had been attacking the men in the corner.

Demoralized, the shocked Reapers got to their feet and lashed out at anyone within arms reach. From behind the wall of debris, Mike yelled out, "Attack, and don't let any of them escape."

As the Reapers tried to back out of the compound, one of the artillery men behind the wall of rubble yelled out, "Clear a path."

The Islanders scattered as the metal shrapnel blasted out of the cannon. The Reapers running to the closest gate were knocked to the ground. Many of them had multiple pieces of cutlery, eating utensils, buttons and metal slag sticking out of them.

Victoria trailed behind the handful that made it to the far gate. Seeing her go, Mike yelled out, "Get them."

The crew from the ship rushed after them. Outside the gateway, only one Reaper took the time to reload and fire at them. The musket ball barely broke the skin of one of the Islander's shoulders. Several strands of her blood red hair floated to the ground as she continued her pursuit.

None of the rest missed a step. Nancy stopped at the edge of the garden. The arms of the young girl were still tied around a musket. Its muzzle was stuck in ground twisting her body sideways. Blood was oozing from the cuts across her throat and both ankles.

******

Paul looked back at Victoria and saw the blood dripping from her shoulder. "You are not going to make it."

"It is just my shoulder."

"You know that you are leaving behind a blood trail that a blind man could follow." Paul glanced at the other men. "We are not going to make it as long as she is with us."

Victoria tried to grab her pistol. Paul smacked her across the face and knocked her onto her side. With his foot on her wrist, he picked up her pistol. "You won't need this anymore."

Grabbing her good arm, he dragged her to the ledge of a cliff. The surf hammered at the rocks below them. Victoria grabbed a bush and held on as he tried to kick her over the side.

A shot whisked by Paul's head. He ducked below the surrounding bushes and began creeping away. "This is all your fault."

Victoria attempted to crawl behind some rocks as two Islanders spotted her. As they grabbed her legs and pulled her away from the edge, she cried out, "Don't do anything rash. Without me, my men will never surrender."

The two men looked at each other. "Maybe we should take her to Mike."

Nancy walked up to Victoria and looked into her eyes. "I think she would say anything to stay alive. One of her own men just tried to kill her."

Victoria chuckled as she gazed back at her. "They are my family. Sometimes families squabble."

"Liar!" Nancy pulled out her dagger and jabbed it against Victoria's throat. "You are nothing but a heartless child killer."

One of the men grabbed her hand. Even though her blade barely penetrating Victoria's windpipe, the blood gushing out of the wound along with her mouth enraged the hidden Reapers.

As a volley of shots rang out, the Islanders dashed for cover. One Islander was hit in the side. Paul couldn't hold the three other men back. As Victoria dropped to her knees, the enraged men drew their knives and screamed as they charged the group of Islanders. Paul stepped back, "You will all be killed!"

Their screams drowned him out. The two men leading the charge were shot. As they crumbled to the ground in front of him, the third Reaper leaped over their bodies. With his long blade, he slashed an Islander's arm and another's thigh. As he reached Victoria, he grabbed her good arm and began to pull her away.

Nancy finished reloading her pistol. Holding it at shoulder height, she ran towards them. Her hastened shot cut off a piece of the man's ear.

Paul fired his pistol and hit Nancy's gun arm. After tossing his pistol away, he pulled out his knife and dagger as he charged the Islanders.

His hair raising screams rattled two of the Islanders as they took aim. Despite being only a few metres away, one missed. The other hit his chest. The impact knocked Paul to the ground. His chest armour had stopped the bullet but he had dropped his knife.

As Paul tried to get up, three Islanders jumped on top of him. He thrust his dagger into one of the Islander's shoulders as they rolled him onto his stomach. Even pinned to the ground he kicked and fought back with every ounce of energy he had.

One of Islanders picked up a rock and used it to hammer his dagger through the back of Paul's armour. Killing was not a part of his upbringing. Tears came to his eyes as he cried out, "Just die will you. Just go away and leave us alone."

The last Reaper wrapped his arm around Victoria while dangling his knife in the air. "Leave her alone. She is our queen. None of us would be alive if it wasn't for her."

One of the Islanders kicked the knife from the man's hand. "He is no threat. I can't kill a defenceless man." Seeing Victoria clutching her neck, he added, "Lets take them back to the compound and let their lives rest on Mike's shoulders."

Nancy yelled out, "I say kill them here."

The man looked at her. "Then we would be no better than they are."

Chapter Thirty - One

On the third day, Grant led his men along with some of the miners into the encampment. The pits and trenches restricted the beasts' involvement. Parked along the sides, their gunners were ordered to kill anyone that tried to escape.

Most of the Townies in the outside trenches, were slaughtered without a fight. Barely being able to lift their rifles, they simply accepted their fate. The further in they went, the more resistance they encountered. A sudden volley of bullets drove Grant and his men into the trenches.

Grant rolled a couple dead bodies in front of the trench he was in and used them as a marker. While crawling out of the encampment, a sniper shot the back of his shoulder. The bullet had travelled up the back of his body armour and under his shoulder protectors.

Two of his men ran over and dragged him the rest of the way out. Grant looked at Eric. "Tell the artillery men to blast them into hamburger." Gazing toward the encampment, he added, "They are hidden in the trenches just beyond those stacked bodies. Our men are in the trenches on this side of them."

As the cannons roared, a miner told Grant, "Maybe we should take you over to get fixed."

Grant looked over at the earth dwellers' make-shift field hospital. "I'm not sure that's a good idea."

The maskless miner gazed at the blood seeping out of Grant's wound. "I don't think you have a choice."

Two miners helped Grant to the hospital. Karen looked up from her patient she was stitching up. She dropped her needle, pulled a dagger out of her belt and ran toward him. It took Joe and both miners to hold her back. "You butcher. Why would any one of us want to help you? You have been craving our flesh from the day you were born."

The trader walked over to them and said, "Because we need him and so do you."

Joe wrapped his arms around Karen as she spewed out, "We don't need him!"

The trader gazed toward the mine. "But the miners do. Their machinery is getting too old. It is beyond repair. They are lucky it lasted this long. Even if they move their gardens outside they can't work it. Their suits are not designed for hard labour. They need people that can handle the sunlight to grow crops for them. The people I brought here were supposed to help the miners. They were clean and I had seen how they grew crops in the sun. Now they need Grant and his men to do the work for them."

With her teeth clenched together, she screamed out, "Why him?"

"Because he lived up to the agreement they made with the previous mayor. The town was doomed. Even then Grant was amongst the select few slated to survive." The old captain studied the face of the crowd that was forming around them. "It wasn't his fault that Killy's men decided to turn the Islanders into jerky. By the time we got back to town it was over. I had hand picked the families on those ships. They were the best I could find."

Gloria went over and helped a miner remove Grant's shirt and body armour. As she examined the wound she glanced at Karen. "It's imbedded in the bone. You are much better at extracting bullets than I am."

Karen glared at her. "He let Killy butcher a live, pregnant woman and pounded my body like a smith's anvil. I say lop off his arm and let him bleed to death."

Grant gazed at Karen. "I was the mayor. I had to give the people what they wanted. If I didn't get it, they would've rebelled." He looked away as he added, "Maybe I did consider you as a piece of meat that I could do with as I wished. If it wasn't me, it would have been Killy and his men doing the pounding and eventually the slicing."

Mary elbowed her why through the crowd. "I'll extract the bullet."

As Mary went over to help Gloria, Joe asked Grant, "So you turned on Killy to save the miners?"

Through clenched teeth, Grant answered, "Yes, the town was dying. Most of the people in it were full of numerous toxins and riddled with various forms of cancer. Why should the healthy have to suffer just to prolong the agony of the dying. The introduction of the Reapers only made things trickier."

******

Most of the remaining black powder was exhausted by the cannons battering the encampment. There was only enough left for the muskets. Before the dust could settle, Eric led the men into the encampment. Amongst the debris he bent over to examine the remains of a solar water distiller. Instead of urine, the Townies were putting in pounded slices of meat. "They were extracting water from the dead. They must of got that from the Reapers."

Eric unscrewed the collection bottle behind the distiller's condensing hood and took a drink. As shots rang out, he yelled out, "Don't leave any of them alive. Make sure you kill them all." Following Grants orders, Dead or alive, every Townie was either beheaded or received a bullet to the forehead.

******

Months later. The flesh of the men and women that died in the battle had been either consumed or turned into compost. Despite all of Grant's efforts, even as the first surface crop was being harvested, the women and the earth dwellers were still skittish around his men.

As Grant bit into his first beet, he looked up and saw that Karen was working only two rows over from him. Joe watched him stand up and walk over to her. "We have to move on. You know how hard I have worked at getting my men to change their ways. I am sorry about the past, but that was a different time and under completely different circumstances."

Karen looked at him. "You were the hunter. We were your prey. Moving on is much easier for you. Fear is what kept us alive." She stood up and rubbed her enlarged belly. "Maybe the next generation will be a little more trusting."

Grant looked down at her belly. "It will. Be it boy or girl, I will give it no reason to fear me."

Joe stood behind him with his knife in hand. "And I'll be there if you do."

******

Six months after the battle, Mike spotted a mast sticking out of the water. By the time the Fresh Start finally reached port, the New Hope had it's cannons pointed at it. Simon spotted Daniel and yelled down, "Hold your fire."

With a ship in dry dock and a refurbished catamaran lashed to the dock, the Fresh Start dropped anchor. Two rowboats come out to meet them. While still in the rowboat, Daniel saw a strange woman standing next to Mike.

As Mike offered him a hand getting onto the pier, Daniel asked, "Who is she? She is not an Islander."

Mike used his hand to gesture a small degree of respect toward the woman. "This is Victoria. She has been helping me run the island."

Daniel saw the battle scars on Victoria's face, neck and arms. After a few seconds he blurted out, "She is a Reaper."

"She was their queen. She had managed to keep over a hundred families alive on a floating pile of garbage. The battle had destroyed our gardens and killed over half our men. We have more disfigured and handicapped than we do fit. We needed someone that could make the tough decisions that had to be made."

"But a Reaper?"

Victoria stepped forward. In a raspy voice, she said, "Yes I am a Reaper. I had reaped whatever my people needed to stay alive." She glanced at Mike. "Many of my decisions were not popular, but they had to be made."

Patrick climbed out of a rowboat and walked up to them. "So, you have met Victoria."

Daniel looked at him. As Patrick gave Victoria a hug, Daniel shook his head. "What is going on?"

Patrick smiled at Daniel. "I convinced Mike to spare her life." He glanced at Victoria and than back at Daniel. "If he liked it or not, at the time, he needed her help. I became both her bodyguard and mediator through the island's rebuilding phase. Needless to say, over time, we grew quite fond of each other."

Sarah stood on the pier as David got out of the rowboat and climbed up the ladder. Wrapping her arms around him, she said, "I was praying that you would find a way to get back to me."

David used his thumb to brushed the tears off her cheeks. "When I heard that a ship washed up in the Rainbow Sea, I was overjoyed. The oil workers patched it up and helped us give it back its original name." After squeezing her tightly, he added, "It must have been named the 'Fresh Start' for a reason."

Sarah looked into his eyes and said, "You're right. Now I want to have a fresh start with you."

David gently kissed her. Sarah grabbed the back of his head and pulled it towards her's. As their lips briefly parted, he told her, "Me to."

******

In the years that followed, a trade route developed between the island, the oil patch and the mine. With the miners help and encouragement, Grant and his men worked out their differences with most of the remaining women. As for the earth dwellers, a lifetime of being preyed upon was much harder to overcome. Jose and Tara tried to work things out with the men but eventually they followed most of the earth dwellers and made their way to the island.

Kelsey and John stayed behind. In the mine, he didn't need his eyes. His knack for fixing things in the dark became his saviour. All he needed was his hands, wits and the knowledge that Kelsey would always be there by his side.

The End

www.ingramcontent.com/pod-product-compliance
Lightning Source LLC
Chambersburg PA
CBHW061606100726
47898CB00002B/548